CARIBBEAN'S KEEPER

A Novel of Vendetta

by

Brian Boland

CARIBBEAN'S KEEPER

A Novel of Vendetta

by

Brian Boland

WARRIORS PUBLISHING GROUP
NORTH HILLS, CALIFORNIA

Caribbean's Keeper: A Novel of Vendetta

A Warriors Publishing Group book/published by arrangement with the author

The views expressed herein are those of the author and are not to be construed as official views or reflecting the views of the Commandant or of the U. S. Coast Guard.

PRINTING HISTORY
Warriors Publishing Group edition/October 2016

ISBN 978-1-944353-11-7

Library of Congress Control Number: 2016946046

The name "Warriors Publishing Group" and the logo
are trademarks belonging to Warriors Publishing Group

PRINTED IN THE UNITED STATES OF AMERICA

10 9 8 7 6 5 4 3 2 1

Dedicated to Beth and Elli, who believe in me—
even when I don't.

CHAPTER 1 – *DELANEY*

IT WAS HIGH SUMMER and dawn broke early in the Florida Straits. Cole stood silent on the bridge wing, his waist against the railing, and stared east as the black sky surrendered to quiet shades of purple. With a steady hum and the rolling sound of whitewater off the bow, the Coast Guard Cutter *Delaney* steamed north at eight knots, plowing ahead through the lukewarm waters of the Gulf Stream. Soon the sky would come alive with vivid shades of red and orange before daylight finally took hold and brought with it another humid tropical day.

This day was, in many ways, a near repeat of every day for the past two years. Cole's alarm had gone off at three in the morning. He had rolled out of his rack and fumbled in the darkness for the mini-refrigerator by his feet. Opening a can of Red Bull, he sat on the edge of his rack by himself and chugged the sweet caffeinated concoction that started each new day. With a final slurp, he looked down and steadied himself, trying in vain to shake the weeks of fatigue from his body before the start of another day at sea.

Sometimes he sat for a minute or two, but never for much longer as it was best to get moving. He crushed the can in his fist, stood up, pulled on his heavy blue utility pants, threw a clean blue U.S. Coast Guard t-shirt over his arms, tucked it in, and cinched up the black webbed belt around his waist. Tucking his pants into steel-toed black leather boots, Cole left his stateroom and started his rounds before assuming the deck watch on the bridge.

He always started at the fantail, where from the dark air-conditioned innards of the ship he'd emerge through a watertight door and take the day's first deep breath of salty air. Each morning, Cole stood at the stern and watched the white trail of wake disappear into the blackness of the ocean and a sky devoid of light. The stern would rise and roll with the sea swell beneath and it was a favorite moment of Cole's day as he stood alone in the predawn air with the sea as his only companion. He'd sigh, kick at some rusting stanchion, then work his way forward during his rounds—but this morning was different.

As Cole stood there with his hands in his pockets, a voice called out from behind him in the darkness. "LT, I think I owe you my life."

Cole turned quickly, surprised to see the old man, with his arm in a sling and a bandage over his right eye, standing just to the right and behind him.

Cole took a long breath to catch his nerves and smiled at the sailor, saying, "No Sir, I wouldn't go that far."

The man took a step to stand beside Cole then stared out at the horizon and paused before speaking again. "That's not what some of the crew said. I heard them talking last night that you insisted on checking on my boat. They said the captain went so far as to tell you to shut up, but you persisted. And for that, I'm alive."

Cole smirked just a bit, as he knew it was true. He looked down and enjoyed the fact that the crew spoke highly of his actions the day before.

"Well, Sir, I was just doing my job."

The old man smiled too and both of them stood in silence, looking out at the sea as *Delaney* gently rolled over a swell. They stood for some time, both appreciating the moment. For the old man, the sea had nearly taken his life the day before. For Cole, he'd realized a lifelong dream. On watch the previous afternoon, Cole had spotted the old man's sailboat 20 miles off the coast of Cuba. Cole had sensed something was wrong when he saw the jib luffing against the stiff easterly breeze. As *Delaney* reached her closest point of approach, still nearly two miles away, Cole focused through his binoculars and saw no one on deck and that both jib sheets were swinging wildly from the clew.

As Cole stood and thought back to that moment, the old man broke the silence. "Not all men are cut out for the sea, LT. But I reckon you're one of the few who can take her on. You seem to understand her." He paused for another moment, then continued. "Now if you'll excuse me, I might try to close my eyes for a bit before we pull in. When do you think we'll tie up?"

Cole looked down at his watch instinctively, but knew already in his head of the day's plan. "We'll be at the sea buoy at 0800, and probably pierside by 0900."

The old man nodded and said once more to Cole, "Thank you, LT."

"Not a problem there, Skipper. It was my pleasure."

With that, the old man walked back inside the innards of *Delaney* and Cole was once again alone on the fantail. It was true what the man had said, but Cole wasn't the type to take such credit. Cole's instincts, and his years of racing sailboats offshore, had told him something was amiss, but when he'd reported it, OPS had wanted nothing to do with the boat. When Cole pressed the issue, Commander Walters had come to bridge, but she too had dismissed Cole's concerns. It wasn't until Wheeler, Cole's roommate, had taken Cole's side that both Walters and OPS relented and agreed to divert to the sailboat and send over a boarding team.

Wheeler led the boarding team and within minutes of pulling alongside, he had radioed back for a corpsman. The old man, sailing alone from Belize to Key West, had fallen during a squall and broken his arm the day before. His forehead, just above his right eye, was also badly cut, leaving him in shock from the blood loss. Worse still, his rudder had broken free and nearly sunk the boat. With a broken arm and bleeding head, the old man had patched the rudder post as best he could and then passed out. By the time the boarding team had brought the sailor aboard, he was badly dehydrated and in shock from his injuries. Wheeler had tried to save the boat as well, but the leaking rudder post was too far gone, and she had sunk within a few hours of *Delaney's* arrival.

Cole stood there on the fantail for a moment, overwhelmed with pride. His goal since he was young had been to make a difference like that. Many times on *Delaney* he'd been a part of the team effort, and no doubt had saved many a migrant or lost mariner from the sea. But this rescue was different. Cole knew it was his own actions and his alone that had saved the old man. Just as his emotions nearly overwhelmed him, Cole snapped himself out of it and remembered that he had rounds to finish. Now was not the time to reminisce.

Cole continued making his way forward, checking that the small boat was properly secured, hatches were closed, and that the aging cutter was ready enough for a new day. His last stop was the messdeck, where he poured himself a bowl of Frosted Mini-Wheats and sat alone below the dim red lights in silence. Regardless of what the cooks had served for dinner the night before, the messdeck always smelled the same—garbage thinly masked by an over-dependence on bleach. It smelled and was clean enough, but there was always the faintest trace of soggy meat or something fried that wafted through the entire space. Silently lifting each spoonful of cereal to his mouth that morning, Cole ate his breakfast and thought some more of the old man and what courage it must take to tackle the sea alone.

His next stop was three decks above in the Combat Information Center, commonly known as CIC. Inside, he'd check with the petty officers on duty for any new tasking or intelligence that had come over the radios since the previous evening. Rarely was there anything worth mentioning. The array of radar screens, communications equipment, and sensor systems looked like something out of a movie. The thought made Cole smile a bit. Most mornings he'd do little more than joke with the sleepy petty officers on duty and remind them to give him a heads up if anything out of the ordinary developed. From CIC, he'd leave through the same door, walk down a dimly lit passageway, then up three steps, through another door, and onto the bridge.

The bridge team consisted of six crewmembers: a navigator, a helmsman, two lookouts, a boatswain's mate, and the officer of the deck. Two radar consoles emitted a dim green light and Cole could just make out the tired faces as they went about their watch. Radios crackled softly as Cole plotted the ship's position on a paper chart, matched it to the radar picture, and read through Walters' orders for the night. At precisely 0800, Cole was to have *Delaney* one nautical mile south of the Key West sea buoy. Anything less would not be tolerated, or so said Walters, the ship's commanding officer. Cole's plot had showed that a slight increase in speed was needed, but otherwise the task at hand was a simple one. The radar picture was clear and nothing but deep tropical water stood between *Delaney* and the sea buoy, some 35 miles to the north. Cole walked over to Lora—the officer of the deck—and firing off his trademark half-assed salute, stated, "I offer my relief."

Lora looked at him for a moment with the nervousness she always tried to hide, and saluted back. "I stand relieved." She passed her binoculars to him and sped down below without another word. Lora kept a low profile and this morning was no different. In some ways, Cole envied her.

Cole exhaled with force and called out in the dark, "Helmsman, all ahead six."

The helmsman barked back, "All ahead six, aye," then a moment later, "Sir, my engines are all ahead six."

Cole answered, "Very well," then walked out of the bridge and onto the bridge wing. With any sort of headwind, it offered a clean breeze and some relief from the thick air. This morning, however, a light breeze blew from the south and was completely negated as *Delaney* steamed north. It was horribly stagnant, made worse by the exhaust that bellowed from the stacks and lingered over the entire bridge. Cole felt the sweat beading on his chest and wondered why he even bothered doing laundry.

The next hour crept by. Cole checked the radar every few minutes for shipping traffic and cross-referenced it with the paper chart, but spent the majority of his time pressed against the railing on the bridge wing, alone with his thoughts under the dark predawn sky. The bridge wing jutted out almost four feet from the side of the ship and hung precariously over the water, some 40 feet below. Cole could look straight down and it almost gave the sense of flying. Occasionally, dolphins swam full speed alongside *Delaney* and illuminated the phosphorescence like a torpedo toward its target. Mostly the bridge wing was quiet and peaceful, two things that made it Cole's favorite spot. He enjoyed the solitude of the early morning and took great pleasure in watching the sun come up over the eastern horizon.

Another hour passed. The sun was now up, the orange sky faded to a soft blue, and the deep water was dark, clear, and gently rolling. The southerly breeze barely made a ripple and had it not been for the groundswell pushing in from the west, the Florida Straits may have just as well been a lake. *Delaney's* bow pushed a tumbling white wave in front of her. She pitched up and over a swell before falling back down, her bow cutting deep into the trough left behind as the cycle repeated time and again with near-perfect rhythm.

Another hour passed. On the back end of his watch, Cole made one last round through the bridge, crosschecking the position and dead reckoning his advance to make damn sure he'd be at the sea buoy on time. Cdr. Walters became hysterical if her cutter was even one minute late—or early for that matter. Her leadership was that of an 18th century naval captain, minus the tenacity for warfare or requisite seamanship. She screamed and cursed at the most minor infraction, often becoming so incapacitated by sheer rage that she simply walked off the bridge in a fit. As amusing as it was at times, Cole tried to avoid it. Satisfied that his course and speed over the past few hours had compensated for the drift, he called out one last command. "Helmsman, all ahead five."

The helmsman repeated his standard replies and *Delaney* settled just a bit as her speed came down to around seven knots.

Cole walked back out to the bridge wing, leaned against the railing, and waited.

He had aspired to do great things in the Coast Guard. Cole had raced sailboats all through New England and the Atlantic Ocean as a cadet and reported to *Delaney* convinced that a life at sea was his destiny, but the life of a cutterman had proven more daunting than he imagined. Cole's penchant for seamanship had taken a backseat to his disdain for the command. Onboard *Delaney,* Cole knew he had come up short of their expectations for procedural discipline. It bothered him, but he never could quite figure out how to get in their good graces. Cole had a wild streak in him and he knew it.

He knew how the ship handled and could conn it well, but his sometimes-cavalier attitude had cost him dearly. Several times Walters had threatened to take away Cole's qualifications. Most often, it was because he conned the cutter too close to a suspect vessel or took his boarding team too far in the small boat chasing smugglers. Those antics usually cost him no more than an ass-chewing in front of the other junior officers, but Cole knew that with each of his little adventures he was digging himself a deeper grave. His last two Officer Evaluation Reports had not recommended him for promotion, which meant that his career was a dead end. After two years at sea, he had begun to wonder if he was cut out for the life he was living.

Lieutenant Commander Potts, the executive officer, had made his frustration with Cole quite clear. While Walters was a lunatic, Potts was the one who gave the ship some semblance of order. He was also relentless. Standing well over six feet tall with once-blond hair now going grey, his hands had a tendency to shake when speaking in front of people. Cole never could tell if it was out of anger or simply nerves. Nevertheless, Potts came unglued at the slightest hiccup. To compensate and keep his temper in check, he ruled with an iron fist, and many times that fist was directed at Cole. Cole sensed that Potts still believed in the mission of the Coast Guard, and for that he held a good deal of respect for the man. In any other environment, Cole probably could have gotten along with Potts well enough, but the confines of a 270-foot ship at sea for months at a time was too much for two opposed personalities.

As they neared Key West, Cole was again in hot water with Potts. Several weeks earlier, Cole had led a pursuit off the Caribbean coast of Colombia. They'd been tasked with tracking a drug-running boat for the better part of a day, and as sunset approached, *Delaney* was perfectly positioned to make an intercept just outside of Colombia's territorial seas. Cole was the lead boarding officer and after he'd geared up, Potts had stopped him on the fantail and grabbed Cole by his shoulder, saying, "Don't let this one get away, Cole."

As the boatswain's mates hurried to lower the smallboat over the side, Cole had looked at Potts and nodded, understanding that the entire crew was hungry for a win.

"I got it, Sir. We'll get them."

With that, Cole had mustered his team to the starboard side of the fantail and Cole looked around at the five guys that he would take with him. They were a tough looking bunch, each wearing dark blue overalls with black load-bearing vests over their chests. Each man had a Beretta M9 holstered on their thigh and the two of his most junior members had M4 carbines slung across their chests. Cole's assistant boarding officer, one of the new officers named Jake, stood off to the side as he fidgeted with a radio strapped to his chest and checked in with the bridge before giving Cole a thumbs up. The lead boatswain's mate, a second-class petty officer who Cole affectionately called "Boats," carried a short-barreled 12-gauge shotgun and smiled just a bit when Cole's eyes met his. After they all strapped their helmets on, adjusted their night vision goggles, and flipped them up, Cole briefed them on what he knew.

"All right, guys, it's a Go-Fast and we've got a C-130 overhead that's had eyes on it for the past six hours. Our plan is to stand off by a mile and stalk once the sun goes down. The Herc will vector us in and we'll stand by for use-of-force clearance. Everyone understand?"

Cole looked around as each man softly nodded.

Cole continued, talking directly to his second class petty officer. "Boats, I want you on the rail ready with the shotgun if they engage when we close in. You know the drill: clear to shoot for personal defense."

His boatswain's mate nodded and smiled a bigger grin. Cole couldn't help but laugh. The rest of the team smiled as well, and Cole asked if there were any questions. Having none, Cole and his team stepped over to the port side, and one by one they cautiously climbed down the Jacob's ladder and hopped down onto the pitching smallboat.

Already onboard was the engineer seated aft and the coxswain forward at the wheel. As Cole and his crew settled into their seats and strapped in, Cole smacked Jake on the back and grinned, saying, "Now the fun starts."

The smallboat sped away from *Delaney* as the sun disappeared behind some low clouds on the western horizon. Jake was seated next to Cole and established comms with the C-130 overhead as the coxswain steadied on an intercept course. Cole kept comms with *Delaney* and checked in to report their position. For the next half hour, things went smooth as the smallboat took a position one mile aft and to the starboard side of the suspect Go-Fast. Through his goggles, Cole could make out the Go-Fast's wake. The Caribbean was calm and the fading twilight revealed nothing but a few light rain showers in the area.

At some point, the Go-Fast had caught wind of something amiss and made a rapid turn back to the south. It was an all-too-often occurrence. The smugglers likely had night-vision goggles and had seen the silhouette of either the C-130 or *Delaney* in the distance. The aircraft overhead relayed their turn to Jake, who instructed the coxswain to energize the blue lights and give chase.

Cole nodded and tried to think ahead to the next move. The coxswain jammed the throttles, and Cole felt the smallboat surge up and onto its V hull as it sliced towards its target. It was now an old-fashioned chase, and Cole grinned and then gritted his teeth as he was jolted from side to side. One of Cole's junior team members howled like a mad dog, and they all smiled as the boat reached top speed.

Cole relayed it all to *Delaney*, but had a hard time over the screaming engines of the smallboat to clearly hear anything back from the cutter. With continued vectors from the aircraft overhead, the coxswain made a slow turn to the left and came within 25 yards of the Go-Fast's stern before paralleling its course due south.

As they drove into a light rain, Cole took a moment to look around and admire his crew. The coxswain showed a steel resolve on his face as he expertly worked the throttle and wheel to keep a tight formation with the Go-Fast. All around him, Cole's team readied for the attack as the smallboat surged up and over swells. On the port side of the smallboat, Cole's leading petty officer with the shotgun repositioned himself to hold his sights on the Go-Fast, now no more than ten yards ahead in the dark.

Jake grabbed Cole's shoulder and yelled, "I've lost comms with the Herc."

Cole thought for a second, then looked forward at the Go-Fast and remembered Potts' words. Cole then looked back at his boatswain's mate who grinned at Cole through the rain, silently encouraging him to continue the chase.

"Fuck it," said Cole and he motioned with his left hand to continue the chase. It was pitch black now, and all Cole could see ahead was the white wake of the Go-Fast as it ran south for Colombia. He flipped his goggles down and still could only make out the green blurred wake of the Go-Fast. Cole tried again with no success to get comms with *Delaney*. It wasn't until after they emerged out of the rain squall several minutes later that Cole heard *Delaney* calling for him.

"Bravo, Conn, Bravo, Conn, acknowledge."

Cole yelled back into the radio, "Conn, Bravo, Go ahead."

Cole heard the concern in the voice on the other end when it said, "Bravo, Conn, RTB, I say again, RTB."

Just as Cole acknowledged the call, Jake yelled to him, "I got comms again. We're ten miles from Colombia. The C-130 says we're inside their TTWs. We gotta turn around!"

Cole looked ahead once more at the Go-Fast's wake through his NVGs and realized he'd lost this one. Moreover, he'd busted a sovereign nation's territorial seas. He tapped the coxswain on the shoulder and motioned to turn around. The coxswain shook his head to say no, but Cole signaled him again to turn around. With disappointment and frustration on the faces of his entire crew, Cole flipped his goggles up and sat back for the long ride back to *Delaney*.

He wasn't back onboard more than five minutes before Cole found himself once again being dressed down by Potts.

"Damn it, Cole. Do you even realize what a mess you've created?"

Cole, knowing better, still argued, "Sir, you told me not to let them get away."

Potts grew even more upset and yelled, "There are rules, Cole, and you don't seem to ever take that into account. I'm telling you right now, this isn't the end of this one for you. Now get the fuck out of my face."

And so, weeks after that night, Cole stood on the bridge wing and thought back to that chase. His watch nearly over, Cole compared that chase to that previous afternoon and reflected quietly on the blurred lines between right and wrong. He knew it was wrong to keep the chase up, but a drug bust had been a mere 30 yards from him, and the entire crew of *Delaney* was hungry for it. Had he been successful, he thought, perhaps Potts would have had a different reaction. But luck was rarely on Cole's side these days.

He thought too of the old man now sleeping on the couch in the wardroom down below. *Had I been wrong to push the issue with Commander Walters and OPS about the sailboat?* In all likelihood, Potts and Walters didn't like him anymore because of it, but the sailor who was alive because of Cole would probably argue the opposite. There were no easy answers to any of Cole's questions.

After a few minutes, Cole's mind steadied once he heard Wheeler moving about on the bridge. Cole's roommate and a classmate from the academy, Wheeler was a golden child. He was tall, an accomplished athlete, and well-liked by the crew for his ability to filter the crap from above and spare the crew from Walters' wrath. In short, Wheeler had the system licked and the sky was the limit for him.

Wheeler did everything Potts asked of him and never questioned why, putting him on the fast track to success and standing in stark contrast to Cole. This morning he had come up to relieve Cole for the transit into Key West. Cole watched from the bridge wing as Wheeler made his round of the bridge, quickly devoured an apple, then tossed it in the trash as he stopped at the radar console. Cole watched with irritation as Wheeler chewed the rest of the apple and stared at the radar for a minute or two. Cole knew damn well the radar picture was clear and no traffic stood between *Delaney* and the sea buoy, now just a few miles to the north. From the bridge wing, Cole looked north ahead of the cutter and there was nothing but water. Reluctantly, he walked into the bridge to see what nonsense Wheeler had come up with.

"What's this guy here doing?" Wheeler asked without looking up at Cole.

"Come on man, that's not a contact." Cole gritted his teeth already knowing where this conversation would end.

"It looks like something." Wheeler's eyes remained focused on the black screen as the radar scanned around and around and a faint green blip popped up every third or fourth sweep.

"Wheeler, why are you such a bitch?" Cole said. He was having a bit a fun now.

Wheeler ignored the provocation and calmly replied, "Did you run a plot on this guy?"

Fuck, Cole thought, knowing that Wheeler would not relieve him of the deck until he plotted out a maneuvering solution for the phantom blip. Perhaps Wheeler actually convinced himself it was a contact, or perhaps Wheeler was screwing with Cole—either way, Cole had to plot it out. He took a blank maneuvering board from the chart table and started laying out the solution on paper. It was difficult to do since the suspect blip disappeared for half a minute at a time before reappearing, but Cole dutifully went through the steps before showing Wheeler that whatever it was, it wasn't moving anywhere and posed no threat to *Delaney*.

Wheeler looked at the plot and gave Cole a terse, "Very well, I offer my relief."

He saluted Cole with a smirk giving away the fact that the radar blip was just a quick joke at Cole's expense.

Cole saluted back smiling, "You're such a prick sometimes." He walked back out on the bridge wing, still smiling a bit at Wheeler's little prank. They were polar opposites, but as roommates they got along well enough to screw with each other incessantly. Wheeler didn't dare show it in front of others, but he liked Cole, too.

Not yet eight in the morning, Key West was at last in sight. Soon, the party catamarans would anchor just off the reef and tourists would splash over the side with their cheap pastel-colored snorkels and fins. Cuddy cabins and center-console power boats, crewed by half-drunk and sunburned weekend fishermen, would dot the shallow waters between the reef and the shore. The cruise ships' engines were still lit off and faint trails of their exhaust were carried north with the sea breeze. Cole looked at Key West and knew the little town of misfits and modern-day pirates was coming alive. He'd spent many nights drunk like any good sailor cavorting up and down Duval Street. He knew the good restaurants tucked into quiet corners where the cruise ship crowd dared not go. He knew the bars that served good spiced rum and had more than a few favorite weathered bar stools overlooking the harbor. Cole daydreamed often about settling down in the little town known as the Conch Republic.

Meanwhile, back on the bridge, more and more members of the crew were taking their positions. They marched up and silently settled in for the slow transit. To Cole, it resembled a clown show. The bridge was barely big enough for six, but each time *Delaney* pulled into port, more than 25 crew members were crammed onto it. There was a navigator, a back-up navigator, Lora overseeing both the navigators, and a seaman to record the minutiae in a little green notebook. They huddled around the chart table and bumped against each other as they went about their assigned tasks. There were two more seamen on each bridge wing as bearing recorders who shouted bearings to landmarks for the navigator inside who compared their references to the GPS position plotted on paper. There were also two lookouts who most often defeated their own purpose by standing next to each other and focusing their efforts on watching the show inside the bridge rather than scanning for potential conflicts ahead.

There was a helmsman and a throttleman who physically manipulated the rudder and throttles respectively. Then there were half-a-dozen petty officers on sound-powered phones who did little but stand by in case of some unspecified catastrophic failure. For the hours-long transit, they would lean against whatever bulkhead kept them out the way and focus all their energies on keeping their eyes open. Sometimes they would laugh, seemingly to themselves, but really because someone had made a crude joke over the phones that only they could hear. There was a chief boatswains' mate and a senior boatswains' mate who supervised the deck crew that would ultimately throw the mooring lines over to the pier at the end of a mooring evolution. For the most part, they stood out of the way and passed the time making idle chatter.

Then there were the officers. Lora was the navigator for this evolution and stood by the chart table. In theory she was in charge of the plot, but in reality she stood silent as the enlisted folks around her did their job and paid little attention to her presence. Lieutenant Grouse, the operations officer, was pacing from station to station, making sure everyone was on the same page. Everyone called him "OPS" and he was much older than his peers, having spent his life at sea with the Coast Guard. He reminded Cole more of a grandfather type than a sailor and Cole stayed away from him most of the time since OPS didn't care much for Cole either. He wasn't a bad guy, but he kept a low profile, biding his time until he could be reassigned off of *Delaney* to another cutter.

Wheeler barked out commands over the loud and chaotic scene developing on the bridge. He was smart enough to recognize the ridiculousness of it, but played along in the interest of not ending up like Cole. Potts stood in a corner, looping his binoculars around his neck and quietly took in the bridge scene before Walters came up. The rest of the deck officers all grabbed radios or binoculars and did their best to look important.

Cole was tasked with the radar. Still standing on the bridge wing, Cole saw Potts giving him the death stare and picked up on the angry man's cues ordering him to man the radar. Cole exhaled rather loudly, walked into the chaos of the bridge, and stood over the radar console. Potts passed by him and whispered as he went, "Keep your shit together Cole and come see me after we've tied up."

"Captain on the bridge!" came out from a chorus of watchstanders as Walters' short frame emerged from below decks. Her curly short red hair was tucked up under her ball cap and her pock-marked face wore its normal expression of anger. She said not a single word to anyone as she made her way to the captain's chair. It sat against the aft bulkhead, facing forward, elevated above the bridge. She climbed up and sat down, convinced in her own mind that she was the master of this ship. OPS approached her and reported that all stations were manned and ready. She nodded and he backed away without turning his back to her.

Wheeler was next. He saluted her and reported the ship's position just south of the sea buoy. Again she nodded and instructed him to enter the shipping channel. Wheeler saluted a second time, replying, "Aye, aye, Captain." He walked back over to the front of the bridge wing and stood next to Potts as *Delaney* crept closer to Key West.

"Who was eating an apple?" Walters asked, her face turning a few shades ruddier. From her perch, she was looking over and down into the trash where Wheeler had tossed it.

The entire bridge went silent. Twenty-something sets of eyes looked around for someone to step forward and take the fall. Cole looked at Wheeler and Wheeler looked back at him with an expression of dread.

"That was me, Captain."

Everyone stared at Cole. From the console, he turned to face Walters and readied himself for an ass-chewing.

"Figures." She muttered the words without looking at Cole and shifted her gaze to look ahead of the cutter.

Slowly, the crew went back to their tasks and as they did, Cole caught Wheeler staring at him. When they made eye contact, Wheeler nodded subtly in appreciation. Cole nodded back and *Delaney* continued at a snail's pace.

The deep, dark blue of open water gave way to shades of green as *Delaney* neared the Key West reef line. Coral heads appeared as dark spots below and only the channel, with *Delaney* in the middle, remained a dark blue. When she passed the reef line, the westerly swells subsided and *Delaney* steadied herself in the calmer waters. Protected by the reef, there was nothing more than a light chop now and the rising sun reflected off thousands of dwarfed crests. Inside the reef, small boats bobbed and motored their way aimlessly about. The palm trees of Key West were close enough now that Cole could see the southerly breeze colliding with and dying against the swaying fronds. *Delaney* inched past the green and red channel markers and veered west around the southernmost point, then north again past the cruise ship terminals.

Cole was busy watching the tourists mill about Mallory Square, less than 100 yards to the east, when OPS barked at him, "Radar, what is this sailboat doing in front of us?"

One of the dozen tourist party boats was idle in the channel, floating between *Delaney* and the Key West Coast Guard base. The radar would do little to determine the sailboat's course, and

Cole knew that OPS yelled at him simply to buy some time and appease Walters. Just as it did every day, the catamaran would set a sail to give paying tourists the false sense of sailing, then motor its way south to the reef. On the radar, it was far too close to interpret, but Cole pretended to plot it.

Wheeler, with a fake irritation in his voice, ordered, "Helmsman, All Stop!"

"All Stop. Aye, Sir," came from the helmsman, followed quickly with, "Sir, my engines are all stop."

OPS again asked Cole what the sailboat was doing as the tension on the bridge peaked. The radar plot was pointless at a range of less than 50 yards, but Cole replied back "Sir, they appear to be tracking due south." It was a total guess, based entirely on the fact that the catamaran did the same damn thing every day. Wheeler, OPS, and Potts all acted the part and exhaled loudly.

Walters squirmed in her seat and her head peered back and forth like a frustrated turtle. "Damn blow-boaters," was all she could manage in her growing frustration. The Coast Guard base was less than 200 yards away and the delay was not more than a minute, but her anger was real. Cole guessed that she was the only one on the bridge who was actually upset, but the crew did their best to act the part.

As the catamaran started to make some headway to the south, Wheeler barked a new set of commands and *Delaney* slowly aligned herself with the pier. Wheeler knew how to drive the ship, as he had a true sailor's sense about him. He'd back down on one engine, then forward on the other. He'd reverse both engines, then twist the ship again, each time inching closer and closer to the pier. Potts normally took over at this point, but Wheeler had earned his trust. Cole was off the radar by now and enjoyed watching Wheeler conn the ship into place. With a line over, Wheeler sent out a flurry of new commands, reversed the rudder hard, went ahead for a moment on both engines, then called out to put over the rest of the lines. Wheeler kept his composure throughout the process, and in Cole's mind would make a great captain one day.

Two dozen boatswain's mates were now hard at work pulling the 2,000 tons of ship the last few feet to the pier. They worked well together. They could yell obscenities at each other and a moment later be laughing as if nothing had ever come between them. The chief boatswain's mate and leading petty officer kept quiet for the most part, occasionally barking an order when they saw fit, but for the most part they let their subordinates do their jobs. Cole enjoyed this part of the Coast Guard. The camaraderie of the enlisted men and women was something he'd rarely felt in the wardroom. But just then, he caught Walters fidgeting in her chair with a look of disgust on her face and Cole shook off any romantic notions of the sea services. The southerly breeze pushed *Delaney* gently against the pier, and Cole left the bridge before OPS announced to secure from the sea detail.

Cole made his way down a passageway and into his stateroom. Wheeler would take his time on the bridge ensuring that every last detail was accounted for before coming down to their stateroom, so Cole was left alone with his thoughts. He took off his boots, blue pants and shirt, and gave himself a fresh coating of deodorant. After changing into his flip flops, faded cotton shorts, and a wrinkled button-down linen shirt, Cole felt much better than he had all morning. He went over to the sink and washed his hands under the cold water, rubbing them both over his face and through his disheveled hair. Taking his washcloth and soaking it as well, he wiped his face and scrubbed hard, as if to wash away the past few months.

He had not forgotten Potts' order to see him before he headed out for liberty, so Cole walked back down the passageway again to Potts' stateroom, where he was already back at his desk, firing off emails. Cole knocked and Potts called him in. Cole took a seat by the door and waited. Potts ignored him for a minute as he proofed the email, hit send, then spun around in his chair and stared at Cole.

"Cole, I told you that your little stunt off Colombia was going to cost you."

Cole nodded and felt the butterflies forming in his stomach. Perhaps this time he'd be restricted to the ship. With Key West's bars only a few hundred yards away, Cole dreaded the thought of being stuck on *Delaney* for the next few days.

"Headquarters, on my request and recommendation, has decided to separate you from the service."

"Do what?" Cole said.

"You're done Cole. I've frankly had enough of your shit and now you've managed to piss of Colombia and the rest of the Coast Guard as well. So go pack your things. It's time for you to move on."

"That's it? Just like that, you're kicking me out?" Cole was floored.

"Cole, you got some real issues you need to work out. I really do hope you sort this shit out and get your act together, but you are not a good officer and I can't have someone like you in my Coast Guard."

Cole thought for a moment and replied forcefully, "I think that sailor down below might say different about me."

Potts just shook his head and ignored Cole as he dug through a stack of papers on his cluttered desk and pulled out a single sheet. He looked down at it and said, "The results of your suitability board came in a few days ago, but I didn't want to drop this on you while we were at sea. Who knows what you might have done."

Potts read from the letter, "Lieutenant Junior Grade Cole Williams, due to sustained poor performance, you are officially separated from active service on this date. Your severance pay amounts to six months basic pay and you hereby forfeit all rights and privileges of active duty service." Potts paused for a second, handed the sheet to Cole, and put his hand out.

Cole thought for a moment that he wanted to shake hands, but that wasn't the case.

"I need your identification card, Cole."

Cole dug into his wallet and gave his ID card over to Potts.

"Good luck Cole. Now get off my boat."

Cole said nothing.

Astonished that it was all over in a matter of seconds, Cole walked back to his stateroom. In his shorts, shirt, and flip flops, the air conditioned passageway was cold and Cole felt the shock overcome his body. Frustrated and angry, he grabbed his sea bag and stuffed a few random bits of clothing into it along with some personal effects, took one last look around his stateroom just to make sure he hadn't left anything he needed, and noticed his piled-up uniform still on his rack. He paused for a second, then left it there and slammed the door. Down the passageway again, Cole made his way through two watertight doors, into the hangar, and finally out onto the flight deck. His feet felt numb from the air conditioning inside and the sun immediately went to work warming his core. Many of the crew were still tying up loose ends, but the brow was already over. Cole made his way over to the side with his sea bag slung over one shoulder. He could feel a single bead of sweat making its way down his chest.

Allison stopped him. Another classmate from the academy, she'd been on the ship for two years with Cole, but had worked for the engineering officer. Her choice in jobs was a calculated decision on her part to avoid Walters and she was smart for doing so. Allison was always nice to Cole and watched with compassion as Cole was repeatedly raked over the coals by the command. Most of the junior officers avoided him, but Allison was always kind and could joke around with him after his beatings were through to raise his spirits.

She asked, "Cole, where are you going?"

Cole smiled and looked over his shoulder in the direction of Duval Street. "Potts just fired me. Apparently he had a suitability board behind my back and the Coast Guard opted to let me go. I figure I'll find a hotel for a few nights then sort things out from there. I've got a few months' pay from the severance, so I'm good for a while."

Allison gave a slight nod as she pieced together that Cole had just been kicked to the curb.

"Cole, I'm so sorry. Can I do anything?" She asked with a friendly voice and her tone asked much more than a simple question. Cole realized he would miss their friendship and in his last few minutes aboard the cutter, Allison was saying just as much.

"Nah, I think I'm better by myself."

Allison hugged him and held both his shoulders with her hands, saying, "Come out tonight. You'll hurt my feelings if you don't."

Cole knew she was worried about him and agreed to meet later that night. Cole didn't show it, but he was worried about himself as well. With that, he took one last look at *Delaney* and turned for the pier.

CHAPTER 2 – THE CONCH REPUBLIC

COLE WALKED DOWN the aging pier away from *Delaney* with his eyes partly focused on the bright blue water of the small harbor, home to the Coast Guard's fleet of cutters and boats that patrolled the Keys and the Florida Straits. The morning air smelled of salt and subtle hints of gasoline mixed with engine oil carried along by the gentle breeze. A cruise ship's whistle sounded in the distance, signaling one either arriving or departing from the downtown waterfront, only a 15-minute walk away. He slowed to keep the sweat from building too fast and looked with half-hearted curiosity at the evenly spaced patrol boats tied up pierside. Their white hulls and orange Coast Guard stripes were clean and well maintained, a testament to the orderly discipline of a seagoing military service—the same one that had just kicked him out. Blue fitted canvas covers were lashed down over their deck guns as the small flotilla bobbed gently and baked under the climbing Caribbean sun. Their mooring lines were neatly made up to rusted cleats bolted to the pier, while a radio played country music from inside the garage of the small-boat station as petty officers and non-rates tended to their daily chores. A half dozen or so of them tinkered quietly on an engine of one boat as Cole passed within earshot without saying a word. A resting black lab with tired eyes, the mascot of sorts for the station, looked up at Cole from the shade of a palm tree and rolled over slowly, going back to its morning nap. It was warm, the breeze was light, and the bright sun reflected off the turquoise water and the bleached concrete, forcing Cole to squint as he walked. In so many ways, it was the ideal Coast Guard lifestyle.

From there, Cole passed through the side gate that led to a shortcut downtown. He had come and gone through that gate more times than he could count, often drunk and stumbling back to *Delaney* after a night of partying with the crew. The port calls always came and went too fast. *Delaney* had patrolled for weeks in the Florida Straits, working all hours of the day and night interdicting migrants in everything from homemade rafts to stolen power boats. Their near-daily interdictions were interspersed with the occasional search-and-rescue case that broke the monotony of law enforcement. The crew's reward for their hard work was Key West for a night, maybe two at most, and only long enough to fill the ship's tanks with diesel, replenish the food stores, and give the crew a night to blow off steam. The entire crew always worked at a furious pace to finish up the odds and ends of tying up, focused entirely on their first taste of alcohol, loud music, and debauchery that waited for them downtown.

The truth was that Cole felt relieved to pass through the gate again, this time without the looming last call that always signaled his impending return to the ship. Once off the base, he made his way down Trumbo Road, right around a corner, and onto the wooden boardwalk that wrapped itself around Key West's inner harbor. Most of the party catamarans were already gone for the day. So too were the dive boats, all making their way out to the reef overloaded with amateur divers and their rented gear. The charter flats boats floated quietly in smaller slips next to the boardwalk. Their captains, most devoid of expression, passed the time either sitting at the consoles with their tanned bare feet up on the wheel, or seated on benches along the boardwalk, watching and hoping silently for some business to materialize from the morning foot traffic.

The boardwalk was slowly coming alive, but still quiet as most of Key West's residents and visitors were asleep or at best slowly working their way to a state of low consciousness. The bartenders were busy cutting limes and lemons, and their bar staff carried cases of beer back and forth, filling up the ice chests before the start of another drinking day. Cole stopped briefly at Turtle Kraals to watch some tarpon swim under the dock and disappear into the depth of the basin before he continued on his way downtown.

It was now approaching 11 o'clock and Cole's seabag weighed heavy on his shoulder. His back wet with the onset of a good midday sweat, Cole realized he had nowhere to go. The sting of failure and the weight of the unknown once again grew heavy. Ahead was the open-air Schooner Wharf, an oasis of sorts, and Cole knew from experience that its rum drinks were always a good blend. Dropping his bag at the bar, Cole eased himself onto a heavy wooden stool and followed a seam of the wooden bar top with his fingers, his elbows pressed against the rail. Soon thereafter the bartender approached without a word, knowing from the expression on Cole's face that he was there for business.

"Rum and Coke please, with a lime."

The bartender, a slender older woman with a leathered face and unkempt hair, looked at him for a moment before replying with a coarse voice, "Honey, we call that a Cuba Libre around here."

Part biker chick and part hippie, she smiled as Cole acknowledged with a smirk, "I'll have one of them as well then, please."

She brought his drink in a small white plastic cup and a wedge of lime rested atop the mountain of ice now stained dark with a bubbling blend of Coke and spiced rum. Cole squeezed the lime and drizzled its juice over the ice, stirring with his pointer finger. Taking a mouthful for his first sip, Cole held it for a moment, relishing the burn of rum and the fizzle of soda, before swallowing and setting the cup back down. Nearly a third of the drink was gone. He looked slowly over each of his shoulders, taking in the sights, sounds, and smells of Key West. It had a certain charm to it, a mystery that never quite revealed itself until one was dizzy from drink and burned by the sun. All too often it came as a fleeting moment of clarity amidst a drunken haze, and was all but lost by the next sip. Key West's allure was addictive and, with drink in hand, Cole had his first fix. The bartender brought him a second without asking and Cole took well-spaced smaller sips, taking his time as the rum warmed his core and slowed his worried mind. His momentary mild panic eased to a passive bliss as the rhythm of Key West became increasingly louder.

Almost an hour had passed. The crew from *Delaney* would be on Duval Street by now. The bars along the boardwalk that Cole loved so much were an afterthought for them. They wouldn't reach the Schooner Wharf until well after midnight, as they made their way back to the side gate. Cole liked the inner harbor more than Duval Street and always tried to steer the party crowd there earlier in the night, rarely with any success. He thought Duval Street, while an experience in itself, was more a sideshow than the real Key West. And so Cole sat, content among strangers, for a few more hours as he tended to his dizzy mind.

The sun passed overhead and worked its way west in choreographed fashion for the sunset party at Mallory Square. Cole paced himself, managing the rum on his brain and making small talk with the passing patrons that came and went throughout the day. Feeling the first hint of late-afternoon air, Cole settled his tab and slung his sea bag over his shoulder once more. Past the boardwalk, he finally hit Duval Street. The uncontrolled chaos of Key West was bursting with energy. A cruise ship, two perhaps, were most certainly tied up as sun-burned tourists nearly stumbled over top of each other while sipping fruity drinks and making their way from bar to bar. They wore straw cowboy hats, flower-patterned bathing suits, and Hawaiian shirts. Pure joy beamed from their faces as they soaked up each warm second of a vacation they had probably been waiting on for months.

Intermixed were the Key West regulars—misfits in normal society who had run from all over the country to call the Conch Republic home. They moved with purpose, towards their shifts as bartenders, bouncers, strippers, and entertainers. Their faces wore years of hard living, and not yet on the clock, they made no effort to hide the toll of decades under the sun with substances running through their veins. Cole slowed amidst the human traffic and ducked inside the lobby of the La Concha hotel. The front door closed behind him, the sounds dissipated, and the tidiness of its lobby was a study in contrasts. The air conditioning almost gave him a chill as it cooled the beads of sweat on his chest and back. Walking up to the desk he asked about a room for a few nights. The receptionist smiled, swiped his credit card, and sent him on his way with a plastic room key in hand. Up an elevator and down the pastel-themed hallway, he opened a door and walked into his dark room. Dropping his sea bag on the floor next to a king-sized bed, Cole opened the curtains overlooking Key West.

The room was silent. Floors below, Duval Street was booming. The bars were blasting reggae and Jimmy Buffett and top-40 dance songs. People were drinking, screaming, yelling, and thinking to themselves that this must be heaven on earth. Farther down the road, performers were taping together their makeshift stages at Mallory Square, hoping to God that the impending audience would be generous with their tips. Bartenders were busy shuffling back and forth, filling the never-ending orders for drinks and bar food. From his room, Cole felt nothing. There was no rush, no sense of urgency to quell his thirst, no need to hurry for anything or anyone. It was far removed from *Delaney,* and he relished the feeling. He looked forward to sleeping for hours in that bed, with its clean linen and warm comforter. He walked over to the thermostat, cranked it down a few notches so that he would sleep well under all the blankets, and picked up his sea bag.

Dumping it out on the bed, he took the few sets of clothes he had with him and put them away in drawers and hung the button-down shirts on hangers. He had six t-shirts from *Delaney,* each a faded blue with the crest of the ship over the left breast. Folding each up the same way he'd been taught at the academy, he put them away in drawers as well, and then tossed the sea bag over in a corner. With a brief respite from the madness of Duval Street, he found himself drawn back into it and the clean cool fragrant smell of the room seemed too artificial for his liking. The bass of a dance song was a faint bump in the distance, and Cole headed back down to the madness.

Walking again through the lobby, he passed through the front glass door and stepped out into the noise and the smells. Not too far down Duval Street, he took a secluded corner seat at Fogarty's and ordered the fish tacos, a dish he ate each time the opportunity presented itself. Sipping on a rum drink, he ate quickly and in silence, having not eaten anything since a bowl of cereal on the messdeck earlier that morning before his last watch. The moment wasn't lost on him. Like a prisoner freed from jail, this meal tasted better than any he'd had before. Cole had eaten the same plate dozens of times, but on this occasion it lifted his spirits.

With his belly full and his teeth numb from the booze, Cole settled his bill and descended again into the absurdity of Duval Street, ready to say good-bye to his shipmates and occasional friends from *Delaney*. They were easy to find at Fat Tuesdays. More than a dozen Slushee machines churned behind the bar, each a different color but remarkably similar in taste after one had consumed enough of them. The dozen or so junior officers were in the middle of the bar like a pack of wolves devouring a young deer. Walking up the steps, Cole laughed to himself at the sight of them, already drunk and smiling like it was the best night of their lives. He saw in them a new camaraderie. Perhaps it had been there all along. The thought saddened him for a moment, but he pushed it aside and put both his arms around Wheeler in a gentle headlock of sorts, as the whole crowd seemed happy to see him alive and smiling.

Wheeler hugged Cole with strong arms and shook Cole's shoulders after he let go.

"Brother, I owe you for the apple thing."

Cole shrugged, "Don't sweat it man. I was screwed either way."

Wheeler looked down to hide his discomfort before replying, "You got a bad deal on this one Cole. I would have done the same thing off Colombia."

Cole laughed, saying, "No you wouldn't, Wheeler. You don't make my kind of mistakes."

Wheeler hugged Cole again and they both smiled, then turned back into the fray. Cole took solace in Wheeler's appreciation. *If only the past two years had gone that way*, he thought.

The party went on through the night. The crowd meandered down and back up Duval Street, stopping sometimes for ten minutes and other times for two hours. Beers intermixed with rum drinks passed from hand to hand and Cole enjoyed his last night with the wardroom. Potts, Walters, and OPS were nowhere to be seen, and Cole's former shipmates let their guard down a bit around him. But even as they smiled and laughed as friends, underneath it all was an unspoken distance between Cole and his former shipmates. They all knew he'd just been kicked out. And as the bars began to shut down after midnight, Cole found himself on the receiving end of half-assed high-fives and handshakes. Allison gave him a long hug and wished him all the best, and Cole knew she meant it. He thought for a moment to try and kiss her, but things were confusing enough so he fought off the urge. He preferred her friendship over drunken lust. Under the lights of a sidewalk painted with neon signs, Cole parted ways and walked alone back to La Concha.

He awoke early the next morning with the familiar post-party thirst and a mild hangover. Lying awake in his bed, the morning light creeping through curtains he had forgotten to close, the room seemed oddly quiet. Unlike *Delaney*, it didn't roll and pitch or shudder under the force of a passing wave. No pipes protruded from the walls nor were there the constant thuds and rattles of a ship at sea. It was only seven o'clock, but Cole had slept for a good uninterrupted stretch, something that rarely happened at sea. He felt quite good, even with his head partially swollen and his tongue imitating a cotton ball.

He stood up and dressed himself with the same clothes he'd worn the night before, fastening only the two middle buttons on a familiar linen shirt. He drank water from his palm under the faucet until the cotton feeling subsided, and, grabbing his wallet and room key, made his way downstairs. If he hurried, he could beat the tourists to Blue Heaven and scarf down some banana bread with butter without waiting in line. When he stepped outside of the hotel, the sidewalk was shaded, still hidden from the rising sun as storefront owners swept out the debris from the night before. Some simply hosed it off the curb. Plastic cups, beads, cigarette butts, and the occasional shirt all gave subtle clues to the party from the previous night, and the air smelled cool with the faintest hint of stale beer.

Blue Heaven hid itself down a backstreet, a landmark breakfast place for visitors and locals alike. By eight in the morning, the line would stretch out the door. Cole walked in at 0720 and sat at the shantytown-styled bar perched on a sand floor. Coffee and banana bread gave him new energy and he passed the time watching a rooster chase chickens around the plastic patio furniture that served as the outdoor dining room. *Delaney* would be underway at 0900, and Cole hoped to watch her out to sea from Mallory Square. He ate the last crumb of bread soaked in butter, finished one more cup of coffee, settled his bill with an attractive raven-haired bartender, and was on his way.

The walk to Mallory Square was pleasant in the morning air. The breeze blew soft against Cole's face as he walked, a light mood settling in around him as taxis and scooters made their way up and down the street. Key West went to sleep each night like a stumbling drunken fool, but the town recovered each morning with a renewed vigor and freshness that kept its inhabitants coming back for more. Reaching the square, Cole pressed his forearms against the railing and looked out over the bluish-green water, breathing the salt air deep into his lungs. Sunset Key, across the channel, was manicured and the resort-style bungalows tucked among palm trees had a look of tropical luxury. The white sand beaches were all freshly raked. It was the kind of picturesque landscape one saw in advertisements, and was the image most thought of when the word *Caribbean* was spoken. Just to the north, Wisteria Island sat windswept and barren. The gnarled underbrush that covered the island looked inhospitable and cruel. The mess of mangrove and brush extended itself out over the water, a stretch of sandy beach barely visible underneath. Cole looked back and forth at the two islands, wondering which of the two was the true Caribbean.

Meanwhile *Delaney* was backing away from the pier at the Coast Guard base a few hundred yards to the north and east. Her stern crept closer to Wisteria Island until she shifted her rudders and swung hard in place, pointing her bow south toward open water. In his mind, Cole could hear the barking of orders and see Walters fidgeting in her chair and craning her neck as the two dozen crew members shuffled about on the bridge. *Delaney* inched ahead until she was centered in the channel and picked up speed as it approached Mallory Square. The lookouts were leaning against the railing talking to each other, and Cole couldn't help but let out a hearty laugh and shake his head.

The boatswain's mates were hard at work on the weather decks, dragging the heavy waterlogged mooring lines back and forth, stowing them below decks until their next port call. He could almost hear them ribbing each other and re-telling tales from the night before. Crew members stood on the flight deck, resting their arms on the railing and staring back towards Key West, no doubt with faded memories of the previous night replaying in their heads. *Delaney* knifed ahead through the calm waters and disappeared around Cut Bravo, pointing back towards the straits. The ship disappeared and Cole felt a deep and bittersweet sadness.

All at once he also felt a longing for the swells under his feet and the dark open sea. In less than a day, he already missed it. Standing only a few feet above the water, Cole felt detached from the sea and some gnawing urge to be on it again occupied his mind. The same longing for adventure burned in his soul and he watched with curiosity as cruising sailboats and center consoles motored past. Surely he could pick up a job with the U.S. Customs agents, or the local police, or even as a Fish and Wildlife Conservation agent. It was time to turn a new leaf and as the first beads of sweat formed on his upper lip, Cole left the square and headed back towards the boardwalk.

He went back to his hotel and cleaned himself up as best he could. After a shower and shave, Cole changed into some clean clothes and looked at himself in the mirror. He looked for some time and assured himself that he would do just fine in whatever job lay ahead. With that, he headed down to the lobby and pulled up a chair next to a courtesy phone. Thumbing through a phone book, he found numbers for the Key West police, the local Fish and Wildlife Conservation Commission office, and the U.S. Customs office. He dialed each and managed to set up appointments throughout the day to fill out applications. Feeling confident, he set out and made his way around town. The local police department seemed promising and was interested in Cole's experience. The officer Cole spoke with made it sound like a sure thing and the paperwork was nothing more than a formality. When it asked for his past supervisor, Cole hesitated for a second, but then listed Potts and his email address on *Delaney*.

Once done there, Cole did the same thing with the Fish and Wildlife Conservation Commission, who also seemed interested in his skills as a boarding officer. After the same paperwork drill, Cole left feeling good about his prospects. His last stop for the day was with the U.S. Customs office. An agent met him at the front door and walked Cole back to a conference room where they both sat down. In his third meeting of the day, Cole felt good and answered the agent's questions assertively. After some time, the question came up about Cole's employment with the Coast Guard.

Cole was as honest as he felt was appropriate, but the agent pressed the issue as to why Cole had separated so suddenly. Feeling no need to hide the truth, Cole explained the incident off of Colombia and saw the expression change on the agent's face. The agent nodded along as Cole explained his situation. After a few more minutes, the agent looked away from Cole for a moment, then back at him and said matter-of-factly, "Sorry, Cole, but I just don't think you'd make it past the selection process with a history like that."

Cole thought for a second and tried to think of something to say, but nothing came to his mind. It was awkward as the agent escorted Cole back out and shook his hand before sending him off. It was not the end to his day that Cole had expected, but he knew he still had a good chance with the other local agencies. By then it was late afternoon, and Cole walked for a bit around the town to clear his head. He knew it would be a few days before he'd hear back from the police or the Fish and Wildlife agents, and even longer before he'd go through their initial training and start a job, so Cole weighed his options as he walked down to the boardwalk and along the waterfront.

The afternoon was on its last breath when Cole walked up to find the *Yankee Freedom II* tied to her berth. She was a high-speed catamaran that had just come back in from one of her daily trips. The passengers now gone, some of the crew walked about cleaning up from the day. Cole walked out onto the pier and caught some movement in the cabin. He called out a loud, "Hello." A tanned stranger of Cole's age stepped out onto the aft deck and said hello back.

Cole cleared his throat and asked matter-of-factly, "Don't suppose you're hiring any deckhands?"

The figure smiled, laughing almost at Cole's direct line of questioning and asked back, "Do you know your way around a boat?"

Cole's turn to smile, he replied with a chuckle, "More than I care to admit. My name is Cole and I'm just looking for some work around here. I just got out of the Coast Guard, so yeah, I'm pretty good on a boat."

His counterpart replied, "I'm Kevin and I run the deckhands. If you're serious, we can talk over a beer."

Kevin looked the part. He was about Cole's height, of similar build, and wore a faded pair of cotton shorts low on his waist with a white t-shirt stained as one would imagine from a day's work in the sun and salt. He had short dark hair and a distinct laugh that revealed a laissez-faire approach to all things in life.

Cole offered to buy the first round.

Needing to clean a few things up, Kevin invited Cole up before ducking back inside the cabin. Cole, now alone on the aft deck, instinctively went about tightening the lines over to the dock and cleaned up the bitter ends, coiling them neatly beside their cleats. The cat bobbed gently and the fiberglass deck felt good under Cole's feet. He kicked off his flip flops and reflected on the significance of the moment. He was on a boat again, but this time on his own terms. Suddenly the ocean wasn't so far away and by simply standing on a deck devoid of military protocol and nonsensical tension, Cole felt a renewed appreciation for the calming force of the sea. It was a feeling he'd cherished as a cadet at the Coast Guard Academy each time he set sail down the Thames River, pointed towards Long Island Sound and the cold Atlantic Ocean beyond. The sea always meant freedom, and here Cole felt it once again. On the deck of this catamaran, a boat he'd known for only a few minutes, he recognized in himself that his love for adventure and open water had never left him. Two years on *Delaney* had only buried that feeling, and it had remained hidden and dormant until this moment.

Kevin emerged from the enclosed cabin and looked down momentarily at the lines Cole had tightened and seemed somewhat impressed. It was almost a look of disbelief. It took Kevin a minute to piece together in his mind the fact that Cole had enough good sense to do something without being asked. Cole watched Kevin's facial expression change and sensed immediately that the two would be friends. Kevin shook his head and let out another one of his hearty laughs.

They chatted about nothing on the walk up the dock and agreed to beers at Turtle Kraals. Over the course of an hour and several rounds of Corona, Cole agreed to start the next day as a deckhand. It paid just over minimum wage, but would be plenty for Cole to sort things out over the remaining summer until something more steady opened up with law enforcement. On top of that, the job offered hours each day on the open water between Key West and Fort Jefferson. It was easy work: show up at six in the morning, set up the fruit and bagels for breakfast, clean the main cabin, and wait for the tourists to board a little after seven. The trip took a bit over two hours each way, and Kevin pointed out the downsides of dealing with seasick passengers, all things Cole was familiar with from his time in the Coast Guard.

They chatted idly about girls, places they'd lived, things they'd seen, and the addictive nature of warm tropical water. Kevin had moved down from central Florida and said he couldn't stand to leave the fishing. The catamaran job paid the bills while he lived a life others could only envy. Cole sensed that Kevin was more intelligent then he let on and quickly developed a measure of respect for his professed way of life.

Well after the sun had set over the Keys, Cole and Kevin shook hands. Kevin went on his way and Cole ordered a plate of fish tacos to settle his stomach. He ate by himself, one last bottle of beer sweating next to him before he made his way back to La Concha for the night. Key West was alive as he walked back up Duval Street. He thought that perhaps he was now a regular. In a town of misfits, he wondered, *What does one need to become a local?* His mind pondered such inconsequential questions as he walked alone up the sidewalk. The bar music blended in with the raucous noise as Key West repeated its same drunken mistakes yet again. He turned in to his room a little after nine and smiled under the crisp and clean cotton sheets, ecstatic at the thought of eight hours of uninterrupted sleep.

He woke early at a half past five and brewed the junk coffee in his room. Dressing quickly and in silence, he grabbed the coffee to go in a Styrofoam cup and made his way down Duval Street to the *Yankee Freedom II*. The feeling of a first day at work was new to him, and he enjoyed the thought of the day ahead. Meeting Kevin at the dock, Cole caught a Yankee Freedom t-shirt Kevin threw at him and replaced his button down shirt with it. Hopping aboard, Cole went to work with little direction from Kevin. He helped carry crates from the dock, set up the meager breakfast foods, and introduced himself to the few other crew members wandering about.

The tourists showed up shortly after seven. Cole was polite and realized that his smile was contagious. It was easy work. The sun was up, the engines were running, and Cole could hardly wait to slip the lines off the cleats and smell salt air in his lungs again. With the last of the guests aboard, the nimble cat cut through the light chop of the harbor and pointed south, her engines vibrating the deck beneath Cole's bare feet. She cut the same path through the water Cole had steamed so many times before on *Delaney*, but this time was different. Cole pictured himself content like the boatswain's mates on the decks of *Delaney*. His pace slowed as he stowed the last of the lines and the cat picked up speed southbound approaching the sea buoy. She rocked more as the open swells pushed under her bow and the cat made an easy turn to the west. Quickly coming up on speed, Cole's work was done for the next two hours. Perhaps he'd take a photo or two at the request of some tourists, or even pose for one, but the next two hours left him mostly alone with his thoughts.

Twenty minutes after rounding the reef, Kevin approached Cole on the aft deck and the two stood facing out over the water.

Kevin said, "If this is something you wanna do, you've got the job. I was just impressed you were here early this morning."

Cole replied, "Yeah, man. I think this is good for me."

"Cool." Kevin didn't say much after that. The two stood side by side, their arms against the railing and their shirts blowing in the breeze. The sun was warm and the breeze was stiff as the

Yankee Freedom dug through a groundswell and pointed towards the Dry Tortugas.

Two hours later, Kevin and Cole made their way to the bridge as Fort Jefferson came into view. The cat slowed as she neared the island, and Cole was struck by its secluded charm. Dating back to the middle of the 18th century, the fort served as an outpost against piracy and commanded control of the straits. It was monstrous and a sight to behold. Her massive brick walls pressed up against the shallow waters of a larger lagoon. During the Civil War, it had housed hundreds of army deserters. Cole knew the history of the fort and smiled to himself in appreciation of the mindset of a deserter. He felt like one himself in some ways and imagined what life must have been like for a prisoner on such a remote stretch of islands.

As the cat approached the dock, Cole hopped over first and tied her off to several rusting cleats on a weathered wooden dock. Helping passengers off, he smiled and directed them towards the beach. Some brought snorkels and masks, others walked through the abandoned fort or took guided tours with the park rangers. Others were already drunk from the ride over and flopped themselves down on the sandy beach, happy to be on terra firma. Everyone seemed to enjoy themselves.

Cole had a few hours to burn before the cat would head back towards Key West. He walked the quiet side of the island by himself and stopped at an open field littered with half-a-dozen homemade rafts. They were leftovers from Cuban migrants hoping to make landfall in the United States. To buck the Gulf Stream and end up west of Key West was quite a feat. Most had a crude engine, many from an old lawnmower or other small power equipment. The rafts were made of wood, plastic, Styrofoam, and even worn tractor tires. Each showed unappreciated craftsmanship. The vessels had been born out of the desire to escape communist poverty at any cost, and Cole admired the clever way the migrants had fashioned them. Cole walked past each of them, baking under the sun, awed by the fierce determination required to cast off from Cuba in the middle of the night, pointing straight at the northern darkness. All odds were against a successful landing. All too often, they were swept up by the Gulf Stream and never heard from again. Cole knew from first-hand experience that dehydration drove many insane and they simply rolled off their rafts to the circling sharks rather than face another hour of agony at sea. Some would fight among themselves and many would simply let death take them by the hand.

He'd picked hundreds off of rafts just like these. Some had fought Cole, the fire still burning in their cores to reach American shores. Most though were too weak to resist and many more were glad to be rescued at sea. Their impending return to Cuba was never a good thought, but those who still cherished life knew that beatings and prison sentences at the hands of Cuban authorities were better than a slow and painful death at sea.

Kevin walked up as Cole stood silent next to the sturdiest of the rafts.

"Gotta wonder what they're thinking to try something like this." Kevin obviously shared Cole's respect.

"I've interdicted hundreds of these and I'm always amazed at their effort," Cole responded, grabbing the rail of a raft with both his hands as if to give it a once-over before taking it out for a spin.

"No one knows what to do with the rafts that end up here, so the park rangers just drag them up into the grass and they sit here for years," said Kevin, who walked around to the other side of the raft and peaked underneath at the hull.

Cole asked, "You ever see these on the trips between Key West and here?"

Kevin replied, "Nah, I always figured you guys picked 'em up before they made it this far north."

Cole laughed a bit out loud and answered back, "You'd be surprised, man. Most never make it in these things. We'd catch maybe half of them. A quarter might make it and the rest end up cooking under the sun. The ones that make it have enough money to pay a smuggler to pick them up in something fast."

Kevin looked Cole in the eyes and replied, "You don't say." He grinned just a bit as he said it.

They walked back to the dock together. There was nothing more to say about the rafts. Just as he had as a boarding officer, Cole felt an immense respect for any human who would set off with his family in search of something better. Always focused on the law enforcement mission before, Cole allowed himself to look subjectively at the choice so many Cubans made to flee their homeland. The rafts pulled up on the beach of Fort Jefferson were just a fraction of a much larger and endemic problem. It seemed appropriate that Fort Jefferson, a last bastion for America's borders, still stood a silent watch over a smuggler's paradise.

CHAPTER 3 — CUBA LIBRE

A WEEK PASSED and still Cole heard nothing from the applications he'd put in. He checked out of the hotel after the first week and, with Kevin's invitation, Cole moved in with him. In exchange for stocking food and booze in the fridge, Kevin gave Cole a couch in the corner of his apartment just a few blocks from downtown Key West on a quiet side street. The old palm trees gave plenty of shade throughout the day and helped to mask the insanity only a few hundred yards away. Kevin's apartment was cut out of what had been a larger house, and the rooms still held much of the grandeur of its former existence. There was one main living room with dark and worn hardwood floors, where Cole's couch sat in a corner under a large window. There was always sand on the floor, and it stuck to Cole's feet when he walked barefoot. Off of the living room there was a bathroom, a small kitchen, and Kevin's room. The two struck up a good friendship and Cole embraced a simple routine well-balanced between work and pleasure.

After a second week passed, Cole stopped by the Key West police office to check on his application on one of his days off. After a few minutes, the same officer with whom Cole had met the first time came out and escorted Cole back to his office. Offering Cole a seat, the officer sat behind his desk and took a long breath before explaining, "Cole, I heard back from your command on *Delaney*. Frankly, they didn't have many good things to say and I don't think we can offer you a job without some better recommendations."

Cole felt his mouth go dry. He couldn't think of a thing to say in response.

The officer continued, "I'm really sorry, Cole. You do seem like a good guy, but my hands are tied on this one."

Cole nodded and thanked the officer for his time. With that, he left the office and walked back towards Kevin's. Cole tried his best not to let it rattle him, but he knew that Potts was not going to ever give him a good recommendation for anything. It was no surprise then that Cole hadn't heard back from the Fish and Wildlife office either, as Cole had listed Potts' contact info. The magnitude of Cole's situation sunk in as he walked back up the steps at Kevin's apartment. His only employment to speak of was *Delaney,* and while he had a degree from the Coast Guard Academy, he had no good work experience that would get him in the door with anything related to law enforcement. Cole took a beer from the fridge and nursed it on the small porch outside of Kevin's apartment. He thought for a second to just pack up his things and leave the Keys, but the thought of some office job and a suit bored him. Cole took a long sip from his beer and realized that he was now truly on his own. Still, he refused to give up.

For the next two weeks, almost every morning Cole was up and out of the door just after five for a jog down to the beach and back. He'd finish up with push-ups on the front porch and take a quick shower before heading out the door to the *Yankee Freedom.* He basked in his newfound existence as a free spirit, but he was always on time for work, unable to shake the military punctuality of his former life. If the night before had gone too late, Cole slept under a palm tree at Fort Jefferson for an hour or two in the middle of the day while the tourists played on the island. If he wasn't tired, he'd lounge around the upper deck of the *Yankee Freedom* and make small talk with the crew.

Almost every night centered around pretty girls Kevin and Cole would pick up from the *Yankee Freedom.* They'd come from all over the country to Key West, and Cole played up his quasi-local status to the best of his abilities. Together, Cole and Kevin tried as hard as they could to treat each night as if it were the greatest of their lives, mirroring the mood of the young women so often in their company. They lived like kings. Cole grew his hair down past his ears and it turned a muddied blond from the sun. He shaved once a week or so, almost always sporting something between stubble and a beard, and he never shaved on Mondays, as it was his unique way to distinguish himself from the laboring masses. Cole was fit and tanned from days under the tropical sun. After more than a month, Cole had forgotten about his problems with Potts and his failed attempts to get back in with law enforcement. He accepted the fact that he'd inadvertently burned that bridge and found in himself a renewed vigor for life.

He worked five days a week, normally matching Kevin's schedule, but occasionally he found himself with a day off and nothing to do. Kevin's apartment was semi-furnished and the owner had left an entire wall of books on heavy ornate wooden shelves in the living room. On those days when Cole was alone, he grabbed one of the novels and made his way to the Schooner Wharf just before noon. Nursing something laced with rum, he'd read for hours, stopping occasionally for conversations with passers-by. He read Hemingway's *The Old Man and the Sea* in one sitting, thinking only of the horrible taste of fish oil and wondering for some time if there were still men in Cuba so hardened as the old man.

As the summer pressed on, Cole migrated further and further from Duval Street. Kevin had a 23-foot Mako center console. It was older than either Kevin or Cole and still sported its original inboard diesel engine. Aptly named *Aquaholic,* she never reached a full plane, but Cole loved the reliable hum and smell of the old diesel engine's exhaust. The fiberglass deck beneath his bare feet would rattle as Kevin pushed up the throttles and the old boat felt sturdier than the newer and fancier center-consoles that jetted around the Keys. The *Aquaholic* had character and charm, fitting in perfectly with the Keys. Oftentimes they'd get off work as the sunset neared and take the days' catch of ladies for a cruise around the Keys at night. Kevin kept his boat at a dock in Garrison Bight, and each night they'd pass the Coast Guard base coming west out of Fleming Key Cut. Cole found himself a bit quiet as the cutters came into view. Months had passed, but still Cole wondered if he would ever be able to forget his past. However, the giggles and smiles of their female company never let Cole dwell too long on it.

Kevin would, on occasion, disappear for a day or two. Cole never thought much of it nor did he care, until curiosity finally got the best of him. They were both working on the *Yankee Freedom* one afternoon late in the summer when Cole noticed Kevin wearing a Rolex watch.

"What's up with the watch man?"

Kevin shrugged it off and the two stared each other down in a light-hearted manner.

"Seriously man, I've never seen that before." For reasons even he wasn't sure about Cole found himself unable to drop the subject.

"You want one?" Kevin was playing mind games and the two continued coiling lines as the *Yankee Freedom* approached Fort Jefferson.

"Maybe I do," Cole said as he dropped a coiled line to the deck, smiled, and pushed the issue, but Kevin went quiet.

They tied up at Fort Jefferson, put on their friendly faces, and helped the pile of tourists off the boat and onto the island for their day of leisure. Kevin and Cole cleaned up the loose ends and made their way into the shade of a patch of palm trees.

Kevin offered up a veiled explanation.

"Listen man, I do some work on the side, the kind of shit you might not like."

Cole looked him straight in the eyes and asked, "What the fuck are you talking about?"

Kevin, for the first time since Cole had met him, looked a bit uneasy. "I know you had a rough time in the Coast Guard, but I don't really know where you stand with all this migrant shit we've talked about."

Cole's mind raced as he put the pieces together. Kevin, for as long as he'd known him, took off for a day or two every few weeks and Cole never asked questions. But now Kevin was offering up something mischievous that Cole had never caught onto.

"What are you into man?" Cole smiled to relieve Kevin's clearly mixed conscience.

"No one gets hurt. I just help some people out," said Kevin, clearly on the defensive.

Cole fired back, "I've got no allegiance to anything, if that's what you're getting at."

Kevin relaxed a bit and explained, "I drive a boat sometimes, any boat really, down to Cuba and back."

He was finally at ease, as if in a casual conversation, like any of the other hundred conversations they'd had together. "There's a ton of shit going on down here, and I get into it every now and then. It pays like crazy. I pick up a boat somewhere, run due south with the throttles down, pull up to some spot, load up some people, and drive them back up north. It's as simple as that."

Cole smiled, partly because he couldn't believe it was going on this whole time, and partly to relieve Kevin's anxiety over the conversation. "I could teach you a thing or two about driving a boat."

Kevin laughed, "Bullshit you could."

Cole, with a straight face, asked, "Can I go with you next time?"

Kevin thought for a moment and answered, "Dude, they might not dig the Coast Guard thing, but I'll ask."

The conversation ended as quickly as it had begun. Cole and Kevin relaxed in the shade until early afternoon when they prepped the *Yankee Freedom* for the return trip home and helped the same tourists, now sunburned and cranky with the onset of fatigue, back onto the giant cat for the trip home.

Days went by and nothing else came up from their conversation. Cole hadn't stopped thinking about it, but didn't want to push the issue. Two weeks passed and still nothing was mentioned between Cole and Kevin.

On a sleepy Monday night, the two of them were sitting on the porch outside Kevin's apartment with a bottle of Captain Morgan and a liter of pineapple juice. Both half drunk and with the last traces of daylight disappearing to the west, Kevin spoke up. "What are you up to tomorrow night?"

Cole answered, "Hopefully a blond. I'm tired of brunettes." He reached for the rum.

Kevin was looking right at his eyes. "Seriously, man. You got anything going on tomorrow night?"

Cole set the bottle back down. "No, I got nothing." He felt the onset of butterflies, but kept it to himself.

"We'll leave here around nine or so and it'll be an all-nighter. You cool with that?"

Cole gritted his back teeth, swallowed for a brief second, and answered, "Hell, yeah man. I'm in."

They poured another round and Kevin provided some details. They'd both call in to the *Yankee Freedom* and ask for a day off. Kevin knew from experience that the captain wouldn't care one bit. After the day's work, they'd head home and sleep until about eight in the evening. After that, they'd head down to Kevin's boat and go from there. Cole didn't need to bring anything, do anything, or say anything. Kevin made it clear that Cole was along for the ride. It went without saying that no one needed to know a damn thing about the whole affair.

"You cool with this?" Kevin was easing himself up from the chair while looking at Cole with as serious of a face as he could muster after a bottle of rum.

"Yeah, brother. Time to step it up a bit."

The two walked back off the porch and into the apartment. Kevin, walking in front of Cole, reached down behind a table and flung a pair of women's panties back at Cole's head. Cole ducked and kicked Kevin in the back lightly as Kevin stumbled forward, laughing.

"Those are yours boss. Way too big for my taste." Cole was smiling. The mood was light again and they both turned in for the evening. Cole knew it was a turning point in his life, but he felt no reason to dwell on the matter.

The next day, Cole was up early for his morning run. He showered and checked in at the *Yankee Freedom* like he did every day. Kevin was there a few minutes later, and the day pressed on like any other. Cole almost thought Kevin had forgotten about their conversation entirely. They spent the downtime chatting with the rest of the crew, but Cole found himself preoccupied with any sign from Kevin that their mission was still a go. Kevin didn't give away anything. Had it been a late-night boarding in the Coast Guard, Cole would have spent considerable time studying the weather, the seas, and the mission, but Kevin gave no indication of any such research.

They tied back up to the pier in Key West in the afternoon and grabbed a quick dinner of fish tacos on the way home. After reaching the apartment, Kevin said he was hitting the sack and would wake up at eight. Cole wanted more details, but Kevin shut his door and Cole was left with his mind racing. He tried to sleep a bit on the couch, but to no avail. He laid there for two hours, watching the digital clock on the television, knowing that his chances of sleeping were nonexistent.

A bit before eight, Kevin emerged from his room with a grin on his face. He chugged two glasses of water from the faucet in the tiny kitchen, advised Cole to do the same, and went about grabbing a few odds and ends around the apartment. Cole drank three full glasses, remembering all too well the feeling of dehydration from his days as a Coast Guard boarding officer toiling under the tropical sun. He felt like a fish out of water as Kevin moved about the living room with purpose. Kevin had a cell phone, a small backpack Cole had never seen before, and a handheld GPS with a suction cup mount.

Kevin grinned and asked, "You ready, dude?"

Cole fired back, "Fucking A, man. Let's go."

As they walked out the door, Cole realized he was wearing one of his old blue *Delaney* t-shirts, faded even more so by the past few months in the sun. The crest of the cutter was still visible though and it made Cole smile at the thought of his former shipmates realizing what he was up to now.

The two made their way down to Garrison Bight and onto the *Aquaholic*. Kevin fired up the old diesel and Cole untied her from the cleats on the dock, giving her a good push away from the splintered wooden pilings. As Kevin started a slow motor out of the bight, he called someone on the cell phone and talked for almost a minute. Kevin jotted something down on a piece of paper then hung up. The old Mako blended in with the dozens of other pleasure boats out for a balmy evening in the Florida Keys. They waved at boats crossing their paths, made their way out past the Coast Guard base, and turned sharply to the north. Kevin opened up the throttles and played with the GPS. He wove a meandering course back and forth until finally the GPS gave him something to work with.

Kevin drove for almost half an hour before ducking the *Aquaholic* behind a small uninhabited key well north of Key West. The sun was down and twilight was fast losing its daily battle to the darkness. The air had cooled just a bit and the nighttime sky felt good. Cole was seated on the bow when he spotted something in the darkness ahead. Almost out of nowhere, a pristine Grady-White cuddy cabin emerged, anchored and bobbing in the moonlit flats. Kevin chucked an anchor over the side and threw a line over to the Grady-White. He then hopped onto the cuddy cabin and tied the *Aquaholic* off to the shiny factory-new cleats of the Grady-White.

Kevin put on some latex gloves from the bag and went directly to the wheel, offset slightly to the right of the console. He turned the keys—strangely enough already in the ignition—and her two 250-horsepower outboards came roaring to life, shaking violently at first against their mounts on the transom and then finding their rhythm in idle. Cole smelled the gas exhaust mixed with salt air and remembered the same smell from the rigid hull inflatable boats he'd worked from on *Delaney* for the past two years. Even with those mixed memories, Cole took a deep breath and basked in his surroundings. If the summer had taught him anything, it was that boats were fun again. Kevin tossed him some gloves and Cole hopped over.

"Cut her loose," said Kevin, already mounting the GPS to the console. Cole tossed the line back to the *Aquaholic*, and she disappeared into the darkness as Kevin idled forward through the flats. Cole took a seat to Kevin's left. The sleek hull was immaculate and the engines looked like they had just arrived from the factory. There was hardly any sign that the boat had ever been used.

"All right, man. Fill me in. Where did this come from?" Cole was now standing next to Kevin, his hands braced against the console.

"This one, I don't really know. My guy just gave me the coordinates. Somewhere in southern Florida for sure, but where I don't really know." Kevin scanned the horizon, his left hand on the wheel and his right on the throttles.

He continued talking while his eyes were busy going back and forth from the GPS to the horizon in front of them. "Sometimes I borrow a boat myself, but it gets a bit sketchy, so I prefer to just pick them up like this. It's almost always new, some doctor's new toy or something that we spot tied up in a channel behind a mansion."

Cole put the pieces together as they motored along. The boat had its own GPS, but the handheld was a telltale sign of smugglers, since they could easily chuck it over the side if caught, thus preventing the cops or Coast Guard from knowing where they'd been. Cole could see Kevin knew what he was doing—smugglers almost always went for new boats with more horsepower than they needed. For centuries, speed had been a smuggler's friend. Almost every migrant or drug operation Cole had ever seen used a center console or a cuddy cabin. Once a run was complete, the smugglers would beach the boat somewhere or set it adrift in the backwaters, leaving it for eventual discovery. Most owners got their boats back, albeit with a few more hard-earned hours on the engines.

The two of them passed under a bridge of the famous highway A1A, which ran east and north to the mainland of Florida, and then they continued past Stock Island, on the eastern side of Key West. Once in the channel, Kevin opened her up and the engines surged to life. The boat lifted out of the water before she settled on a plane and the air felt cool against Cole's face. The GPS showed almost 28 knots over the ground. At that rate, they'd hit Cuba in just over three hours.

The seas were calm with a small groundswell that the Grady-White danced over as she screamed southward. Kevin would occasionally yell something to Cole if he saw a light ahead, and twice Kevin brought the boat to a full stop and stepped out from underneath the bimini cover, scanning the sky above them. Cole did the same, knowing they were looking for Coast Guard or U.S. Customs aircraft that patrolled the straits every night. At the same time, Cole knew it was like finding a needle in a haystack. Nights like this were prime smuggling weather, and in all likelihood, Cole and Kevin were not the only game in town.

Cole knew the Coast Guard was on high alert that evening, given the weather. There were almost certainly cutters, aircraft, and small boats all scouring their radars for a little green blip, indicating someone sneaking south. Satisfied each time that no one was in their immediate area, Kevin throttled the engines back up and pressed south. The stars were bright and Cole's mind wandered back to nights on watch on *Delaney*. He'd forgotten how bright the stars were at sea. Moonlight reflected down on the water, and Cole's nerves settled after an hour or so. He was back on the open water and could feel the ocean air on his skin. It was exhilarating and the Grady-White was a solid boat out on the water. Cole almost forgot entirely about what they were doing as he enjoyed the ride.

After midnight, Kevin brought the boat to a stop. He squinted and looked forward, standing up on his toes. Cole looked too and could see faint lights to their left.

Havana.

"Holy shit, that's Havana," Cole said as the reality set in.

Kevin never stopped looking forward. "Yup."

"We're heading west of Havana, but here's where we start to worry about the Cuban Border Guard. Do you see anything ahead of us that looks like a boat?"

Cole scanned back and forth, his eyes well trained to pick up the faintest hint of a running light. He'd tracked boats at night, but with the help of radar. The Grady-White had one, but Cole knew it was short range and if anything came up as a blip, it would probably be too late, so they left it turned off.

Cole pressed his lips together, taking one more slow and deliberate scan. "I don't see anything."

He stepped to the back and took a leak off the stern as Kevin continued to scan forward for any signs of danger. To the north, all Cole saw was a dark sea. He walked back forward and looked again for trouble, but there was none.

Kevin pressed the throttles ahead, keeping the speed back a bit. They worked slightly west of their original course and before long, Cole saw the rocky coast of Cuba in front of him. It started out as a dark jagged line rising from the horizon and took on a more defined shape as they crept closer. Kevin stopped a few more times, and they both scanned ahead and behind. The only sound was the motor at an idle purr and the water lapping against the hull.

With the landscape emerging in front of them, Kevin spent more time looking down at the GPS. He played the throttle and slowed down gradually. Cole kept his eyes out and on the water in front of him. He could see the outline of trees now and the moonlight against palm fronds. There was a rocky coastline in front of them and some sort of small coral peninsula on the bow. A wave broke over a reef in the distance every few seconds, its whitewater seemingly floating on an invisible plain. Kevin drove straight at the peninsula then made a hard right turn and slowed the boat as they entered a large bay. A fire smoldered somewhere in the distance and its smell caught Cole's attention. Unlike a wood fire in the States, a fire in the Caribbean burned mostly green brush—no doubt cut by hand and machete—and its odor was a sweeter and more complex scent. Whoever the farmer was who'd cleared brush that day was certainly asleep by now, and the smoldering remnants of his day's labor drifted in the midnight land breeze out and over the water.

Even in the middle of the night, Cole could see it was a beautiful bay with coral heads dotting the water. There were no lights and the bay was calm like glass. The moon cast slivers of light down as it climbed above them and over a low layer of scattered backlit clouds. Kevin sent Cole forward with a flashlight and told him to point it towards a small sandy area nestled behind the peninsula and to flash it three times quickly. Cole complied.

From somewhere in the brush beyond the beach, three flashes came back towards them. Kevin was as serious as Cole had ever seen him. He pushed the bow right up to the beach and it nudged the sandy bottom a few feet shy of the dry shore. Bodies emerged from the brush and Cole counted eight of them. One more, a man, stayed halfway between the brush and the water. He whistled softly at Kevin and called out, "Ocho, si?"

Kevin called back, "Bueno." The man hurried back into the brush and disappeared.

The passengers wore ragged clothes and each carried a bag about the size of a teenager's backpack. Kevin and Cole helped them up one at a time and sent them down into the crowded cuddy cabin. They were all thin and their skin dirty, likely from the daylong trip to this much-anticipated rendezvous in the middle of nowhere. They talked to each other softly, some holding hands, and seemed to reassure each other that things were going well. There were two men, but the rest were women and two appeared to be teenage girls. After the last one was onboard and down below, Kevin jumped back to the wheel and reversed out. The motors churned up an immense cloud of sand and the water was clear enough that Cole could see it under the moonlight. *Not good for an engine*, Cole thought.

"Drive it like you stole it, huh?" Cole was looking at Kevin as he said it.

Kevin grinned.

They backtracked out of the bay the same way they'd entered. Kevin was cautious around the coral heads as a hole in the hull this far from home could spell disaster, and both knew Cuban prison was no fun. After clearing the bay and pointing due north, Kevin opened up the throttles again and the Grady-White surged up and into a rhythmic plane as they screamed back to the north. Cole looked at his watch and saw it was after one in the morning. With the added weight below, they were making 25 knots over the ground. Kevin explained that they wouldn't stop on the way back like they had heading south, because if they were stopped now, they'd be screwed. This was simply a mad dash. On the trip south, they could have always claimed stupidity or error as their reason for heading into the Florida Straits in the middle of the night. But with eight illegal migrants in the cabin, there was no bullshitting their way out of this one.

Cole knew that many smugglers would find themselves the subject of hot pursuit as they neared the Florida coast. Customs, Coast Guard, local police, even Florida Wildlife Conservation officers often joined the chase to catch smugglers and defend the integrity of the U.S. border. Cole had been on more than a few chases himself and knew that more than half of the migrants made it to dry land, meeting the "Wet Foot/Dry Foot" policy of the United States. If a Cuban touched dry land, he or she was welcome to stay. That was the goal, and it didn't matter if they were in handcuffs ten seconds after setting foot on solid ground. They just needed to touch sacred American soil.

Cole also knew that many made it to the coast without ever being detected. Planes, helicopters, ships, and boats patrolled the waters every day and night, but it was a vast expanse to cover and smugglers knew their routes well. Their chance of success was quite good, or else they wouldn't bother with the risks. The

Cubans who built homemade rafts and attempted to paddle their way north with a trash bag full of their worldly possessions were the unfortunate ones who often died of dehydration or found themselves caught in the Gulf Stream, unwillingly pushed east, then north and into the Atlantic. Cole had seen every stage of death as a boarding officer. He'd carried men and women reduced to skin and bones, many too weak to even stand. In some ways, he knew more than he realized about the eight souls in the cabin below.

In all likelihood these migrants onboard the Grady-White were well connected in Florida. Someone, maybe a dad or an uncle, had found their fortune in America and paid a hefty sum to give their family the best shot at reaching Florida. The Cubans who took to rafts and paddled the 90 miles were the most desperate. The eight below were fortunate, and they knew it. Cole looked down at them from time to time and saw the fear of uncertainty on their faces as they were jolted back and forth by the boat as she screamed north.

He smiled at one lady who kept staring at him and gave her a thumbs up. "Bueno."

She relaxed a bit, but kept an eye on Cole, looking for the first signs of trouble as they edged closer to Florida. Two hours went by at full speed. Cole scanned the horizon and then the fuel meter on Kevin's console. They had a quarter tank left. Kevin exchanged a look with Cole and then back down at his GPS.

"Thirty minutes, bro."

It was now four in the morning. Key West was a faint beacon on the horizon. Kevin kept it on their right side and once again scanned the horizon, comparing what he could see with what his GPS showed on its tiny display. They rounded the uninhabited islands to the west of Key West then turned sharply to the east. Kevin wove the boat at speed around shoal after shoal and brought her to idle after nearly 20 minutes, showing a near-photographic memory of the shallows surrounding Key West. He picked up the phone again and made a call.

"Normal dropoff?" Kevin nodded as he listened.

"Cool man, give me ten minutes." He put the phone down and pushed the throttles forward. Cole could see on the GPS that a marker was sitting where they'd dropped off the *Aquaholic*. Kevin spotted the bay after some time and slowed the boat. Next to *Aquaholic* was yet another center console. The eight passengers below were whispering and each of them were trying to look out of the tiny portholes of the cramped cabin. Cole looked down and said, "Bueno," once again. The older lady smiled back at him this time. Cole could see, and smell, that someone had vomited on the trip, yet none of the other migrants complained.

Kevin pulled up next to his boat and shut the engines down. They'd run hard for more than six hours and the fuel tanks were all but drained. On the third boat were two men who waved at Kevin. As the migrants stepped up and out of the cabin, they scanned around them, unsure of exactly where they were. Some stretched their arms out and yawned. One of the teenage girls let out a loud screech and ran across Kevin's boat and into the arms of one of the men on the third boat. He hugged her and motioned with his pointer finger for the rest of them to be quiet. He couldn't hide a contagious smile as the other seven climbed across Kevin's boat before exchanging hugs. Cole thought it was surely a long-awaited family reunion, but he watched with indifference. There was no right or wrong in what he'd just been a part of—there were valid and well-intentioned arguments on both sides of the debate over illegal immigration. All Cole knew was that he'd just tasted adrenaline once again and he liked it.

The driver of the third boat tossed an envelope onto the deck of Kevin's boat, threw off his mooring line, and idled off into the darkness. Kevin went back to his boat for a plastic two-gallon jug of gas. Cole, already back on the *Aquaholic*, watched as Kevin poured gas all over the console, deck, and rails of the Grady-White. Thinking for a moment he might burn it, Cole sat on the far rail and looked to Kevin, who just smiled and laughed. "Relax dude, it's just to make sure we didn't leave any prints."

Kevin hopped over to the *Aquaholic* and parted lines with the Grady-White, now sitting quietly again at anchor. He tossed the GPS over the side in the depths of the main channel and took both his and Cole's gloves and stashed them in his pack.

Kevin looked back once and then said to Cole, "Well, we broke it in for some doctor."

The two laughed and relaxed as they motored back to the Garrison Bight docks. Cole tied the *Aquaholic* to a cleat at their usual place, and both of them walked back to the apartment. Hues of blue were beginning to form in the sky as they walked into the living room. Kevin tossed the gloves into the trash and went straight to the refrigerator. Tossing Cole a beer, he grabbed one himself, and the two took their usual seats on the front porch. Daylight was breaking. A rooster came alive somewhere in the distance and, with that, it was just another day in Key West.

Cole took a giant sip of his Dos Equis and focused his energies on remembering the smell of that smoldering fire somewhere on the wilds of the Cuban coast. On an empty stomach, the beer worked quick on Cole's mind. He fancied himself as a modern-day pirate, now sharing in an ancient profession of arms, wit, and bravado. As they sat there with their feet on the railing and their chairs kicked back on hind legs, Cole thought about the family that was reunited. He'd now seen the entire spectrum of southern Florida's illegal migrant epidemic. It had plagued the country since its inception and Cole took a second deep sip of his beer as he tried to figure out where he stood on the issue.

"What's your take on all of this?" He was looking at Kevin.

Kevin pulled the envelope from his pocket, opened it, and counted out bills with one hand. He put ten one-hundred dollar bills on the table and pushed them over to Cole. "That's how I feel about that."

Cole counted them himself then folded and stashed the money in his pocket. "All right, then. Good enough for me."

Kevin looked back out at the quiet street in front of them and finished off his beer. "You're in, bro?" His tone indicated more of a question than a statement.

Cole laughed for a second and nodded. His mind was clouded, partly by fatigue and partly from the beer. It was a dangerous decision. He thought back to the feeling of being on the water, the rush of breaking someone else's rules, and the roll of hundred-dollar bills in his pocket. He thought too of the Coast Guard, the years he'd spent pursuing a dream, and how it had all fallen apart in front of him.

"Sign me up," was all Cole said.

CHAPTER 4 – INDIAN SUMMER

TWO WEEKS PASSED before Cole brought the subject up again with Kevin. They were under a palm tree on Fort Jefferson sitting idly under the noon sun when Cole spoke up.

"So when are we going again?"

Kevin laughed to himself, his arms up and crossed behind his head as he lay prostrate on the sandy grass. His eyes were closed when he answered. "It's all you, bro. I like to go alone, plus the money is best when you go by yourself."

"So I just call your guy?" asked Cole, who was sitting forward with his arms draped over his knees and his heels dug into the sand. He yawned as he spoke.

"Pretty much, man. I'll give you his number. Don't save it in your phone, just keep it written down somewhere. He's a bit funny about his phones."

Cole nodded, looking down between his feet and spent some time thinking about what he was asking for. Criminal networks—and that was what this was—were a slippery slope. That much Cole knew. Where it ended he had no idea. He thought about finding his own limits and he thought about jail, then he pondered the look on Potts' face if he ever found out his errant junior officer was rotting in some Cuban prison. He also thought about extending his middle finger to Potts as he sped past on a midnight run and the satisfaction of doing something well. That thought took hold. Cole was his own captain, master of his own destiny. He took a deep breath and solidified a plan in his mind.

Nearly a month after their first run, Kevin handed Cole a piece of paper one evening and told him to call the number written on it. Cole took the note, stuffed it in his pocket, and played the part as

if nothing had happened. They were in the midst of another raucous night and Kevin had been gone for about ten minutes when
he returned with the note. Cole figured Kevin had been off talking
to Miguel, "the guy," and Cole's chance rested on the other end of
that phone number.

Cole nursed his drinks for the rest of the night, slowly
sobering up to the thought of his first run as a captain. A young
woman, pretty and barely in her twenties, had latched onto him
earlier in the day. They'd been out on the *Aquaholic* and Kevin
acted as a good wingman with her friends while Cole played the
requisite games he'd become so good at. He was a bit burned by
the sun and felt the dried salt on his skin from a swim he'd taken
with her earlier. With smuggling on his mind, he'd slipped though
and the night was slowing down. Worse yet, he'd forgotten her
name, a major transgression in the game of drunken lust. She'd
caught his mood change as well.

With her fingers clutching the pockets of his shorts and her
body pressed against his, she momentarily had his attention.

"What's got you so down?" she asked playfully and bit lightly
on her lower lip, her head tilted to one side as she pulled herself
even closer against Cole. Her fingers were now locked through his
belt loops.

"Just a long day, I suppose." Cole feigned interest, but
couldn't shake his mind away from the thoughts in his head.

"Something's got you down." She pulled his waist harder
against her hips.

"How do you know that?" Cole looked into her pretty eyes.

"I can just tell, and I want to have fun." She smiled shyly.

Cole, recognizing the cues at hand, went into recovery mode.
"You're a sweet girl, Crystal," he said, thinking she looked like a
Crystal. It was too late when he remembered that Crystal was the
week before. *Damn this rum,* he thought.

"It's Brittany."

She released her grips, pushed herself away from Cole and
slapped him on the left cheek. Clearly insulted and regaining her
senses, she separated from the intimacy moments before.

Growing increasingly mad, she yelled, "You're drunk."

"So are you." Cole laughed just a bit and pulled back thinking for a second she might swing again.

By this point, her friends had parted ways with Kevin and were on their way to her defense. The fat one looked like she could do some damage and Cole knew he'd been beat. Kevin was still casually leaning against the railing at the bar, looking at Cole, and laughing his ass off. The girls departed back onto Duval Street and Cole made his way over to Kevin, watching the girls as they disappeared down the street.

"That was awesome," Kevin said as he finished up the rest of his drink and looked at his watch. It was just after midnight and Duval Street was at full speed.

"I'm done." Cole tossed his plastic cup in the trash and the two departed. Kevin was still laughing as they rounded a corner and walked back on the side streets.

"Fucking Duval Street." Cole was laughing now too, looking down and shaking his head.

"You gonna file charges?" Kevin punched Cole in the shoulder.

"Nah, she hits like you."

Cole called the number Kevin had written down, but it wasn't until a few days later that he heard from Miguel. Cole was to meet him at Garrison Bight on his day off later that week an hour before noon. The call was short and the words were few. Cole put his phone away wondering if it had even just happened. It seemed rather anticlimactic. He went about his normal routine for the next few days, always thinking in the back of his mind about the trip ahead.

At the appointed time, Cole sauntered down to Garrison Bight, wholly unsure of what to expect. He walked up and down the docks twice with a good sweat under the noonday sun. Nothing but the typical boats lined the dock. He thought about grabbing a beer at the Thai Island restaurant to save the seemingly wasted walk. Standing on the far end and now late for their meeting, an older Hispanic man approached Cole.

"Amigo, you are here for the jet ski tour?"

Cole looked behind him then back at the unexpectedly short man talking to him and shook his head answering no. The old guy persisted.

"Amigo, it's me. Mickey. We spoke on the phone."

Cole squinted and asked, "You're Miguel?"

The short man shook his head and answered, "Si, but everyone just calls me Mickey."

Cole was caught completely off guard and embarrassed with his level of discomfort. *Who is this guy?* He was old, short, had graying shaggy hair, and wore cargo shorts with a t-shirt in the manner one would expect from a teenager. His face was leathered and wrinkled like that of a local. Cole expected some swagger. He expected slick hair, a gold chain, maybe someone in a track suit. This Mickey looked nothing like a kingpin.

"Let's get going and see the sights," Mickey said as he reached out to shake Cole's hand. Cole complied, not letting his eyes leave Mickey's as he looked in vain for some reassurance that this was actually the feared Miguel whom Kevin had talked so much about.

They walked back down the dock and Mickey kept talking about the Keys as if he really were a tour guide. He went on and on about the flats fishing, the tarpon, the restaurants, and the history of the island as if Cole really was a tourist. At the far end of the docks were two jet skis and Mickey stepped across the first to the second and pointed for Cole to jump on the first.

"Amigo, we will have fun, come on."

Cole settled onto the cushioned seat and went to start the engine as Mickey threw a bright yellow life jacket at him. Mickey was already fastening one just like it around his chest.

"Put that on." Mickey pointed back at the jacket then at Cole.

Cole laughed and set it aside. Mickey looked back and forth down the dock and looked sternly at Cole. "My friend, put the fucking life jacket on."

Mickey smiled to relieve the tension and instructed Cole, "We must look the part my friend—always under the radar. It is the most important part."

Cole did as he was told. It was one of those stupidly bright life jackets that no self-respecting sailor would be caught dead in. Cole, in his boardshorts and t-shirt, felt out of place. It was also a perfect disguise to blend into Key West tourism. No one would think twice about two mismatched men on rental jet skis, but he still felt like an idiot.

With both jet skis running, Mickey touched the throttle and idled out of the harbor. Cole followed. They headed back to the west, opened the throttles up passing the Coast Guard base and made their way for the main harbor. Just before entering, Mickey came to a stop. Cole pulled up next to him. They bobbed up and down in the lime green chop of passing boats and Mickey explained the purpose of the trip. He leaned his elbows against the steering column of the jet ski and talked with his hands animating his every word.

"My friend, there is a very nice boat in here. It is your boat. It's been here two days." He motioned with two of his fingers as if that was a big deal. "The owner, he is at a hotel and won't be leaving for another four days. It's gassed up. He doesn't check on it. So tomorrow night, it's your boat."

Cole laughed at the audacity of the plan. "How the hell do I get it out of here?"

Mickey, bobbing in the churned up water and looking like a fool in his cargo shorts and ill-fitting bright yellow life jacket, shook his head dismissively as if he'd made it perfectly clear the first time. With his elbows still on the column, he threw his hands up in seemingly total disbelief. His accent took on a more Hispanic tone reflecting his frustration at repeating himself.

"Amigo, he don't give a shit about his boat. He don't check on it. He just leave it here. It's yours. Maybe he get it back, maybe he don't." At the end of his sentence, Mickey shrugged his shoulders as if a six-figure boat was no big deal to anyone. Cole noted that Mickey pronounced the word *shit* as *chit* with emphasis.

Cole was both confused and amused at the circumstances.

"Got it Mickey. But how do I take it?" He emphasized the last two words as if it would change Mickey's comprehension. To anyone watching they were two men arguing about where to go with the remaining time of their one hour jet ski rental. The skis drifted with the ebbing tide closer to the channel.

"I know where the keys are. No big deal. Then you go, OK?"

Mickey throttled up his jet ski and motioned with his hand for Cole to follow him into the harbor. Cole smiled to himself, shook his head a bit back and forth and followed, fishtailing his jet ski for his own entertainment.

Three quarters of the way down a pier, Mickey doubled back and came to a stop. Cole pulled up again next to him and Mickey mumbled something trivial about Key West's charm. At the same time he motioned behind him and to the right with his head. Cole picked up on the cues, as comical as they were, and saw that Mickey was idling ten yards from an Intrepid center console. It must have been close to 40 feet long and the hull had recently been waxed. She was bigger and sleeker than the Grady-White Cole had run on with Kevin. She was clearly fast and begging to open up on the high seas.

Mickey didn't stay long and motioned for Cole to head back out. They opened up again leaving the harbor and their skis jumped up and over the wake of passing boats as they headed back past the Coast Guard base and towards Garrison Bight. The ride back was fun. Mickey threw a hand behind his back and howled as if he were riding a bull as he bounced over a wave and the engine surged, momentarily sucking air through its intake before settling back down. He looked like a fool and his cargo shorts were wet from the salt spray. He was clearly energized by the thought of sending someone else's boat on a midnight run to Cuba and back. Smuggling was like a drug, and Mickey had just taken a hit. Cole could feel it as well. Mickey reminded Cole of someone's crazy uncle, but he knew Mickey had a firm grasp on the darker business of the Florida Keys. Mickey stopped once more before heading into the harbor and gave Cole some basic instructions.

"The keys are in the compartment on the console. The code for the gate at the pier is twenty twenty-five. Get on the water at eleven. I'll drop a GPS off at your place in the afternoon. If anyone asks, you just tell them you're moving it for Mr. Thompson. Call me when you're a mile south of Key West."

Now Cole couldn't hide his confusion and he didn't like not knowing the details of such a mission.

Mickey laughed. "I've been watching this one. They stashed the keys when they gassed it up and I asked the dockhand whose boat it was. Relax a bit, my friend; Señor Thompson will understand. This is easy. You call me before midnight, OK?"

Cole eased up a bit and nodded his head in approval. They returned the jet skis to the same spot and parted ways without more words. Cole watched Mickey walk away, his t-shirt and shorts wet in spots from the ride. No one in their right mind would guess Mickey's profession. It occurred to Cole that Mickey's appearance was entirely intentional. Mickey may have looked a far cry from the pirates of centuries past, but Cole couldn't help but guess that Mickey ranked somewhere higher in Caribbean lore than most.

As he'd done before, Cole called out of work that Friday. On Thursday, he went about his normal routine on the *Yankee Free-dom*. Kevin never said a word but knew full well Cole was making his first run that night. At the end of the day, Kevin was talking to some girls on the pier while Cole made up the last of the lines and hopped onto the dock. As Cole walked, Kevin looked at him for a brief moment and grinned as Cole went past.

"Have fun, brother." Kevin's grin was a way of testing Cole's determination and at the same time was a genuine wish that the night went well. Kevin's grin reminded Cole briefly of the way

Wheeler would test Cole's resolve before taking a team out on a migrant interdiction; they knew each other well enough that no words were needed. Cole nodded back with confidence and told Kevin to do the same, his eyes briefly looking back to the girls then at Kevin.

Back at the apartment, he crashed on the couch for almost three hours. This time he slept and when he awoke, Cole felt refreshed, unlike the last time. He went over to a cabinet where he kept his money from the last run. He took five hundred-dollar bills and put them in his pocket. It was a gamble, but if he ran into trouble on the Cuban side, bribes were never out of the question to get out of a tight spot. Besides the cash, he took only his driver's license. He left his passport, figuring that any interaction with Cuban or U.S. Customs wouldn't involve getting a stamp. He was wearing the same shorts he'd worked in that day and they were faded from the past few months. He'd traded out his *Yankee Freedom* shirt for a dirty button down linen one that he'd meant to wash for a week but hadn't gotten around to. On his feet were a pair of new running shoes, because he thought if it came down to it they'd be better than flip flops. They were the only thing he'd spent any of his money on from the last trip. It was dark, the sun having set almost two hours before, when Cole walked out onto the porch and saw the handheld GPS sitting on a chair.

"Son of a bitch," Cole said out loud but under his breath as he picked it up and hit the power button. It had a full charge and three waypoints saved in it, labeled "A," "B," and "C." By the looks of it, the thing was brand new. He stuffed it in the other pocket of his shorts and walked back inside. Cole ate half a sandwich and drank as much water as he could stand before heading out the door, down the steps, and towards Duval Street.

It was loud and for a Thursday night the town was in full swing. He walked with the crowd and ran through scenarios in his head. He would stop a few times on the run south to listen for helicopters or planes and scan the horizon for the familiar lights of Coast Guard cutters. On the run back north, just as Kevin had done, he'd go all out and hope to avoid the hornet's nest of local, state, and federal authorities that were most certainly out that night looking for his kind.

Rounding the corner to the marina, he passed the Schooner Wharf and wished for a second he could sit as he did so many nights and soak up a few rum drinks making small talk with the patrons. It was a balmy early-fall evening, the kind that felt just right in the Keys, but Cole knew he had work to do. With a deep breath he pressed on to the gated dock and entered the code as he'd been instructed. The gate clicked open and Cole strolled down the dock like it was his business. No one noticed. A few of the yachts were lit up with festivities on the back decks. Empty beer cans and half-empty bottles of rum littered the makeshift tables as conversations came and went. Muffled music came from the cabin of one boat and a woman's high-pitched laugh rose up from the cabin of another. The sounds trailed off as Cole neared the end of the dock. Cole's boat was dark and bobbed silently in her slip. She was as pretty as he remembered and wore two oversized outboard engines on her back end. They were immaculate. He stood there on the dock for a moment or two and felt butterflies build in the pit of his stomach.

"Fuck it," he said as he hopped onboard and went straight to the console. Sure as Mickey had promised, the keys were on a foam keychain and Cole fired up the two engines. They shook to life on their mounts and settled to an idle. Cole took a few seconds to familiarize himself with the setup. There was a wheel and two throttles, all of which were perfectly polished chrome. Neutral, forward, and reverse were marked on the bottom of the quadrant. There were more gauges than Cole needed, but RPM and fuel were easy enough to read. Again as Mickey had promised, she had a full tank of gas.

Someone called down to Cole from the dock, "Sweet boat man."

Cole froze for just a second before turning around to see an overweight middle-aged man with a plastic cup in his hand and a flower print shirt over his belly. He must have heard the engines start up and come up from one of the other boats.

"Thanks." Cole threw off the two spring lines and untied the bow lines before hurrying back to the wheel.

"It's late, man. Where are you going?" They guy was slightly unsteady and Cole figured there was a good chance he wouldn't even remember the encounter.

"I'm moving the boat for Mr. Thompson. Can you grab those stern lines for me?"

Without putting his drink down, the fat guy looked down with his head and neck, but the rest of his body remained in its unsteadily upright posture. He was clearly more intoxicated than Cole first thought.

"Can you just untie them for me?" Cole almost felt bad for the guy and it was clear he had not the faintest idea of how to untie the line from a cleat. Not wanting to stay any longer, Cole untied the lines on his end and tossed them into the water and away from the engines.

"Can you just pull those lines in for me?" Cole asked.

The fat guy smiled at the simplified request and reached down with one hand, his other wholly focused on not losing his drink.

"You got it man. That really is a sweet boat."

Looking forward and speaking to himself, Cole mouthed, "I know."

He idled forward out of the slip, and turned once to nod back at the fat guy, who was still smiling.

He idled ahead for some time until well clear of the marina, and after entering the main channel, he pointed the boat south. Past Tank Island, or Sunset Key as it was known now with its immaculate cottages, Cole jammed the throttles to half speed and she lifted up and out of the water. The bow rode high and with another push of the throttles, she came up on a plane. Settling into a rhythm with the light chop, Cole scanned behind him as downtown faded in the darkness. Passing Fort Zachary Taylor, and with the dark Florida Straits in front of him, Cole turned hard to the east so as to give off the appearance he was simply heading for another key. After a few more minutes of running east, he eased off the throttles and let the boat settle. Still inside the reef line, the water was calm except for a light land breeze and ripples coming from the north.

He phoned Mickey. It was 2300 when Mickey answered and asked if everything had worked out so far. Relieved to be away from the lights, Cole told Mickey he was good to go.

"Point Alpha has some great fishing. I caught twelve just the other day. You should check it out. Call me when you're back inside the reef line," Mickey said and hung up.

It seemed simple enough. Cole wondered if all the coded language was really necessary, but then again Mickey was one of the pros who wasn't sitting in jail and he probably knew best.

Cole pulled the GPS from his pocket and highlighted Point A. Moments later, the GPS drew a straight line in that direction and Cole whipped the Intrepid around and back to the south. He pointed at the sea buoy marking the main channel and again opened the throttles up to a full plane. At 30 knots over the ground, he was cruising and still hadn't opened her up all the way.

Passing the channel markers at the mouth, the boat surged up and down now with the open swell. Cole slammed the throttles down and she lurched ahead, only the last few feet of her hull even touching the water. She was hard to control and took even the gently rolling swells with difficulty. *Too much power,* he thought. Cole braced his lower back against the seat and his feet against the console to keep himself in place. After ten minutes, he'd had enough. The boat was making 43 knots over the ground but the ride was brutal. She felt like a bull at a rodeo, surely hell bent on kicking him off. Cole settled at 30 knots for the rest of the trip.

He stopped twice, just as Kevin had shown him. Scanning the horizon and the sky, he was happy to see no lights but the stars and lingered each time to take a gulping breath of the nighttime air. He sighted Cuba just after two in the morning. It was nearly three when he was within shouting distance of land. Point Alpha was outside Havana but not so far that he couldn't see its lights to his west. Paralleling the coast, the GPS got him within 50 yards of a small beach in an exposed cove. He nosed the boat in towards the 30 or so yards of beach and felt her drive the deep V-hull into the sand. He smelled the exhaust of his engines first then as the breeze caught up with him, the familiar smell of a tropical night took hold. The moonlight bounced off palm fronds as they gently played back and forth as Cole looked around for any signs of his cargo.

A flashlight came on in some tall grass just beyond the sand. Cole toggled the navigation lights on and off three times then left them off, as he'd done all night. Bodies emerged onto the sand and towards the boat. Sure enough, Cole counted 12. They were all dressed in the same manner as he'd always seen from *Delaney*. Dirty clothes, holes crudely patched with yarn, and worn-out shoes. Cole knew someone had money back home to pay for this trip and so long as he held up his end of the bargain, their life of destitution would soon be over.

With all 12 up and over the bow, they settled in various places. One man remained on the beach until Cole had backed her away then he disappeared back up the beach and into the grass. In such a small cove, Cole put his port engine in reverse and his starboard engine ahead to spin her around in place. The nose came around wildly and Cole smiled at the amount of power at his fingertips. Some of the migrants lost their footing as the bow spun around and Cole apologized as best he could in Spanish, saying, "Lo siento." Then he smiled.

An older man smiled back at him and mumbled something to the rest as they reached around for handholds and prepared themselves for the ride north. Cole again spoke. "Vamanos." *Let's go.*

The older man shook a fist in the air and repeated Cole's words. "Vamanos!" His enthusiasm was contagious.

Cole motored at half speed until clear of the points of land that blocked his view. Scanning left and right, happy to see not a single boat in his vicinity, Cole opened her back up to 30 knots and pointed north. He had more than half a tank of gas and once on speed, he felt good about the trip so far. It was just after three in the morning.

The first hour went off without a hitch. The passengers had mostly sat down, but a few stood up, their arms braced in any way they could find to steady themselves as the boat leapt up and over the swells marching in from the west. Cole thought himself lucky that they ran with the Gulf Stream. Had they run from the east, they would have stood up tall against the current and made the ride unpleasant.

Approaching five in the morning, Cole noticed several of the Cubans looking back to his port quarter and pointing. Three of them were talking. Cole glanced over his shoulder quickly but couldn't see what they were talking about. They were looking at him now and asking questions in Spanish. Over the wailing engines, he couldn't hear what they were saying. He looked again over his left shoulder and saw a red flashing light above the horizon, not too far behind him. He looked ahead to process what it might be. Checking his GPS, he was 25 miles from the sea buoy. He had less than an hour to go.

Cole looked again behind him and clearly saw the silhouette of a helicopter. It was low and clearly flying along with him. "Fuck," was all Cole could manage under his breath. He felt butterflies again. He yelled out over the engines, "Sientate," thinking that it meant something along the lines of sit down. It must have, as the migrants all sat and pressed their backs against the sides for support.

Cole punched the throttles. The boat gave him another ten knots and he was making 40 over the ground. She felt unsteady, as she had before, but now Cole needed the speed. With only her back end dancing off the tops of waves, the boat jolted from side to side, forcing Cole to spread his legs further apart to absorb the impact.

He was still heading north, towards the Key West sea buoy, and the wind stirred up tears in the corners of his eyes. The Coast Guard station at Key West would respond, that much he knew. It was anyone's guess whether or not they had small boats coming from Marathon and Islamorada. Worse yet, he had no idea what Customs and local police were doing. He knew well enough though that the crews of more than half a dozen units were now being roused from their sleep and running towards their boats, all to give chase for him. There was even a chance *Delaney* was out that night and Cole wondered if Wheeler was preparing his boarding team somewhere in the distance.

Eighteen miles to go. Cole had to assume the worst. Boats were already under way and making best speed to close in on him. His chances rested on outrunning them, something his Intrepid was capable of. But if they were intercepting from the north, there was little he could do but thread the needle between them and hope to shake them off in shallow water. He strained to think clearly and analytically about his plan, but each time the boat soared off the back end of a wave and slammed back down, he would lose his most recent thought and had to begin again. He pushed the throttles again, but they were already maxed out.

His best plan was to risk the boat by running straight over the reef, a route that no lawman would take. They wanted to catch him, but they wouldn't risk their own boats or their lives by running over the reef at night. It was a gamble in that there was no way to tell where the coral heads sat. They could be six inches or six feet under the water. The move was smuggling's version of a Hail Mary throw by a desperate quarterback. If they didn't follow him over the reef, he'd have enough time to run her up somewhere and go from there. This all assumed that he made it through their initial intercept and lucked out with a deeper pocket over the reef. If he hit the reef, the boat would tear open and wreck, throwing him and his passengers into the air.

The helicopter was still behind him and flew a lazy pattern on his stern, going from one side to the other. He focused his eyes ahead, scanning for the blue lights of law enforcement but saw none. If they were blacked out, he wouldn't see them until they were right on top. Cole was 12 miles from the sea buoy.

At eight miles, he saw the blue lights—two sets of them almost side by side, they were heading directly at him. He pushed the throttles again, but they were still maxed. He scolded himself for doing so as it was nothing more than a game of nerves at this point. Looking back to his left, he couldn't see the helicopter. To his right he couldn't see it either. He looked back left and right again and it was gone. *Perhaps they'd run out of gas and headed home?* he thought. Cole knew he lucked out on that one. His odds were now improving.

Four miles from the sea buoy, he could make out the wake from both the boats coming out to meet him. He kept on his course directly at them, with a closure rate of more than 60 knots. Suddenly, one broke off to his right but the other kept on with a high-speed game of chicken. Seconds later, one boat passed in an instant close enough that Cole could clearly see the faces from the boat staring at him. His Intrepid rolled hard to the right then went completely into the air off the wake of his pursuer. It landed horribly and nearly threw Cole to the deck. Recovering, he made a 30-degree turn to the east and pointed now at the unlit line of coral only a mile or so ahead. Looking back to his right, the first boat had come around and was now almost abeam at less than a mile. It must have been U.S. Customs as it seemed to match Cole's speed and slowly closed the gap as it angled in. Cole was impressed for a second at the coxswain's timing of the maneuver. The reef was less than a mile away. The boat crew pursuing him would have to act quickly to stop him. The first boat, belonging to the Coast Guard, had lost too much ground in its intercept and was no longer a concern despite their pursuit from a half mile or so back.

Cole turned 15 degrees back to the west to buy some time from the closing pursuit. He looked at his GPS just as the blue dot marking his position crossed the reef. He held his breath and clenched the wheel for the impending impact with the reef, but it never came, and she glided right over it and into the shallows. With the swells subsided, he had another three knots of speed and screamed towards the dark coast ahead of him. He turned harder to the east towards the darkest islands. Key West was far to his left and some smaller islands were directly ahead. He didn't look back, but knew that the Customs coxswain had broken off the chase at the reef. He brought the speed back to 15 knots.

He yelled ahead to the migrants to hold on and waited for the boat to hit bottom. When she finally did, it came on slowly at first. He heard and felt the propellers digging into the sandy bottom. As the hull caught hold it slammed him against the console and his chest pressed hard against the wheel. His feet came up and off the deck as she dug in and finally came to a stop. One engine was still grinding at half speed and kicked up a horrible sludge of water and sand. Cole killed the engines, and it was quiet for the first time in hours. Cole's ears were ringing. He looked back behind him and saw nothing but the calm waters of the protected shallows as it trailed off into the darkness behind him.

The migrants, all 12 of them, were already hopping over the side and into the knee deep water. They understood dry feet meant *terra firma* and they literally ran up to the beach, only 20 yards in front of them, where they huddled up close. Somewhere to the east, a dog was barking, reassuring Cole that he wasn't far from civilization. He basked in the silence for a few more seconds before he heard the faint rumble of a helicopter. More than likely it was state or local police on their way to track him and his cargo down. He hopped over the side, into the knee-deep water, and made his way up to the beach, mad that his new running shoes were now soaked.

CHAPTER 5 — POINTS SOUTH

THE MIGRANTS WERE GONE. They'd surely been briefed about what to do in the event plans changed and clearly, the plan had changed. Cole was standing up under the overhang of some palm fronds as he fumbled for his phone—the dog still barking in the background and the helicopter still a ways off. Dialing Mickey, Cole tried his best to explain what had happened.

Mickey cut him off before Cole even got a full sentence out. "What the fuck man, you woke up the cavalry. Where are you?"

Cole thought about it but didn't know. "I dunno. I'm somewhere east of Key West. The cargo is good and dry, but I don't know where they are at. They split pretty quick."

"OK. You go hide. Let things settle down. I'll call you in a few hours." Mickey pronounced the word *you* as *jew*.

Cole hung up the phone and tucked it back in his pocket. Mickey wasn't much help and Cole was mad at himself for letting things get so out of control. He meandered his way around the small beach a bit until finding a trail, then followed it some 50 yards or so until he spotted some lights. Proceeding carefully, Cole figured out that he was butted up against someone's backyard. Sure enough the lights were all on in the house and Cole ducked behind a patch of palmetto grass and sat down in the cool sand, his back against the trunk of a palm tree. It was early morning and the stars were still bright with enough moonlight to see a good ways in any direction. Cole knew he was not in a good spot and the chopping sound of helicopter blades in the distance was his greatest concern.

Cole told himself to be smart. His mind got away from him for a second and he forced his thinking to slow down. He was facing the house, the beach behind him, and he saw a gravel driveway to the right. Cole knew cops would be here soon and hiding in someone's backyard was not a good option. Bent at the waist, he hustled over to the driveway, ducking behind trash cans and a minivan. The driveway led out to a road and he made a quick run for it to get some distance between him and the boat. The gravel crunched under his wet shoes as he ran and Cole felt the onset of blisters on his feet. He could hear the helicopter closer now and as he approached what must have been the main road on the Key, he could see the helicopter to his east, its spotlight combing back and forth.

He took off in a full sprint, hitting the main two-lane road where he saw another gravel drive opposite the one he'd just come up. Cole sprinted north 100 yards or so until it opened up in an empty lot. There was a rocky beach just to the north then dark open water beyond that. If it was anything like the rest of the Keys, it would be knee-deep water for hundreds of yards and full of shells, rocks, and the occasional coral head. Swimming for it wasn't an option—the helicopter would spot him in minutes. But going back wasn't an option either and Cole exhaled loudly, fighting back the first tinges of desperation.

In the lot were a few abandoned and dilapidated overturned boat hulls. The helicopter wouldn't be able to see him under the hulls, even if it had infrared cameras. At the same time, the cops would probably bring dogs to sniff Cole's trail. With that in mind, he jogged towards the water and ran in up to his knees, then turned west and waded back around the mangroves to where one of the hulls was overturned about 50 yards away. His feet were cold and made it all the more difficult to walk over the uneven rocky bottom, but he was able to grab the phone in one hand and flop the rest of his body in the water to wash his scent as best he could. He rolled a few times then waded directly towards the hull, shivering as he walked.

Cole was careful to take as few steps as possible as he crawled up to and under the boat. With the glow of the phone, he looked around his cramped hideout then curled up under the bow and waited. Cole was soaked. Shivering in the chilly pre-dawn air, he was frustrated, but knew he'd have to sit tight for a while. This was not where Cole hoped to be, and as the sky grew lighter to the east, he heard the helicopter pass overhead several times—a constant reminder of his current predicament.

Less than 15 minutes from when he'd beached, police sirens sounded in the distance. Cole figured the cops were on the main road when the sirens cut out and he heard a car door slam shut. The helicopter passed overhead again, but he never saw the bright spotlight near his hideout and it seemed that the helicopter kept its speed up. His stomach was in his throat as 30 minutes passed by before daylight took hold and warmed him up enough to stop shivering. With a bit more light, he looked at his surroundings, finding he was was sitting amid small rocks with some old fishing net down by his feet. Grabbing it, he made it into a bed of sorts to ease the pain of sitting on jagged rocks for the past hour. He began to relax and soon nodded off.

Cole woke to the cell phone vibrating in his pocket. He was groggy and slow to answer.

Mickey was yelling at him, "What the fuck man. Where you at?"

"I'm under a boat, Mickey." Cole saw the clock on the phone telling him it was past ten in the morning. He'd been asleep for almost four hours.

"What the fuck you mean, you under a boat?" Mickey seemed confused.

"I'm under a fucking boat, Mickey. I don't know what boat. I don't know where. Thanks for asking, though."

Mickey relaxed his voice a bit, "Well, I'm out here looking for you. I'm on a jet ski."

Mickey's pronunciation of *jet* substituted a *yet* for *jet* and Cole again laughed quietly and shook his head. The humor of it helped ease his mind. He wanted to say, "So jew are on a yet ski?" but knew Mickey wouldn't get the joke, especially at this particular point in time.

Mickey continued, "They were all over Sugarloaf Key this morning. The news said the police picked up the twelve already. Where you at on the key?"

Cole connected the dots in his head. Sugarloaf Key made sense. He'd turned east during the chase and Sugarloaf wasn't too far. He scolded himself for not thinking about it during the chase—if he'd been any further to the west, he might have ended up on the Navy base and his chances of hiding out would have been slim to none. It was dumb luck that he ended up on a sparsely populated key. Better lucky than good—but he'd have to do better next time.

He answered Mickey, "I'm on the north bank of the Key. Hang on."

Cole thumbed through the phone until he found a GPS menu that gave him the coordinates and he read them off to Mickey.

Mickey took the coordinates and told Cole again to sit tight—he was on his way.

Cole relaxed a bit. The pressure was off, and he'd kept his cool through the toughest parts and was now on the home stretch. His mouth was dry to the point that he had a hard time swallowing and his tongue was stuck to the roof of his mouth. His clothes had fared no better than his body, having been soaked for almost 12 hours. The salt that had dried on his skin itched to no end, and as Cole shrugged it off and waited, he thought about drinking a beer and taking a hot shower.

He was a long way off from where he'd been a few months ago. As he sat, soaking wet under an abandoned skiff waiting for Mickey, Cole did a bit of self-reflection. Smugglers had run all manner of contraband through these waters for centuries. Cole's career had started off on one side of the law and he'd found that life dull. Moreover, he'd been told over and over again that he was not good at it. The Coast Guard small boat from the night before summed it up well. They were duty-bound to respond but had played it safe when it came down to it. There were operating procedures the crew had followed and that particular coxswain wasn't willing to venture outside of those parameters to make the intercept. The U.S. Customs boat was similar. While the coxswain had shown some damn good seamanship in timing his intercept, he'd bailed when Cole approached the reef line.

Their hearts weren't in it like Cole's was. As he sat there Cole realized that he'd just put every ounce of energy he had into avoiding capture and had come out on top because of it. Cole knew he'd won because he'd worked harder and taken more risks. There was far more at stake for him than for the boat crews that came after him. He felt a renewed sense of courage, the kind that comes from doing something well entirely on your own. He'd risked everything and basked in the satisfaction of it under the rotted hull of an abandoned boat as he waited. His soaked clothes, the blisters on his feet, and the fatigue that wore heavy on his mind were akin to a badge of honor.

It wasn't long before he heard the hum of Mickey's 'yet ski.' Peeking under the hull, he saw Mickey idling up towards him and scanning back and forth in the sky for trouble. Cole crawled out and waded to Mickey.

"Let's go man!" Mickey was still scanning the sky.

Cole joked, "You didn't bring one for me?"

Mickey was not amused. "Get on the fucking jet ski."

"Only if I can drive," Cole quipped.

Mickey was not happy. "Get on the mother-fucking jet ski or I'll leave your dumbass for the cops."

Cole climbed on the back and Mickey throttled ahead out towards a creek taking them south to the open flats.

As Mickey punched the throttle, Cole yelled over the engine, "Nice Yet Ski Mickey."

Mickey yelled back at Cole, "What did you say?"

Cole was laughing as they screamed back west to Key West. "Nothing," he replied, almost as an afterthought.

The warm sun and breeze against his face were a welcome relief from the hours he'd just spent huddled under the skiff. Life was good once again. His fingers were still a bit numb from the nighttime chill, but the sun warmed the back of his shoulders and Cole smiled.

Mickey dropped him off at a dock inside Garrison Bight, from which Cole walked several blocks back to Kevin's apartment. As he meshed back into the midday atmosphere of Key West, Cole realized he was free and clear. Hours before he was a wanted man, but now he was just another face on the street in dirty clothes. A police car slowed as he cut down a side street and Cole waved with a smile as it passed. He laughed out loud after the officer drove past him.

Rounding the last corner, he walked up the steps to the apartment. He strolled inside directly to the refrigerator and grabbed a Dos Equis. Popping the cap off, he downed half of it in his first swig before kicking off his sandy shoes and making his way to the shower. Hotter than he normally had it, the shower shook the last bits of cold from his core. He took long, deliberate blinks under the steaming water and felt the crusted salt melt from his body, taking the opportunity to finish his beer with another swig. The salt from his skin burned the corners of his eyes as the hot water trickled down from his matted and sun-bleached hair. He soaped up then stood under the water in silence for another minute or two.

The beer soaked his brain. His teeth felt slightly numb and he paused to fully embrace the loss of balance that ensued. Drying off, he threw on some clean shorts and pulled a button-down cotton shirt around his shoulders, not taking the time to button it up. Armed with another Dos Equis, he stepped out of the air conditioned apartment and took his usual seat on the porch. Cole managed his buzz with the second beer and leaned his head back against the wall and watched the afternoon's cumulus clouds climb towards the heavens.

Hours went by. Cole thought he had a respectable collection of bottles on the table when Kevin finally made his way back from work. As Kevin came up the steps, they made eye contact and Cole knew his drunken smile probably looked stupid and mischievous at the same time. Kevin was laughing and shaking his head as he disappeared into the apartment. Moments later he came back out with two more beers.

"You're nuts." Kevin took a good long sip from his bottle.

Cole took it as a compliment. "Tag along sometime, I'll show you a thing or two."

Kevin just smiled and kicked his feet up on the railing. "Mickey says you ran straight over the reef. That's a fine line between brilliant and desperate."

Cole thought for a second and steadied his mind. He was serious when he replied to Kevin. "I know, man, but what the fuck were my options? I'm running aground either way at that point."

Kevin nodded his head in agreement. "How did you know they wouldn't follow you?"

Cole smiled. "I didn't. I just assumed they wouldn't. I fell back on what I know and I've seen it too many damn times. We— or they—won't push things, and my only option was to exploit that."

They were both silent for a moment. Cole took the first sip of the beer Kevin had brought for him. He broke the silence and stated matter-of-factly, "I got the job done. That's all."

They tapped bottles in a drunkard's salute to Cole's efforts and both took another sip.

"Mickey thinks you're nuts." Kevin was looking at Cole's face for a reaction.

"Mickey is also getting his money because of me."

Kevin nodded in agreement.

No sooner had Cole mentioned Mickey by name when the man himself came walking down the sidewalk with his hands in his pockets. Kevin and Cole both waved hello. Mickey walked halfway up the steps and tossed an envelope onto the table.

Cole harkened back to *The Old Man and the Sea* and quipped, "Tell me about the baseball," in his best drunk impression of a Cuban accent.

Mickey and Kevin both looked at him like he was out of his mind.

Kevin spoke first, asking, "What the fuck did you just say?" Then he laughed. Mickey followed. "He not only crazy, he nuts."

Mickey shook his head and tried to avoid laughing but couldn't ignore the absurdity of it all.

Cole was a bit disappointed that neither of them understood the reference. "You both should read more Hemingway." He sat back and took another sip of his beer.

Mickey shook his head again and walked down the steps. Turning back towards Cole and Kevin, he spoke softly. "You did good amigo. I'll be in touch." Mickey disappeared around the corner and was gone.

"So what do you do when they're on your ass?" Cole asked.

Kevin was quiet for a moment and replied. "No idea. Never happened. But I might have pushed through the channel before turning to shake them."

Cole was shocked. Kevin had never been chased. He seemed like a veteran, but now Cole, in his first run, had set the bar pretty high for outrunning the law. Cole had a new appreciation for what he'd pulled off.

Kevin, his feet still crossed over the railing and the beer in his hand, opened up.

"I've never been chased, at least that I knew of. I haven't really thought about it much, but I don't think I'd stop either. I just don't know that I'd run a boat at full speed across the fucking reef. You could have split her in half."

Cole took the hypothetical as constructive criticism.

He answered with his best explanation. "I honestly hadn't thought about it either. But I knew the Coast Guard wouldn't follow me and I doubted Customs would either. I was just playing the odds since it seemed like the best way to shake them. Maybe it was reckless, but so is what we're doing out there."

Kevin nodded in agreement. "Have you eaten anything?"

Cole shook his head no and realized he hadn't had anything to eat in almost 24 hours.

Kevin suggested they go get some dinner out in town. They both finished their beers and staggered around the apartment for flip flops, keys, wallets, and the like. The sun was falling to the west and the blue sky showed the first signs of morphing colors for the impending sunset. Cole felt better than he had in a long, long time.

They walked the few blocks to El Siboney, and took a corner seat inside. Cole was lit up beyond where he'd been for quite some time. He had four hours of bad sleep in the past 24 and had hardly eaten anything. Kevin did his best to catch up and the two worked their way through several more rounds of Dos Equis.

Ordering grouper, Cole and Kevin both dug into steaming plates of black beans and rice, topped with a blackened filet of fresh fish. Halfway through, Cole came back to his senses enough to think again about the past day. The envelope Mickey had dropped off had enough cash for Cole to live for several months without working again, but Cole knew he'd be better off keeping his day job. There was no telling when Mickey might call again.

Cole cleaned the plate and slowly lost his appetite for more beer. His mouth burned a bit from the blackened grouper and his nose was running. The air conditioning was cranked in the restaurant and Cole felt his fingers getting cold again. His body was fading pretty quickly and he knew it. While a good part of him wanted to set Duval Street on fire, he knew the smarter option was to call it a night. They both settled up and left a generous tip among the scattered array of empty bottles on their table before taking a leisurely walk back to the apartment. Cole barely made it to the couch before he was in a deep sleep.

Waking early the next morning, Cole was back to his normal self. He suited up to go for his morning run but his shoes were still soaked. Behind the couch, he fumbled for his old pair and laced them up, taking off running from the porch, down the steps, and onto the street. He was full of life. He ran fast and took deep breaths, making it down to Roosevelt Boulevard before he really opened up along the boardwalk. He felt a bit of the hangover, but it was the mild kind that he could easily run right through. He'd work up a good sweat and by the time he was back at Kevin's he'd be at 100 percent.

Cole finished up on the side street by the apartment and took a few minutes to walk around back and forth and catch his breath. Once steadied, he headed inside, took another shower, dressed and was out the door with Kevin down to the *Yankee Freedom*. He went to work like the last day had never happened.

As she plowed into open water and the catamaran came up to speed, Cole spent a bit more time on the open back deck as he coiled lines and straightened things out. The cat rolled gently in the groundswell, every now and then digging deeper than usual into a wave. When she did, he felt the boat drive into the swell, then rocket back out, up, and over into the next one. Salt spray caught his face a few times, but it was pleasant and nothing like the stinging he'd felt at full throttle two days before. Finished with his work for the time being, he rested both his forearms on the railing and stared out at the sea in front of him.

It wasn't a particularly bad day, but the wind had come up from the northwest and Cole watched gusts push across the crests of the swell, driving up bits of spray as the cat's wake crossed theirs. The water was a dark and inviting shade of blue, unlike water he'd see anywhere else. Strung out lines of orange seaweed marked the tide and currents that swirled in all directions. He knew that mahi-mahi schooled up under the weeds and saw the gulls circling above the bigger patches, confirming the presence of fish below. Birds swooped down as flying fish popped up from the depths on the backside of the swells, flying just a few inches above the water for a few seconds before disappearing into the face of another wave. The hum of the engines, the rolling of the cat, and the smell of exhaust swirling in the air satisfied Cole's senses, giving him a feeling of weightlessness and freedom that for so long he'd thought was lost. All the while, this same sea kept his secrets tucked in her depths.

Having slept more than eight hours the night before, Cole had too much energy to hole up under a palm tree on Fort Jefferson. He spent his downtime walking around the island and ended up back by the migrant rafts that were pulled up high on the beach. They were the same ones from the last time he had poked around. Cole kicked at the side of one of them and despite its worn appearance, the wood was still solid. Someone had put time and craftsmanship into it. Cole wondered if someone like Hemingway's Old Man had built it. He wondered too if the crew of this raft had made it to American shores. That someone could row 90 miles across the Gulf Stream still seemed impossible, but here on the beach was proof that some did indeed. Cole tried for a moment to put himself on a wooden boat in middle of the straits, no land in sight, and armed only with oars.

Ain't that some shit, he said to himself and walked back over the catamaran to get her ready for the return trip.

He spent the entire leg back to Key West on the fantail, looking out over the water and thought about those rafts. He was interrupted from time to time by seasick tourists, and he did his best to help them steady their nerves. Some were unsteady on their feet, others puked and rallied, while some were green and looked like they would forever hate the sea. Cole gave them the basic tips. *Look out on the horizon, take a few deep breaths, think about something other than the boat.* The ones who ended up on the fantail were usually too deep in the throes of seasickness and resigned themselves to riding it out on the back deck. Cole felt bad for them, but at the same time he knew that not all men were cut out for the sea.

He made another run almost a month later. It was cake. He'd nosed up on yet another crescent beach just east of Havana. The palm fronds reflected moonlight, the smell of burning brush lingered in the air, and another dozen migrants scurried out from under the trees and onto yet another stolen center console. Screaming back to the north with his passengers tucked up on the bow, Cole scanned the skies more than he did the horizon, looking for aircraft anti-collision lights, a telltale sign he was in trouble. But they never showed.

He ran just west of Key West, up to some uninhabited Key, and met Mickey with another boat. Cole hopped over to Mickey's cuddy cabin and was greeted by a smiling man who shook Cole's hand and said *gracias, muchas gracias*, more times than Cole could count before hopping over to the center console and motoring off to the east. Mickey patted Cole on the back and took him back once again to Garrison Bight. An envelope of cash in his pocket, Cole walked in the dark alone back to the apartment and inside. He slept for an hour or two and woke up to Kevin walking around the kitchen.

Cole spoke first, "That was an easy one." He was rolling over on the couch, his arms outstretched over his head as he shook the fatigue off and steadied himself on his feet.

Kevin was making a pot of coffee. "That's how it's supposed to be."

"Well, shit, why didn't anyone tell me that the first time?" Cole laughed and grabbed his shoes. He decided to skip the morning run after the previous night's excitement and told Kevin he'd meet him at the cat.

"No coffee?" Kevin seemed unusually offended.

"Nah, your coffee tastes like shit. I'll see you in a bit."

"You're gonna work today?" Kevin laughed as Cole walked out the door while pulling a t-shirt over his head as he did.

"Why not?" Cole closed the door behind him.

He treated himself to a breakfast of champions at Blue Heaven. He was ahead of the morning crowd and sipped coffee at the eccentric bar while he devoured a plate of eggs, bacon, and banana bread.

"Quite the appetite." The girl behind the bar was making small talk.

"One of those nights, if you know what I mean." Cole stopped eating just long enough to flash his shit-eating grin at her. She was cute, but Cole didn't intend to put on a show for her.

"I know what you mean." She was now leaning against the bar.

Cole had two hours of sleep on him at best, and he was on his way to a full day of work. She was clearly sending signals, but he didn't have the energy or the desire to play along. He tipped well and threw her a half-assed salute as he made his way back out onto the street and down to the *Yankee Freedom*, albeit an hour later than usual.

He powered his way through the morning routine and settled under a large palm tree just before noon. An hour and a half later, he felt more tired than he had the night before and it took all his energy to get up and prep the boat for the return leg. Kevin passed by him on the dock and deliberately knocked his shoulder into Cole, which threw Cole off balance in his current state.

Kevin laughed. "You look like shit dude."

Cole regained his footing and laughed as well. "Yeah, but I have a roll of hundreds that will make a real nice pillow tonight."

Kevin shook his head and hopped onto the cat. Cole followed a moment later and went to work.

They were both laying out food and drinks for the return leg in the main cabin when Kevin seemed to offer some genuine advice.

"Look, man; you're killing yourself. Take it easy for a bit. The work's always gonna be there."

Cole nodded, "I know."

He continued on with the mundane tasks before him and thought about Kevin's advice. Kevin was the type to seize life by the balls. He took risks not for the sake of pushing his limits, but rather as a means to an end. Living the good life, which is what he did, was the end for Kevin. Running migrants gave him an influx of cash to keep on keeping on. It was gas for his boat, new dive gear if he needed it, or simply some extra dollars in his pocket to make a night on Duval Street a memorable one.

In a way, Cole envied him. For Cole, the adrenaline was an end in itself. He'd hardly spent any of the money he'd made. Some new running shoes, and few shirts when his others were practically falling off his shoulders—that was it. He ate well, but well below his means. Behind some books on the shelf next to his couch, Cole had 10,000 dollars rolled up with rubber bands. He liked to pull out the rolls from time to time, but it wasn't nearly as satisfying as the feeling of driving a hull up onto the sand under the radar of the Cuban and American governments. It was nothing compared to the feeling of running a boat to her limits under a midnight moon. He knew the water more intimately than he ever had before, and that was what he sought from life.

Each run he made left him exhausted, both physically and mentally. But the fatigue was gone by the next morning and the addiction to adrenaline never ebbed. It was only a matter of days before Cole felt it creeping into his veins again and he wasn't sure it was something he could control. Even if he wanted to, Cole felt he was going down a path from which he couldn't turn around. It scared him, but at the same time it was exciting.

A week went by before Mickey called. Cole made yet another uneventful run. The temperature had come down quite a bit as fall was setting in and as Cole walked back in the darkness to the apartment, he wasn't as satisfied as usual. Kevin was asleep in his room as Cole mixed up a Captain and Coke. Squeezing a lime over the top of it and stirring with his finger, he pulled a sweatshirt over his head and took his seat on the front porch. He put half the drink in his mouth and held it for a moment, taking in the last few minutes of darkness, then swallowed. He dialed Mickey.

"What the hell you up for? It's five-thirty in the morning, kid." Mickey sounded half asleep.

With his feet crossed and pressed against the banister, he held the phone in one hand and the half-empty plastic cup in the other. Cole finished the drink, leaving nothing but the ice and a coke-stained wedge of lime in the bottom. Setting the drink down, Cole spoke matter-of-factly into the phone.

"I want more, Mickey."

CHAPTER 6 — HABANAS

MICKEY HAD NOT BEEN in the mood to discuss business that morning before the sun was up. He told Cole to sleep it off and they'd talk the next day. Cole had the day off, so after ending the call with Mickey, he mixed up another Cuba Libre to celebrate the sunrise. By the time he'd stirred it and taken his seat, the sky had turned a lighter shade of blue and wispy clouds were backlit by the rising sun. Cole was drunk but happy, and his mind was alive with thoughts of what might lay in store.

He turned in for some sleep once the temperature started to come up. Cole guessed that in the darkness of the night, it had dropped into the low 60s and it felt clean and crisp. As the day progressed, it would end up somewhere in the upper 70s or low 80s—enough to feel hot under the Florida sun. With the AC humming and the curtains drawn, Cole slept well past noon and finally began to stir shortly before two in the afternoon. Kevin was nowhere to be found, so Cole worked through a pot of coffee, then went for a quick jog to the airport and back.

He'd missed a call from Mickey and had a text message suggesting they meet for a late lunch. Cole showered up and changed into some clean clothes. He pulled on a pair of jeans, flip flops, and his trademark button-down linen shirt. Stepping out the door, the midday sun was warm, but the air felt cooler against his skin and he enjoyed the leisurely walk downtown. It was by far his favorite time of year. While the rest of country was preparing itself for winter, the Keys were coming into their prime. The nights were cool, but each day the sun did its best to keep temperatures comfortable during the day. The Gulf Stream never let the water cool too much to stop anyone from a midday swim. The vacationers still flocked to Duval Street and basked in their long weekends away from the snow and wind up north.

Cole took the long way around to Margaret Street and settled onto a barstool at Turtle Kraals, overlooking the marina. There he ordered a skirt steak and another Cuba Libre. He'd been sober for a few hours by that point and figured the most productive part of his day was already over. Mickey showed up 15 minutes later and pulled up a stool next to Cole. It was mid-afternoon and the two had an entire corner of the restaurant to themselves. A steady breeze rolled in off the water, and the mix of boats bobbed back and forth in their slips. On the sailboats, halyards and shackles slapped against aluminum masts. Feeling dizzy from his drink, Cole likened it to a chorus of off-key bells rung by an orchestra of idiots. It was a sound that Cole loved. He couldn't help but take a deep breath and smile.

Mickey sat silent for some time as he perused the menu and Cole waited patiently, sipping on his drink. After ordering some ceviche and a Dos Equis, Mickey put his menu down and crossed his arms, looking at Cole with a stern face.

"I don't get you, Cole." He paused. "You make good money, you good at what you do, you live the good life, but you still telling me you want to do something else?"

Cole laughed a bit and realized that Mickey accentuated the J in words like 'you' when he was irritated. It wasn't all the time, but right now he really emphasized them. Here Mickey seemed to act more like a concerned father than the ringleader of an international smuggling operation.

"What the fuck do you care, Mickey?"

Mickey tossed his hands in the air, up and over his head in an exaggerated manner. "OK, then, I don't care. I no give a damn. You just tell me what you want and maybe I can help."

Cole finished off his drink. He held it almost inverted for an extra second or two to suck down the last few drops of coke and rum. The glass was now empty, the stained lime stuck between the remaining ice cubes. He wanted to open up and pour out his problems, but Mickey was no shrink, and Cole wasn't about to show any sign of weakness to a seasoned criminal. *Delaney* was always in the back of Cole's mind. The honest truth was he didn't know what he wanted, but every run to Cuba and back only fueled his appetite for open water, fast boats, and adventure. Perhaps it was reckless and stupid, but Cole felt that each time he made a run, he was stuffing it in Potts' face. He wanted more of that feeling.

Cole knew he was only skimming the surface of the Caribbean underworld. He was ready to take off the training wheels and hoped that Mickey could point him in the right, or more appropriately wrong, direction. He didn't fully understand why he wanted to make his way south, he just felt an undeniable longing for a new chapter. As nice as it was, Key West felt small and constricting. Every time he cruised past the Coast Guard base, it reminded him of his shortcomings. He felt like it choked him. "What else you got Mickey?"

Mickey laughed. "What the fuck you mean, 'what else I got?'" Mickey tried to make fun of Cole's southern drawl but it came out wrong when crossed with Mickey's Spanish accent. The two of them laughed and it broke whatever tension had built since the conversation started.

"Hook me up with some of your buddies further south." Cole figured Mickey had connections.

Mickey's eyes grew big for a second then back to normal. From his pocket, he pulled out a phone, read a text message, typed a short reply, then put the phone back in his pocket. Shaking his head a bit, he took a long sip from his beer. He began to speak just as he swallowed.

"You're asking to get into something you might not get out of. Plus in most people's eyes, you're a snitch—at least you were a snitch, working for the man. I send you to see some people and they probably just shoot you in the head." He meant what he was saying. Migrants were one thing, but cocaine, pot, and cash were things people lost their lives over.

Mickey continued, "I send you down there and you screw up, I look bad and you die—that's how things work, Cole." He paused. "You are asking for a lot."

Cole argued back, "I've got discipline Mickey—you know that. I get the job done no matter what. All I'm asking for is a contact. Someone to talk to. I'll take care of myself from there."

Mickey was quiet and took a deep breath followed by another long sip from his beer. "You ever been to Panama?"

Cole hadn't. He'd seen its coastline from the bridge of *Delaney*, but had never set foot on solid ground. Cole thought back to the distant lights on the horizon that he'd seen so many times and tried to hide the excitement that grew as he mulled it over. "No, Mickey. I haven't."

"Well, why don't you buy some tickets. I'll make a call for you."

The two finished up lunch and the conversation turned light. Mickey surely had plenty of tips and advice, but he kept them to himself. Cole figured it was Mickey's style to let him learn those lessons himself. As they parted ways, Mickey looked Cole over and shook his head, as if he already regretted his promise to help Cole on his way south.

A month later, Cole found himself at the Key West International Airport early in the morning. It wasn't much, consisting of a 5,000-foot runway barely big enough for a jet to get in and land. Most of the traffic was regional airlines and a healthy dose of turboprops moving the tourist crowd in from larger airports to the north. The terminal itself was a single room with a few check-in counters. A duffel bag by his side, Cole quietly waited for his plane and watched the tourists come in and out. Kevin had loaned the bag to him as Cole figured his seabag would stick out too much. He wore a newer pair of jeans, having spent a bit of his money on some new clothes for the trip. His shirt, fresh off the hanger, felt a bit stiff compared to his older ones. Once he sweat in it a bit and put it through a wash cycle or two it would hang off his shoulders like his others.

The airport pressed up against the water and Cole could smell the cool air coming in through the open windows. In the shade of the terminal, it was nice enough that Cole briefly thought of turning off the whole thing. *Why do I want to leave when it feels as good as it did on that day?* He rested his head against the wall behind him and crossed his legs in front of him. With a ticket, cash, and passport in his hand, he felt committed to at least trying something different. If things didn't work, he could always come back to Key West. There would always be another winter and a load of migrants waiting in the brush of Cuba's north coast.

Soon enough, he hopped aboard a small turboprop to Tampa. Climbing up and away from Key West, he looked out the window and saw the Keys below him. For a moment or two he again questioned his decision to leave. The green water, the dotted sandy beaches, and the underwater forests of seagrass and reef seemed so far away now and he missed them already. Before long, the plane climbed through a layer of clouds and the Florida Keys were all but a memory.

From Tampa, he took a larger jet over to Dallas where he had half the day to waste before his flight to Panama City, Panama. With his duffel bag over his shoulder, he wandered the airport for an hour before finding himself completely bored. The smells were like any airport. The food court stunk of pizza and hot pretzels. Kiosks sold crappy pillows and trinkets for passers-by to occupy their time. He thought about settling into a bar stool and drinking himself to a stupor, but the atmosphere of the airport just didn't seem right. He made his way through the security checkpoint and then outside. It was late December and the air was cold. He still had his flip flops on and felt a bit out of place amongst the honking horns, exhaust fumes, and hustle of Dallas.

Cole waved for a cab as an idea popped into his head.

He hopped in and the cab driver looked into the rearview mirror waiting for Cole to give him directions. Cole gave a light-hearted smile and said, "I need some boots."

The cab driver asked if he had anywhere in mind and Cole shook his head. "Whatever is close works for me." And with that, they were off.

Dallas was a huge city and the eight-lane highways were a far cry from the quiet side streets of Key West that Cole had called home for the last five months. It was rather depressing and not at all what Cole had hoped Texas would look like. He knew that outside the city limits, the state was beautiful and an endless unforgiving rugged terrain stretched in every direction. But in the back of a cab amongst the gridlock, Cole couldn't wait to get on his way.

After some time, the cab pulled into a large department store, Cavender's, and Cole gave the driver two 20-dollar bills.

"Give me twenty minutes. I'll be back."

The driver nodded and reclined his seat back a bit, pulling his trucker hat over his eyes.

Cole walked through the automatic doors and made his way over to the boots. An entire wall was covered in western boots. Cole walked the length of it and back, grabbing a few and giving them the once over. None particularly caught his attention until he found a square-toed pair with a Texas flag color scheme. They were all leather, but the sides were stained with a blue star on the outside and red and white striping on the inner side. He asked the teenage girl behind a counter for a size ten and she brought them out a few minutes later.

"You need to wear socks to try them on." She was waiting as if Cole was magically going to shit out a pair of socks.

"Well, I guess I need to buy some socks, then. What do you have for warmer weather?"

The girl came back with a three-pack of lightweight wool socks and Cole pulled them up and over his ankles. He hadn't worn a pair of socks like that in almost six months. When he ran in Key West, he wore the shorter ankle-high ones, and even then it was only for half an hour or so. He realized just how weathered and tanned his feet were from the salt air and sun. Pulling both boots on over his new socks, he walked around for a bit and the girl returned to the counter and consumed herself with something on her cell phone.

On the wall adjacent to the boots, there was another towering section of western hats. Cole stood there in his State-of-Texas boots and chewed on his lip for a minute.

Why not? he thought.

He picked up a few and tried them on, feeling a bit awkward at first but also liking the way they looked. The felt ones were most certainly going to be too warm, so he moved on to some made of straw and others of palm leaves. The majority were white or off-white in color, but a few were stained darker and Cole found one that was just a shade or two short of jet black. It was a palm leaf material that felt good against his head and the leather band inside gripped his forehead, holding it firmly in place on top of his bleached hair.

Cole looked at himself in the mirror, his boots on his feet and a cowboy hat on his head. He pulled the brim just a bit lower to hide his face in its shadow and smiled a devilish grin.

"Yippee Ki-Yay, motherfucker," he said with certainty and tipped his hat to himself.

He checked out and walked back to the cab, his flip flops now in his hand and his new boots on his feet. It was awkward getting into the cab with his hat on, but he did his best to play the part. The driver looked back in the mirror again and Cole asked to get back to the airport. He must have at least looked passable since the cab driver paid no attention to Cole's new attire. Cole then stashed his flip-flops inside his duffel bag and they were headed back to the airport.

Back at Dallas International, Cole passed security again and went back to the terminal. He felt a bit awkward still, but no one seemed to give him a second look. Apparently he was pulling off the cowboy thing. He found a Mexican cantina—or at least an airport bar pretending to be one—and pulled up a stool. He wiggled his feet in his boots and rolled his ankles around trying to break in the leather a bit.

The bartender came over and asked Cole what he wanted to drink. She was his age, her hair bleached blond and she had a curvy figure accentuated by jeans hanging low on her hips. Her hands were pressed firmly against the bar, but she kept her distance.

"Captain and Coke please, with a lime."

She looked at him for a second, her head tilted slightly to one side and said, "I figured you for a whiskey guy."

"Maybe if you'll have one with me."

She laughed for a second, looked down at the floor, then back at Cole.

"You're trouble, aren't you boy?"

Cole grinned because he'd made her smile. "Wanna find out?"

"Oh, God. I was right. You are trouble," She laughed out loud as she spoke and went back to make his drink.

As a matter of fact, I am, Cole thought.

He took his time with the drink. The bargirl didn't show as much interest in him as he'd hoped, but she made small talk along the way. Cole nursed two more as the hours went by and eventually he ordered a plate of chicken tacos.

"Where are you heading there, Cowboy?" The bar traffic had slowed a bit and she was a few feet away cleaning glasses as Cole was working through the tacos.

"I'm on my way to Panama." He looked at her momentarily then back down at his plate. He was dangling the bait and playing it cool to see if she bit.

"And what are you doing down there?" She was nibbling on the hook.

"I'm a bible salesman, Miss." He accentuated his southern accent and smiled his devilish grin again.

She laughed. "You're a liar is what you are," she said, moving back to clean up the bar.

Cole finished up his plate, emptied his glass, and left two 20-dollar bills to cover the tab. It was a healthy tip as he'd enjoyed her brief company and the conversation.

"You're a pretty girl. Have a good one."

He tipped his hat, then turned before she could respond and walked out of the cantina towards his gate, not looking back. He knew she was watching and it lifted his spirits.

Later that afternoon, he boarded the massive jet bound for Panama City. He'd spent extra money for a first-class seat and had another rum drink in his hand before the plane even took off. It put him over the edge and he reclined the leather seat back and quickly fell asleep, his dark cowboy hat pulled over his eyes and his feet crossed in front of him.

He woke some hours later. It was dark and quiet in the cabin. From 30-something thousand feet, it was near darkness outside. There was still light to the west, but as he sat looking east, the day was near done. A flashing strobe light above the plane flickered every few seconds, and he saw a faint red light at the tip of the wing behind him. There was a screen on the back of the seat in front of him, and he toggled through the menu until a map appeared with an airplane icon indicating their position. They were in the basin, well south of Cuba, Jamaica, and the Caymans.

Half an hour later, the pilot came over the intercom and advised them of their initial descent into Panama City. Cole chugged a bottle of water to clean himself up a bit. Below, he could see the lights of some smaller towns on the Caribbean coast. As the plane descended further, it pushed through and around some towering cumulus clouds and the ride became bumpy. Still high among the clouds, the jet crossed Panama, just a thin dark spit of land separating the Caribbean from the Pacific, and Cole saw the vast expanse of the dark Pacific in front of him. The plane turned right back towards Panama and descended further. The western sky was barely a shade of red on the horizon and entirely black above. As the jet settled on its final course into Panama, Cole stared down at lights of dozens of ships anchored outside the Panama Canal, patiently waiting their turn to hit the canal and continue their voyage east.

After touching down and a long taxi in, Cole grabbed his duffel bag from the overhead and made his way inside the terminal. He could feel the humidity and the heat, even in the nighttime air. It was all new and interesting to him. People moved at a frenzied pace and the culture felt loud and intentionally chaotic. People yelled at each other. As Cole watched, more and more it seemed to be a norm. It was like a big city, but the languages, sights, and sounds were unique. Cole ran his fingers across the stubble on his chin and wiped the fatigue away from his face. He threw his duffel bag over his shoulder and walked briskly towards the exit.

Mickey hadn't given him much, just a name—David. Down an escalator, Cole walked out the sliding glass doors to the outside. The heat hit him and there was no breeze to soften its punch. Cole unbuttoned two of the buttons on his shirt to let in a bit more air, but it was to no avail. He stood a foot back from the curb and took it all in. Cabs pulled in and out, the women wore too much makeup, men all wore jeans and many of them wore gold necklaces or other pieces of jewelry. Cars honked for the sake of honking. The Spanish language came hard and fast from all directions and Cole stood silently listening to it. The air was muggy and exhaust won out as the dominant smell.

A man in jeans and a Nike t-shirt hopped out of a white van that had just pulled up. He approached Cole with a smile and said in very good English, "You have gotta be Cole."

Cole looked the stranger in the eye, nodded his head and extended his hand. The man took a firm grip and the two shook hands.

"I'm David and I will show you around a bit. Please come with me."

The two climbed in. It was a smaller European-style van with windows all around and three rows of seats. David sat in the middle row and Cole was in the first. The driver said nothing as he navigated through the congestion and onto the highway. It was past nine o'clock at night but the traffic was still heavy as the highway paralleled the Pacific towards downtown Panama City. After 20 minutes, Cole could see the city in front of him, its towering buildings and bright lights rivaling that of any big city in the states.

David spouted off random facts about Panama. There was construction everywhere and as they hit the main streets of the business district, thumping music echoed amid the car horns and bright lights. There were casinos, bars, and restaurants along the way. The sidewalks were lined with people going about their business. It took them another 20 minutes to get to the far side of town. As they left the bright lights and turned down some smaller streets, Cole looked around a bit more, trying not to give away the sinking feeling in his gut.

David picked up on it and reassured Cole, "Don't worry, my friend. We just need to make one stop and we'll head back to the hotel. Everything is cool."

Everything was not cool. They were now in the ghetto and only one out of every six street lights worked. There was graffiti on the walls of just about every building and at least half of them looked deserted, their windows busted and the doors either boarded up or kicked in. Fences all had barbed wire across their tops.

David spoke calmly, "Give it a few more years and this will all be luxury condos. The beach is only a few hundred yards from here. Primo real estate."

The driver took three quick turns, and they pulled up to what was most certainly an abandoned building. Graffiti covered the walls. A man stood outside the door of the building and David motioned for Cole to step out.

"David, what the fuck is this?"

David spoke quickly, "You gotta trust me on this one. Don't get excited. This will be a few minutes and we'll be on our way. If you freak out on me, it's gonna be trouble. Just stay cool and we're good, OK?"

Out of options, Cole stepped out of the van.

"Hola," was all he said to the man outside the door and the plainly clothed guard nodded his head back at Cole.

David walked them inside. It was total darkness save for some light from a room at the end of the hallway. The two walked down the dark corridor and turned into a room, where there were a few lights plugged into the wall. Three men stood talking in the middle of the room and looked at Cole as he walked in.

Cole again said "Hola," and made a slight waving gesture with his thumb, pointer, and middle finger. His mouth was dry. One of the men, in his late 40s by Cole's estimate, rubbed his chin with his fingers and looked at David. David nodded and spoke rapid Spanish. The two had a quick conversation and Cole could only pick up the words "gringo," "Estados Unidos," and of course "Mickey." They all seemed to say Mickey's name as if it carried a good deal of weight.

The man finished up talking with David and walked over to Cole. He extended his hand and the two shook. At first Cole thought it broke the tension, but afterwards he could still feel it heating up the room even more than the stagnant air.

"You got some balls, my man."

The man had his hands on his hips now and shook his head. He spoke the same way Mickey did, substituting a *J* for the *Y* in *you*. But this time it wasn't funny.

"Why you wanna come down here and drive boats?"

Cole took a deep breath to hold his composure and said, "Well, I'm good at it. I'm comfortable on the water and driving boats like I do makes good money for you and for me."

The man shook his head no, "You make good money in Florida."

Cole replied, "I can make better money here."

"Were you really in the fucking Coast Guard?"

Cole laughed just a bit and replied, "Well, yeah, I was, but they didn't like me."

Now the man laughed a bit too. "Well, shit, my friend. I can see why."

"Are you sure you're not undercover?" The man seemed calm and cool but the question was a serious one.

Cole thought for a second. Part of him wanted to just laugh, but he knew he had to be convincing. Mickey had warned him about this. Cole wanted to explain how much Potts had hated his guts, how he'd been thrown out with the trash and couldn't give two shits about the damn Coast Guard, but he maintained his composure.

"I've been running a lot of migrants to be undercover, don't you think? I'll give you any information on me you'd like if that will assure you that I am no longer interested in doing anything for the fucking Coast Guard." He emphasized 'fucking' when he said it.

"No." The man shook his head. "We've looked into you. You seem legit. And like I said—you've got some fucking balls to walk in here."

The other two in the room walked out, leaving Cole, David, and the new guy in the room by themselves.

The older man continued, "We'll put you to work. It'll be a few days. You'll go on a run with some of my guys, help them out and we'll see how you do. This is the big leagues, Señor Cole."

Cole nodded. "Well, Sir, I can assure you that I'm varsity."

The older man and David laughed, then picked up another fast-paced conversation in Spanish. They used their hands when they talked, just like Mickey. Cole couldn't understand what they were talking about, but from the more controlled gestures of their hands, he figured things were calm enough not to worry.

The old man turned to Cole again. "There is something you must understand."

He cleared his throat. "There are very real consequences when you move something that costs a lot of money. Jail is not something you worry about here. If you get caught and go to jail, so be it. You get out one day and things are OK. But if you talk to save yourself or don't do what you've been asked to do, there are very real consequences."

Cole softly nodded. *Understood.*

The man motioned for them to walk out of the room. "There is something you must see."

Cole, David, and the man walked back down the hall they'd just come down and turned left into a dark room he'd passed when he first walked in. As he entered the doorway, tucking his head a bit to fit his hat through the frame, the lights came on. The other two men were in there standing next to a younger guy sitting in a chair. Cole could see that the kid had his hands tied behind his back and his face was a bit beat up. It wasn't horrible, but clearly the kid had taken a few punches. He had on a pair of jeans and a basketball jersey. He had no shoes on and looked straight ahead without much of an expression on his face.

The older man spoke. "This kid, he fucked up."

He pointed with his finger at the kid.

The older man walked over to the kid and the first two men stepped back against the wall. The kid took a deep breath and exhaled with a bit of a shudder.

The older man continued. "He got caught and tried to talk his way out of jail. Now, jail in Panama is no fun. Anyone who goes in has a decent chance of getting fucked up. There are different gangs and groups and cartels and all of that shit." He motioned with one hand in a circular gesture as if the rival cartels were no big deal.

"But Cole, I promise you we will do our best to look out for you if you get caught."

He pointed at the kid again. "But this kid didn't trust me. He got caught and he started talking. And because he started talking, I lost some stuff I didn't want to lose. And when I lose stuff, I gotta explain to my boss why I fucked up. And he's gotta explain to his boss why he fucked up. And together, we gotta take some steps to make sure none of our people fuck up again. This shit ain't personal, it's business."

He paused and looked at Cole before asking, "Do you understand, Cole?"

"Yes, I do. Clearly."

The man stared at Cole, nodding gently to indicate he was convinced he'd made his point.

It seemed the meeting was over, but David took a deep breath and Cole didn't like the vibe that came with it.

The older man repeated himself. "It's not personal, it's just business."

He reached behind his shirt and drew a stainless steel snub-nosed revolver from the small of his back. The kid looked to his right at the gun and yelled. Cole didn't have to speak Spanish to understand what the kid was saying. *He was sorry...It would never happen again...He'd do anything to make it right.* The kid was sweating now and squirming in the chair, his legs underneath him trying to get some traction, but there was nowhere he could go. His words fell on deaf ears.

In one smooth motion, the older man pressed the gun up to the kid's head and pulled the trigger. It was a blur to Cole. The kid screaming was muted by the sound of the gunshot bouncing off the walls of the little room. After the shot, smoke lingered and obscured details from the room. It must have been a magnum caliber to shake the room like it did. Cole's ears were ringing, and his feet felt unsteady for a second or two from the blast. He was feet away from the muzzle, but it felt as though someone had just punched him in the face. The kid was slumped over and no longer screaming, his head having rolled forward and his body only partly propped up by his two hands tied together behind the chair. The smell of gunpowder dominated the room. Cole saw dark blood all over the kid's head and turned away in disgust.

Cole's heart was beating so loud he feared they would all hear it. He was sweating too. The older man wiped the muzzle with his shirt and returned the gun to the small of his back. "We're done here."

Cole took one last look at the kid's lifeless body as it sat in a contorted mess on the chair. He'd been alive ten seconds before, and now he was dead. Mickey hadn't lied. Cole's feet felt drunk underneath him and he gritted his teeth to get his balance back, taking a deep gunpowder-laced breath. As they walked out of the building and back into the nighttime air, it was a welcome relief from the heat and stench inside. Cole took another deep breath and looked up at the sky. There were stars and a few clouds were backlit by the moon. The light breeze hit the sweat on Cole's face and chest, cooling him.

The older man extended his hand to Cole. Cole shook it without thinking.

"We'll be in touch, Cole. Until then, enjoy yourself."

"Gracias," was all Cole could manage. It was surreal. The guy had just shot a kid in the head and now he was telling Cole to enjoy himself.

David patted Cole on the back and motioned him back to the van. The driver was still sitting in his seat, expressionless, reading a newspaper.

Sitting down in their same seats, David perked back up and said, "All right, I'll show you the hotel. It's nice, the Marriott downtown. There's a bar across the street, Habana's—we'll have a drink."

CHAPTER 7 — PANGAS

THE VAN PULLED UP along the sloping crescent driveway of the Marriott hotel. There were two policemen, dressed in military garb, with their backs against the outer wall when Cole stepped out. Each had a rifle slung over their shoulder and seemed bored by security duty at the hotel. David opened the back of the van, handed Cole his duffel bag, and the two began to walk inside. As they walked in, Cole turned and behind him across the congested street, he saw an outdoor bar with loud dance music blaring over the speakers. It was overrun by stunningly good-looking women. As David and Cole walked through the glass doors, David laughed.

"So you want to get a drink now or what?"

Cole laughed and nodded his head, turning back towards the lobby. As the doors closed behind them, the sounds of the club faded and the cold air-conditioned lobby chilled the bit of sweat on Cole's back left from the vinyl seats of the van. David spoke in Spanish to the man behind the counter and in short order, Cole had a plastic room key in his hand. He figured everyone in the hotel knew what the hell he was doing down there, but he tried his best to hide it. The man behind the counter casually nodded at Cole and extended his hand towards the elevators. The expression on the man's face told Cole that his secret was already out.

"So much for a low profile, huh?" Cole looked at David.

David smiled and replied, "It's fine, my friend."

David walked with Cole over to the elevators. "Meet me across the street in a few. I'll save you a seat."

"Cool." Cole stepped into the elevator and selected the 12th floor. The doors closed and he was finally alone. He huffed out a breath and looked at himself in the elevator's mirror. His hair was a mess, longer than it should be and dirty blond still from the months in Key West. After his travels, his shirt now hung on his shoulders and there were drops of sweat that had soaked through in a few random spots on his chest. Cole looked in the mirror again and recalled the kid getting shot. He wondered what, if anything, the kid felt as the old man pressed the barrel up to his head. The kid knew he was dead the second they'd tied him to the chair, and he had played it cool right up until the moment the older man pulled the gun.

Had he tried to maintain his composure and simply lost it at the end? Or did he really think he could bargain his way to freedom with a drug cartel? Cole took another long exaggerated breath. He wondered if he could have kept calm like the kid. *Could I have slowed my breathing and accepted my fate without a final desperate and uncontrollable outburst?* He did not plan to get himself into that situation in the first place, so he shook the thoughts from his mind and looked down at the carpet in the elevator. The truth was it scared the living shit out of him.

The elevator opened up on the 12th floor and Cole made his way down to his room. Opening the door, he dropped his duffel on the bed and opened up the curtains looking down at the city street. It was a bit like La Concha on Duval Street. Twelve stories up, he couldn't hear the music or smell the warmth of the Latin American city life, but he knew it was there waiting for him. The room was quiet. The air conditioner purred like a kitten. Cole dialed it down a few degrees and drew the curtains again. He opened the mini fridge and pulled out a Miller High Life. It was most certainly there for gringos like himself. No self-respecting local would touch the stuff, of that much he was certain. Cracking the bottle cap open on the lip of the dresser, he tipped it back and drained half the bottle in one swoop. His thirst taking hold, Cole drained the rest with a second swig.

Feeling rejuvenated, he slid the card key in his pocket, tucked his wallet in his other front pocket to keep it from prying hands on the streets below, and made his way back to the lobby, out the front doors, and hustled across the street.

Habana's was booming. Cole figured it out before he even got across the street. It was a brothel that happened to sell booze and cigars on the side. Beautiful women stood around sipping Red Bulls, and damn near every single one of them made eye contact with Cole. There were more than 20 ladies at the ready and probably more hidden behind their wall of tight dresses and long dark hair. Stout men stood guard over the few parking spots in front and only allowed in drivers they recognized. David motioned Cole over to a small table with plastic chairs set up against the front railing. He held a sweating Dos Equis up and Cole took it in his right hand. The music thumped and lights danced across the busy floor. Key West had never seen a night like this.

Cole took a sip as a spotless Mercedes pulled up in front of the bar and the men out front yelled furiously at each other. Within seconds, a taxi cab driver was back in his cab and moved it to clear a parking spot. The Mercedes, without ever stopping its roll, slid right into the spot. The men continued yelling, some at the traffic on the street and others at the ladies standing around the bar. Five women came down the front steps and walked to the car. A few seconds later, the men yelled again, dismissing all but one of the women and the car's passenger door opened. The girl, young with shiny and straight black hair, smiled and slid into the passenger seat, her heels making it somewhat awkward as she tried to get in. Her tight black and white dress made it doubly difficult as she struggled to sit down.

The men blocked traffic, the Mercedes slipped back into the fray, and the remaining four women stepped back up to the bar and went back to their conversations. Cole drank half the beer and spun around 90 degrees to David, who had a big smile on his face. "Different world, huh?"

Cole nodded as he slowly swung around again to check out the innards of the bar. A beautiful young woman caught his eyes and walked over to Cole. She wore a short white dress that glowed from the blue lights and her hair was dark brown, straight, and long to the small of her back. She said something to David in Spanish and Cole heard none of it over the thumping speakers. A few blue strobe lights flickered behind the bar and a scattering of other colors danced around the ceiling and walls, half-obscuring her from his eyes. Seconds later, she put the palm of her hand on the back of his head and played with his hair. Her hand was soft and her fingers tickled the back of his neck.

She smiled and spoke more Spanish. Cole only heard *chico* as she exaggerated her words in an effort to draw Cole's attention to her lips. It worked. She sat in his lap and shook her butt just a bit as she settled onto his thighs. David was laughing loudly. Cole reached around and put his left hand firmly on her thigh and took another sip from his beer. Her skin was soft, cool, and delicate to the touch. He shrugged his shoulders to David as if to give the impression it was no big deal. He tried hard but failed to hide a smile behind the mouth of his beer.

As Cole tried to act the part, a van pulled up to the prime parking spots out front and the men again went about clearing traffic and yelling back and forth. Out stepped some Americans. Cole knew immediately they were military. By Cole's count, there were 12 of them, all wearing shorts, t-shirts, and flip flops. With their attire and their short hair, they stood out from the unofficial Central American dress code of long pants and flashy jewelry. They were in high spirits and shook hands with the men on guard duty as they made their way up the steps and towards the bar. Ladies flocked to them, drinks were poured, and beers appeared by the dozen.

David shooed away Cole's lady friend and leaned into the table. The woman stood up from Cole's lap and leaned forward, biting Cole's ear just a bit as she turned to walk away back into the madness. David snapped his fingers twice to get Cole's attention. "Now we are working, my friend, so pay attention."

Cole nodded and took another sip from his beer. He was still grinning.

David continued, "Those guys, go talk to them. Figure out who they are and where they were tonight. They are U.S. military and fly out of the Panamanian base here looking for our business going north. The way they're drinking, they probably got a bust. Go get me the details."

Cole chewed his lip for a second and finished his Dos Equis. It was probably a test to see if he was really ready to turn his back on his country. Had he been sober, it may have taken some thought, but in his present state, Cole was up for anything. "Roger that."

David pointed at Cole as he stood up. "And stop saying 'roger that,' OK?"

Cole laughed and leaned in a bit. "Roger that." He walked around the far wall of the bar and up to a row of stools where the Americans were huddled. Each of them double-fisted drinks, and some had already latched onto a few of the working women who were quick to recognize the men as potential business.

With his back to the Americans, Cole ordered another Dos Equis. Grabbing the beer and taking his first sip, he slowly spun around, ending up next to one of the younger Americans.

"What's up, man?" Cole nodded calmly.

The young guy stared at him for a second then turned his body to face Cole. "Not much. You an American?"

Cole took another sip and smiled. "Yeah, down here for a little rest. How about you?"

The guy, probably just a few years older than Cole, finished one of his beers with a mouthful and struggled for a second to swallow before wiping a drip off his lip and grinning like a cat. "Not really supposed to say."

Before Cole could even respond, the other guys were giving Cole's acquaintance a world of shit. One of them threw a handful of peanuts at him. "Hey, Secret Agent Man, tell him what you do!"

"Don't tell him; you'll have to kill him!" said another.

"Tell him the truth, you fucking air ninja!"

They were all laughing uncontrollably. One poured the ice from an empty drink over another's head. More peanuts flew back and forth. The ladies kept clear of the ruckus, but stayed close to keep watch over their men.

The guy Cole talked to first finally settled down a bit and spoke quietly to Cole, his elbows pressed against the bar as he motioned for another beer. "We're a Coast Guard C-130 crew, down here for a few weeks. Don't mind the boys, they're just celebrating a bit."

Cole grew a bit nervous if any of them might recognize him, but he didn't seem to know any of them and they were well on their way to a drunken stupor, far beyond the point of distant facial recognition.

Cole offered to buy the guy a beer and he quickly accepted. Over the next round, Cole got more details through light conversation. The American more or less laid out their night's activity. With their radar and infrared camera, they'd latched onto a Go-Fast coming out of Colombia and orbited on top until a Panamanian Navy ship interdicted it in Panama's territorial waters. Apparently there had been a bit of a gunfight between the two boats, and the C-130 crew had watched the whole thing from 1,000 feet. The guy went into great details about what a gunfight looks like through an infrared camera, describing the rate of fire between the Panamanians and the smugglers. He described it like a video game, except it doled out real death less than a quarter mile beneath them.

The Coasties had found the boat, successfully vectored in the Panamanians—who were always hungry for a fight—and stopped that evening's drug run. It was a good bust for the good guys and they were blowing off steam from near non-stop operations over the past two weeks before heading home in a day or two.

Cole took a beer in return from the American and changed the conversation to women about 30 minutes later. By that point, the rest of the crew was out of their heads. Two of them had lost their flip flops on the dirty floor and were trying in vain to get them back on their feet. The others were laughing as the two shoeless clowns put left flip flops on their right feet and confused each other's for their own. More peanuts flew back and forth. The bartender shook his head and laughed it off—just another night in

Panama. After almost an hour, Cole looked back to see David still sitting patiently at the table.

Two of the Americans started wrestling and Cole's drinking buddy broke off the conversation to break up the fight lest they get themselves kicked out. The American stuck two new beers in each of their hands and sat them down at the bar. He yelled something at both of them, and they shook hands grudgingly. Making his way back over to Cole, the American laughed a bit.

Cole looked at the bar where the two errant crewmen were seated, back to being best of friends.

"You look like you've got your hands full."

The guy nodded and laughed, sipping from another beer before he replied. "Yeah, you stick these guys in a plane for twelve hours a day and there's gonna be some infighting. But it's still a damn good way to make a living. I love 'em."

The American must have been one of the pilots. He was younger than most of the other guys, but could lay down the law if it came to it. Cole figured he might have been a lieutenant, but didn't want to ask too many questions. Cole tipped his beer against the lieutenant's and they parted ways.

Cole shuffled between the ladies and the bar's other patrons back to David. Some of the girls reached out and grazed him with their hands as he walked by. He was unable to hide a sly smile as he walked. They were all gorgeous, every last one of them. Sitting back down, David leaned in. Cole summarized the details, and David looked pleased. He took out his phone and consumed himself with a text message he was sending out.

Cole looked back towards the Coastie crew. The two guys were back to fighting and the lieutenant was once again breaking it up. It was well past midnight, and the entire crew seemed good and drunk. The lieutenant was busy gathering his guys, and Cole laughed as he watched the show. Each time the lieutenant got one of them up or away from the bar, another one would slip back into the fray for another drink and he had to go round them back up. The lieutenant would have had an easier time herding feral cats.

After ten minutes, Cole heard him cussing at a few of them as he instructed one of the older guys to put a girl down that he had picked up over his shoulders. Even the security guys controlling the parking were laughing and joking to themselves as the aircrew slowly made its way out of the bar and across the street towards the Marriott. Cole heard one of the younger crew complaining from the far curb that the lieutenant had ruined it and that one of the girls had really liked him. The rest of the Coasties were across the street by then, but the lieutenant was busy dodging traffic trying in vain to get his last wayward crew member to the safety of his hotel room. The kid was probably no older than 19 or 20, only a few years younger than the lieutenant. The rest of the crew, now gathered on the far side of the street, seemed older and a bit more seasoned, eager to watch the lieutenant flex his muscle against a drunk kid's logic.

As the scene played out, everyone at the bar from the prostitutes to the bartenders and the security guys watched and laughed, smacking each other in the shoulder at each new turn. The lieutenant would run around the back end of a car stuck in traffic as the younger guy ran around the front and back towards the bar. The lieutenant, clearly not as tipsy as the kid, finally caught up to him and spun the kid around back towards the hotel with a headlock.

"GO!" barked the lieutenant. He kicked the younger guy in the ass as he pushed him across the street.

The kid stumbled forward and steadied himself yelling, "Dammit, Sir. She likes me!" He pointed back towards the club in defiance. The whole bar erupted in laughter and the pretty hooker at the center of all the trouble blew a kiss back at the crew across the street and they cheered loudly, throwing their fists into the air. Now even the police at the Marriott were laughing and pointing.

Cars were honking their horns at the show, and Cole sat back in his chair remembering fondly the bond that came from working side by side with the same guys day in and day out. Cole again thought back to *Delaney* and wondered if there wasn't something he'd missed all along. But at that moment, the lieutenant didn't give two shits about any sense of brotherhood. He barked out again and pointed towards the hotel. "Go!"

In a last act of vengeance, the young kid took a flip flop off his foot and threw it at the lieutenant. He missed by a long shot, but the bar applauded and cheered the kid for his effort. The lieutenant now ran after him and the two made it across the street to the welcoming cheers of the rest of their crew. The kid stumbled again, almost falling down, and mumbled something about wanting his sandal back before the lieutenant grabbed the back of the kid's t-shirt with a fist and dragged him into the hotel. They disappeared inside the hotel and the bar settled back down to its normal pace.

David was shaking his head and laughing. "You Americans, you are crazy."

Cole finished off a beer. He'd long ago lost track of how many he'd put down throughout the night. David sent another text then closed his phone.

"That was twenty million dollars that we lost tonight because of those guys." David said it matter-of-factly, but Cole was impressed by the amount of money.

David flipped his phone back open and read another text. He flipped it closed and tipped his bottle to Cole. "Looks like you're up tomorrow, my friend."

"What do you mean, I'm up?"

"You gonna make a run to make up the losses from those drunks tonight. You ready?"

Cole's heart thumped a bit in his chest and he felt it in his stomach. The run tonight had ended in a gunfight. The lieutenant had said it looked like a bloodbath from what they could see through their infrared camera. The Panamanians played by a different set of rules and often opted to shoot first and ask questions later. Cole thought about what he'd gotten into. Guns never even came into the mix running across the Florida Straits. The Customs guys, the Coasties, even the local police never even drew a weapon against someone unless they were being shot at themselves. And no one Cole knew carried a gun. Kevin certainly hadn't. Cole hadn't shot one since he'd left *Delaney*.

Cole looked back at David and asked, "Yeah. What time are we meeting?"

David read another text, sent one back and turned his attention back to Cole. "Let's meet in the lobby at noon."

Cole nodded and asked, "Am I checking out?"

David shook his head no. "No, no, you should be back here a day or two after, sipping rum and smoking cigars to your heart's content." He smiled to lighten the mood.

The two parted ways, and Cole made his way across the street and back to his room in the Marriott. Despite the unknown of the next day, he had little trouble getting to sleep.

The following morning, he was up just after eight. After a break-fast from the hotel coffee shop and a few cups of coffee, Cole spent almost an hour in the hotel gym. He worked out hard, but couldn't take his mind away from thoughts about the run he was going to make. He hated the fact that he didn't have any details. He didn't even know what to bring.

Taking a shower in his room, he dressed in a pair of shorts, his running shoes, and the same shirt he'd worn on the flight down. He had a light water repellent jacket and brought it along just in case. He also tucked five hundred-dollar bills into his pocket along with his passport and locked up the rest of the cash he'd brought in the safe in the room. Making his way downstairs, he had some time to kill before noon, so he made his way into the sports bar in the back corner and ordered a Cuban sandwich and water.

Young Panamanian women wore soccer jerseys and knee-high socks to match the sports theme in the bar. It seemed out of place in Panama, but the other patrons didn't seem to mind. It was someone's interpretation of an American sports bar. Flat screens showed soccer games from around the world. Cole's food came with a heaping portion of french fries, and he made sure to down half a dozen glasses of water to hydrate before the trip. He sat by himself and paid little attention to the televisions, his mind consumed by the task ahead.

Finishing up, he walked to the lobby and found David waiting for him. They greeted each other like old friends and made their way out of the lobby into the midday sun. It was hot and the heat reflected off of the buildings, only making it worse. The night before was warm, but now, at noon, it was entirely uncomfortable, but still the locals on the street all wore jeans. Cole looked around the daytime traffic and couldn't figure out how people could hustle around without sweating through their clothes.

David directed Cole over to a waiting van. Climbing in, the air conditioning was running at full strength, and Cole settled into his seat against a window. He looked across the street to the now-quiet Habana's and thought about the previous evening. It was a far cry from the debauchery of the night before as one older gentlemen swept the floors and a few men sat around smoking cigars in the shade. The van inched into the traffic, where horns blasted, people seemed to jump out in front of the traffic at the last second, and no one gave a damn about stop signs or traffic lights. It was chaos, but somehow it worked.

David said nothing as the van pressed on through the city. It meandered through some side streets, into even less inviting parts of town, and finally merged into the moving traffic of what served as a main highway. They were heading north, paralleling the Panama Canal. As the van made its way out of Panama City, the country opened up around them. They were finally on a two-lane highway through open fields where cattle grazed. There were lean-tos built of scrap metal dotting the landscape and kids rode bikes down dusty trails. Some fields were growing crops and others were overgrown tangles of brush. It looked inhospitable, but there was a tropical feel and the occasional thick canopy of a jungle offered brief respites from the sun. They drove clear across the country to the Caribbean side, and three hours passed before they came to a stop on a dead-end gravel road. In front of the van sat a small bay with the rusted-out hull of a barge aground in the middle. A few small workboats bobbed gently in the breeze, and on the far side of the harbor against a backdrop of palm trees, two flatbed trucks were being offloaded by a bunch of guys to a panga floating ten yards off the beach. Cole and David walked over to the trucks and one of the men broke off from loading to greet them.

"Is this the cowboy?" He extended his hand to Cole.

Cole took a firm grasp and grinned.

David piped up and said, "This is your guy. His name is Cole. He's making his first run down here, but he has a bit of a reputation from running boats up north."

The man looked pleased. "Great, great, you are early which is good. We will have her loaded and gassed up in about an hour. You just relax and we'll finish getting her ready."

The panga looked to be in decent shape. Pangas were unique to Central America. They were the workboat of every fisherman from Mexico on down. Built of fiberglass, they were usually painted in pastel colors with beautifully upward sloping bows and graceful lines. Normally, they were an open cockpit with a small center console just forward of the engines. This one had two outboards, both carrying 275-horsepower engines. Sometimes pangas had only one, and Cole was thankful this one had two motors in the event that one seized up on him. Both the outboards looked to be in good shape and newer than the panga itself.

Perhaps it was stolen or perhaps it was reserved for jobs like this, but from the dings and scratches along the hull, Cole figured it had seen its fair share of time on the open water. With a wide bow and the upslope, pangas could handle open water better than the sportier models in the States. Pangas weren't built to dazzle or set speed records, but they were a workhorse and many seagoing men trusted their lives to these boats. Cole had never driven one, but he had always admired their lines when he was a boarding officer working in the Caribbean.

The six men finished loading bales onto the deck of the panga and began spreading fishing nets and gear over the top to give off the appearance of legitimate intentions. It was almost five in the afternoon when the last of the two external plastic fuel tanks were topped off. Cole knew that most smugglers used big drums and thought it clever that this panga was outfitted with square plastic tanks painted white to blend in with the white fiberglass bench seats. Even from ten feet away, he had a hard time spotting any tell-tale signs of drugs.

The same man came back to Cole and gave him a quick rundown. Two of his guys would go with Cole. One, Hector, was just along for the ride if anything came up, but the other, Diego, was a whiz with engines and would handle any mechanical trouble that came up on the run. Diego was a veteran and the old man assured Cole that he was in good hands. Diego had an athletic build and moved quickly around the panga, giving Cole a thumbs-up when they made eye contact. Hector, on the other hand, was pudgy and angry with Cole's presence. After exchanging looks with Cole, Hector looked down at the water and muttered a few words under his breath. Diego yelled something back at Hector, putting him in his place, then flashed a smile back at Cole to let him know all was well.

The old man handed Cole a handheld GPS and explained that this trip would go a bit under 300 miles of open water to the border of Costa Rica and Nicaragua. The waypoint saved in the GPS was a river mouth where Cole would have to cross a shallow sandbar then take a left turn up the river to a small set of shacks. Diego and Hector would know where to drop off the boat. They planned for it to take 12 hours. Casting off a few hours before sunset, Cole would be there in the morning before the sun was up.

Along with the GPS, the man gave Cole a smaller bag. Cole took it and it felt heavy. He unzipped the bag just a bit and saw a Glock pistol and a half-dozen magazines. Crouching down, Cole set the bag on the dirt. Picking up the Glock, he could tell it hadn't been cleaned in a long long time. Salt had dried all over the frame and it had been shot since its last cleaning. Gunpowder residue was caked all over the forward end of the slide. Cole inserted a magazine, felt it click in place, and racked the slide with the gun pointed down and away from the others. It chambered a round with just a bit more grit than normal. If he had to take a dirty gun with him, a Glock was a good choice. It would run with just about any amount of dirt and grime covering its innards. He tucked the pistol in the small of his back, tightened his belt a bit to hold it firm, then tossed in his jacket with the spare magazines and zipped the bag back up.

Meanwhile, the man and David went back and forth in Spanish and Cole couldn't pick up any of it. Turning to Cole, David asked if he had any questions. "Yeah. How do I get back here?"

The other man chimed in. "Don't worry cowboy, we'll take care of that. You just get this boat and this load to Nicaragua."

Cole could do little but accept the man at his word. "Well, OK then. See you when I see you."

Cole took his shoes off and held them in his hand as he walked through the knee deep water over to the panga. The shallow water was warm and felt wonderful against his bare feet. He tossed the bag of magazines and his shoes over the side and onto the deck. Diego extended a hand and helped Cole up and over. Standing onboard for the first time, he felt the sturdy deck beneath his feet and the rough finish of the fiberglass. When built, no one had bothered to take the extra time to sand it down for aesthetics, but as Cole walked around inspecting the fuel lines and the console, he felt confident she could handle the open water.

There were two keys in the ignition. Cole turned one and the first engine kicked and moaned for a brief second before coming to life, spitting a stream of cooling water out the side. He turned the second key and she was alive moments later as well. He adjusted the trim a bit and his two crew settled into seats forward of Cole. They sat facing away from him, their hands pressed against the seat behind them and made small talk. *No big deal*, Cole thought, although he knew that a boatload of cocaine was, in fact, a big fucking deal. Here he was, once again, crossing a threshold. But here on the quiet Caribbean coast of Panama, it seemed far enough removed from *Delaney* that there was little need for concern. He smiled and gave a half-assed salute to David and the other man as he backed the panga away from the shoreline.

There was plenty of room, but he twisted the motors anyway, putting the left one clutch ahead and reversing the right. The bow spun around smartly into the wind and Cole idled ahead through the small harbor. He didn't look back at David or the safety of the shoreline, knowing that he couldn't turn around at this point. Before him stood a challenge, and Cole was hell-bent to see it through to success. He motored slowly for some time and felt the sea breeze pick up against his face. The color of the water was somewhere between green and blue and puffs of wind danced across the surface as he rounded a sandbar and saw a monstrous jetty in front of him. It was a great feeling to be out of the city and back on the water. Despite the risk of being caught, or lost at sea, or hunted down by another cartel, Cole was thankful to be on the open water again.

To his left, he could see the unending line of tankers anchored off the canal waiting for their turn to cross Panama. Ahead and to his right there was a break in the jetty and beyond it the Caribbean Sea. Cole turned slightly right and pointed for the channel. Diego looked back at Cole and gave him a thumbs up. Hector sat facing forward, slumped as if he was pouting. Diego, throwing his fist up into the air, yelled, "Vamanos!"

Cole throttled up to about 15 knots. The bow rose up and out of the water then settled down just shy of a full plane as a cool and stiff breeze filled in. The water was deeper and a darker blue as they crossed the entrance and hit the full expanse of the Caribbean. There was a chop of about three feet, but the panga held her course well. Cole worked the throttles a bit until she found her rhythm amongst the waves, the whitecaps, and the sea spray.

Fuck Hector, he thought. Cole yelled back at Diego, "Vamanos!" *Let's Go.*

CHAPTER 8 – EL CARIBE

THE SKY SHOWED the first signs of sunset as Cole leaned back against the raised seat behind him. It wasn't enough to sit down on properly, but pressing his back against it took some of the load off his feet and stabilized his footing amid the rolls. He ran at just under 20 knots until almost eight o'clock in the evening. Looking ahead, the last hints of light disappeared behind a low cloud on the horizon. He had been driving northwest since he passed the jetty and had covered only 30 miles. Land no longer visible, Cole grasped the magnitude of this run. Had it been Florida, he'd be a third of the way there, but now in the open Caribbean, he had covered only a small fraction.

Cole brought the throttles back to idle and the panga slowed. Her bow pushed one last wave ahead then settled. Hector and Diego looked back at Cole and saw that he was scanning the sky around them. Cole took his time looking for any signs of aircraft. Seeing none, he scanned the horizon all around for ships and also saw nothing. He was all alone on the sea as the panga bobbed and the two outboards hummed against their mounts. There was a good breeze from the north and it was full of cool air, chilled even more as the night took hold. Cole grabbed his jacket and zipped it halfway up. His arms, face, and legs were already covered in a fine film of dried salt from the sea spray and humid air. Taking a deep breath, Cole smiled at the two up front.

"Vamanos," Cole yelled again. They both just laughed, muttering back and forth, probably calling him names in Spanish.

Cole pushed the throttles halfway up, and the bow rocked up and over the water. He turned her northward with a half-spin of the wheel and matched her to the reference on his GPS. It was the only light on the boat, and Cole kept it tucked in front of the throttle quadrant. Satisfied with his course, he looked at the magnetic compass and committed 335 degrees to memory. If the GPS died, a compass was all he had to go off of. Cole punched the throttles and felt the panga surge up and ahead.

Unlike the overpowered center-consoles he'd run in Florida, the 550 horses pushing this panga were perfectly tuned to this boat and its cargo. She easily made 30 knots and danced with grace over the swells. It was a simple design, and Cole appreciated its seakeeping. What a panga lacked in sleek design, she more than made up for with subtle grace.

Hours went by and they continued screaming northward. Cole made minor corrections to his course, bringing her more and more to the left by five degrees. Currents and winds factored into his drift, and he worried more and more about the GPS losing its charge. After almost six hours, she still showed half of a battery, but Cole worried about it. Finding the weakest link in a chain was in his nature and a single GPS was a gaping hole in his plan.

It was after midnight when he brought the throttles back again. He scanned the horizon once more, seeing nothing but the stars. Towering columns of cumulus clouds were backlit by the moon, and it was a beautiful thing to see. Cole looked to the tops and saw the ominous cumulonimbus peaks creeping skyward. Far to the northeast, he saw some lightning concealed in the innards of one particularly large buildup.

Satisfied again that he was alone, he sat on the seat for a moment and drank warm water from a milk jug that Diego had brought him. Ignoring Cole, Hector went about swapping fuel lines from one tank to another and Cole took comfort in the knowledge that he was halfway there. His body was tired, but his mind was alive and sharp. Dipping both his hands in the dark water over the side of the boat, Cole rubbed them together to loosen his muscles. He'd gripped the wheel for more than six hours and felt the fatigue setting in on his body. He twisted left and right to stretch his back as Diego gave Cole a thumbs up and took a new seated position leaning against the side of the panga.

Cole throttled up again and they picked up speed northward. Another hour passed. Cole's feet hurt and cold had set in on his weakening body. Feeling the effects of exposure, Cole shook his head violently to ward it off as another hour passed. The engines screamed and the panga held her course well. He was thankful that she needed such little input from the wheel to hold her course.

Just as his mind drifted to other things, Hector yelled something and pointed to the sky. Diego climbed up from the deck and braced as he looked up in the same direction. Cole was squinting, but couldn't see what they were talking about. It couldn't be good.

Cole heard one of them say "airplane" in broken English. They were both yelling and pointing and yelling more back at Cole. Then Cole saw it. Against the moonlit sky and not too far south of them, the silhouette of a plane came into view. It was low, maybe 1,000 feet, and had no lights on. There was no chance of it being a commercial flight or anything other than what Cole feared it was. It was a few miles from them, paralleling their course just off Cole's right shoulder. A minute went by and the plane made a slow lumbering turn towards Cole.

Fuck. Cole had some time to think, but he knew they'd spotted him. Hector and Diego were talking to each other and left Cole to his own thoughts. It was a big ocean, but Cole had no way of knowing who the plane was talking to. It passed off Cole's right side and was now ahead of them, but turning back around. It disappeared behind some clouds, then reappeared moments later, pointed at the panga.

Cole kept the throttles down and pressed on at 30 knots. The plane was dead ahead and pointed at him. It descended to the point that it almost seemed to be touching the surface. Cole could see moonlight reflecting off its fuselage and it couldn't have been more than 100 feet above the sea. At a half-mile or so in front of Cole, the plane energized every light it had. Cole squinted as the illumination damn near blinded him and the plane passed in a split second right over the top of the panga. It was so damn low that Hector and Diego ducked. Even Cole couldn't help but duck down a bit as it screamed overhead. The massive propellers drowned out the sound of Cole's engines and he recognized it as a P-3 Orion as it climbed up and away behind him. It's exhaust warmed the nighttime air momentarily, and Cole smelled the burnt jet fuel in its wake. The U.S. Navy and U.S. Customs both flew them down here, and it had passed over him so quickly he couldn't see any markings to figure out who it was.

It would take a few minutes for the P-3 to come back around. There was nothing the plane could do by itself except annoy him for the next three or four hours. But the P-3 crew was surely talking to every ship within 100 miles. And there was no doubt in Cole's mind that every ship in the fight was turning in his direction.

He'd spent many nights on *Delaney* chasing down Go-Fasts. All too often, Cole and *Delaney* missed their targets. It was next to impossible to find a Go-Fast and all the more difficult at night. If a warship wasn't perfectly positioned to intercept a panga, it stood no chance of catching up to them. Cole knew he was still in decent shape. The P-3 came back around and settled into an orbit around Cole. Diego and Hector were still pointing and talking wildly. Cole calmed his nerves and focused on the next few hours. Any fatigue was gone and he was now at full strength with the help of adrenaline coursing through his veins.

To his west, Cole saw a good line of thunderstorms. It was early in the morning and he still had four or even five hours before the sunrise. Ahead of him were clear skies and to the east were smaller clouds. He knew enough about flying to be sure the P-3 would keep its distance from the thunderstorms. From the bridge of *Delaney*, he'd spent hours listening to the secure radio communications between the planes as they negotiated the horrific summer weather in the tropics. Many times they could not complete searches due to the convective storms. He figured the clouds to the west might give him some separation from the P-3.

He turned 45 degrees to the west and headed for an intercept with the meanest-looking thunderhead. The P-3 held its orbit for the next hour and Cole carefully scanned the horizon for any lights or silhouettes of ships, but he saw none. The P-3 made another low pass of Cole, this time coming up from behind him and startling him as its engines screamed overhead. Cole cursed the plane and its pilots under his breath. He again felt the hot exhaust and smelled the burnt fuel, figuring that the pilots were probably just bored at this point and looking for ways to entertain themselves. What Cole didn't know was if they had company on the way. He remembered the conversation about the gunfight with the Coastie crew.

His mind wandered. *Maybe these two jackasses are playing with me while they wait for the real show to begin? Maybe me and my small crew are already dead and we'll be the last ones to figure it out.* The thunderstorm was picking up a bit ahead of him now, and he felt some cooler air across his face as he got closer. It was a mature storm, now dumping its cold air from tens of thousands of feet above him onto the surface of the sea and lightning lit the innards of the dark clouds every few seconds. The wind shifted as he pointed directly into the middle of it. He could see a squall line of rain not too far ahead.

Cole kept the throttles up and looked behind him. The P-3 had fallen back a bit in his trail and was flying a lazy S-pattern behind him. The rain first hit as a mist, cold against his face. For a second, Cole felt relief from the salt that covered his body. He reached up and zipped his jacket all the way, pulling its hood over his head. Just as quickly as he'd felt the mist, it opened up into a downpour, and Cole couldn't see more than 50 feet in front of him. He looked down at the GPS and verified that a correction to the north would put him back on course. He'd added half an hour to his trip by deviating, but in rain like this, the P-3 had surely lost him. Cole figured they would try to wait him out, but at least he'd shaken them for the time being.

Heading slightly west of north, the driving rain held up for some time. Lightning and thunder were intermittent, but a few bolts flashed down and out of the clouds, striking the water around him. Diego and Hector huddled against each other and were done talking. At this point, they were cold and wet and trying their best to wait out the storm as Cole powered through it. Adrenaline had warmed Cole initially, but as he pressed through the storm for the next half hour, he was cold once again. He felt his hands cramp around the wheel and his fingertips were numb. He was thirsty, but didn't take the time to find his bottle of water.

The wind died as he drove under the center of the storm. Rain poured from a bucket over his head and his shorts stuck against his thighs. If there was any silver lining, it was the fact that the fresh water had rinsed away the salt and his skin no longer itched. Looking down at his GPS, Cole was just under 60 miles from the rendezvous.

It was nearing four in the morning when he emerged from the rain. He was north of the sheltering storm cell and had covered nearly 45 miles in driving rain. At first, he was still under a heavy low-cloud deck and the sky was obscured. With no horizon that he could see, the sea blended into the dark grey sky. It was a picture worth painting and its beauty took Cole's mind off of his current troubles. As time passed, the clouds opened up again and Cole yelled at the two up front. They looked back at him and Cole motioned for them to look around the sky. They spent a minute or two canvassing the stars back and forth then smiled back at Cole. Diego gave Cole a big toothy grin and a thumbs up. The P-3 was gone. They were probably on their way back to base, having ceded victory to Cole. Cole laughed, shook his head, and wondered if they were headed to *Habana's* to toast Cole's prowess. Probably not, but Cole kept the thought in his head for amusement. Once again, he'd beaten them with calculated risk. His feet throbbed, his hands were painful against the wheel, and his back felt like he'd carried a ton of bricks, but he was on the home stretch.

By five a.m., the sky to the east was purple and red. Cole zoomed out the GPS screen to look at how far he'd travelled through the night. It gave him hope he was almost done. As the stars faded and the eastern horizon turned orange, Cole could make out the tree line to his west. He cross-referenced his GPS again and knew he was within a few miles of the river bank.

With the morning light, Cole's fatigue faded. To the east was daylight. Above him hung all the shades of a Caribbean morning that he loved so much. The water reflected the first glimmers of sunlight, and Cole could see the rolling waves and mist marking the reefline ahead. Salt spray rose up from the swells and was carried by the morning land breeze. Cole throttled back as he hit the waypoint and he turned off the GPS. It had been 12 hours. Even with the delay from the P-3, he'd made great time. He was now gliding through the water and standing on his toes looking for the river mouth. With a swell from the northeast, it was hard to pick up, but Cole thought he saw an opening where the waves were not as severe. He had no way of knowing how big they were as they crashed over the reef, but if he hit the middle of a channel the waves would roll right through and so would he.

Cole inched closer to the shoreline and paralleled it northward. The panga rolled with each passing swell and at the top of each crest, he could see over the waves to the sandy shoreline. Further north, he spotted the river. As he smiled, Diego yelled something in Spanish and pointed seaward again. A larger set of waves had snuck up behind Cole and he was still south of the river mouth. By the looks of the swell, Cole wasn't going to make it back out before the first wave broke. He jammed the throttles and paralleled the building waves. The lip of the first wave formed just as the panga surged over the top of it. Airborne for just a second, the panga slammed back down on the backside of the wave. Cole steadied himself before seeing the next wave was even bigger, probably six feet on its face, and driving towards him. With the throttle still down, Cole looked back to his left towards the land and saw the channel only a few hundred yards away. He then looked back to his right and saw that the wave was already breaking.

Whitewater was rushing towards him and all Cole could do was drive further inshore away from the breaking wave to buy some time. The motors struggled a bit in the churned up shallows and Cole knew he was only in a few feet of water. If a wave caught him, he'd wreck the boat and lose his cargo. With no other option, he raced for the river mouth and waited. It was only a few seconds before he found deeper water—the river—and the wave petered out, but it felt like an eternity. The stress lifted as he brought the throttles back and saw deep dark blue water around him. The two up front shook their heads, but both gave Cole a grin. Cole ran both his hands through his matted hair in disbelief.

He pointed her up the river and looked back to bid the Caribbean goodbye for now. He was hard on himself for slipping too far inshore and nearly having been caught by the surprise swell. He'd fixated on one thing, finding the river, and nearly lost the boat because of it. Cole shook it off and thought again that it's better to be lucky than good. His cowboy seamanship had worked.

Daylight had taken full hold, and while it was still early morning, the sun reflected off the palms that sat motionless in the now-still morning air. Mangroves and brush stretched out to the waterline, and the river turned brownish as Cole passed a narrow opening between two shallow spits of coral. There was nowhere to pull up to and not a soul in sight.

Cole heard birds in the trees and the smell of lush vegetation overtook that of the salt air. Diego looked back at Cole and motioned with one hand to take a left into what looked like a small inlet. It seemed like another world. Just inside the cut, there were a few dilapidated buildings with rusting tin roofs. Two scrap-wood docks jutted out into the river, but Diego motioned Cole further along. The panga now crept through still water at a walking pace as Cole played the throttles back and forth from idle. Under a palm canopy 15 yards ahead, Cole saw an older man waving from the bank. He stood on a web of a tree roots and was barefoot in shorts and a dirty shirt.

Cole nudged up to the shore and the older man took a line from the bow of the panga and tied it off to a tree. Cole's crew hopped over and tied off the stern, bringing it in close against the shore. The second guy disappeared momentarily and came back with a tattered burlap tarp. All three men then went about pulling the tarp over the hull. Under a canopy, tucked up against the bank of a nameless river and hidden under a tarp, no plane would ever spot Cole's panga now. He was safe once again.

The old man walked Cole and his crew 20 yards up a dirt trail to a shack with an open porch. Three hammocks were strung in the shade of its crumbling roof, and they all sat down at a table just past the hammocks. The older man called out and a woman, also older, came from inside with a pitcher and three glasses, each worn like sea glass and filled with ice. Where on earth she'd found ice Cole didn't know. She poured each of them a glass and Cole took a deep long sip of the thick red juice. Diego lifted his glass, said "Papaya," and Cole thought it was the sweetest-tasting drink he'd ever had. Each of them drained their first glasses and their spirits soared. It had been a roller coaster of emotion over the last 12 hours, and despite the taste of the juice, Cole knew he'd reached his limits and would soon need sleep.

The old man reappeared from inside with a bottle. Pulling the cork, Cole knew it was rum, and he gave himself a double shot in his glass, the ice now beginning to melt. Diego and Hector followed suit and topped their glasses off with papaya juice. Cole stirred his with his finger which now had regained its feeling from the night's cold rain. He finished half the glass and the buzz nearly knocked him off his chair. He smiled and laughed as his two crew seemed at ease again for the first time since he'd met them. They all toasted one another.

The woman brought out a plate of tortillas and black beans. She followed that with a plate of cooked fish, all cut into smaller bits and still steaming. Cole dug in with his crew, filling his mouth with enormous bites of the tortillas filled with beans and fish. He polished off his drink and made another. The pitcher was empty by the time the men set it back down. Cole noticed that the woman and the man served them quickly, but avoided eye contact and did not seem entirely pleased with the arrangements. It dawned on Cole that they were perhaps not willingly hosting such an event.

Strong-arm tactics were a way of life for smuggling, and this old couple most likely had no option other than to accommodate the demands of the drug cartel that laid claim to this forgotten stretch of coast. This river that Cole had driven up was a perfect hideout. Tucked against the border of two countries, it had easy access to the Caribbean and enough lagoons and coves surrounded by jungle to hide an army of pangas as they made their way northward with loads of cocaine.

It put a dent in Cole's buzz for a moment and each time the woman reappeared and topped off their drinks or plates, he felt the slightest twinges of guilt for imposing on them. Half an hour into his stay, Diego and Hector climbed into hammocks and pulled the floppy sides up and around them. Cole thanked the man and crawled into a hammock of his own, staring up at the makeshift roof over his head. There was not a single man-made sound to be heard. Birds flew overhead and cackled and a dog barked somewhere in the distance. There was no breeze, but under the shade of a tall tropical canopy in the morning, the air was cool enough for Cole to fall asleep moments later.

He woke shortly after noon and saw his crew still asleep in their hammocks. Walking inside the single room of the shack, Cole found himself in what served as a kitchen, bedroom, and general store. There was a shelf of canned goods, most with handwritten labels, and two cases of soda on the floor. By the kitchen, there were some unopened bags of flour or sugar, neither of which had any markings. Over by the stove, steam came from a pot sitting on top. The older man walked in from the back door and greeted Cole with a polite yet distant *Hola*. The woman came in from the front and stirred whatever was cooking in the pot, placing an iron lid back over it when she was done. She paid little attention to Cole.

On a shelf by the door was a framed picture of a boy, no older than 16. Cole picked it up and saw that the photo itself was worn, its edges frayed and some water stains distorted the colors. The boy had an innocent smile on his face. Cole stared at it for a moment before the old man spoke up, saying, "Mi hijo." *My son.*

Cole looked back to see that the man had stopped whatever he'd been doing moments before and now stood facing Cole. Cole looked at the photo again and set it back on the shelf.

Cole asked, "Donde?"

The man stared into Cole's eyes, "Muerte." *Dead.*

Cole paused, not knowing what to say. He spoke softly, "Lo siento." *I'm sorry.*

The man shook his head, stared at the dirt floor, then went back to sorting things on the counter. As he did, he spoke more in Spanish, and repeated "las drogas" several times, again shaking his head. His eyes watered, but the old man didn't cry.

The drugs.

Cole put it together in his head. The man had lost his son to the business of running drugs. Worse still, each time men like Cole tied up, it reopened the wound.

Cole mouthed the words again, "Lo siento," and walked out. He crawled back into his hammock, but couldn't sleep.

It was late afternoon when the old man roused Cole and his partners. He spoke to Diego and Hector in Spanish and they motioned for Cole to come quickly. They walked the same trail back down to the water and Cole saw yet another panga tied to his, which was still under the tarp. Cole's crew motioned for him to climb aboard and he did, stopping only for a second to grab his jacket, the bag, and shoes from his panga. Two men drove the second panga and slapped Cole on his back as his partners replayed the nights' activities. Cole couldn't understand the Spanish, but figured soon enough that they unanimously approved of his actions to avoid the P-3 the night before.

It was hot in the afternoon sun and once out on the river, there was no canopy to block it. They motored out of the cove, back into the main body of the river and Cole stuck his hand over the side and into its muddy ripples. The water was warm to the touch, almost too warm. No doubt the river wandered from miles inland, picking up silt along the way and warming itself under the sun. The panga moved along at ten knots or so, pushing a small wake off her stern that Cole watched roll gently up to the mangrove shore and disappear. Crossing the choke point again, Cole smelled the sea and saw the reef line several hundred yards ahead of him. The sea breeze was a welcome relief from the motionless air that blanketed the river, but Cole was still tired and sore from the night before. As waves crashed and rolled in, he felt partly defeated by the Caribbean. Here she was alive and rolling while Cole had just barely recovered over the past half a day. It humbled him as they motored along. *Anyone who dared not respect this sea is a damn fool,* Cole thought.

His body ached and his eyes still felt burned by the salt, but Cole knew a hot shower was still a long ways off. Motoring out the channel, the panga rolled up and over a few swells that pushed through and the small boat crossed the reef line once again. Cole felt a shudder as one of the larger waves broke violently over the reef, the same line he'd gotten too close to the day before. He still did not have his strength back and was wary of another trip.

Not more than 200 yards further offshore, a coastal fishing boat rolled gently in the swells. The panga pulled up next to it and all three, Cole included, hopped over onto the wooden deck. More hammocks were strung on the back deck, which was partially covered by a tarp to block the sun. The driver of the panga whistled and waved goodbye, turning once again towards the shore. Diego smiled at Cole and pointed south, saying simply, "Panama." He then crawled into one of the hammocks and did not speak again. Hector made some small talk with the crew then did the same, leaving Cole on the deck, his hands in his pockets and his back against the railing.

One fisherman emerged from below decks onto the fantail and dumped a bucket of fish scales over the side. He greeted Cole, but gave no indication of an itinerary. Cole found a seat on a bench along the starboard side as the fishing boat's engine hummed louder and she made a slow labored turn to the south. Cole figured she was their ride home and would probably take all night or more to cover the distance. From the smell of it, the boat had indeed been fishing and was picking up some extra cash along the way by transporting Cole and his crew back to Panama. The same fisherman brought Cole a fully cooked fish, scales and all, on a tin plate and handed it to him. Cole thanked him and began to peal the skin back with his hand and pulled pieces of meat from its bones with his bare fingers. It was plain, but filling. This crew seemed more welcoming than the older man and woman back in Nicaragua. Perhaps this crew willingly took on the risk of the drug trade, but either way Cole felt much more at ease with the apparent kindness.

The deck of the wood boat curved to allow water to freely find its way off the weather deck in heavy seas or storms. Its hull was painted white, and the deck had been white at one time too, but now was grey and weathered from the sun, salt, and endless days of gear dragged across it. There were a few patches of paint left, but the owner had long ago realized the futility of keeping her pretty. Nevertheless, her wooden deck was worn smooth under Cole's bare feet and had a charm of its own. There were two lids over what must have been the fish holds below, and a neatly rolled net was tucked against the stern among a pile of buoys. The wheelhouse had once been painted green, but it too was now a faded salt-worn grey. Some other crew spoke back and forth down below, but Cole couldn't find the strength to go below and see what they were up to. He brought the plate back to the wheelhouse when he was done and set it down just inside. He then walked back to the bench and turned to look out at the dark blue water and light blue sky around him.

Cole sat there for some time, his elbows and forearms against the railing, watching the sun slowly fall from the sky. He remembered doing the same from the deck of the *Yankee Freedom* with Kevin, but that seemed like a world away. As the boat rolled along, Cole was quite content. He'd worked hard to get to this moment and he basked in it, incredibly relaxed. A groundswell pushed in from the east and the boat rolled through the troughs of each swell, then up and over peaks with grace. If she could tell stories, Cole would have listened all night. With sunset approaching, a cooler breeze blew from the northeast and swirled around the open back deck. The water was that same beautiful dark blue that marked open sea, and as the daylight faded, Cole was lost in his own thoughts. He took deep exaggerated breaths, filling his lungs with air.

The sun now gone, Cole climbed into a hammock that afforded him a clear view off the stern and he watched the wake disappear into the darkness behind the boat. He thought of his morning rounds on *Delaney*, where he'd done the same thing from the fantail. He wondered what Walters and that cursed cutter were up to, then shook away the thoughts to enjoy his present surroundings. There were no storms like the night before and the air was cool as the boat's motor hummed Cole to sleep, and he nodded off for a night at sea.

CHAPTER 9 – BANANA WARS

COLE WOKE LONG after the sun was up. He was almost cold in the morning chill and fresh breeze that had picked up with the sun. The sea was dotted with occasional white caps and with no land in sight, nor any other boats in view, Cole felt the same weightlessness as the evening before. He basked in his complete lack of responsibility and threw his hands behind his head, driving his fingers through his salt-crusted hair again and again as he stretched and chased the fatigue away. He didn't care how long the transit took, it was a wonderful feeling and he held onto it with a smile he couldn't hide. As he stretched once again and twisted his torso around in his hammock, he heard his two companions talking from their hammocks. He yawned and settled back into his nest.

Half an hour went by and the boat chugged along with a steady but gentle roll that rocked Cole back and forth. The engine hummed from below and traces of exhaust wafted in the breeze that carried with it the ever-present salt air. Cole finally rolled himself around and stepped out, his bare feet touching the deck for the first time in almost nine hours. The weather-worn wood was wet with dew and slippery. He took a leak off the stern and walked forward to the cabin, poking his head down below long enough to catch a whiff of coffee.

"Cafe?" Cole smiled and looked at one of the deckhands below, who nodded yes, poured Cole a cup in a dirty mug, and passed it up to him. Cole wrapped both hands around the cup to fight off the chill and leaned his waist against the rail, looking out over the water. Diego called out to him in Spanish and Cole looked back to him with a smile, lifted the mug, and said, "Vamanos!"

Both Diego and Hector laughed. Morale was high. Off the starboard bow, there was indeed some land. It wasn't enough to make out anything distinguishable, but Cole was certain it was land. He saw the cumulus clouds building as the ground warmed in the sun and figured that he was no more than five or ten miles from shore. Cole finished off his coffee, filled it again from down below, and took a seat on an empty crate near the stern. He felt the vibrations of the motor against the transom and could sense the engines' strain as the old boat chugged along. He hadn't been in the wheelhouse yet, nor had he met the captain. He knew there was no need, no formalities to speak of, and no nonsensical madness as the boat approached land. It was the complete opposite of *Delaney*.

Cole went forward to the wheelhouse and saw the captain at the helm, but said nothing. He was an older man, his skin tanned like leather and his hands were rough from a life of hard work. Whoever he was, this was a familiar route, one which needed no charts, navigator, lookout, or radar. The captain could find the channel with his eyes closed, guided only by the changing wind and waves. With nothing but his fingertips on the wheel and throttle, the old man felt the sea and steered his course by instinct alone. Cole held immense respect for this captain and did not want to disturb him. He walked back aft and sat, pressing the back of his head against the transom and slowly worked through his second cup of coffee, enjoying the sounds and tranquility.

He thought briefly about the old man's words back in Nicaragua.

Las drogas. The drugs.

Cole was part of it now. He'd seen the war on drugs from both ends. It was a nasty business, but so too was life. Cole shook the thoughts from his head and stared out at the rolling blue sea in front of him.

Hours passed before they rounded the same jetty Cole had driven through nearly two days before. The engines slowed and the boat settled on the calmer waters inside the sea wall. The heat from the sun grew with each passing minute. Without a breeze on the open sea, it was uncomfortably hot once again. The old boat motored up to the small bay from where Cole had left and a panga approached with a few men speaking back and forth with Cole's two crew. They spoke quickly and excitedly before hopping over to the panga. Cole stuck his head inside the cabin once more and called out his thanks to the unseen Captain. He hopped over to the panga and they motored in to the beach, where David was waiting with another van. Shaking hands with Cole, David hurried them over to the van and Cole climbed in. It was the first time he'd felt air conditioning in two days, and it felt great.

From there, the drive back to Panama City was uneventful. Traffic built along the way as Panamanians went about their midday business, but Cole enjoyed the ride. At one point, he pulled the Glock from the small of his back and dropped the magazine out before racking the slide and clearing the chamber. He did it quickly without looking and put the magazine and gun back in the small duffel bag with the rest of his gear. The grittiness of it still bothered him, as did its general lack of cleanliness.

Cole asked David, "Can you get me some motor oil and some rags so I can clean this damn thing?"

David looked down at the gun then back at Cole. "What's wrong with it? You didn't shoot it, did you?"

Cole shook his head, "No, but it's filthy. I could use a good holster as well."

David nodded, answering, "Yeah, sure. I'll get you some stuff tonight."

Cole knew it was his military upbringing that wouldn't let the gun's condition slide. He wondered if that discipline would be with him for the rest of his life. It had been over six months now since he'd left *Delaney*, but ever since he'd first fired a gun, it had been drilled into him to keep his weapon clean. He let it go for the time being as the van meandered its way back into downtown Panama City.

As the van pulled up to the hotel, David patted Cole on the shoulder as they stepped out. "Nice job my friend. Now you enjoy yourself for a few days and get your strength back."

Cole took the bag and his jacket through the lobby, over to the elevators and up to his room. It had been made up since he'd left, and the air conditioning was turned up too much for Cole's taste. He set the thermostat back to the upper 60s and grabbed a Miller High Life from the refrigerator. Opening it on the edge of the windowsill, he took a long sip and looked down at the street below, then took the beer with him into the shower. He turned the water on hot and stood there for some time as it washed two days of salt out of his hair and off his skin. Fatigue and hunger hit him as he finished the beer and dried off.

Not long after, Cole heard a knock at the door. A bellman had a small paper bag in his hand and gave it to Cole, saying something about David. Cole nodded and the bellman walked away without another word. Closing the door and walking back to the small couch in his room, Cole set the bag down on the coffee table and opened it up. There was a small unmarked plastic bottle of some type of oil, a rag, some cotton patches, and a cleaning brush. Also in the bag was a generic tan leather holster with belt clips. David had kept his word.

Cole cracked another bottle open and set about cleaning his gun. He opened up the duffel bag and took out the Glock and magazines. He first emptied the magazines, all seven of them, and stripped them apart. Two had rusted springs inside and Cole set them aside as no good. The remaining five he cleaned with the rags and oil, giving the springs and innards a good thorough wipedown. Out of High Life, he switched to Panama, a beer he thought not as good as the Miller, but a close second after a few sips. With a bit of a buzz as he took a long sip of his third beer on an empty stomach, he sorted through the ammo. It was .40 caliber and of mixed headstamps, meaning someone had loaded the magazines from various places. Two of the magazines had hollow-point rounds, and the rest were standard ball ammo. Most of it looked to be in good enough shape and Cole loaded the five good magazines again and set them aside.

He went onto the gun itself. It was a Glock 23, more or less the standard for federal law enforcement agencies in the states.

Cole had never shot that particular model, but every Glock was alike. He locked the slide back and checked that it was indeed empty before letting the slide forward and pulling the trigger again. Pulling the slide back again just a bit, he pushed the slide lock down and removed the slide and barrel. They were filthy inside and out. He took another sip from his beer before removing the guide rod and barrel from the slide.

With nothing but time on his hands, Cole slowly and methodically went about his cleaning. He let the oil sit for some time in the barrel and worked the brush back and forth inside and out until he felt the heat generated by friction against the barrel. He repeated the same step several times to remove all the deposits and ran a rag through it each time. On the outside of the barrel and the slide, he oiled and wiped clean every surface. With his fingers and the back end of the cleaning rod, he was able to remove the firing pin assembly and did the same with it. He looked at the various pieces strewn about the table and felt confident the gun was up to standard. He quickly reassembled it, pulling the trigger once the slide was back on. It felt smooth again as he racked the slide several times and walked over to the window. Aiming at the lamp in the corner, he pulled the trigger and saw the front sight twitch just a bit to the left when he squeezed.

Adjusting his grip, he racked the slide and squeezed the trigger again. He took a long breath, holding the gun in his hands, and looked down at the street below. He was in no mood to be social and it was just past 10 p.m. when he loaded a magazine back in the gun, racked it to load one in the chamber and ejected the magazine to top it back off before reinserting. If he had it, he might as well keep it at the ready. Setting it on the nightstand next to his bed, Cole finished off his beer and flipped the lights off. He was exhausted but spent some time contemplating his situation. He was thousands of miles from home, had no trusted friends to fall back on, and now was a certified drug runner. There was no going back from this point. He doubted his choices for some time, but ultimately pushed them aside, convincing himself he had no other options, and soon fell asleep.

Cole didn't hear from David for several days. After he woke each morning, he would sip coffee at a shop across the street and then spend the middle part of the day in the hotel gym or pool. At night he'd have a few drinks with the girls working at Habana's. He took a liking to one in particular, Maria, who seemed sweet and would chat with him in broken English for long stretches. From Colombia, she was in Panama to make money and one day hoped to bring it back to her family. Maria had propositioned Cole early on for the *full sexo*, but he had dismissed her with a smile and they had developed a mutual understanding of each other since then. She would giggle when he wore his cowboy hat and spoke to her with an exaggerated southern accent. He watched with curiosity and a bit of jealousy when someone picked her up. She was slender and his height, always wearing some tight dress and walking like a woman. It played on his emotions, and he enjoyed their time together.

When David finally did catch up with him days later, he told Cole of another run the next day. Feeling the same butterflies in his stomach, Cole fought them back with his own reassurance that he knew what he was doing this time. His first run gave him experience and confidence, much like his first run in Key West.

The following day, the same pattern played out as the first run. By the time he was underway late in the afternoon, he felt quite good as they motored along leisurely waiting for the sun to go down. And when nighttime took hold, Cole pushed the throttles and spun the panga due north. The first surge of power that lifted the boat was his favorite part of the trip. It turned into an easy run with no aircraft or ships in his way. The weather was the same and he tied up the next morning with a boat full of kilos of cocaine that much closer to their North American destination. He lounged in the same hammock the following day, caught a different fishing boat back the following evening, and once again made it back to the Marriott tired, but feeling a sense of accomplishment.

Two months went by with the same routine. At times, Cole made one run every week, sometimes two. David was apologetic when he went back to back, but Cole didn't mind at all. He viewed it as a job, not unlike any other and he felt that his hard work would pay off in more ways than one.

David had given Cole a debit card from a local bank along with a PIN to access it. It was an easier way to get paid than cash. David smiled when he handed it over and told Cole he had just under 100,000 dollars on it. Hard work had certainly paid off. With nothing of significance to spend it on, Cole tucked the card away in the safe in his room. If he kept at it, he could probably settle down well before any honest man's retirement.

He varied his routes a bit, sometimes sticking closer to shore and occasionally venturing eastward, but none of the dozen or so trips were much different than his first. He had no other problems with aircraft. On three trips he'd seen lights on the horizon, but had altered his course each time to keep a healthy distance between them and hopefully stay under their radar, assuming they were even looking for him in the first place. The Caribbean was a big body of water and Cole knew he was a small target well-concealed under a blanket of darkness.

During his third month at the job, Cole was surprised one afternoon when the old man woke him up earlier than usual along with Diego and Hector. They all spoke quickly to each other and Cole only caught the word *problema* twice, but it was enough to tell him something wasn't right. They all gathered their belongings and hurried down to the panga, tied off in the same spot as last time. This time however, the tarp was gone and two large packages were on Cole's panga with another panga tied off to his. Three guys then spoke with Diego. Cole was picking up more and more Spanish, but they all spoke so quickly that he was unable to follow the conversation.

Diego then relayed the problem to Cole. Hector looked upset, but then again Hector always looked upset, so Cole wasn't overly alarmed. This second panga was transporting a payment back to Panama when one of its engines had seized up. It was beyond repair and left them with one good engine. They had limped along at just under 15 knots since the night before and came in looking for help. The driver of the other panga handed Cole a satellite phone and said, "David," just as Cole took it in his hands.

Cole held it up to his ear and said, "Hello."

On the other end, David laid it out to Cole in a few short sentences. This was a large payment going south that needed to get to Panama quickly. The other crew, almost out of gas and time, had pulled into the same bay where Cole was resting since they knew it was friendly territory and could offer some assistance. David asked Cole if he could turn it around on his panga and get it the rest of the way to Panama.

Cole thought about it for a moment and replied, "It's a bit early in the day to be making a run."

David answered, "Yes, this is true, but money isn't safe just sitting there—and frankly, neither are you, if word gets out."

Cole processed David's logic and it made sense. Drug cartels were cutthroat. So too were the petty criminals if they heard about a load of money just sitting on the bank of a quiet river. Cole thought about the old man's dead son. *Was it an afternoon like this that had gotten out of control?*

"All right, David. We'll get going here soon."

Cole motioned to his two crew with his fingers and said *vamanos,* with some reluctance this time. The panga needed gas and the old man went back and forth up the trail a few times with cans. Both Cole and his crew carried cans as well from a rusted tank behind the shack. It took them time, but they finally topped off both the plastic tanks on the panga and Cole fired up the engines. The old woman appeared with some tortillas wrapped in plastic and Cole smiled back at her with a heartfelt thanks. She didn't make eye contact with him and Cole was certain she was happy to see them go. The old man passed them plastic gallon jugs of water, and with that, Cole spun the panga around in the narrow channel and set off.

As he motored out, Cole looked down at the two packages on the deck. Each was the size of a large backpack and wrapped in black plastic. Cole knew Diego and Hector well enough to recognize their uneasiness. The sun would not set for another few hours. If the other panga had run all day, they ran a good risk of being detected. And if detected, that meant the cavalry was probably out looking for them.

Cole didn't wait to cross the reef. As soon as he passed the two spits of coral marking the entrance, Cole pushed the throttles up and they were off. Within minutes, it felt like just another run, headed south this time. Cole set his compass to run just a bit east of south, to parallel the coast all the way to the bay nearly 300 miles away. He pressed his back against the seat behind him and settled in for the long haul. As the hours passed and the sun dropped to the west, Cole fell into his usual rhythm.

When sunset neared, Cole passed the time by taking in the evening colors. But not more than a minute after the sun was gone, Diego pointed to a plane above them to the east. Cole saw it almost immediately against the twilight. *Damn it*. He was closer to land than usual and knew of nowhere in Costa Rica where he could put the panga ashore. Moreover, he knew that Costa Rica would let the plane within its airspace to chase a smuggler. The worst case was that the first crew had been spotted, and the focus of all the ships and aircraft in the Caribbean would be to reacquire and catch Cole with his cargo. That meant there was a good chance ships were nearby. And Cole knew that ships had guns.

By the time nighttime hit, Cole was already at full speed direct to the rendezvous point. He looked at his GPS again and realized he had never recharged it. He'd never made a second run, so the thought had never crossed his mind. He had less than half a charge and was still close to 200 miles from the bay. The plane was still in an orbit over him, and this time they didn't drop down to make low passes. To Cole, this was an ominous sign since it likely meant the pilots were busy talking to other players. He was uneasy and mad at himself as he screamed southward.

Several hours passed, but eventually Cole saw a dreaded silhouette in the distance. His crew saw it as well and pointed, but he was already focused entirely on what it was. A second later, flashing blue lights illuminated on the silhouette and Cole knew immediately it was the Coast Guard. He saw light reflect on the distinctive orange hull as it drove on an intercept course for Cole, closing in from the east. They had likely been tracking him for some time and now the only question was whether or not he could outrun them. Cole had been in a few chases on the right end of the law and knew that the initial intercept could make or break a drug bust. If the coxswain driving knew what he was doing, Cole was evenly matched against him. The cutter was likely also close by, but stood no chance of catching Cole with his panga making 32 knots.

Cole also knew that some cutters had upgraded to newer and faster small boats that could outrun him. It was all up to chance at this point. Making things more complicated, there were some specially trained boat crews who were authorized to use disabling fire against the engines of drug runners. As the intercept tightened, Cole turned 30 degrees to the right to buy himself some time. The Coast Guard small boat adjusted its course as well and Cole spent more time looking at the small boat than he did his own course. In reality it was only a matter of minutes, but each second was excruciatingly slow for Cole. His crew sat forward on the bow and could do nothing but watch and hope for the best.

Cole remembered his first chase and how he ran the reef line off Key West to shake his pursuers, but knew he would not be so lucky tonight on the open sea. As the small boat's intercept crept closer, Cole caught a good look at it under the moonlight and it looked too large to be the same small boat he'd ridden in. A few seconds later, he caught another glance and confirmed his fears. It was a newer boat, capable of "Over The Horizon" pursuit and Cole remembered listening to all the speculation about its new capabilities. This also raised the likelihood that the crew onboard the OTH was planning to shoot out his engines.

With his pursuer now barely 50 yards off his port quarter, Cole realized the OTH was matching his speed. There would be a lengthy dialogue between the small boat and the cutter to authorize warning shots and then disabling fire. There was a chance that the commanding officer would not authorize it, but that was too slim of a margin for Cole to count on. As his panga sped south through the calm Caribbean Sea, Cole weighed his options and knew they were quickly running out.

He looked back once or twice more then up at his two crew members who were looking at Cole for any sign of hope. Above the noise of the engines and the wind, Cole heard himself take a deep breath and he settled his mind on what seemed like a long shot. With his left hand still on the wheel, Cole reached for the holster on the small of his back with his right hand and pulled out the Glock. He kept his finger off the trigger guard and looked back again at the OTH chasing him. He knew they were Coasties, just like he had been. He knew they'd been after him for some time, but also that they were probably just kids, no different than the boatswains' mates and machinists' mates he'd known on *Delaney*.

He braced his legs on the deck and turned back towards them, pointing the gun a good 45 degrees left of the OTH and a good 30 degrees above the horizon, making sure to aim so wide and high that he stood no chance of hitting a thing and pulled the trigger. The gun recoiled in his hand and an orange flash shot forward for a split second. He pulled the trigger again. He fired yet again and followed it with eleven more rapid fire shots into the night sky. Each time his wrist snapped back in his hand and the muzzle lit up as the burning gunpowder exited the barrel.

Even over the roar of the engines, Cole's ears were ringing when he finally emptied the magazine and the slide locked back. He dropped his hand to his side and looked down at the gun, not bothering to check that it was unloaded. Tossing it down on the deck at his feet, Cole pushed it aside and behind him. Looking back at the blue lights, he saw that they had indeed turned away from him. He hated to do it, but escalation was Cole's only chance of ending the pursuit. He knew the Coasties had standing orders on a chase and had bet that they were not going to continue to close the distance with him if he was shooting. At night, the OTH would have had no way of knowing if he was firing at them or away from them. The muzzle blast and sound would have been all they could see, and if they were on night vision goggles, it would have been almost blinding at that distance.

Cole waited for some time before looking back again and the blue lights were nowhere to be seen. All Cole could make out was the sharp V shape of his wake as it trailed off in the distance. If the coxswain was smart, he would have turned the lights off to avoid giving an enemy an easy target. The boat crew was out of the fight and it was unlikely they would rejoin that evening. Cole's crew said nothing as they were smart enough to realize the magnitude of what Cole had done to keep them out of handcuffs. It was a huge risk that had paid off. Alone again under the moon, Cole raced southward for the rest of the night. His GPS had almost no battery left when he spotted a faint glow off the bow and in the distance. It was below the horizon, but it matched up with what his GPS was telling him. He referenced the compass and the lights bore 130 degrees magnetic. He committed the course to his head and turned off the GPS in case he needed it again later.

After another 45 minutes, he could clearly see the lights of Colon and the tankers and freighters at anchor inside the jetty. Relief set in as he throttled back and searched for a break in the jetty. Paralleling the rocks, it wasn't long before he cut inside the jetty at the main entrance and paralleled it again on the inside. He soon spotted familiar markers and slowed, motoring into the small harbor. Taking the throttles to idle, Cole pulled out the satellite phone and called David.

David was quick to answer and told Cole to stay out a bit until he called again. Cole acknowledged and thought about why he couldn't just tie up himself. It dawned on him that David would make sure some security was in place first before Cole motored in with tens of millions of dollars in drug money. As he sat on the side of the boat and waited with the engines at idle, he reached down to the Glock, found another magazine in his bag and reloaded before tucking the gun again into the holster on the small of his back. Twenty minutes later, David called and told Cole to come on in. Throttling ahead just a bit, Cole crept around the abandoned hulls in the bay and finally around the large rusted remains of the barge and saw two trucks with the parking lights on and facing the water.

Cole suddenly became concerned. The thought of things going bad on land had not crossed his mind, but he knew this was likely contested turf. He exhaled with force when he heard David's voice from the beach. The panga dug her bow into the coarse sandy bottom and Cole killed the engines after what had seemed like an eternity. The silence was a welcome relief from the past 11 hours. Having set off well before sunset, it was still nighttime as Cole grabbed his things, waded ashore and rubbed his eyes. Around him were at least four men he could see, each with a rifle close to their chests. They were 20 or so yards back from the beach and evenly spaced to form a good perimeter as Cole's two crewmen helped offload and carry the two packages to shore. Loading each into a separate truck, David hurried Cole into the back of one of them and the driver made quick work of speeding away, the back tires spinning up dust and rocks as he accelerated.

As they pulled onto one of the main roads, both trucks slowed down a bit to blend back in with the light early morning traffic. In Cole's truck, there was a driver and one of the men with a rifle sitting shotgun. Cole sat in the middle of the backseat of the truck with David to his right and the other guard to his left. Cole looked down and saw that the guard held some short barreled version of an M4. From the looks of both the gunmen, they seemed to be able to handle themselves. Neither paid any attention to anything inside the truck as they scanned the passing traffic for any signs of trouble.

David wanted to know how the trip had gone.

Cole wasn't sure where to start. "Well, I got it here. But we ran into a problem about halfway through. I'm pretty sure they were Coast Guard."

David's eyes sharpened and he asked, "What happened?"

"I couldn't shake them, they were faster than me, so I emptied a magazine behind me and they broke off the chase."

David shuffled in his seat. "You shot at them?" His eyes were bigger now.

"No, not at them, just behind me to give the impression I was. I figured that might shake them and it did. I'm pretty sure they were going to shoot the engines out and that wasn't gonna work out too well for you or me."

David sat back and looked ahead. He pulled his phone out and patted Cole on the knee twice saying, "OK, my friend. You did OK."

Cole couldn't pick up much of the conversation that David had on the phone, but it seemed like David was answering a lot of questions. Cole didn't like to think of who was on the other end of David's phone calls. He hoped that the trucks weren't taking him somewhere like they'd taken that kid on Cole's first night. Mad at the situation, Cole did his best to hide it, but he was not happy.

When David hung up, Cole couldn't hold back anymore and he opened up. "What the fuck, David. You didn't tell me I couldn't use the gun. Some ground rules would have been a fucking nice thing to have."

No one in the truck seemed to notice or care that Cole was pissed.

David stopped him before he could continue and said, "No, no, no, you are OK, Cole. We are all right; you are all right. We take you back to the hotel. You need some rest. Everything is OK."

He patted Cole again on the knee. Over the next hour, not much was said. As Panama City appeared in the distance, Cole dreaded the next 20 minutes as they drove through the worst parts of town. He wondered if they were going to pull into some empty building and drag him to a room. Shuffling a bit in his seat, Cole realized he still had the Glock tucked under his shirt. It reassured him since if he was on his way to get a bullet in the head, someone probably would have taken the gun from him already.

Nevertheless, Cole was uneasy about his prospects and resigned himself to fight it out with the 13 rounds in the gun if it came down to it. Knowing he wouldn't win against the guards, Cole sure as shit wasn't going to let them just walk him into a room, tie his hands behind his back, and watch him squirm.

Fortunately, it never came down to that. Three hours after he'd beached the panga, the trucks pulled up to the Marriott and offloaded Cole. David said he'd be in touch and with that the trucks were gone, leaving Cole by himself in front of the main doors. It was mid-morning by then. Above the buildings and the noise, Cole could see the sun creeping skyward. He took a long breath and exhaled, the stench of the city a welcome relief and much more preferable than the stench he recalled from the room where the kid had been killed. The thought rattled his nerves.

Cole walked inside and up to his room. From the bag, he pulled one more round from another magazine and dropped the magazine out of the gun, loaded his back to capacity and reinserted it, leaving it on the nightstand. *Fourteen rounds now.* It did little to comfort him. Standing by the window for some time, Cole looked down at the city beneath him. *Perhaps I've done enough. Perhaps I should get out while I still can.* The truth was he didn't know if he could get out. The thought of quitting anything so soon after *Delaney* gnawed at him, but at the same time he realized his decisions always seemed to leave him in a tight spot. There were no good answers and he had no one to blame but himself. Such was life, and with that he crawled under the blankets of his bed and soon fell asleep.

CHAPTER 10 — WHEELS UP

COLE WOKE LATER in the afternoon and stepped back into his regular routine as best he could. With no messages from David and nothing to do, he worked out then ate at the sports bar downstairs, finishing off a few Panamas with his Cuban sandwich. With the afternoon sun starting to fall, he headed to Habana's and lit a cigar before taking a prime seat for the nighttime show. Sipping a Dos Equis, he put his feet up on the railing in front of him and crossed his cowboy boots over each other, then pulled the brim of his hat down low.

All things considered, he felt good. The sleep had cleared his mind, but the previous night still hung heavy on his conscience. He had escalated and figured out quickly that David had to answer a lot of questions. The drug trade was a tricky thing, and Cole felt isolated without any information beyond David's facial expressions. As with anything else, not knowing was gnawing away at him. Taking a long deep drag from his cigar, Cole blew the smoke up and over his head and tried to think of something else. He spent several hours making light conversation with the girls before heading back to the Marriott and falling asleep again.

Several days, each the same as the first, passed before David caught up with Cole. They met at the coffee shop across the street early one morning and David explained at length. He spoke with his hands and seemed to use very deliberate words in finding a delicate way to explain Cole's predicament. "There is an understanding down here among the different families that we like the status quo."

Cole let David continue searching for words for some time before he cut in, saying, "I get it, David. Just tell me what you need to tell me."

David shrugged his shoulders before taking a long sigh. "Cole, for my boss, you did good bringing the money in—but for the other bosses, it's not so good. There are more boats now, more planes, and a lot of people think you made things worse. Trust me. Everyone, and I mean everyone, knows about it."

David was back to talking with his hands. Cole could tell that despite trying to hide it, David was concerned.

"If there is more pressure from the United States because of this, that means more drugs will be caught and less money to be made. You see?"

Cole knew that already. "Well, what the fuck was I supposed to do?"

"No, no, you did OK. There is no good answer. Some guys would not shoot, some guys maybe they do. You, you're a damn cowboy, so you shoot." David laughed a bit and pointed at Cole's boots with a smile. Cole looked away, partly amused, but still mad at the situation.

"So what do I do now?"

David shifted in his seat and leaned in a bit. "You take it easy for a bit, let things calm down, and everything goes back to normal in a few weeks. OK?"

The thought of sitting around his hotel room for a few weeks with nothing to do wasn't particularly pleasant. Cole wanted to make money and more importantly, he wanted to push the throttles up as the sun faded and feel salt spray against his face as he roared north with a load of cocaine.

"This is shitty, David, but there's not much I can do, is there?"

David shook his head. "I'm afraid not, my friend. You sit tight. Things will be OK."

Days passed and Cole could do nothing but sleep in, lounge around the hotel pool, and spend his nights across the street at Habana's. He kept waiting for a call or message from David, but nothing came. No one at the hotel or across the street seemed to act any differently, but Cole couldn't help but be tense. The heat and the smell of the city bothered him more with each passing day. Even with the heat, he always wore his jeans after sunset to blend in with the locals, and would take short walks around the surrounding blocks most nights before turning in for the evening. He usually left his cowboy hat in the room to avoid standing out too much. His hair was a blond shaggy tangle on his head, and he knew he drew enough attention as is.

Almost a week after he and David had last spoke, Cole was once again on the last inches of a cigar when he smashed it out on an ashtray at Habana's. He shared a few drinks with Maria and as she sat across the table from him, Cole smiled at how pretty she looked with her long dark hair and light blue dress. She laughed at him for it. It was only nine o'clock, but the night was slow. Cole smiled to say goodnight and stood up to take a walk. They kissed each other on the cheek and she held his hand for just a moment with a flirtatious smile before walking back into the crowd. Ever the businesswoman, Cole thought as they parted ways.

Cole walked down the concrete steps and onto the sidewalk, heading left towards a casino. With his boots on, a button-down shirt only half buttoned across his chest, and well-worn jeans snug against his waist, Cole blended in as well as he could. His Glock in its holster felt natural now that he'd been carrying it for over two months.

The night was warm and he meandered past the casino, up a quieter street, then down towards a main drag. He knew the city streets well enough to explore them and still find his way back to familiar parts. No one paid any particular attention to him on his nightly strolls, and it gave him some time to stretch his legs and gather his thoughts.

The city was chafing him and Cole was getting restless, just like he had in Key West. Perhaps it was time to cut his losses and find something new. He'd made a good deal of money, enough to keep him living well for the next few years, provided he picked back up with Mickey running the straits. He thought and walked and went back and forth with his ideas for some time. Maybe David was right and things would settle down, but he had been dormant for more than a week and there were no indications of things picking up again any time soon. Cole had no way of knowing what conversations were going on about him.

Cole walked farther than normal when he finally turned for home. Continuing down a main street amongst the bustling Panamanian night life, he zig-zagged his way back up to the Marriott. Up a side street, he saw the main road for the hotel two blocks further up another smaller side street. Cole turned and walked, his mind now settling back down as he thought about one more drink before turning in for the night. The street was dark with no traffic on its narrow two lanes. He could see people up ahead on the cross-street two blocks in front of him in the street lights, but it was close to total darkness where he walked and the tall buildings on both sides blocked most of the sky.

Cole heard a car behind him and instinctively turned to look for just a second. It was a dirty white sedan, no different than the million other cars that clogged Panama City. As he turned back and continued walking, something didn't sit right. He thought about it again and looked behind once more. The car was driving too slowly, even for a side street. It was 30 yards behind him. No one drives that slow in Panama, he thought. With his second glance, he knew whoever was driving had seen Cole look twice. Keeping his same pace, Cole saw a set of elevated cement steps in front of him leading to a doorway. Beyond the steps was a driveway with a few trash cans tucked against a low concrete wall. As he passed the steps, he side stepped to the right and into the driveway before turning around to see the car still approaching.

The back window was rolled down as the car came within ten yards and slowed even more. Cole couldn't see the driver or anyone else, but he felt his heart pound in his chest and he gritted his teeth, exhaling as he lifted his shirt with his left hand and postured the palm of his right hand against the backstrap of his Glock. As he methodically wrapped his fingers around the grip, his fears were confirmed. From the backseat, the barrel of a gun appeared with a dark figure sitting in the middle seat. Cole drew as the gunman opened up. From less than ten yards, the muzzle blast lit up orange inside the car three or four times in rapid succession and the sound was deafening. In the middle of those first shots, Cole dropped to his right knee and pressed his side against the low concrete wall, gripping the gun with both hands. The back of his left shoulder burned like a fire as he pressed it against the wall. Fixing his eyes on the white dot of the front sight, Cole steadied his aim for a split second, and he touched the trigger with the pad of his finger. Surprising even himself, Cole methodically returned fire at the car. His first shot rattled him a bit and he sent the next three rounds high over the top of the car.

With the gunman still firing at him, Cole regained his composure and his next two shots silenced the gun in the backseat. He couldn't see his target, but at such a close range, he had aimed at the center of the rear window and found his mark. The car's tires smoked as the driver stepped on the gas for a quick getaway. Cole, now holding the advantage, swept his sights to the front passenger door as it passed by him. Still crouched, he sent four more shots in rapid succession at less than five yards through the window as it sped past him. At least one of the bullets also found its target as the car veered hard to the left and smashed head first into a light pole. Still running when it came to a stop, the brake lights were on along with the left blinker.

From his crouched position, Cole looked back up the street from where the car had come and he saw nothing. It was quiet again. His ears were ringing and his shoulder still burned, as if he'd cut it against the wall. The faint smell of gunpowder quickly blended in with Panama City like nothing had happened. Cole scanned back to his right, then left again before standing up. Looking at his shoulder, there was blood. So much so that he felt it running down his arm. He couldn't see it, but the thought sunk in that a bullet had caught him behind his shoulder. He held the

Glock with both hands and kept it pointed at the car as he took a few steps towards it.

"Damn it," Cole cursed when he realized he'd lost count of how many shots he'd taken. Halfway to the car, the passenger door opened and Cole saw a man step out, seemingly unhurt until he turned to face Cole with blood all over the front of his shirt. The man seemed startled to see Cole approach and turned back to reach into the car. Cole took no chances and fired off two quick shots at center mass and the man slumped onto the pavement, one arm still reaching into the car. Cole raced to the trunk before swinging around to the rear window from where the gunman had opened up. Inside, Cole saw the shooter slumped over in his seat. He then looked up front and saw the driver's head smashed partly through the windshield. Cole walked forward and kicked hard at the man on the ground. Seeing no reaction, Cole stepped over him and looked more closely at the driver. Cole couldn't tell if he had shot him since the impact of the crash had done so much damage to the driver, but he was also clearly dead.

Cole looked at the guy in the backseat who was not moving and took a moment to release the magazine. There was one round left in it. With one in the chamber, he had two shots left. The Marriott was not far away, and the street was quiet. Pain was setting in and Cole could feel his shoulder muscles tightening. Blood stained the back of his shirt. He saw people a block ahead on the main street, and none of them seemed to know or care that there had just been a shootout 50 yards away.

Cole reholstered his gun, and realized he was panting. He tried to swallow, but couldn't. His mouth was dry. Sweat covered his forehead and he felt it running down his chest as he crossed the street back to the sidewalk and walked quickly towards the busier main street. He wiped his eyes and tried to swallow again, but still couldn't. He shook a bit and his ears were ringing even louder now than they had before.

When he hit the main intersection, Cole scanned all four corners, then wiped the sweat from his forehead with the back of his right hand and then against his jeans. He turned right on a sidewalk congested with people. It was just after ten when he saw the lights from the casino and he knew the Marriott was close. He felt more secure on the busy street among the pedestrians and heavy traffic. No one seemed to notice the left side of his shirt was stained with blood.

As he walked, Cole processed. Whatever had just happened wasn't good. It wasn't a robbery—it was an attempted murder. Someone wanted him dead. Cole's mind raced as he played scenarios in his head. Was it another cartel? Was it his cartel? Was it David? His first reaction was disbelief, but he shook that from his head and scolded himself for thinking he was any different than anyone else in the business.

He again tried to swallow but couldn't. Needing a drink in more ways than one, Cole turned for Habana's. A few of the regulars smiled at him with no idea what Cole had just done. *This fucking city*, he thought. The music thumped, still not loud enough to drown out the ringing in his ears. His breathing had slowed and he could no longer feel his pulse in his chest, but his nerves were still on edge. The pain in his shoulder was a dull, constant ache and wasn't going to fix itself anytime soon.

He stood back against the bar and watched the crowd for any signs of trouble, but saw none. Taking a beer with his right hand, he cupped his left hand around the neck to wet it, then pressed his palm against his head. It felt cool for just a second and it was enough to give him a pause to gather his thoughts. He wondered if the cops had found the car yet. Perhaps someone had called the police by now about gunfire. Perhaps not. It was Panama, after all.

If anything, the cops would collect the dead like they did every night and bring them downtown. They would gather their evidence and Cole knew he had left spent brass cases. He tried hard to think if he had touched anything on the street or the car, but was confident he hadn't. A gun was easy to replace, and if need be he would lose the Glock on his hip for another one. He'd have to tell David and this was certainly going to escalate things again. The thought made him take a deep and reluctant breath.

Cole also knew he'd just won a gunfight, and with that thought he finished off the beer with a second long sip. He ordered another, took a smaller sip, and suddenly felt that same tingling feeling from when he was on the open sea. It was nothing to celebrate, but being alive always felt better when death had just moments ago been so close. The beer didn't stop the pain from spreading beyond his shoulder. And unlike crossing the reef off Key West or shaking the P-3 in a thunderstorm, this time Cole was left in bad shape. This time there were consequences and the warm blood against his back reminded him of his own mortality.

He took a deep breath and another sip from his Dos Equis. Maria caught his attention from a table in the middle of the fray. She was sitting with another girl and they were sipping Red Bulls. She smiled at him and mouthed something in Spanish. He smiled back and walked a direct path to her and pulled a chair in close. Sitting down, he put one hand on her lower back and leaned in to her ear, whispering, "Vamanos."

She sat back and looked at him with an inquisitive smile and asked, "Donde?" She shook her head just a bit with the question and her long hair swayed with it.

When she said it, she curled a finger around the ends of her hair and couldn't hide her curiosity. Cole leaned in again, a bit unsteady, and spoke in English, "Let's go."

She was still playing with her hair and looked at him with a suspicious grin, before she spotted the blood on his shirt and her jaw dropped. Her eyes stayed locked with his for several seconds as she went back and forth in her head before she mouthed, "OK."

They both stood up and Maria left her Red Bull on the table, bidding goodnight to her friend. Cole walked her across the street and into the Marriott. The air conditioning gave him the chills immediately and he realized how much he had sweat over the past 15 minutes. His shirt was soaked. Maria walked by his side through the lobby and held his forearm with her soft hand as they made their way to the elevator. As it started climbing to Cole's floor, she grabbed him close and they faced each other.

"Are you OK, cowboy?" she asked as she turned Cole a bit to look at his left side. As she tilted her head to one side, Cole ran his fingers behind her ear and tucked some of her hair away from her face.

"Stop it," she said as she examined his left side. "You're bleeding, Cole."

She was leaning in close to him, her chest pressed against his, when the elevator door opened and they walked side by side down the hallway to his room. Cole was starting to feel dizzy, perhaps from the beer, or the loss of the blood, or the air conditioning chilling his soaked skin. She held his right arm and leaned in to support his body against hers as they walked into the room.

Closing the door behind them, Maria took Cole to the bathroom and helped him get the shirt off his back. She cursed in Spanish and with the mirror, Cole could see a good-sized gash behind his left shoulder. It must have been one of the first shots that got him, or maybe even a ricouchet off the cement wall, but it had nicked him bad enough to be a concern. Cole knew he was lucky. It hurt like hell, but it could have been far worse. If he'd crouched a foot in the wrong direction when the car passed, he'd likely be dead.

Maria went out of the bathroom to the phone by the bed and called someone. Cole didn't know who nor did he care. He pressed both his hands against the counter of the sink and dropped his head down, closing his eyes and gritting his teeth. He was in bad shape. He sat down on the edge of the bathtub and worked his boots off with his right hand. His socks took longer to pull off with one hand. Maria came back and in and helped him to his feet.

"I called a doctor," she said while kicking Cole's boots out of the way.

Cole looked at her and asked, "How long?"

Maria patted him on his back and replied, "Soon. He is a friend and will help you. Why don't you try to take a shower and clean up a bit?"

Cole nodded his head in agreement. With that, Maria went back into the main room and Cole slowly worked his way into the

shower. He tried to clean the wound, but it hurt beyond his toler-
ance even to get wet, so he left it alone, opting to wash away the
sweat and blood from the rest of his body.

When he finished, Cole dried off as best he could with his one
good arm and awkwardly held the towel around his waist as he
walked out of the bathroom. Maria's dress was on the floor by the
bed. He stopped in his tracks and found himself dizzy once again,
this time in a good way. Turning away from the bed, he saw that
Maria had pulled on a pair of his boxers and one of his *Delaney* t-
shirts. For the first time since she'd seen his wound, she smiled
and laughed, saying, "Don't get any ideas, cowboy. You're in no
shape for anything."

Cole laughed because Maria knew the thought had crossed his
mind. She brought him a pair of shorts and helped him pull them
on. With his right hand, he cupped the side of her face and stared
at her until she looked away.

"Thank you." It was all he could manage. Maria held his hand
and helped him lie down on his side. She then sat with him until
someone knocked at the door. Cole had left the gun in the bathroom and sat up quickly to retrieve it. Maria stopped him and held
his shoulder until he laid back down.

She answered the door and brought in a middle-aged man with
a duffel bag. Introducing himself as a doctor and friend, Cole relaxed enough to let the man examine his shoulder. Maria and the
doctor spoke some more before the man patted Cole on the shoulder and assured both him and Maria that he could stitch Cole up
with no problems.

On his side facing away from Maria and the doctor, Cole
could only guess that it was iodine that burned on the open wound.
Maria reached across his chest to hold his hand. Stitches followed
and Cole passed out before the work was done.

He woke the next morning with daylight creeping through the curtains and saw Maria laying next to him. She was on her side facing

him and her arms were curled around a pillow. She was still asleep, and Cole didn't want to wake her. He stayed in bed for some time, in and out of sleep himself with his one good arm intertwined with hers. When she finally did wake up, Maria was quick to smile at him, and Cole wondered if she hadn't been up for some time and had simply kept her eyes closed to avoid the morning. Cole smiled back at her and paused to take in her pretty features. His left shoulder was stiff, but his arm didn't feel all that bad.

He fired up the coffee maker by the mini-fridge and made two cups. Passing one to Maria, the two sat in bed sipping their coffee and touched their feet against each others under the covers, laughing when they did. It was close to noon by the time Maria put her dress back on and fixed her hair as best she could in the bathroom. When she came out, Cole watched her around the room as she looked around for her things. He tossed the *Delaney* t-shirt she'd worn the night before back at her, saying, "Keep it." She smiled and stuffed it into her purse.

He asked, "How much do I owe you?"

Maria looked back at him, stopping momentarily before putting her shoes back on. She walked back over to Cole and sat on the side of the bed with him. "Nothing."

Cole asked, "But what about the doctor?"

Maria shook her head, "He is a friend. There is no charge."

She got up to leave and Cole grabbed at her hand. "Don't leave. Please."

The truth was Cole didn't want to be alone. With a bullet hole in the back of his shoulder and no one he could trust, Maria was all he had and he owed her dearly. Maria nodded that she would stay and sat back down on the bed.

She smiled and asked, "So what do we do now?"

He flashed a grin and said, "I think I've got a plan." Cole stood up, walked over to the phone, and dialed David.

Before Cole could get a word out, David asked in a sharp tone, "Are you part of this shit, Cole?"

Cole was not entirely surprised that David already knew something had gone down. "Would you rather me have rolled over and died?"

"Damn it, Cole. You're more trouble than you know."

Cole laughed to himself. "What did you hear?"

David replied, "What did I hear? What did I *hear*? I hear that some fucking cowboy is killing guys down dark alleys. I hear that some guy is shooting at the Coast Guard and then comes back to Panama and turns the city into the Wild West. That's what I hear."

Cole quipped back, "Yeah, because Panama was so peaceful until I got here."

David calmed down a bit and said, "You sit tight. I fucking mean it. I'll be over in a bit."

Cole hung up the phone and remembered that he hadn't reloaded from the night before. He took the gun from the bathroom and the bag of cleaning supplies over to the table, unloaded it, and gave it a quick run through with the oil and rags. Whatever pain meds he had from the night before were starting to wear off. Maria offered to get some more, but Cole preferred to tough it out and keep his senses sharp. Loading the gun again with a full magazine, he put his jeans back on and a new shirt then tucked the gun back in its holster. With gauze and tape over the stitches on his back, he buttoned his shirt, snugged up his belt to hold the gun's weight, and sat back down with Maria, waiting for David.

He looked at her, sitting next to him on the bed and thought for a long second before he spoke. "I owe you a lot."

She shook her head back and forth playfully. She could tell his arm was starting to hurt. "We should go and I can get you some more medicine."

Cole declined, saying, "No, there's something else I want to do. Just give me some time." With that, she leaned against his good side and they talked like they had so many times before. Maria didn't know it, but Cole had a plan in his head to repay Maria's kindness.

Two hours later, David knocked at his door. It was after three in the afternoon. The two shook hands, and Cole pulled two beers from the refrigerator, passing one to David. David eyed Maria and looked back at Cole with a grin. Cole locked eyes with David and said, "It isn't what you think."

David laughed. "It never is."

Cole replied, "I mean it. Don't say a word."

They both took large sips and got down to business. "Cole, I won't lie to you. You pissed off the other cartels with the shooting at the Americans. You've disrupted a balance that we all like down here. On the plus side, you brought in some good cash that we would have lost otherwise, so my boss is still OK with everything, but some of the others are not so much."

Cole processed for a moment and asked, "So who the fuck tried to kill me, David?"

David took another sip and paused. He looked at Cole as if to suggest he was going to say something heavy. "You gotta get the fuck out of town for a while."

Cole was looking back directly at David. "OK. How the fuck do you suggest I do that?"

David laughed. "No worries, my friend. We'll get you out of here. You go sit tight and let this thing settle down. You've got some cash; there are plenty of places to sit and be comfortable. We've got a plane going out tonight if you'd like."

"Where to?"

"A couple of places, but he'll end up in Martinique, I believe. Maybe Aruba on the way, just to drop off some things."

Cole figured it was another run. With his shoulder, he was in no shape to push through the night. "Are we moving stuff?"

David shook his head and answered, "No, no, we don't use planes much right now for that kind of business. The Colombians have gotten too good at shooting them down. All of it is legit, or at least as legit as it gets for us."

Cole accepted the offer. "When do we leave?"

David finished his beer. "Now."

Cole thought for a moment, looked at Maria, and replied, "We gotta run by the bank first."

David asked, "Why?"

"Something I need to take care of."

David looked back at Maria, then at Cole. "Does this have something to do with her?"

Cole nodded, "Yup."

From the bed where she sat, Maria tilted her head as if to ask Cole what he was up to. Cole just smiled at her.

Cole packed up a few of his things, including some extra tape and gauze the doctor had left, and they all set off. David had a van waiting, and Cole climbed in with Maria, the two of them sitting in the backseat. David climbed in up front. She seemed uneasy and Cole reassured her with his hand on her knee. It was mid-afternoon, and Cole scanned Habana's one last time as the van pulled away.

It felt like he was geared up for another run north, but the van took different turns as it made its way through town. Cole remembered the drive in on his first night and found himself almost nostalgic for the past few months in Panama. Part of him wanted badly to turn and drive north to set his hands on a panga again or spend a lazy morning in a hammock in Nicaragua sipping a rum drink. But with each adventure, Cole knew he was only deeper into a world from which he may not get out. *Am I simply another cog in the wheel, or am I actually part of the problem?* He questioned his decisions and he didn't like the answers that festered in his mind.

He pushed those thoughts away as the van pulled up to a large bank. Maria, Cole, and David all stepped out and walked into the air-conditioned lobby. Cole asked Maria to wait for them up front, and David walked with Cole up to a well-dressed middle-aged woman seated at a desk in a corner. Cole explained to David that he wanted to sign his account over to Maria. David shook his head to say no, telling Cole it was a mistake. Cole persisted and reluctantly David translated Cole's request.

As the woman drew up paperwork, David again tried to talk Cole out of it. "Cole, you've got a lot of cash here. Don't be stupid because of one night. There are a lot of pretty girls here."

Cole gritted his teeth. He'd made nothing but mistakes in Panama. Left for dead and unwilling to trust even David, Cole wanted nothing to do with the money he'd made over the past months. He looked over his shoulder at Maria. She was seated facing away from them and he thought back to how she'd held him up the night before. He thought about their first conversation and how she'd explained that one day she'd bring back her money to her family in Colombia. There were lots of pretty girls in Panama, but he held a special place in his heart for Maria. Not only had she been there for him at his lowest point, but Cole had gotten to know her over the months and, to him, she was so much more than just another working girl.

As the woman finished the paperwork and turned it around on the desk for Cole to see, he asked David to go get Maria. David shook his head one last time and stood up. "You are nuts, Cole."

"Just go get Maria. Please."

Maria walked over a few moments later and Cole asked her to sit down. The woman behind the desk sat expressionless as Cole took Maria's hand.

He asked her, "Maria, would you leave Panama if you could?

She smiled a nervous smile and replied, "Well, one day, yes. Why?"

Cole pointed down at the papers. "I want you to have this."

She looked down and saw a cash value of just over $120,000 at the bottom of the page. Confused, she looked back at Cole.

He explained it to her. "I'm leaving, but I want you to have this. I want you to go home, if that's what you want to do. Or go somewhere, anywhere. Start a new life. Do you understand?"

Maria looked back down at the paper, then at Cole. "But why, Cole?"

Cole paused for a second, then answered, "Because I want to know what it feels like to do something good."

Maria started to cry. She wiped the first tears away, but couldn't hide her emotion. "Why me?"

Cole smiled at her, saying, "You're the only good I've known in the world in a long time and it would make me happy to know you're happy."

From her seat next to him, Maria wrapped her arms around his neck and pulled him in close, pressing her face against his neck.

Cole laughed a bit. He hugged her back and held her for a moment to take in all of her charm. "Come on now, sign the papers for me."

Maria complied and the woman took the papers off, leaving Cole and Maria to themselves.

Maria was still fighting back tears.

Cole asked, "Will you leave?"

She nodded yes. "I will go home, to Colombia." When she said the word Colombia, she teared up again and Cole knew Maria meant it.

The woman returned with a credit card and a checkbook, discussing it for a minute with Maria in Spanish before all three stood up and shook hands. Outside the bank, Maria hugged Cole and didn't let go for some time. Cole embraced her firmly with his good arm and managed to wrap his left arm around her as well.

Cole asked, "Are you good to go from here or do you need a ride?"

Maria replied, "No, I'm good. I'm going to get my things and say goodbye to some friends. I will fly home tomorrow, maybe the next day."

"To Colombia?" Cole asked.

Maria smiled, teared up again for a second, and then shook her head, saying, "Yes, to Colombia."

She paused for a second to compose herself, then hugged Cole one more time. As she held him tight, she asked, "Will you come with me?"

He patted her back, but shook his head to say no. "I can't. I have to take care of some things. But maybe I'll see you again one day, Maria."

She hugged him again with force and kissed his lips. It caught Cole by surprise, but he kissed her back and it only reaffirmed the feelings he held for her. With one last hug and a smile from Maria, they parted ways. Maria looked back twice as she walked down the sidewalk and disappeared. He stood there for some time until David called out from the van and motioned for Cole to get moving. Cole stood for a few moments more, replaying the last few minutes over in his head, before he climbed into the van. With his drug money now gone, Cole was left with his severance, which was honest—albeit bittersweet—money to get along with for the time being.

As they drove east to the airport along the Pacific, Cole thought about the Caribbean and wondered if he would have the chance again to roar across the waves under a full moon. If he was washed up and simply didn't know it, he felt sorry for himself. It was short-lived, but in many ways he was just happy to be alive. Even from inside the van, he felt a weight off his chest by being outside the city. It was time for something new. Maria would be his lasting memory of Panama City. One day he hoped to forget the blood and the death and the drugs, but he would hold onto the thought of Maria.

As they motored along in and out of afternoon traffic, David asked Cole for the gun back. "You gotta dump that thing. The cops are looking for it now."

David extended his hand out for Cole to give it to him. Cole instinctively didn't like the idea of not having a gun with him and reassured himself by patting it with his right hand.

He looked back at David. "I'll give it to you at the airport."

David laughed and said, "You worry too much my friend. Besides, now you got no money, so why would I even mess with you?"

They both laughed a bit at the joke. The truth was Cole felt better being broke than if he left a rich man. It was money he'd earned, but he valued a cleaner conscience more than cash.

The rest of the drive was uneventful and when they approached the airport, the van turned down a separate road from the main terminal.

"Where are we going?" Cole watched as they drove right past the main passenger area.

David pointed further down the road and said, "We don't bother with customs. Everything is good, my friend. Don't worry."

When they finally pulled up to a nearly empty ramp, Cole saw a man step out of a smaller twin-engine plane and walk towards the van. David stepped out first and walked over, shaking hands with the guy. Cole was next and they all stood around the hot ramp in the afternoon sun sizing each other up.

David made introductions. "Cole, this is Murph. He's one of our pilots."

Murph extended his hand and Cole obliged. Murph was older than Cole by probably ten years, balding a bit, and wore sandals with khaki shorts and a wrinkled short-sleeve shirt. He was tan, but looked to be an American. He had a smile on his face. Cole could tell that Murph was trying to figure Cole out just as much as Cole was trying to sort out a new face.

"He's running to Curacao and then to Martinique with some papers and documents for us," said David. "You can ride along and stop wherever."

Cole nodded to accept and walked to the van to grab his bag. As he walked back over to the plane with his bag over his shoulder, he reached into his holster and handed David the Glock. David took it, slipped it into the small of his back, and exchanged a firm nod with Cole. Without much in the way of goodbyes, Murph showed Cole to the step up behind the wing and Cole climbed in.

He couldn't stand up straight in the cramped cabin, but there were a few seats scattered about and two briefcases off to one side. Cole took a seat right behind a bulkhead that separated the cabin from the cockpit.

Murph pulled some chocks out from under the landing gear and threw them into the back of the plane. Through the small round windows, Cole saw him pulling at things and smacking different parts of the plane, giving it a once over. Once up into the cabin, he walked forward and whacked Cole on the back of the head and pointed forward. "This ain't the fucking airlines, kid. Sit up front and do something useful. I don't trust you if I can't see you."

It caught Cole off guard, but he followed Murph further forward, and after seeing Murph climb over a console and sit down, Cole repeated the same balancing act and settled into the right seat. Murph was furiously flipping switches and pulling handles and soon enough both engines roared to life. For the first time, Cole found himself somewhere hotter than Panama City. With no air flow, the cockpit must have been over 100 degrees. He was soaked in sweat, wiping it from his eyes and trying to figure out how to put on the headset Murph had handed him. For Cole it was completely foreign, but as Murph began a slow taxi, Cole realized he had his ticket out of Panama.

MURPH TAXIED FOR WHAT seemed like an eternity. It was hotter than hell itself and the sun baked everything under the windshield. Ahead and to the left, Cole watched intently as a massive airliner lumbered up into the sky and disappeared into a scattered layer of clouds. Even over the two engines of Murph's plane, Cole could hear the jet roaring up and away. After a few minutes more, the air conditioning was finally blowing cool air into the cockpit, and Cole could feel the temperature dropping. Murph continued on at a steady clip down the taxiway. He seemed busy talking with the ground controllers and running through his checklists, so Cole kept to himself and took in his surroundings. Jet fuel smelled remarkably different than the gasoline he burned in an outboard engine. He thought back to the P-3 that buzzed him weeks ago. It seemed like an eternity had passed since that night.

Looking back to his right, Cole saw that he was only a few feet from the propeller turning on the right wing. It seemed odd that he was so close to it, and for the life of him, Cole couldn't figure out how it was going to lift this plane into the air. He'd flown commercial flights more times than he could count, but from the passenger seat of an airliner, he had always assumed things would work out. Now, in the copilot's seat, he looked around at the gauges and needles that flickered back and forth and wondered what the hell was going to happen. He sat there looking down at the instruments until Murph punched him in the shoulder to snap Cole out of it.

Glancing over at Murph, Cole saw that he was pointing up ahead and to the right. "See that blue building over there?"

Cole looked ahead and could see a two-story structure that looked just as run down as everything else in Panama outside the main drag of the city. Antennas protruded from the top, but the grounds around it looked better maintained than most of Panama. It was most certainly military.

"Yeah, the two-story one. What is it?"

Murph grinned and said, "That's the Panamanian military. That's their air base. They'll fuck you up if they catch you. Shoot you without thinking twice about it."

As Murph taxied past, Cole had a good view of the base. There were a few old planes laying around on the sidelines, most worn down beyond recognition and certainly not in any flying condition. But there were two Hueys, straight out of a Vietnam War movie, with some guys in flight suits walking around them. For a moment, they looked straight at Cole as he looked back at them, only 40 or 50 yards away as Murph taxied past. All Cole could do was wave. One of the guys in a flight suit threw a wave back at Cole and went back to securing something inside the helicopter.

"Funny," Murph said without looking at Cole.

Still looking out the window at the various planes and helicopters lining the ramp of the military base, Cole asked, "What's funny?"

Murph took a 90 degree turn at the end of the taxiway and stopped the plane just short of the massive runway. "Funny that they're gearing up to go look for you and you're sitting right here in my damn plane."

Cole was looking straight ahead now and settled back a bit in the seat. "I'm glad you find it entertaining, Murph."

Murph punched Cole again. From inside the cramped cockpit, Murph practically had to lean all the way to his left against the cabin to get enough space to rear back his right hand and punch Cole, but still he did it again and laughed out loud.

"Seriously man, they're stone cold killers. You're lucky to get out of here alive."

Before Cole could say anything back, Murph was talking to the tower and he popped the parking brake loose. Pushing the throttles up a bit, Cole felt the tail sway back and forth as the plane accelerated in a lazy turn to line up with the runway centerline.

Before Murph even was aligned with it, he jammed the throttles up and the plane swerved hard as he turned it further left and they accelerated even more. The dashed centerline began to pass underneath the nose faster and faster.

Cole felt himself pressed into the seat as Murph pulled her up and with a subtle thump, they were in the air. The wings dipped back and forth for a moment or two and she swayed a few more times as Murph worked the rudder with his feet and the wings with his left hand on the yoke. It was uncomfortable at first, but soon Murph found the plane's sweet spot and they were on their way.

Murph called out, "Gear up." He had his left hand on the yoke and his right hand draped over the two throttles. Cole didn't know what he was talking about.

"Gear up, you dumbass." Murph was looking at Cole now with a stern face.

"What the hell are you talking about?" Cole had no idea what Murph was looking for.

Murph reared back like he was going punch Cole again, but he stopped short of it and instead pointed with his finger to a handle with a round clear plastic knob on it just in front of Cole's left knee.

"You see that knob there?" Murph was pointing straight at it.

"Yeah," Cole replied.

"Well, flip it up, you retard."

Cole reached down and flipped it up. A few clunks followed and the handle glowed red briefly before three indicators all displayed 'up' and the clunks stopped.

"Never flown before, huh?"

Murph was settled back into his seat as he flipped a few more switches and they climbed up into the setting sun. The Pacific was a sea of yellow sunlight reflecting off the surface below them and daylight was showing its first signs of retreat. Cole didn't respond to Murph as he was consumed by the view of the vast sea in front of him. They were flying out into the Pacific and Cole leaned up and forward a bit to look down at it. No sooner had he caught a glimpse of the water below them when Murph checked in with air traffic controllers and started a turn to the left.

They climbed even higher, and as Murph came through 180 degrees of a turn, they were facing a giant wall of mountains on the nose. Cole looked down out the window to his right and saw nothing but green. He could make out some dirt roads leading in from the coast and the rusting metal roofs of houses dotting the landscape, but not much more. Most of the landscape was just a dark shade of green in the late afternoon light. Panama City was to his left across the cockpit, and he couldn't make out any detail other than the mass of buildings and light reflecting off windows. But to his right was a part of the country he'd not yet explored. It looked different from the air. He was all at once entirely relieved to be out of the city and took a slow deep breath. Panama's never-ending party wore him down more than anything, and now that he was out, he felt like he'd made the right decision. It was indeed time to get out.

In a few short months, Panama had chewed him up and spit him out. He was lucky to be alive, just as Murph had said. He thought for a moment about the gunfight, but now not even 24 hours later, it too was a blur and he struggled to remember the details. The muzzle blast from the car, the recoil from his gun as he ducked for cover and did his best to make his shots count, the brass clinking off the pavement, the smell of gunpowder in the humid thick air, and the silence afterwards when the shooting had finally stopped was stuck in his mind. His shoulder too was a reminder of how close he came to not making it out. He ran through it again in his head then just as quickly sent the thoughts away and stared out the window at the green country below.

With the air conditioning finally getting full control of the cockpit, it cooled off nicely and Cole sat forward for a second to pull his shirt off of his sweat-soaked back. The bandage felt like it was holding up all right. He sat back again, much more comfortable.

"I've never flown in the cockpit before." Cole looked for a second at Murph then back ahead at the mountains in front of them.

"First time for everything," replied Murph and he seemed more relaxed now that he was in the air.

Cole asked, "So what's your story then?"

Murph grinned a bit and pushed a few more buttons before taking his hands off the yoke. "She'll fly herself from here."

"Autopilot?" Cole wasn't sure what he was talking about.

"Yup, this thing is the shit. King Air with all the bells and whistles," Murph quipped as he settled back a bit more in his seat.

He went back to Cole's question. "I've been flying down here for a little over ten years. Started running shit back and forth to Hispaniola when I was about your age. Never really done anything else."

"Where'd you learn to fly?"

Murph took a deeper breath. "I started out in Florida at a flight school, but right about when I was ready to finish, I flew a little too low past a girl's house and it kind of went downhill from there. I finally got my license but couldn't really get a good job anywhere, so I packed up and made my way down here."

Cole was quiet for a moment, realizing that Murph was just like him. He looked up ahead at the mountains and could see that the plane was climbing over them. The altimeter was spinning through 10,000 feet, that much he could understand. There were some dark buildups ahead at the peak of some of the mountains, and in line with where Murph was flying.

"Is that weather a problem?"

Murph looked up ahead and squinted before responding. "You worry a lot, you know that? I heard you're some cowboy or something, shooting it out like the wild west and here you are asking me about puffy clouds and shit."

Cole laughed. "Just seems a bit different in a plane, that's all. And yeah, I guess I made a bit of a name for myself down here."

Murph laughed too and seemed to ease up even more as their altitude increased and the cabin cooled. He seemed satisfied that

Cole wasn't all that bad of a guy. As they reached the top of the mountains and leveled out, the landscape disappeared beneath them. They were in the clouds and bounced around a bit more than Cole liked. Rain followed, and the plane jolted up and down at an alarming rate. When Cole had driven through a thunderstorm, he bounced around a bit, but a plane added a new uncomfortable dimension. Without seeing a thing in front of him, Cole felt the back end yaw left and right like it did on takeoff and he took a deep breath.

Cole mumbled, "Ain't this some shit."

Murph just sat there in his seat, occasionally twisting a knob on a small radar screen in front of him, but otherwise not seeming to give two shits about mountains or thunderstorms, or the rain that was pummeling the windshield. When the turbulence kicked them around even more, Murph pulled back on the throttles a bit, but just as soon as the plane settled again, he jammed them back up. Cole looked out at the propeller turning just feet away from him and saw the flicker of a strobe light every few seconds against the otherwise dark mass of clouds outside. He wanted to ask Murph about any more mountains since at that particular place and time neither of them could see shit in front of them, but knew Murph would just blow it off so he didn't bother. Cole pressed his head against the seat and waited.

In a matter of minutes, they were through the worst of it. The clouds backed off and Cole caught his first glimpse of the Caribbean in front of him. From 17,000 feet, he could see clear across the coastline of Panama. The Caribbean shoreline, now darker with the sun behind the mountains and obscured by the clouds they'd just pushed through, was dotted with flickers of lights. Some were from ships at anchor, others from the small remote villages that dotted the north coast. The cockpit was cool and the plane settled in the undisturbed air, her propellers driving them eastward with a steady hum.

"Well, shit. This ain't half bad," Cole nodded.

"I'm glad it's to your standard." Murph reached behind his seat and pulled out a small collapsible travel cooler. Setting it down in his lap, he unzipped the top and pulled out two Dos Equis bottles, both sweating from a bath in ice.

"You've got to be shitting me," Cole said in disbelief.

"Beverage service." Murph passed one to Cole then opened his with a bottle opener that he pulled from the side pocket.

Passing the opener to Cole, Murph took a good long sip and set the beer between his legs before dialing in a new frequency and adjusting a few more switches in the plane.

"Is there a movie too?" Cole popped the top off his beer and held it out for Murph to toast.

Tipping the neck of his beer against Cole's, Murph took another sip and talked to someone else on the radio before changing his course just a bit with the turn of a small wheel on the console between them.

Cole took another sip and asked, "So what do you move down here?"

Murph looked at him for a second then stared straight ahead at the dark night in front of them.

"Used to run drugs, like you. But the governments, Colombia mostly, got real good real quick at shooting planes down. Once they got their first taste of it, there was nothing stopping them. The U.S. was supplying them with equipment and it was a pretty lethal combo. This was right when I was getting into it. Guys were getting shot to shit and never heard of again."

He took another sip from his beer and rubbed his lip with his thumb. "I figured what the hell, I'll give it a try. I made two runs out of Colombia before they caught me. I had this crotch-rocket of a plane come up from behind and wag his wings right next to me. I mean, I could literally see the fucker's face. I flicked the guy off and figured I was done. He was calling out on the radio for me to land, but I was getting pretty close to the beach line and figured I would make a run for open water, trying to get to twelve miles."

Murph quit for a second, looked at one of the gauges, and took another sip. Cole kept quiet as he had a sense that this story was going somewhere and that his adventures to date paled in comparison.

"So anyway, sure as shit, he pulls behind in a loose trail and lights me up. I mean, I can hear bullets tearing into the plane. It was just a single engine Cessna, no match at all for whatever he was shooting me up with. And then the engine started smoking, fuel was leaking out of the wings, and I put her in a descent to the jungle. He blew right past me one more time as I was descending to rub it in my face. I killed the engine and lined up to ditch on a flat part of the landscape."

Cole was struck by it. "Shit, man. That's one hell of a story."

They were both looking straight ahead and the silence was uncomfortable. Murph seemed like he was replaying it in his head.

Cole pressed. "You gotta tell me the ending. I mean you're still here, so what the fuck happened?"

Murph paused and shook his head back and forth as if to say he didn't even understand it himself. "I don't really know. I put her down in the jungle and somehow walked away from it. The plane was a wreck, but I climbed out through the windshield that was busted out and waited."

Cole was puzzled. "You waited? You just sat there and waited?"

Murph laughed and replied, "Yeah, I fucking waited. I was in the middle of the damn jungle wearing a pair of flip flops. What else was I gonna do?"

The two laughed. It was a hell of a story and the two seemed to appreciate each other's company for the next two hours. Cole laid out his whole story about *Delaney*, the migrant runs, and his decision to press further south. Murph seemed somewhat impressed with Cole's stories as well and before long they were starting a slow descent down into the island of Curacao.

Having never been there, Cole focused his attention outside the cockpit and strained to make out details about the island in front of him in the dark Caribbean sky. Murph took her off autopilot and handled the plane like a pro. He'd cut them both off at one beer for that leg, but had promised another once they were wheels up.

As they neared the airport, Murph called out, "Gear down."

Taking that as his cue, Cole reached down and flopped the same lever down. Similar clunks followed and the plane surged just a bit before the three indicators all displayed 'down' and Cole was happy with his first flying lesson.

Murph eased the plane onto the runway and from a pilot's view, Cole saw firsthand the balancing act of bringing a flying piece of metal back onto the ground with grace. He was impressed. The landing was far more involved and intricate than tying a ship up to a pier. They taxied clear of the runway and over to another empty ramp, where a lone blue van waited in a corner. Taxiing over towards it, Murph instructed Cole to hop out the back with both of the briefcases behind his seat and give them to the guy in the van.

Cole complied and in a matter of minutes they were taxiing again with Murph flipping switches and tuning radios. He paused briefly and pointed again up past the runway to a large hangar and some monstrous planes sitting on the dark ramp.

"See them, that's a U.S. base down here. Those planes are the ones out looking for you every night."

Cole squinted to make out the silhouettes of the planes, but in the darkness he couldn't see clear enough to make much out of them. He wondered if that same P-3 wasn't parked up there somewhere. It was an odd twist of fate that he was now practically kicked to the curb by David, and here he was twice in one day and in very different places looking practically eye to eye with the same guys trying every night to catch him.

The planes were huge, sitting quietly on the ramp as Murph taxied them past. It was asymmetric warfare in every sense of the term. Cole set out with a boat, a motor, and a GPS. In front of him was an array of some of the most technologically advanced warplanes in the U.S. inventory, all focused on finding guys just like him and slowing the flow of drugs to North America.

Murph spun the plane around again and lined up on the dark runway, this time waiting until he was lined up properly before gunning the engines. Seconds later they were accelerating. The plane's landing lights lit the pavement in front of them and an array of different colored lights marked each side of the runway with a single row of lights down the centerline. Other than the runway, it was dark. Cole felt the nose pitch up briefly before the familiar thump indicating they were in the air.

Murph called for the gear and Cole flipped the same lever again without missing a beat. Once pointed east and on autopilot, Murph pulled out two more beers and the two of them toasted the evening. "I assume you didn't want to stay in Curacao?"

Cole took a sip and replied, "No. Let's see what else El Caribe has to offer."

From 19,000 feet, it was total darkness below and above. There were some scattered thunderstorms along the route, but nothing like the ones they'd pushed through over Panama. Cole could see the stars above him and enough of the moon was out to bounce some light off the Caribbean below. Cole was now adjusted to the hum of the engines and compared to running a boat hundreds of miles, an airplane was certainly an easier ride.

The flight to Martinique was just about two hours, and Cole pressed Murph for more details. Murph in turn laid out the pros and cons of running drugs by air. It had taken the better part of a day for anyone to find him after he'd ditched the plane. By the time the Colombian military arrived, he'd burned the whole thing down to ashes and, from the story he told, he met the Colombians with open arms and a shit-eating grin on his face. Without evidence, they had nothing that could have proved Murph's guilt, as it had all gone up in flames. The Colombians put him in jail anyway, but in a matter of months, he was out and on his way.

Since then, almost eight years ago, Murph had been moving mostly above-the-table shipments around the southern Caribbean. Sometimes he flew people from place to place, picking them up, dropping them off, and waiting for days at the nicest hotels money could buy. He told Cole that the two briefcases were nothing more than checks and documents as far as he knew. Like any other business, there was a paper trail. It was well guarded, but there was still a paper trail, and that was Murph's niche in the business. If he wasn't chauffeuring the middle management from meeting to meeting, he was moving their administrative necessities. From time to time he'd test out a new route or move cocaine if David was in a pinch, but it was a good life that Murph had carved out for himself.

Cole was relieved that the cartel had kept its word and hadn't sent Murph on his way empty handed. He compared his situation to Murph's and the two agreed that Cole still had a decent chance of making something of it. In the interim, Murph would show him a good time in Martinique once they landed. As they started their descent into Fort-de-France, Cole couldn't help but smile.

Murph touched down again and taxied to a smaller ramp lined with planes similar to their King Air. He shut down quickly and the two stepped off the plane into the nighttime sky. Cole took a deep and long breath of the air. It was tropical just like Panama, but a strong steady breeze blew from the east and the air smelled fresh and full of salt. There was no city stench like Panama City nor was there the constant thumping of dance music from Habana's. It was peaceful, at last. With his bag over his shoulder, Cole followed Murph inside the small terminal where Murph had a green Volkswagen rental car waiting, and the two were off.

Murph drove like a madman through the streets, entering and exiting rotary intersections like he'd been at it his whole life. He grinned and giggled with each hard turn. Cole couldn't help but laugh as well with his window down and the cool evening air in his face. The local radio station played something in French and Murph cranked it up as he hit red line speeds on the straightaways then played the gears down in the turns.

Even though it was dark, Cole could sense the island was far different from the western side of the Caribbean. A refreshing breeze rolled in undisturbed from the Atlantic. The smell took him back to the first night he'd beached on the north coast of Cuba. The tops of palm trees moved with the wind, and the buildings were more spaced out and colorful than the congestion of Panama. It was getting late, but people were still lingering around the small cafes that lined the roads.

Murph pulled off the main highway, and Cole strained to read the street signs. It was all foreign to him, a new language. He hoped that enough time would pass here that he would come to learn a few phrases. With one last hard turn, Murph settled the car into a parking spot and the two hopped out and walked into the entrance of the Hotel Bakoua. The lobby was open-air and had smooth tile floors. Soft music played from a radio behind the desk. It was remarkably quiet and Cole was again struck by the contrast. In broken English, the woman at the counter checked both of them into their rooms and gave them keys. From the reception area, the two walked around a corner, down some steps, and to the bar that overlooked the pool and the bay below. They were elevated on a cliff and Cole fought for a moment to keep a smile from creeping across his face.

Murph saw Cole's reaction, laughed, and pulled a stool up at the bar. Cole followed and the old man behind the bar brought them a plate of green olives and peanuts. They both drank rum punch and snacked on the peanuts for an hour or so, still swapping stories about wild nights, women, and the places they'd been. It was almost midnight when they turned in. Murph set off down towards his room and Cole found a sign pointing him to the left and down an open-air walkway to the end. To his left was a steep rock embankment covered in small flowers and brush. To the right was a single row of rooms with the beach on the far side. He found his number on the last room on the right and walked in, not knowing what to expect.

Like he always did, he set the thermostat a few degrees lower and walked over to the sliding glass doors. Opening them and stepping out onto his balcony, he saw a sand beach below and two dozen sailboats at anchor in the small cove to the left. He could hear the breeze whistle through their aluminum masts and halyards. Listening to it, he thought of Key West for a moment. So much had happened since he'd left the Conch Republic. He took one last deep breath and turned in for the evening.

He awoke the following morning later than usual. With nothing to do, he made some coffee in the room and went again out on his balcony. He'd missed it the night before, but the balcony wrapped around to the left and opened up onto a covered deck, almost hanging over the coral jetty below him. Taking a seat on a bench and throwing his bare feet up on the table, he shook his head and grinned at his fortune.

It wasn't long before he heard Murph calling up to him from the beach below, "You lucky son of a bitch."

Cole grinned even wider and quipped, "Better to be lucky than good Murph."

Murph shook his head and looked away towards the water for a second before returning with a light-hearted smile. "Get down here, man. You gotta see this."

Cole finished his coffee and made his way back through the room and down a set of wooden steps to the beach. He had on only a pair of board shorts and tucked the room key in a pocket. Murph walked quickly back down the beach, almost to the water, before motioning with his head for Cole to look out into the water behind him. There, two tanned and pretty girls were topless and lounging around in a foot or two of water. Cole stopped dead in his tracks and looked back at Murph, who was now the one with a smile on his face. "Welcome to France, buddy."

From there, the two of them made their way out onto a small dock and walkway that led out to another bar jutting into the small cove. Once there they drank themselves quickly into a mess and recounted the previous 24 hours. The bartender again brought out peanuts and green olives, which did little to help manage the rum punch that soaked their bellies.

The bartender eventually gave them the cold shoulder, and with their cups empty and their minds clouded, they settled back into some chairs on the beach and set about watching the French girls that walked past. They were all beautiful and paid little attention to the two drunk Americans. At some point Cole had nodded off and woke around noon under the shade of a palm tree. Murph had found another drink somehow and was fidgeting in his chair, unable to sit still and appeared to be looking for mischief.

"What's up, man?" Cole was still waking up from his nap.

Murph was scanning the cove and said, "I'm bored. There's a drink for you on the table."

Cole rolled over and sat up, reaching for the rum punch and he took a good long sip. It brought him back to life.

Beyond the bar, a young couple was seated in a pedal boat and they slowly chugged along out into the cove cutting a wide circular path. Even with the language barrier, it was clear the women was loudly nagging the man, who seemed to be trying to explain himself for some perceived transgression. Taking another sip from his punch, Murph set it down and spoke under his breath. "Watch this. I'll give her something to bitch about."

Cole said nothing, but watched Murph walk calmly out into the water and dive under for a moment before taking a few strokes out. He seemed to be lining himself up with the pedal boat and Cole chewed at his lip for a second trying to figure out what Murph was up to. He took another sip from his drink to finish it off and watched intently as the couple unknowingly made their way closer to Murph.

When he was within a few feet of them, he waved hello and they waved back, the woman stopping her tirade for just a moment, before Murph turned to make his way to the beach. As they passed him, Murph suddenly dove underwater again and emerged just inches from behind the pedal boat as it took a leisurely course further out into the cove. He was up to something and out of sight of the couple as they pedaled along. Seconds passed, and Murph finally slipped back under the water and emerged with some distance between him and the boat, this time making his way on in. Stepping out of the water, he again walked matter-of-factly back to his seat, dried off with a towel, and cleaned the rest of the melted ice and rum punch from his drink.

"What was that all about?" Cole had missed whatever Murph was up to.

Murph grinned and extended his right palm out with his fist closed before opening it and revealing the two hull plugs from the pedal boat. Cole looked for a second at the plugs then back out at the pedal boat making its way into the deeper water of the cove. The two young lovers were now giving each other silent treatment.

"No fucking way."

Murph was now sitting back down on his chair and laughing hysterically. Cole followed suit. They both looked out at the cove to try and see if the boat was getting any lower in the water but couldn't tell. But not more than a minute later, they heard the first yell. From its pitch, it must have been the woman, and she clearly had realized their boat was sinking. Cole and Murph looked out again, this time squinting harder and both giggling like little girls. The man driving was trying to turn the boat around, but it was now sinking lower and lower into the water and not responding to the two of them pedaling frantically.

The woman yelled some more towards shore and the man followed suit, both of them waving their hands in the air towards the beach. After a few seconds, the woman slapped the man and yelled at him once again. With the two of them yelling, Cole and Murph had to steady themselves so as not to fall out of their seats. The couple had caught the attention of the boy working the dock who was now yelling back at them and motioning with his hands for them to pedal faster. Guests on the beach were now standing up and talking as the couple on the boat yelled at the boy on the dock and the boy yelled back at them. It took a serious turn when the dock boy finally jumped in the water to swim after them.

Moments later, the pedal boat finally succumbed to Murph's sabotage, and with a titanic-esque dramatic list to one side, it finally went under. The couple, now without a boat, swam back to shore and the woman was out of breath by the time she reached the shore, not so much from the swim, but more from her tirade against her man while they swam the 30 yards to shore. The dock boy swam out to the boat and was the only one left yelling after it had sunk before he realized the futility of it all and swam back to the dock.

It had caused quite a scene. Murph buried the two plugs in the sand and suggested that he and Cole make a run for some lunch at the bar by the lobby. Cole agreed. They both tried to contain their laughter, but could take no more than ten steps before one of them would start laughing again and it inevitably triggered the other to do the same. It was in this condition that the two of them made their way up the steps and sat at the bar, ordering sandwiches and another round of rum punch.

Cole had to wipe his eyes from the sweat and laughter, finally controlling himself when his drink arrived. Murph was still giggling, his forearms against the bar and his head bent low as he tried to regain his composure. Cole took a sip from his drink and as he set his glass back down on the bar, he saw a girl walk down from the lobby. Her long hair, dark and curly, bounced around her shoulders with each step and her skin was olive with a slight tan.

She walked up to the bartender and spoke in French with him, no more than five yards from Cole. Cole watched the words roll off her lips and wanted desperately to understand her language. She carried a clipboard with her and must have worked at the hotel from the way the two of them talked. A long green cotton dress hung from thin straps over her bare shoulders and she couldn't have been more than 22 or 23, but she carried herself like she was older, or at least more mature than her age. Cole stared motionless. She was thin at the waist and through her dress Cole could see subtle but curved hips. The top of her dress hung low and Cole saw enough of her to lose his normally cool composure around beautiful girls. His mouth went dry. He bit down on his teeth, exhaled to steady himself, and just as he did, she looked away from the bartender and directly at Cole.

He was caught staring right at her and she knew it. He didn't look away, nor could he at that moment even if he had tried. She held her gaze for a few seconds more, tilting her head just a bit as she did. Her eyes were dark and beautiful as they looked directly into Cole's. For a moment, she looked as if she might smile just before she turned and walked back towards the lobby.

CHAPTER 12 – AMOUR

MURPH SLAPPED COLE on the back to snap him back to life. "Ohhhhh shit, Cole," Murph was shaking his head as he spoke. "I've seen that look before."

Cole took a handful of peanuts from the tray on the bar and blinked a few times to get his thoughts in order. "What look?" He tossed a few peanuts in his mouth and took a sip from his drink, still trying to regain his mental footing.

"The one you just had when you locked eyes on that pretty little thing that just rolled through."

"Yeah, she's a cutie, that's for sure," he replied casually, but kept the other more intense thoughts to himself.

What he wanted to do was describe every detail of who he'd just seen and the effect she had on him, but Cole knew better than that. Murph wouldn't have any of that talk in his present state. Cole had been around girls from all walks of life over the past months, many of them beautiful in so many different ways, but he couldn't shake the girl in the green dress from his mind. There was something different about the way she walked, the way she had looked at him deliberately longer than expected and then walked away.

He thought for a moment of taking a walk up the steps to the lobby to find her, but he knew well enough that he was drunk and sweating and would need a better game plan to make a worthwhile impression. Still, he found himself looking back up the steps, hoping he'd catch another glimpse of her.

Murph finished off the dish of peanuts and emptied his drink. The bartender made his way over and looked at Murph for confirmation to fill it back up. Murph nodded in the affirmative and the bartender shifted his gaze to Cole. He looked at the bartender for a moment then asked plainly, "Who is the girl?"

The bartender leaned in, apparently not understanding English very well.

Cole pointed back up the steps. "The girl. The girl in the dress. Who is she?"

The bartender looked confused for a moment and still he stared at Cole.

"La chica?" Cole said it a bit louder.

Murph chimed in, "Fucking brilliant Cole, he doesn't know English so you try Spanish in a French-speaking country?"

"Shut up Murph," Cole said it without taking his attention away from the bartender.

"La chica?" Cole was desperate.

The bartender grinned a bit then let out a soft chuckle. "Isabella."

Cole mouthed it to himself, *Isabella*, and the bartender laughed some more than spoke rapid French as he shook his finger at Cole and laughed.

"Merci." *Thanks.*

It was all Cole knew of the language and the bartender nodded, walking back to a corner of the bar to mix up two more drinks. It was getting late, and the first hints of sunset painted the tops of the scattered cumulus clouds that hung over the island. Cole was tired. As the bartender brought Murph and Cole their last round, he again spoke French to Cole, who wished once more to understand what the old man was saying. After a minute, the bartender retired to a quiet corner and took a seat. No one else was moving about and the hotel seemed all but abandoned.

It was the farthest thing from Panama City, where on the other side of the Caribbean the lights and sounds were most certainly booming. Here, there was a steady breeze pushing in from the east that wafted through the open-air bar and pressed against Cole's back. It was so quiet that he could hear the wind against the trees. Cole took a few minutes to soak it all in.

Murph finished his drink and parted ways, stumbling at times down the steps to his room. Cole did the same, down a long set to his floor, then down the same corridor to his room at the end. The whole time he thought again about turning around, but knew in his present state that he best wait until the morning. Entering his dark room, he pulled the curtains apart and slid the glass door open, stepping out onto the balcony overlooking the bay. To his left he looked out over the anchorage, with most boats entirely dark save for their anchor lights at the tops of their masts. He could hear the ripples of water slapping against their hulls and watched as they all turned slowly in rhythm with the subtle changes of the wind. The sun was setting off to the west, across the Caribbean. He thought about Panama once more, trying to keep his adventures in a positive light, but the more he fought it, the more Cole realized he'd gone too far with it all.

On the other hand, Cole felt that he could stay in a place like Martinique for a while. With his hands against the railing, he took deeper breaths and thought about Isabella. He would stay, he decided, until he had the chance to meet her. Even if she wanted nothing to do with him, he might stay longer in Martinique.

Back in his room, Cole pulled the bandage off his shoulder and looked at his newly formed scab as best he could in the mirror. It was still a bit red, but seemed to have closed up all right. With a light conscience, he turned in for the night, pulling the comforter almost over his head as he fell asleep.

He met Murph the following morning over breakfast. After enough cups of coffee and some pastries, Murph said he would be leaving that afternoon. There was some serious work he had to do. David had mentioned some shipments coming from Venezuela, and despite his initial protest, Murph was on the hook to make a move. He made it clear Cole could come along and island hop with him, but Cole was by then committed to sticking around for a while. He thanked Murph for everything but politely declined.

"It's the girl, isn't it?"

Cole shook his head to say no, but Murph just laughed. "I saw it last night. You're hooked. She's got you whether you like it or not."

Cole shook his head again, laughed, and replied, "No, it's not that. I could use some down time and this place has a vibe to it that I think might be good for me."

With that, Murph stood up and shook hands with Cole. He then wrote a number down on a napkin. "If you want to get in touch with me, call this number. Leave a message if I don't answer. I usually check it every week or so. It's my own number, so it's off David's radar, if you know what I mean."

Cole tucked it in his pocket and again shook Murph's hand. "Good times, Murph. Thanks for everything."

"Any time, bud." With that, Murph turned and walked away.

Cole sipped on a few more cups of coffee as the morning warmed up and the breeze filled in. By noon, he was down on the beach. Cole extended his left arm and worked it back and forth, feeling for any tenderness or signs of infection. Feeling none, he smiled at his good luck and figured that some saltwater might be just what he needed. He took a long swim out into the anchorage, and took turns at each mooring ball diving down to the bottom, anywhere from 20 to 30 feet down, then resurfacing and continuing on. At the end of the field, he turned and repeated his freedives on his way in. By the time he was back at the beach, he'd been in the water close to an hour and was thoroughly exhausted.

He spread out on a lounge chair and pulled his palm leaf hat down low over his eyes for the next few hours. By late afternoon, he had an appetite and meandered his way over to the dock and bar that sat out over the water. By himself now, he wondered about Murph and felt just a bit alone as he ordered a sandwich and rum punch. There were a few couples at tables around him, but once again it still seemed to be a quiet time of year and the hotel wasn't even half full.

Cole took his time with the sandwich and as he started on his second drink, he heard a faint hum in the distance that grew in intensity from a still unknown direction. Looking up from his drink, the others at the bar were looking around as well as the noise steadily grew. It was an airplane, of that much Cole was certain, but he couldn't see it. And then from the east, it screamed over at almost treetop level directly above the hotel then continued on in a steep climbing turn out over the anchorage and to the west.

Cole laughed out loud and howled at the peak of the engines' roar overhead. The bar shook just a bit and Cole felt the engines' thump in his chest. He recognized the plane when it passed overhead. It was Murph, at his usual antics and flying like a cowboy. The other patrons had all ducked, almost under their tables and now talked wildly and pointed to the west in the direction Murph had gone. Cole tipped his drink up in Murph's direction, finished it, and ordered another to toast his friend.

The fly-by had drawn out some of the other guests as well who now stood on the beach and looked around at the blue sky and puffs of clouds. They were too late to have seen it, but they'd all heard the rumble and roar when Murph practically clipped the top of the hotel as he passed. On the steps leading up to the main lobby, he saw a few people talking. He fixed his sight on one in particular with her back to him. He recognized the hair and felt his heart start to beat quicker. Long, dark, and curly—it had to be her. Forgetting about the drink, he excused himself from his seat and motioned to the bartender that he'd return to settle his bill.

Making his way quickly up the dock, he crossed the beach and slowed down as he got closer to the steps. He could see her face now and it was indeed Isabella, talking to some of the guests. He stayed back until she was done then walked an intercepting path to catch up with her. She noticed him as he came within a few feet. Cole smiled and did his best to say hello.

"Bonjour."

She was almost shy and smiled herself, stopping almost directly in front of him. She spoke French and Cole had no clue what she was saying, but he hung on every word and watched them roll off of her lips. She broke into a smile halfway through a sentence and tilted her head just a bit, locking eyes with Cole.

"I'm sorry, I don't know French at all."

Cole felt his mouth going dry and now, even closer to her than the night before, he saw that she was indeed as beautiful as he'd thought. Her eyes were green and her skin was tanned just a shade or two darker than her natural tone. She wore a skirt down to her knees and a light cotton shirt that fit snugly against her slender waist.

"Do you speak English?" She said it slowly in a heavy French accent, and Cole was relieved that she could understand him, even if only halfway.

"Yes, I do. I'm sorry I don't speak French."

"No, no, it is OK. I am working on my English."

She kept her hands crossed in front of her and Cole had to focus intently on her eyes to not spend too much time admiring her other attributes.

"Well, it's much better than my French."

She laughed and turned away for just a second then back to Cole. When she did, a few curls came out from where she'd tucked them behind her ear and they dangled just over her left eye. She was all at once again stunningly beautiful in a new way and Cole fought hard to keep his composure.

"So you are from America?"

Cole smiled like an idiot without saying a word, consumed entirely by the movement of her lips and her French accent. "Yes, I'm from the States. My name is Cole. How about you?"

She looked confused and asked what he meant by the "States." He nodded and apologized again, explaining the different meaning. She held a soft smile as the two of them worked through a conversation. In any other place and time, it would have been frustrating to have a language barrier like this, but Cole loved it. He spoke slowly and chose his words carefully.

When he was done, she introduced herself, saying simply, "I am Isabella."

She moved her hands for a second as if to suggest uncertainty about a hug or a handshake, then tucked them again back against her waist. It wasn't much, but it gave Cole the first indication that she might like him as well.

In time, she explained that she was in Martinique for the summer on an internship with the hotel. When she didn't know a word she wanted to say, she bit her lower lip and would use her hands in a circular motion, asking, "How do you say…?"

Cole needed no patience to help fill in the gaps, and after a few minutes, he asked what all the commotion had been about.

Isabella explained that someone had seen an airplane and thought it was going to hit the hotel, so she'd come out with the rest of the staff to see for themselves. Cole grinned and looked around to feign the same surprise that everyone else had shown. "Wow, I hope the plane is all right."

Isabella nodded and looked back up and around the sky.

Cole thought about Murph again and laughed just a bit. Had it not been for Murph's stunt, Cole would still be drinking on his own down on the dock. Now he stood not more than three feet from a girl that nearly took his breath away each time she looked him in the eyes. The sun reflected off her almost black hair and each time Cole finally thought he had control of himself again, she would turn or shift her stance in such a way that he was again beside himself.

"Well, I should get back to work upstairs." She shrugged her shoulders just a bit as she said it.

Cole nodded and they both looked at each other for a bit more than a second or two before Cole broke the silence. "Where is there to eat here besides the bar?"

Isabella repeated the question out loud with her French accent and Cole couldn't help but let out a half smile as she figured the question out.

"There are some cafes by the marina that are good."

Cole went all in and asked, "Can I take you to one for dinner tonight?"

"Yes, they have dinner tonight."

Isabella had misunderstood and it took Cole by a bit of a surprise. It had taken some courage to ask her once and now he had to clarify and ask again.

"No, no, I want to go to dinner with you."

This time he pointed at her and smiled.

"With me?" She was caught off guard and looked away almost immediately. Then just as quickly she looked back at Cole with a subtle smile and nodded yes. Her smile grew as she grasped the date he had just proposed.

"Well, OK then. Great. Where can I meet you?"

Isabella thought for a moment then pointed down towards the dock from where Cole had come.

"Seven o'clock?"

She spoke slowly as if the time was more difficult for her to pronounce and Cole nodded yes. "Yes, seven o'clock is great. I will see you then."

"OK."

It was the most captivating pronunciation of two simple letters Cole had ever heard in his life, and he watched her lips as they moved. As she walked back up the steps, Cole leaned against a low fence behind him and tried to shake the smile from his face, but could do nothing to hide it.

He returned to the bar, finished his drink, and settled the tab, signing the bill over to his room. Walking back to the beach, he went for one more quick swim and dried himself off in the sun before returning to his room. He showered and felt the sun and rum punch spinning him into an afternoon nap. Again under the comforter, he replayed in his head the conversation and Isabella's figure that had such an effect on him.

Waking almost two hours later, he dug through the clothes he'd brought with him for something clean. For the first time in almost a year he ironed a shirt to push out the wrinkles then hung it by the closet. His jeans were in fairly good shape, and he ironed them as well to clean them up a bit. He pulled his boots out of his bag and wiped them down with a damp washcloth. Stained dark brown, the once-white cloth had removed months' worth of Panamanian grit from his time in the city. With a cleaning, they looked worn in, but in good shape—much the same as Cole felt. He left the hat, fearing a young French girl might be scared away by too much of a cowboy. It was a bit after six p.m. when Cole dressed himself, took one last look in the mirror, and headed down the corridor to the steps leading down to the dock and bar.

He ordered another rum punch and took his time with it, letting the glass sweat and keep his hand cool. The bar was covered from the setting sun and the late-afternoon breeze blew hard from the east, like it did every evening. Cole looked out over the bay and opened a few buttons to let the breeze hit his chest. It was warm, but a better kind of warm than what he'd felt in Panama City. It was like riding the fishing boats during his runs to the north. When the boat was so close to the water and the breeze blew uninterrupted, it was never uncomfortable, regardless of the temperature.

After 30 minutes, Cole heard his name and Isabella's voice. She was next to him before he turned around and she smiled as if to ask if he was ready to go.

"Sorry, I lost track of time."

He felt his heart thumping again and was frustrated and amused at the same time at his inability to keep his composure.

"No, no, it is OK. I am a little early, I think."

She wet her lips with her tongue just slightly and it sent Cole further into a downward spiral. He couldn't help but laugh at it.

Isabella looked at him for a second, confused, and asked, "What did I say wrong?"

Cole could only shake his head and say, "You didn't say anything wrong. I just think that you are pretty and I want to tell you that each time I see you."

There, I said it, he thought. It was the only way to get back his senses.

Isabella looked away with a bigger smile than he'd seen as of yet before looking back at him and leaning in just a few inches closer. "Thank you, Cole. You are very sweet."

Cole left his drink unfinished at the bar, and with that, they walked side by side up the dock, down the beach at the water's edge, and up an older single-lane driveway to the marina. A channel with rock jetties on each side led in from the bay and opened up into a small harbor with finger piers around three sides of it. It was more than half full of a mixture of boats. Some were larger sailboats, but a good many were sport fishers and center consoles along with a few cabin cruisers. It was a fair mix of just about everything that roamed the Caribbean, some in worse shape than others.

Some folks sat on the open decks of their boats, but most were passing the evening tucked among the half-dozen or so restaurants that jutted up against the concrete wall that formed the perimeter of the harbor. There were also small shops, most of which were closed for the evening. Even with that, there were a good many people out for an evening walk or dinner.

Cole and Isabella walked the full length of the harbor before deciding on a restaurant a block in from the marina. She wore a pair of cotton shorts and a short-sleeve shirt with a loose v-cut across her chest. Led by the waitress to a picnic table by themselves, Cole let Isabella sit first, then sat beside her. She seemed a bit surprised at first, but then smiled when he nudged himself another inch or two closer to her. The side of his knee bumped up against hers, and she pressed back against him.

They were flirting. Cole had to remind himself to remain calm. They talked each other and the places they'd been. Cole spoke of the things he'd seen since leaving the States last fall, and Isabella wanted to know more about America. She'd been there years before, but her study of the English language had left her wanting to know more about the people who spoke it.

She ordered for them both, and promised it would be something good. The waiter returned with two small glasses of rum with a lime and some cane sugar. Isabella Called it Ti Punch, a customary drink in Martinique. She mixed hers with the lime and some sugar before motioning for Cole to do the same. He did, and the two toasted to each other. It was strong but good and the waiter followed with glasses of water.

Isabella took the greatest interest in Cole's explanation of the various accents in the United States. He knew he sounded like a fool, but she laughed and crinkled her nose each time he did an impersonation. When he got to the southern accent, he stayed there for some time and they had a second and third round of Ti Punch. By the time dinner came, Cole was relaxed around Isabella and she seemed to also be enjoying herself.

"You have not told me why you are here, Cole."

Cole steadied himself and looked straight into Isabella's eyes. A lie would be easy and he knew it. The way she looked at him was too much to cast her off like he'd done with other girls. He opted to ease her into the truth, and swore to himself that he would not hide anything from her if she truly wanted to know.

"I was driving boats over in Panama, and eventually just wanted some time away from it, so I caught a ride here."

Isabella pressed further and asked, "But why Martinique?"

Cole shrugged. "Because this is where the first plane I found was going."

She smiled at him and said, "You live very free, Cole."

He paused for a moment or two. His conscience weighed heavy after the past year. He was not yet free. "I'd like to think so," he said with a sigh.

He thought about her observation. "I was in the military for a while, before any of this."

Isabella leaned in with her head, her face expressing disbelief. "I don't believe you," she said playfully.

"No, it's true. I was. I was on a ship for two years and hated every minute of it. I was completely lost with my life. When they finally let me off, I didn't know what to do. I didn't think I'd ever want to be on the water again, and certainly not spend a year bouncing around from place to place. In a way, I'm still sort of lost."

She turned a bit more towards Cole and patted the top of his hand twice with hers before resting her hand on his. "But here you are now, Cole," she said and smiled at him.

He smiled back at her, not wanting her to pull her hand away. It was silent between them, but not as awkward as he'd feared. She pulled her hand away to take another bite from her plate and as she looked down, he admired her again before looking up at the waiter and holding up his empty Ti Punch glass.

Isabella put her fork down and pushed her plate a few inches forward. "I think I am full." She turned her attention back to Cole.

They talked some more about Martinique and things to do. Isabella worked five days out of the week, and at different times of the day. She named off a few of the places she'd been to since she arrived and told Cole of one beautiful spot, *Le Diamant,* that was off to the south. Cole wondered how anything could be better than the views he'd already seen from his hotel, but Isabella seemed certain *Le Diamant* was even more of a sight.

The waiter arrived with two more drinks, and Isabella and Cole both stirred theirs and tipped glasses at each other before polishing off their last for the night. Cole paid the bill with his credit card from the Coast Guard severance. He hadn't touched it since leaving Key West. He flashed back to Panama for a moment and blinked a few times to straighten his thoughts out.

Isabella put her hand on top of his again and all the confused thoughts of Panama vanished. They meandered again around the marina, talking as they went. Cole pointed out features of the boats that he liked or didn't like, and Isabella asked about the differences between America and the Caribbean.

At the far side of the marina, they walked past another hotel that hugged the opposite jetty leading into the harbor. Tall trees lined the water and the jetty rose up a few feet above the dirt to separate the land from the sea. Isabella stepped up on a rock and Cole instinctively reached out and took her hand for balance. She walked along a few of them, hopping across one to another. Cole walked along with her, holding her hand and admiring her charm as she stepped out from one and onto another.

Finally she stepped down and exhaled as Cole turned to face her, his left hand still holding her right. They were further back away from the hotel now, alone among the evenly spaced trees.

Isabella said, "Let's sit for a while." She picked two adjacent rocks and sat down, tapping the other with her palm and motioning for Cole to sit beside her. The rock was warm from the day's sunlight, but there was just enough breeze filtering through the channel to make the air comfortable. A flashing green buoy bobbed just beyond the jetty, marking one side of the channel to sailors coming in from the bay.

Cole looked for some time out into the darkness beyond the jetty and the buoy before Isabella rested her chin on his shoulder. Bits of her hair tickled his neck, and he looked back just to his left, straining his eyes to look into hers.

"You look serious, Cole," she said with a little smirk on her face. Her teeth were white under the moonlight. "What are you thinking about to be so serious?"

She held her chin on his shoulder and he felt her arm come up against his lower back and partly around his waist. She was almost hugging him.

"I was just thinking about the ocean." Cole wiped any hint of seriousness off his face and shifted his attention back to Isabella. He felt her chest against his side and the onset of butterflies kicked in once again.

"Did I tell you already that you're pretty?" Cole looked for any reaction.

"Yes, you told me. I don't mind you telling me again." She lifted her chin off his shoulder but kept her arm around his waist.

Cole took a deep breath and pushed the butterflies back, looking out at the blackness beyond the channel. He was happy—immensely happy—to be sitting on that rock next to Isabella. Still, he looked down at the water inches from his feet and saw the tide moving in and out from the marina. The water, stirred by the stiff easterlies blowing outside, reminded him that the Caribbean would be there waiting whenever he decided to return.

"Should we walk some more?" Cole asked, and Isabella nodded.

He helped her back up, and as she dusted off her shorts, Cole couldn't help but notice her legs and how they led up to slender hips that she brushed with her hands. When she turned and looked at him again, he was grinning.

They walked back around the marina as the night began to wind down for locals and visitors alike. Most boats had only one light on belowdecks as they sat tied up to the wooden slips that wrapped around the harbor. One or two of the restaurants had guests still at the bar, but the waiters and waitresses were busy wiping down tables and pushing in seats.

Cole asked about the hotel and how Isabella had liked it so far. She replied that she was enjoying her time in the Caribbean compared to France. The days were sometimes long, but they went by quick enough, and on days off she was free to do as she pleased. The hotel had a smaller set of apartments next to the Bakoua where she stayed for the summer. Cole walked her along a side street until she stopped in front of a gate.

It took Cole a second to realize it was her apartment. She rolled up on the balls of her feet for a second, then back down as if to say she wasn't sure what to do next.

"Well, I should be going, then," Cole said, facing Isabella and looking in her eyes.

"Thank you very much for dinner, Cole." He could tell she was sincere when she said it, with her French accentuating certain syllables.

"When is your next day off?" Cole asked, reaching out and taking her right hand with the fingers of his left.

Isabella took hold of his and replied, "Tuesday, in two days."

Cole smiled and asked, "Can I take you to *Le Diamant*?"

"Yes, but how? Do you have a car?"

Cole grinned again and said, "No, but for you I'll get one."

"I would like that."

As she backed away, Cole held onto her hand, and she gripped tighter. Cole read the signal and gently pulled her back in, kissing her when their faces met. He brushed the palm of his right hand up against her neck, rubbed the pad of his thumb against her earlobe, and tucked a lock of her curly hair back behind her ear. He leaned in and held his left hand against the lowest part of her back, pulling himself closer. They kissed for some time before Cole pulled away, not wanting to push too far.

Isabella seemed embarrassed by her loss of modesty, but Cole kept the palm of his right hand against her neck again and ran his fingers through her hair, then kissed her one last time.

"Thank you for tonight, Isabella. I will see you Tuesday?"

She smiled back at him. "Yes, Tuesday. *Le Diamant.*"

With that, she unlocked the gate and walked inside. Cole doubled back down the side street then down the same single lane that led back to the beach and the hotel. He had not felt this good in months. If he never saw Panama again, it would be too soon.

Walking up the far steps towards his corner suite, Cole unlocked the door and walked into the air-conditioned dark room. Turning on one light by the bed, he pulled back the curtains and opened the sliding glass door to let in the breeze coming off the bay. Stepping out for a moment, Cole watched the moonlight reflect off the water below in the cove. The boats in the anchorage to his left hadn't moved since that afternoon, and they bobbed gently against their moorings, their anchor lights swaying at the tops of their masts.

Cole heard a knock at the door. Unsure as to who was out this late, he walked back across the room and opened it to see Isabella standing there.

"*Bonjour.*"

Isabella laughed and replied, "At night, we say *Bonsoir.*"

Idiot, he thought. "Well, in that case, *Bonsoir.* How did you know which room was mine?"

"I do work here."

Idiot, he thought again. Cole scolded himself for even asking. He took a deep breath and stepped aside to let Isabella in.

She walked partly in past the doorway and looked at Cole, suddenly a bit unsure of herself.

Cole let the door close behind them, smiled, and wrapped both his arms around the small of her back. Picking her up, Isabella wrapped both her legs around his waist, kissing his neck. Any doubt left her mind as Cole walked over to the bed and let her down on top of the comforter. She laid there looking up at Cole, with her dark curled hair a beautifully tangled mess against the white pillows. She smiled at him when he turned out the light, and Cole laid down beside her.

CHAPTER 13 – BUCCANEER

DAYLIGHT WAS SNEAKING through the curtains when Cole opened his eyes. It was still early, but the sun had climbed up and over the peaks inland and to the east. The air conditioning hummed and the room was still dark save for a few random rays of dancing light. He was on his side, facing away from Isabella. Her right arm was draped across his torso, and her hand was flat against his collarbone. He rolled back towards Isabella and felt her warm body settle against his. She stirred and slid one leg closer to his under the blankets.

Cole ran his hand up and down hers and pulled it in tight against his chest. He didn't dare move again, not wanting to wake Isabella and ruin the most peaceful rest he'd had in years. After a few minutes, he couldn't resist and rolled over onto his right side to face her. Her arm was still across his chest, and she ran it under his left arm and pulled against his shoulder blade with the palm of her hand. She didn't seem to notice the stitches or the thin scab as she pulled him in close. With the little light in the room, Cole could make out curls of hair covering her right eye. He reached over and brushed them aside to see a playful look on her face. She laughed and pulled her bare chest against his, rolling Cole onto his back.

Cole spoke first, barely able to contain a smile. *"Bonjour."*

Isabella giggled again, this time softer, but with the same fervor. There was a warmth to her that Cole felt in his core.

"Bonjour, Cole."

They kissed some more, and ran their hands back and forth against each other's skin. After a few more minutes, Cole rolled over and reached for the phone. He dialed the service number and after a few rings, a woman's voice spoke rapidly and in French.

"Room service?" Not yet entirely awake, Cole's voice was grainy.

The woman continued and Cole sensed her frustration with his lack of French speaking skills.

"Coffee?" Cole held the phone away from his face after he said it and looked back to Isabella, who was holding her hand over her mouth and giggling. He passed the phone to her, but she shook her head and laughed more.

"How do I say coffee?" He whispered and was laughing now at himself as well.

"Cafe," Isabella spoke quietly and laughed again.

"Two Cafe."

Cole squinted his eyes, recognizing his mistake before it even left his lips. He looked back at Isabella who had rolled over on her back and was laughing even harder now, shaking her head. The woman on the other end of the phone continued to yell at Cole, but her insults didn't matter since he couldn't understand what she was saying.

"A little help?" He laughed again.

"*Deux Cafe.*"

Isabella pulled a pillow under her head and rolled back onto it, her eyes still staring intently at Cole.

"And *crêpes!*"

He remembered something in French. It wasn't exactly what he wanted for breakfast, but in a moment of clarity he had to take it.

"Duh Cafe and crepes. Merci!" He hung up the phone. Maybe it would come; maybe it wouldn't. He rolled back over to Isabella, pulling himself on top of her. She kissed him on his lips and ran her hands through his matted hair. Cole pulled at the sheet to clear it from between them. Tucking it behind him, there was nothing between him and Isabella. She ran her fingers across his back.

"Thanks for the help back there," Cole said with a grin.

"They would recognize my voice. I would be in trouble. Besides, you did fine." She reached her head up to kiss him, and he followed hers back down to the pillow. Cole shook his head in disbelief.

Rolling over and out of bed, Cole cinched up his board shorts and walked over to the curtains, pulling them open to see the sun already up and reflecting off the cove in front of his room. He squinted at first before his eyes caught up to the bright light. Turning around, he saw that Isabella had pulled the comforter up almost to her nose. All that remained above were her eyes looking directly at him and her dark hair tucked behind her head.

She pulled the comforter down to reveal her face, and she let out a forceful sigh. "I have to work today." She sighed again, rolling to her right and reaching down for some of her clothes.

Cole hurried over to the bed and crawled back in, reaching over her hip and up to her chest. He pulled himself tight against her and kissed her neck. "You'll stay for breakfast, right?"

"If they hurry."

She leaned back, and Cole pulled the comforter over both of them.

Twenty minutes later, Cole heard a knock at the door and got up to answer. Isabella reached down for her clothes and stood up to dress, smiling at Cole as he nearly tripped making his way to the door. He insisted on taking the tray at the door and repeatedly thanked the hotel worker before closing the door again. Setting it down on the bed, he lifted the lid off the tray to see a healthy pile of crêpes with fruit on the side.

"I didn't do too badly."

Isabella, now dressed, walked over and kissed him on the cheek before fixing herself a cup of coffee and picking a few pieces from the thin pancakes. Cole dropped some sugar in his coffee and motioned for Isabella to follow him. Picking up the plate and his coffee, he walked past the bed and over to the sliding door, nudging it open with the back of his hand, then walked out into the morning air and over to the covered balcony. Isabella followed and sat on a chair looking over the bay. Cole set the food down on the table next to her and sat in a chair on the other side of Isabella. She tucked one leg under her and swung the other gently back and forth, taking little sips and alternating her gaze from the cove in front of them to the anchorage off to the left. She picked again at her food and ate most of the fruit, lifting each piece of melon or strawberry one at a time with her fingers.

They were quiet for some time before Isabella said, "It is beautiful here, don't you think?"

There was a veranda over the balcony that shaded bits of daylight against her face and beyond Isabella all he saw was the sunlight reflecting off the water out to the west. "Yes, it is."

He didn't need to say anything else.

They sat that way for a while before Isabella finished her coffee, took one last bit of crêpe, and stood up. Cole stood as well and walked her back into the room. She looked around one last time then leaned up against Cole, both of her hands wrapped around his neck.

"I'll see you tonight?" Cole asked already knowing the answer.

"Oui," she said back.

"Can you bring some scissors?"

Isabella looked at him for a moment, then asked, "For what?"

Cole grinned, replying, "Nothing much. I just need you to help me with something."

She shrugged her shoulders and said, "OK." She smiled again, kissed Cole, and walked over to the door. Holding it open for her, Cole watched her walk down the steps to the right and disappear. Making his way back into the room, across it and out onto the balcony, he watched Isabella stroll down to the water's edge and then walk along the beach to the other side of the hotel to her apartment. When she was gone, he spent another half hour in the same seat and finished off what was left of the breakfast, replaying the previous night in his mind.

With the day to burn, he set off for a swim out into the anchorage and spent nearly an hour diving to the bottom of each mooring ball and then out to the next. By the time he was at the edge of the anchorage, the water must have been 40 feet deep and it took nearly all his strength to reach the last mooring before he flipped and flutter-kicked his way to the surface. He kept a good pace back in through the anchorage and waved at a few boats as he passed.

Exhausted when he walked back up onto the sand, Cole went back to his room, grabbed his cowboy hat, and made his way back to the beach, where he nestled up under some palm trees on a shaded lounge chair. Tipping his hat down low, he spent the rest of the morning on the beach, watching the vacationers play in the water and on the sand.

By the afternoon, he was hungry, but wanted to wait for a full meal until he was with Isabella again, so he showered and changed into some clean clothes. Heading up to the bar where he'd first seen her, Cole pulled up a stool. The same aging bartender brought over a plate of green olives and peanuts. Cole ordered a Ti Punch to slow his appetite. He nursed it for some time, mixing peanuts and olives after each small sip. After three drinks and almost two hours of sitting, Cole was restless and opted to take a walk.

Onto the beach and past the hotel, he walked along the water's edge rather than cutting up and into the marina. Beyond the Bakoua, the remains of a second hotel sat, overrun by lush tropical vegetation well on its way to reclaiming the structure from what must have been an illustrious past. Past the Bakoua's cove, locals swam in two smaller coves. Cole could see small rock walls overgrown with plants and vines. There was a tiled patio that was almost entirely covered in sand. At one point, it must have been a grand reception area or dance floor, but now only small bits of tile remained and were nearly consumed by the blowing sands.

Cole ventured out onto the last 100 yards of a coral peninsula with palm trees and brush in the middle. It stuck out and up nearly into the middle of the bay and held a commanding view of all approaches into Fort De France. As he rounded a rock ledge, he was not surprised to see a rusted gun emplacement. The tripod was all that remained, bolted into a concrete slab. Looking out over the bay, Cole wondered about the men who'd stood watch over the centuries. Surely even before this emplacement was built, there had been men who stood guard in the days of cannons and ships of sail.

Leaning into the stiff east breeze, Cole smiled as it swept across his face and chest. It was ironic to him that he stood over what once was bitterly contested ground, and yet no more than 100 yards away people bathed and soaked up the sun's rays without any care. He stepped up into the breeze and walked along a narrow path until he found another emplacement. Beyond that was a third, and he saw a break in the undergrowth behind him and slipped in between some trees and shrubs towards the center of the coral peninsula. There was an entire compound, now just a concrete shell of what had been a garrison. Smaller structures, most no bigger than a single room, surrounded a main gathering area. Cole wandered for some time around it. There was graffiti on the walls, and like the abandoned hotel, the Caribbean undergrowth had done its job of reclaiming it.

After wandering the perimeter, Cole walked back out to the foot trail he'd followed and stood once more in the easterly breeze. He felt gusts push up against his chest, and the wind was blowing at times up to 30 knots. It was the same wind that had carried ships from Africa over to the Caribbean and beyond, with their cargo of spices, sugar, rum, and contraband. For the first time in days, Cole thought long and hard about his own travels and the drugs he'd run up to the north. In some way, he was no different than the buccaneers who warred with merchant ships centuries before. Cole thought about the abandoned fort in the greater context of the Caribbean, both the one he knew and the one of centuries past. Looking back to the west, he feared that it was only a matter of time before he turned a boat northward and ran her up to speed. He knew he couldn't hide in Martinique for the rest of his life, no matter how badly he wanted to.

Strolling back to the Bakoua, Cole made sure not to break a sweat before meeting Isabella. When he walked back up the beach, she was sitting on a bench up above where the sand turned into low-cut grass. She smiled when she saw him and waited for him to come take a seat next to her.

"What shall we do for dinner?" Isabella asked. She was wearing a pair of khaki shorts and a white cotton shirt buttoned halfway up. Cole thought there was no way she hadn't tried for the effect it had on him. When she spoke, she held the tip of her tongue between her teeth as she pronounced the words with her soft French accent.

Cole thought for a second. "I like the marina. Is there something there?"

Isabella nodded and they set off up the same path and over into the marina district. They took seats at an outdoor cafe and split a pizza. Cole drank beer and Isabella sipped at a glass of wine, their seats close to each other and facing out towards the docks. She rested her foot over the top of his, and Cole was content to spend the night watching the boats bob back and forth in their slips.

After they finished dinner, they walked around the marina to the far side of the channel and took seats on the rock jetty like the previous night. They talked more about the islands and America. Isabella asked Cole questions and he filled in the gaps, explaining how he'd found his way to Martinique. He hesitated at first, but committed himself to telling her the truth about the drugs. When he talked, she rested her head against his shoulder and listened.

Her affection was undeniable and Cole felt compelled to explain himself. "Would you still like me if I've done some bad things?"

Isabella lifted her head off his shoulder and looked him in the eye. She thought for a moment and held the tip of her tongue again just barely between her teeth.

She asked, "Would you do anything bad to me?"

Cole shook his head and replied, "No, not a chance."

In the back of his mind, Cole worried that he would fall back into the scene he'd left and in some way leave her hurt.

"Would you ever hurt someone else?"

Cole shook his head then thought for a moment. "If they were going to hurt me, then yeah, I think I would."

He thought back to the side street in Panama and how he'd shot the passenger who had turned to go back towards the car. *Surely the guy had reached for a gun, and considering they'd tried to kill me only moments before, killing in turn was the only option.*

"I trust you, Cole." She bit at her lower lip waiting for his reply.

He paused, thinking carefully about the right words. "You are something special to me, Isabella. I won't hurt you."

She smiled, happy with his answer. Cole looked away before she could see his face. Panama was heavy on his mind for some time thereafter.

They walked back through the marina, past Isabella's apartment, and onto the beach. Taking the far steps up to the breezeway, they made their way to Cole's room. Locking the door behind him, Cole walked over to the sliding door, opened it and the two of them walked out onto the veranda. Cole sat on a lounge chair by the railing and Isabella sat in his lap, her head against his chest.

"I almost forgot, I have the scissors," Isabella said as she stood up and went back to the room for her purse.

Returning a minute later, Cole had pulled off his shirt and pointed to his shoulder, saying, "I need you to cut these stitches out."

Isabella ran her fingers across the back of his shoulder and asked, "What is this from?"

Cole dismissed it as nothing, saying, "Just a cut I got in Panama."

She shook her head and touched his shoulder again. "This is more than a cut," she said, before snipping at them, one by one.

When she was done, Cole ran his fingers across the scab that had formed and thought back to that night in Panama. Isabella sat back in his lap and leaned against his chest, asking again, "What happened to you in Panama?"

Cole smiled at her and replied, "A lot, but it's over now."

Content, Isabella rested her head against his chest and Cole played with the curls in her hair. Before long he felt her nod off to sleep. Staying there for some time, Cole watched the night sky before finally picking her up and carrying her back into the room, where he settled both of them into bed. Cole pulled the sheets back and Isabella, half asleep, undressed from the waist up. Then once she'd pulled the sheets back up and over, she smiled shyly at Cole then threw her shorts at him, setting her head down on one of the pillows all the while still staring intently at him.

Cole dropped his shirt and shorts on the floor and crawled in next to her, pulling the sheet up to his neck to ward off the chill of the air conditioning. They pressed themselves against each other and their arms intertwined. With Isabella's head against his neck, Cole felt her curled hair tickle his lips and took a deep breath of the fruit smell of her shampoo. He pulled once more at her to bring her body in closer and then he kissed her on top of her head. They were soon asleep.

When Cole woke, Isabella was already stirring in bed. She kissed him when he first opened his eyes and told him she had to go get some things from her apartment. He watched her dress and re-minded her again just how pretty she was. With a smile, she blew him a kiss and before walking out the door, she turned and said, "Diamant" with her cute French accent.

"I didn't forget," Cole said matter-of-factly and Isabella smiled, disappearing behind the door.

When it shut, Cole took a deep breath and worked his way out of bed. He went for a quick breakfast then over to the lobby. At first he tried to ask for a rental car, but he got nowhere with the older woman behind the counter.

"Taxi?" Cole said it slowly and felt like an idiot for thinking that would make any difference.

But the woman knew the word and picked up the phone, her eyes big as if she'd just figured out a riddle and was proud of herself.

"Taxi, in one hour...one hour..." He said it slower again the second time then pointed at the clock. "One hour, *Merci?*"

The woman smiled, "*Oui*, in one hour, OK."

Satisfied, Cole walked back to his room to grab a few things. He took his wallet and a clean set of clothes, putting them in a small backpack. As he was rummaging through his clothes, Isabella knocked at the door. Cole let her in and took one of the two room keys from the dresser and gave it to her.

"Here, one for you."

Isabella took it and seemed to not understand what he'd just said. In his rush to figure out what to bring, he'd spoken too quickly and lost her. He stopped what he was doing. The truth was that he loved more than anything how she had a way of calming him down. With her French and his English, he had to think about his words carefully and enjoyed watching her think through the things he'd said. He did the same with her words, listening to them and then thinking about their meaning before reacting. Cole knew he could spin himself up when needed, but things worked best with Isabella when he took his time. She forced him to relax and he loved every minute of it. Even better was the fact that she had no idea she did it.

He pointed at the key in her hand and smiled at her. "You keep this. You can come in or go whenever, but I'd prefer it if you just stayed right here."

She thought for a second or two and he saw a smile grow as she tucked the key into the pocket of her shorts.

She looked at him from barely a foot away and spoke. "OK. I like your bed better than mine." She grinned and bit at her lip.

Cole wrapped his hand behind her neck and pulled her in, kissing her quickly on the lips. "We should go." He let go and pointed towards the door.

"OK. We should go."

Her accent was just a bit different, and Cole figured out she was trying to imitate his voice. She was cute even when she was trying to be funny.

They walked the long way around to the parking lot, and Isabella waited outside while Cole walked back in to the lobby. He asked about the taxi and the older woman pointed out to the parking lot and nodded. Cole walked back down the tiled steps, into the midday sunlight, and over to Isabella. When he got to her, he saw a taxi pulling up from the street outside the gates. They walked over and climbed in.

Looking at Isabella, Cole whispered, "Airport."

Isabella took it from there and the driver set off through the streets of the little town, onto the highway and towards the airport. It had been a few days since he'd driven the route with Murph, and there was much more to see with daylight. To the north, there were the highest peaks, but even in the lower part of the island, the roads climbed and descended over rolling hills and through narrow passes. The morning traffic was light and not long after they'd set off, the driver pointed towards a rental car lot.

Cole was relieved to see signs from American companies. He stood a good chance of negotiating a deal on his own. As the driver pulled up, Cole hopped out and asked Isabella to wait with the cab just in case they had no cars to rent.

Walking inside, there was a woman a few years older than Cole behind the counter who greeted him in English.

Cole let out a sigh of relief. "What can I get for a week?"

"Well, Sir, what type of car would you like?"

Cole thought for a second and replied, "Something that a girl will like."

"So you want to impress her?" The woman laughed.

Cole shook his head, "No, not to impress, just something a girl will appreciate."

The woman nodded and smiled, "I have a convertible, just big enough for two."

"Yes, please. That would be great."

Cole passed her his credit card and American driver's license and two minutes later, he held the keys to a red Audi. Walking outside, he motioned for Isabella to come out. As she was stepping out, he gave the driver a handful of bills. Content with the money, which Cole had not counted, the driver waved as he drove off.

They walked over to the far side of the lot, and Cole clicked at different cars until he heard one chirp. When Isabella saw it, she looked back quickly at Cole to be sure it was the right one, and he nodded with a grin. Cole stepped in front of her and opened the passenger door. Isabella kissed him on the cheek and sat down. Cole walked to the driver's side, sat down and fired it up. It was an A4, not the fastest car ever made, but it purred well enough and fit the island atmosphere. Cole put the top down with the push of a button and as he drove off the lot, Isabella sat with her head against the headrest and looked over at him happily.

Soon they were cruising beyond the built-up outskirts of Fort-de-France and passed the turn back towards the Bakoua. They'd been on the road for almost an hour when Cole crested the last hills at the island's southern end and saw the water in front of them. Following a beach road, they stopped for some take-out food and drinks, then continued on until there were open sandy beaches. Cole parked, and they took their bags a few hundred yards further down the beach and set up under a sagging mess of palm trees. A few people walked up and down by the water, but up against the vegetation and under a palm tree, Cole and Isabella were all but alone.

Isabella took off her shirt and skirt, revealing her bikini. Cole was down to his board shorts and they walked for a bit, ending up down at the water's edge. Beyond the small waves rolling in and crashing up to the shore, a rock of an island sat a mile or two offshore. Cole stood there looking at it, the water up around his shins.

"I get it. The diamond."

Isabella wrapped both her hands around his arm and pressed her cheek against his shoulder. "*Oui, Le Diamant.* It's pretty."

Cole walked out until the waves smashed against his chest. He wasn't more than 20 or 30 yards offshore, but he could feel the wind filling in around him. He walked just a bit farther and ducked under the next wave. Resurfacing past it, he was now in deeper water. There must have been a fairly steep shelf, because the water moved around him in ways he hadn't felt for some time. As the next wave lifted him up, he saw Isabella still standing waist deep. He waved at her and she waved back. As the wave passed, she disappeared again and he was alone with the ocean. He took a deep breath and dove down to the bottom, now about 15 feet below him.

The water was noticeably cooler, almost cold at the bottom. He opened his eyes and swam a few yards back towards shore. The salt stung his eyes, but he could see the shelf in front of him a few more yards inshore. He paused for a moment, letting the cool dark water embrace him, before pushing off the bottom with his feet and rocketing back up to the surface. Taking a deep breath at the surface and feeling entirely refreshed, he swam hard to catch the momentum of the next wave and rode along with his body until the whitewater overtook him and the wave passed. He could stand up again and walked back towards Isabella.

Isabella splashed at him with her hand and asked, "Why do you do such things? You scare me."

Cole walked closer and picked her up. He thought, *If she only knew all the things I've done.* He didn't want to disappoint her, or scare her, or hurt her—but he knew himself well enough to worry that he would.

"I didn't mean to scare you. The water just feels too good not to jump in."

As they walked back up the beach to their spot under the tree, Cole looked back beyond the waves and saw the wind dancing up and over the crests, kicking salt spray over the tops. It was good to be with the sea.

They ate their sandwiches, drank their beers, and walked some more down to the far end of the beach before swimming again. Cole didn't leave Isabella this time, but he never entirely shook the thought of how the water had felt at the bottom beyond the waves. Either way, he was happy to play in the shallow water with Isabella. When they were good and tired, they went again back to their spot under the palm tree. It was now the latter half of the afternoon and the beach was almost abandoned.

Isabella was laying on her back on a towel. The sun had started to walk its way down over the hills to the west, and under the shade of the trees, it was dark and cool. Cole was laying on his stomach, propping his shoulders and head up with his elbows.

Looking at Cole, Isabella reached down to the string knot on her hip that held her bikini bottom together, tugging at it until the knot loosened. Cole shifted his elbows and pulled himself in closer to her. With her other hand, she untied the knot on the other side then pulled Cole on top of her. They kissed and laughed. She brought one knee over and rubbed her leg against Cole while he loosened the knot tying his board shorts together. They kissed more and Cole looked up to check that no one was on either end of the beach. They were all alone.

Isabella ran her fingers through his salty hair and pulled his attention back to her. By that point, he didn't care if anyone was walking on the beach. Her lips were salty and he kissed at drops of water on her neck. They were wrapped up in each other and by the time they were through, the sun was an afterthought below the western horizon. There was still some twilight, but it too would soon fade. Tired from their time in the water and under the palm tree, they collected their things and made their way back to the car.

Driving back to the Bakoua in darkness, Isabella rested her left hand on Cole's thigh and her head against the headrest. With the wind, her hair was the same curled and beautiful mess that Cole had admired their first night together. Cole powered through the ups and downs of the winding mountain roads, enjoying the drive and Isabella's company.

Back at the Bakoua, they made their way to Cole's room, settling into the same chairs from the day before to watch the moon come up. The easterly breeze blew with force, and after a day in the sun, it was chilly. As the first stars popped out, Isabella shivered. He smiled at her and motioned to go inside. They took a hot shower, washing the last bits of salt off their faces and dried off before crawling again under the sheets. Cole was in high spirits as Isabella wrapped her arm around his chest and tucked her head into and against his chest.

CHAPTER 14 – HITRON

OVER THE NEXT two weeks, Cole took Isabella all over the island when she wasn't working. At one point, he asked her to quit working altogether, but she refused. Disappointed, he still admired her work ethic, and her even more because of it. And so, on the days she was free, they drove across the island to the east side and spent evenings at quiet bars tucked up against forgotten beaches. Cole had taken a liking to the rum punch and enjoyed the different variations of it at the bars along the way. They spent one afternoon roaming through Saint-Pierre on the northwest coast, picking their way through the remains of a city where nearly 30,000 people had died in the early 20th century when a volcano had erupted. The beaches were still a dark and almost black sand, evidence even after more than a century of the destruction that had roared downhill from Mount Pelee, on the peak that towered over the town.

By the time he finally turned the car back in, both he and Isabella were exhausted. They spent the next two weeks eating at restaurants around the marina and evenings passed by as the two of them sat on the veranda and watched stars come out. Most nights, Isabella asked for a bottle of wine, and while Cole never could enjoy the taste nearly as much as rum, he obliged and the two of them worked through a bottle almost every evening.

Each day, Cole picked up bits and pieces of French and Isabella practiced her English. Conversations went on for hours and Cole relished the tranquility. He couldn't help but be happy when she would say something to him in French for him to repeat. When he did, she giggled and shook her head, hardly ever telling Cole what he'd actually said. Some nights ended before midnight, but many others went into the early hours of the morning. With a moon crossing the sky above them and the ever-present easterly breeze, Cole was content each night to sit until the morning and take in all he could. Most nights, though, Isabella gave him some hint when she wanted to call it a night.

Sometimes it was obvious. She'd get up from her seat and sit on Cole's lap, kissing him and pulling at his shirt. Other nights it was more subtle. She'd be quiet for a bit longer than usual and by the time it caught Cole's attention, she was looking directly into his eyes and he knew she wanted his affection. He never knew what it was that turned the tide. Perhaps it was the things he said in French or perhaps it was nothing, but most often Isabella led him back into the room, turned the lights out, and crawled on top of him.

Well into his second month in Martinique, he awoke one morning to find Isabella already dressing herself for work.

"You know you should just quit, right?" Cole's eyes were blinking as he shook the last bits of sleep away.

Isabella, pulling on her shoes, replied, "I promised them I would work the summer. It would not be fair. Besides, what would I do with all that time?"

"Stay in bed with me for starters." Cole grinned.

"I'll be back in your bed soon either way." Isabella flashed him a smile and adjusted her shirt before turning to walk out the door.

"Oh, Cole, your phone is blinking. There is probably a message for you. Call the front desk. I will see you tonight, *mon amour*." With that she walked out and the door closed behind her.

Cole rolled over to see the phone and indeed there was a small blinking red light. It took some time to figure out how to play the message, but eventually he found the right button. His heart skipped a beat when he heard it. It was David. In so many words, he wanted Cole to get in touch with him. Cole sat for some time thinking about it. In every way, he was happy to have put Panama behind him and did not want to return, especially now.

He went for breakfast to think it over. With a few cups of coffee, he mulled over his options. There really weren't any. Cole knew David would track him down wherever he ran, no matter how remote of a corner in the Caribbean. Perhaps David had a compromise in the works, but Cole had no idea. What he knew was that he'd have to get in touch with David to find out. Moreover, while Cole hated to admit it, the past two months had eaten up the majority of what severance he had left from the Coast Guard.

Returning to his room, he sat on the bed and reluctantly dialed. David picked up and said, "Hello?"

"David, it's Cole, returning your call."

David sounded genuinely happy to hear from him. "I think the weeks have been good to you, Cole. How have you been?"

"Good, yeah. Thanks for the advice. Martinique is something else."

David switched to business. "Like I said, Cole, we just needed some time to let things quiet down. I've got some work for you if you're interested. It's in your neighborhood, too. I assume you want to stick around there for a while."

Cole thought for a second before replying, "Yeah, the island vibe is a bit easier on me than Panama City. What's the job?"

David laughed. "Driving a boat my friend, what else?"

Cole felt butterflies forming in his stomach. "Where to?"

David laid out the plan. "You'll get a ride out to one of our boats around sunset. It'll be an hour or so offshore. Once the sun goes down, you run it up to Saint Croix and call it a day. And Cole, this is a fast one. You'll make forty knots easy."

Cole paused and asked, "When and where do you need me?"

"Great. Glad to hear it, my friend." David was enthusiastic. "Tomorrow afternoon around five at the marina. Look for a red hull and center console. They'll get you out to where you need to be. We'll get you back to Martinique in two days."

Cole said goodbye and hung up the phone. It didn't sound all that bad. Two days on the water and on the other side of the Caribbean. If it got him back in the good graces of David, that was a plus as well. If things had calmed down after Panama, Cole welcomed it.

He went through his usual routine of swimming out into the anchorage and back before taking a nap that afternoon under a palm tree. By the time Isabella tracked him down around sunset, he'd worked up an appetite. They ate at the same restaurant as their first night. After eating, Cole told Isabella he'd be gone for two days. She didn't seem too concerned at first, but she sensed something with the way Cole explained it to her.

"If you are worried Cole, then I am scared."

He shook his head, "No, no, don't be scared. It's a piece of cake."

She persisted, "I can tell you are uneasy and that scares me."

"I'll be fine." He smiled at her and kissed her forehead.

They walked around the marina and to the jetty on the far side of the inlet. They joked with each other and laughed when Cole tried to say things back to her in French. When there was a break in the conversation, Isabella draped her arms over Cole's shoulders and held just a bit tighter than she normally did. Cole knew she was doing all she could to hide her fears and he loved her for it. She was as strong as she was beautiful.

They turned in for the night early that evening. Isabella curled up against Cole as he lay on his back and ran his fingers through her curly hair, playing with each strand before tucking it behind her ear. He felt the rhythm of her breathing and realized soon that she'd fallen fast asleep, her right arm draped over his chest.

They were both up the following morning, and Isabella kissed him before heading out the door. She promised to see him at the marina before he left. With that, Cole was alone with his thoughts. After breakfast, he took a long walk out to the abandoned garrison and sat for some time by the rusting gun emplacements. In town, he bought a sandwich and tucked a second away for the trip that evening. He slept for a few hours that afternoon and woke just a bit after three. Eating again at the bar where he'd first seen Isabella, Cole drank iced water with lemons in it until he was about to burst.

Thanking the bartender, he picked up his backpack with a few necessities from his room and headed down to the marina. He was

15 minutes early, but sure enough there was a red hull with a center console tied off to the concrete bulkhead. Two men, one about Cole's age and the other a bit older were sitting on the bow. They exchanged nods with Cole and he tossed them his bag. Just before hopping down, he heard Isabella coming up behind him.

True to her word, she'd slipped out to come say goodbye. They hugged each other and kissed for a moment.

She held onto him by his waist. "Come back soon, OK?"

There was concern in her voice and she couldn't hide it. Cole assured her he'd be back in two days. They kissed one more time and he pulled her tight against him. Cole felt regret and he hadn't even left the dock yet, but he told himself it would be a quick trip.

He held Isabella's hand for one more moment, then hopped down to the boat. The two men untied her as the engine kicked and snorted to life. The driver reversed then pushed the throttle ahead and motored for the channel. Cole looked back again at Isabella. The breeze was blowing her hair to one side and he could see the outline of her body through the thin cotton shirt pressed against it. She waved and then wiped at her eye with her finger.

She cried a bit. There was no denying it. It tore at Cole's heart, but he was already on his way. All at once he wanted to turn around and call the whole thing off, but at the same time this run was already set in motion and there would be hell to pay if Cole backed out now. He ran both his hands through his hair, looking back at Isabella. She waved one more time and Cole did the same. After that, he was through the channel and she was gone.

The driver pushed the throttles halfway as they passed the last of the buoys marking the channel. Abeam the old garrison, he turned west and pushed them up all the way. Cole felt the clean air against his face and chest. As the boat turned with the wind, it backed off and they raced westward. Running downswell, it was a rough ride and Cole steadied his feet as Martinique trailed off behind them. The driver handled the boat well, turning and reading the backs of each wave as he carved a crisscrossing path until they were well clear of land.

For the next two hours, they ran hard at close to 30 knots. Cole had pushed thoughts of Isabella crying from his mind and focused on his return in two days. He was on the open water once again and the late afternoon sky filled with vibrant shades of yellow and orange against the dark blue water. As the sun started its descent below the western horizon, the driver slowed to idle. He was working off of a handheld GPS, much like Cole had done so many times. They waited for a bit, cutting circles out of the rolling water surrounding them.

When the sun was finally down, the driver pushed ahead for another 20 minutes and then slowed. Both the driver and the other passenger were looking ahead. The one on the bow pointed just left of the bow, and the driver turned to follow. Cole saw a blue tarp on the water draped over something. They driver yelled something in Spanish and someone from under the tarp began pulling it back and yelling back at the driver.

Cole was amazed at the boat that had been concealed. It was a monster, easily 40 feet long with three outboard engines. The entire boat was painted dark blue to include the engines, and she had one large center console about a third of the way forward. There were three guys on it when the driver of the red hull pulled up alongside. They looked like hell. Cole had heard of this tactic before where a boat would drive all night then pull a tarp over the top of it during the day to hide from aircraft and ships. By the next nightfall, it would pull the tarp and make the rest of the trip.

The three men on board looked like they were barely holding on. They'd been under a tarp for more than 12 hours with no breeze or fresh air. The Caribbean sun had practically cooked them. As they climbed over to the red hull, Cole and the older guy from the bow hopped over onto the Go-Fast. The driver stayed on the red hull. Cole looked his crewman over and realized quickly that the guy was stoned. *Whatever*, he thought. Cole looked back a bit unsure since he'd always run with Diego and Hector, but the driver waved and pushed himself away from Cole's new boat.

Cole turned the keys in the ignition and the engines came to life with the usual shudder. The fuel tanks were full along with two more drums behind him. Cole's stoned crew member went about checking the lines for a minute or two before giving Cole a thumbs up and taking a seat up forward among the bales. Cole figured they must have refueled that morning before pulling over the tarp. With a deep breath, Cole worked the wheel back and forth and gave it a once over. The GPS mounted on the console had a decent display screen, far better than the handheld ones he'd used in the past. It had a course to steer and bearing already in place and, with a charge from the boat's battery, would last as long as necessary. Between the gunwale and one of the fuel drums, Cole spied a rifle tucked away. He didn't bother to take it out and function check it, but it looked to be some variant of an AK-47.

It seemed like the big leagues. Here he had a boat most certainly purpose-built for running drugs and a Kalashnikov rifle tucked in the corner. Behind him were the fuel drums and in front of him were close to two dozen bales, of which he was certain were full of cocaine. Cole thought for a moment that he probably could have carried even more than was onboard, but it didn't matter either way. The driver of the red hull waved them off and with a red sky to the west, Cole spun the boat around and pointed northwest, towards Saint Croix, some 300 miles away.

Within minutes, Cole was back in his routine. The sun was gone and blackness blanketed the sky. Cole jammed the throttles up, and the boat surged up over the five-foot chop and powered through it like no other boat he'd driven. When he ran migrants, the boats were shaky at best in any sea state and rode horribly at max power. The pangas were more graceful, but still had to find a niche in any sea state to ride well, oftentimes at less power. But with this behemoth, waves didn't matter, nor did the wind. She plowed through waves and held her course. When she surged up and over a wave, she settled back down evenly and felt solid as she dropped her deep V hull back into the water. Cole glanced down at his GPS and he was covering 40 knots over the ground. He laughed a bit as the wind blew some sea spray against his face. He knew in a few hours he'd be tired of it, but at the moment he enjoyed the ride.

Two hours went by. Already a third of the way there, he heard what sounded like a faint whining from behind him and thought something was wrong with one of the engines. Yelling at his crewman to get his attention, Cole pointed back at the engines. Reluctantly, the stoned guy made his way aft, past the console and stood there for a moment or two, bracing himself against the console and the hull.

"Well, what is it?" Cole yelled but got no reply.

Damn pothead, Cole thought.

He yelled again, "Hey, what is it?"

Still no reply. Cole looked back at the engines then up over his shoulder. His heart sank. It was an MH-65 Dolphin helicopter, off his stern and no more than 100 feet above him. It caught up to Cole then offset to his port side and matched speed. It was HITRON, the armed Coast Guard Helicopter Interdiction Squadron that made a name for themselves employing precision marksmen from the cabin of the helicopter. The crews were trained to shoot out engines of Go-Fasts. Cole had seen them come and go from *Delaney* and they prided themselves on a nearly 100-percent success rate. Operating alone at night and in the middle of the Caribbean, they were no-nonsense pilots and crews that had, over the years, made a significant dent in the amount of narcotics traveling north.

The whining sound was the fenestron, a somewhat unique tail rotor that made a high-pitched whine. Cole was an idiot for not recognizing it when he first heard it. The stoner just stood there next to Cole looking up at the helicopter in disbelief. There was no way of knowing from where the helo had come from, how much gas he had left, or where the ship was off of which he was operating.

Cole looked around for clouds, but there were none. All that was above him were stars and the moon. He clenched his teeth and told himself to think, but he had no options. Popping open the locker under the console, Cole rummaged around as best he could, looking for a flag of any country that he could wave to delay the Coast Guard's approval to stop him, but there were none that he could find.

He looked back up at the helicopter. With the moon more than half illuminated, he could see the gunner in the open cabin and the barrel of his rifle sticking out. He didn't know what it was, either a 240 Golf or M-14, but either way the precision marksman was trained on Cole. Keeping the throttles jammed, Cole zigzagged a bit, but the pilots kept ahead of his evasive turns. There was no use and Cole knew it. He had nowhere to go.

Forcing himself to stay calm, Cole played scenarios out in his head. *Maybe there will be a problem with their approval process and I'd luck out? Maybe they'll run out of gas?* Just as the thought crossed his mind, the gunner opened up with a deafening volley of automatic fire across the bow. Cole saw the spray come up where the rounds impacted the water. Moments later a second volley crossed his bow. Cole knew it was protocol and in another minute or two, the gunner would switch to his .50-caliber rifle and take aim at the engines.

The stoner was sitting down, expressionless and staring ahead. Cole shook his head just as a single shot rang out, and Cole felt the blast against his eardrums. Following the shot, the boat swerved a bit and Cole looked back to see his port engine destroyed. The bullet had impacted the engine and shattered the cowling. It had broken the mount as well, and the remains of the engine were canted to one side. Cole's ears were ringing when the second shot took out the center outboard with similar results.

Fuck. Cole was down to one engine and the boat had slowed to 12 knots.

He had a hard time controlling her and thought about just shutting the last engine down to spare his ears from a third shot. Before he could finish the thought, a third and final shot rang out and the last outboard sputtered and died. Cole's Go-Fast quickly came to a full stop and he was left dead in the water. His ears were painful and he thought perhaps he'd burst an eardrum, but that was the least of his problems. The MH-65 climbed up and into an orbit around him for some time before flying off to the west.

Cole was left alone. Without the engines, the only sound was the waves lapping up against the hull. It was peaceful and eerily quiet. Cole scanned the horizon for a C-130 or P-3, but saw nothing. *How had they tracked me down so early into this run?* On top of that, he was far to the east of the major drug corridors. It didn't make any sense, but then again it didn't matter. Cole sat on the railing of the boat for some time and mulled over his options. Someone was coming for him and he had to act quickly to save himself. If he tossed the bales overboard and they didn't sink, he was screwed. Even if he ditched the drugs, the boarding team would run an Ionscan test and it would surely come up positive.

The only option was to burn it. He had enough gas left in the tanks. He just needed a match. He dug around a bit but found none. Opening up the battery compartment, he pulled the battery out and set it down on the deck then found a knife in the console storage bin. He stripped wire off of some cables coming out of the console and wrapped them in a loose coil. He then gathered a few rags and waited, scanning the horizon for a hull. It was another hour or so before he saw it, on the horizon to the west. It looked like a cutter, maybe even the Coast Guard.

Twenty minutes later, he could see the wake of the small boat coming towards him at less than a mile. Cole went to work. He stabbed the fuel barrels near the bottom and fuel started to spill out. The stoner, unbeknownst to Cole, had been snorting coke from one of the bales for some time and was now a shit hot mess sitting on the deck. Cole motioned for him to jump overboard, but the guy didn't process it.

"Jump, you dumbass. JUMP!" Cole motioned again and the stoner started to stand up.

Cole soaked a few of the rags in gas then set them down next to the battery. With two of the rags that were still dry, he held the wire and touched it against the connectors. It sparked a bit then went out. The boat rolled and the battery slid away from him.

"Fuck. Come on," Cole said as he looked up to see the small boat closing in on him.

He pulled the battery back in close. The smell of gasoline came and went with the breeze and Cole knew he was sitting on a time bomb, but he was committed at this point. He touched the wires again and they sparked. With his other hand covered by a dry cloth, he picked up one of the gas-soaked rags and touched it to the wire. It erupted and nearly singed his entire face when it did. With the rag completely engulfed in flames, Cole dropped it on the deck, grabbed a dry rag, and adjusted it better protect his hand.

Standing up on the bow, Cole threw the burning rag aft and watched it catch a pool of gas by the console. Satisfied that the boat would explode any second, Cole jumped over the side. When he hit the water, he went completely under and took a few strokes away from the boat. He emerged and looked back to see flames rising up from the aft portion of the boat, but it still hadn't spread forward to the drugs. Cole rolled and swam hard away from the boat and as he did, the fuel tanks exploded, sending a wave of heat against the back of his head. Thick smoke bellowed into the night sky and obscured the boat when he looked back.

Satisfied that he was far enough away, Cole treaded in place and watched it burn. Before long, the hull was gone and only bits and pieces still floated in the debris field with flames all around them. Cole wiped at his face and cupped saltwater with his hands, pouring it over his head to wash away any traces of the drugs. The evidence was gone and for that he was relieved. Still, he was now treading water in the middle of the Caribbean at night. The sound of burning and smoldering debris crackled like a wood fire as Cole spun around a few times, looking for the small boat.

When he finally saw it circling the debris, he yelled and waved. The boarding team spotted him and turned in his direction. As they approached, Cole waited patiently until it was nearly beside him. One of the boarding team members pointed a shotgun at Cole as he floated in the water.

Cole lifted both his hands out of the water. "You got me," he said with a grin.

"Cole? Is that you?" It was Wheeler.

He reached down and offered a hand to Cole and pulled him up and over the side. "You have got to be fucking kidding me, Cole," Wheeler said, partly pissed and in complete disbelief.

"Nice to see you, Wheeler."

Cole wiped the water away from his face as he sat on the side of the small boat. One of the boarding team members kept his M9 pistol pointed at Cole.

"What the fuck are you doing down here?" asked Wheeler.

Cole smiled. "Fishing trip. I guess it went bad."

Wheeler shook his head in disbelief. He radioed back to *Delaney,* "One onboard, we're RTB."

Cole spoke up, "No, there are two of us. There's another guy."

Wheeler looked at Cole. "It's just you man. We didn't see anyone else."

"No, there's another guy, he jumped before I did."

"We're taking you back first. Then we'll look some more."

As the small boat sped back to *Delaney,* Cole looked over his shoulder at the debris. There were only few pieces still burning, but almost nothing was left. *What had the stoner thought when I told him to jump? Maybe the son of a bitch didn't know how to swim, or maybe he was paralyzed by fear and the coke running through his veins.* Either way, if Wheeler hadn't found him by now, he was probably gone. Once again, death was Cole's companion and the gravity of it all began to sink in.

Cole wasn't smiling anymore. He looked ahead and saw the dark hull of *Delaney.* It had been almost a year, but now he was going back on *Delaney* and this time he'd be in handcuffs.

Fucking Karma, he thought. The MH-65 was shut down now on the flight deck and Cole could see a group on the fantail waiting for his arrival. He knew the drill.

When the small boat pulled up, Cole climbed the ladder and was quickly cuffed, then led up to the flightdeck. Wheeler was ahead of him and disappeared through the same hatch from which

Cole had walked through when he left the ship the previous summer. The boarding team members led Cole to the starboard side of the hangar and took the handcuff from his left wrist off then attached it to a pipe. They set a blanket down and Cole took a seat on it, his back against the hangar.

The aircrew was doing a post-flight cleanup of their helicopter before they pushed it into the hangar and closed the hangar door behind them. Cole watched in silence as they cleaned up the last bits and pieces. One of the boarding team members sat on a chair a few feet from Cole, keeping an eye on him. The gunner from the MH-65 was stowing a few things inside the cabin and caught Cole looking at him.

Cole asked, "Was that you shooting?" The gunner nodded that it was. "Nice shot, man."

The gunner stopped what he was doing and looked at Cole with a half a grin on his face. He asked, "Is it true what they said, that you were in the Coast Guard?"

Cole laughed and replied, "Yeah, I was. I was on this fucking boat."

The gunner went back to storing his equipment and thought about it for a few seconds. "Ain't that some shit," he said, without looking back at Cole.

Cole nodded, "Yeah. Life's a bitch sometimes." He pressed the back of his head against the bulkhead. His brain was flooded with bad memories of his two years on *Delaney*.

When the gunner was through and the flight crew had put their helicopter to bed, he nodded at Cole before disappearing into the ship. Cole was left with his one guard watching over him and settled, trying to find a comfortable position. The dim red lights were the same as Cole had remembered them. He found them still incredibly depressing.

As he adjusted his legs, a deep sadness came over him. For the first time in hours, he thought of Isabella. She was in Martinique waiting for him. There was no way he'd be back in two days now. He felt it in his stomach when he thought of how much she would worry about him. He had no way to communicate with her. She didn't know it yet, but Cole had managed to hurt her, just as he'd feared.

Cole was angry with himself and playing options in his head when the forward door swung open. Cole looked over to see Potts coming towards him, followed closely by Wheeler. As usual, Potts was agitated. Wheeler was trying to calm him down, but Potts was moving towards Cole like a freight train. As he came to within a foot of Cole, Potts stopped and Cole could see him breathing deeply and exhaling forcibly through his nostrils.

"You little piece of shit." Potts didn't know where to go with it. "What the fuck do you think you're doing, Cole?"

Even with the red lights, Cole could see that Potts was turning red.

Cole wasn't going to back down. *Fuck Potts,* he thought. *You tried to fuck me, well two can play that game.*

"I was fishing. Something went wrong, but I truly appreciate the Coast Guard's assistance. You guys are real heroes." Cole winked at him.

Potts reared back with his right hand and punched Cole in the face. Ducking away in time to deflect the blow to the side of his face, it still shook Cole pretty good. He was dazed for a moment, and when he steadied himself, Wheeler and the boarding team member were pulling Potts away. They got him back towards the door and Potts threw his hands up to cast them off of him and disappeared back into the ship.

Wheeler came back over to Cole. "Fucking A, Cole. You all right?"

Cole nodded. It stung. Cole could feel his left eye swelling shut a bit.

Wheeler looked at Cole's face. "I'll get some ice for you."

Cole shook his head. "Fuck it, Wheeler. I'm fine. Just keep him away from me—for his sake and mine."

Wheeler nodded. "All right, Cole. Get some rest if you can. We're flying you to Guantanamo Bay tomorrow."

Wheeler turned and disappeared back into the ship. Cole knew that beyond that bulkhead were air conditioning and dry beds. Not

20 feet from where he sat was the same damn rack he'd slept in for nearly two years. He preferred to sleep in the hangar rather than see that stateroom again.

His head hurt. His ears were still ringing from the shots and the left side of his head was swelling. He was thirsty and hungry and the salt water had begun to dry against his skin, making him itch. On top of that, the non-skid under the blanket poked through and made it impossible to sit for any amount of time without discomfort. Even with all of that, he thought solely of Isabella and the sadness that ensued left him feeling a low Cole had never known before.

CHAPTER 15 – DECEIVED

COLE SLEPT ON and off through the night. His guard swapped out at some point during the evening, but other than that he saw no one and heard nothing over the damned familiar hum of the ship. With the hangar door closed and no air circulating through the space, it was uncomfortably humid under the red lights. His sweat only made the dried salt water worse when it ran into his eyes. The hardest part, though, was not knowing where he was or where he was going. As was to be expected, no one told him a thing.

After several hours of being awake, Cole was relieved when a few enlisted folks appeared in the hangar and opened the hangar door, revealing the morning sun and blue skies. Still handcuffed, sweating, and uncomfortable, the sight of some blue sky lifted Cole's spirits. The ship rocked gently back and forth on a calm Caribbean morning as she steamed. With the sun rising off the stern, Cole figured they were making their way towards Guantanamo Bay. It was already warm, but as the salt air wafted through the hangar, Cole felt some breeze against his body for the first time in half a day.

Some of the crew looked at him, but most ignored their new prisoner as they went about their morning routine. Cole recognized a few faces, but none dared speak to him. Cole doubted the ones he knew even recognized him under his shaggy hair and a week's worth of an unkempt beard. Allison appeared through the hatch and brought with her a banana and a glass of water. Cole was relieved and excited to see her, but didn't know what to say.

"Hey, stranger." It was all Cole could manage and he said it with genuine despair.

"Your eye looks pretty bad," Allison said as she knelt down beside him, giving Cole the glass.

Cole drank it in two gulps and Allison passed him the banana. "Potts ordered us not to give you anything. He's in a meeting right now in CIC, so you better hurry." She took the glass from him as Cole mouthed the banana.

He felt a bit better. The left side of his face was tender, and he could feel the swelling around his eye. He passed the banana peel back to Allison.

Still kneeling beside Cole, she asked, "Is it true there was another guy with you?"

"Yeah, I don't know what happened to him." Cole looked away from Allison when he said it.

"We looked last night for a while, but never found anything. Now, they want you in Florida today, so we left a bit after midnight."

Both of them were silent.

She asked, "Does it bother you?"

Cole thought for a moment. "I don't even know where to start. The last year hasn't been what I thought it would."

Allison stood up and said, "I think you brought it on yourself, Cole. I worry about you like this. It's not you."

Cole looked up at her. "That's the thing. I don't know who I am anymore. Maybe I really am just a fuckup."

She shook her head disapprovingly and walked away. It hurt him to see her upset and Cole knew he had no one to blame but himself. Having hit a low, Allison was his witness to see Cole at his worst. He pressed his head back against the pipe behind him and looked out at the water behind him. He could see the wake of *Delaney* trailing off to the east. He then remembered everything he hated about that ship. *Why did it have to be Delaney that caught me?* Cole shook his head and took a deep breath.

By the afternoon, the aircrew was pushing the helicopter out onto the flight deck. Cole watched over the next hour as they prepped and fueled the MH-65. When it was time, Wheeler came up to

Cole, uncuffed him from the pipe, handcuffed him again with his hands in front, and brought him over to the cabin door. Cole climbed in and took a seat. Wheeler punched Cole in the shoulder, nodded slightly, and walked away. The same gunner from the night before was sitting next to him.

He leaned over to Cole. "If you try anything in flight, I'll fuck you up worse than whoever did that to your eye last night."

Cole laughed at the nonchalant way the gunner said it. He shook his head, reassuring the gunner, "Don't worry bud. I've lost this fight already."

The gunner grinned and nodded, then put his helmet on and the pilots started the engines. Before long they were airborne, and Cole was thankful to at least be off *Delaney*. The helicopter turned north and flew for almost an hour. In front of them, Cole saw land jutting up out of the dark blue water. He didn't know where they were and it didn't look like Cuba. They flew overland for another hour then landed on a massive runway and taxied in to a ramp surrounded by old concrete hangars. Cole recognized it as an air station. There were four helicopters on the pavement, three HH-65s and an HH-60 Jayhawk. On the far end of the ramp sat a C-130 with its crew scurrying around.

When the MH-65 shut down, the gunner escorted Cole over to the C-130. One of the pilots spoke briefly with the gunner then looked at Cole. He spent a few seconds looking him over before saying, "You are a pretty important mother-fucker, you know that?"

Cole, not knowing what he meant, replied, "Sorry, don't know what you mean."

"They sent us over here from Clearwater to get you to Key West today, and there's a whole damn party of people waiting for you. You must have really pissed someone off."

Cole thought about it and nodded. "Where are we, anyway?"

The pilot laughed and replied, "Borinquen."

Cole looked around and took a deep breath, not wanting to pass on the opportunity to take in the sights and smells of somewhere new. Under any other circumstances, Puerto Rico seemed like a nice place, and a far more pleasant option than Guantanamo Bay.

To relieve any apprehension for the C-130 crew, Cole assured them he wouldn't be any trouble. Two guys in civilian clothes then walked over from the hangar and introduced themselves as Coast Guard Investigative Service agents. They promptly swapped handcuffs with the gunner and took Cole by the arms. He stepped up into the C-130 through the crew entrance door and took a seat in the cargo compartment on a troop seat. Before long, the engines were up and running and the plane shook and rattled as they started a slow taxi. The C-130 felt massive compared to the MH-65 he'd been in before. Cole thought back to the C-130 crew from Panama and saw in this flight crew some of the same mannerisms and friendly back and forth banter as they prepped for takeoff.

The two agents stood a silent watch over Cole as they climbed up and away from Puerto Rico.

Several minutes into the flight, Cole turned to one of them. "I thought we were going to Guantanamo Bay."

One of the agents shook his head. "Change of plans. They want you in Key West," was all he said.

Three hours later they landed. The C-130 had no windows that Cole could see, so it was a boring flight with nothing but the two agents hovering around him. When the plane shut down, they brought him down the same steps to the concrete ramp and there were two black Chevy Suburbans with blue lights flashing under their grilles. They hurried Cole into the first one and drove off. At least now he had a window to look out of.

The plane had landed at the Navy base on Boca Chica and they drove almost 30 minutes to get to Key West. Speeding over the A1A bridge, Cole couldn't help but smile when he saw the familiar blue and green shades of water beneath him. It reminded him of better times. A few minutes later, they were back on Key West's main streets and Cole almost forgot his troubles as he looked around at the familiar intersections and side streets of Key West. He tried to put the window down, but the agent seated next to him stopped him from doing so, instructing him to roll it back up. Cole was forced again to face his prisoner status.

Before long, they pulled into a parking spot in front of an unremarkable multi-story building. Two agents escorted Cole inside, up a set of stairs, and into a conference room. He was still in handcuffs, and they left him by himself. It felt odd to be alone again, as it had been almost a day since he'd been caught. A clock on the wall showed a little after seven p.m. Through the tinted windows, Cole could see the rooftops of Key West and the setting sun to the west. He sat there looking out over the city.

After about 30 minutes, four men walked in. Two were in suits, but the others were in jeans and button-down shirts, their hair unkempt and long. Cole spotted bulges at their hips under their shirts, indicating that they too were agents doing a less than stellar job of hiding their sidearms.

One of the guys in jeans spoke first, asking, "How does it feel, Cole?"

Cole looked at him. "How does what feel?"

The guy laughed and said, "To be sold out like that."

Cole shrugged. "What are you talking about?"

The other guy in jeans took a turn at him. "How the fuck do you think we caught you, Cole? You think we just got lucky with a Go-Fast in the eastern Caribbean? Your boys sold you out. We knew you were coming and we nailed you—and now you're fucked."

Cole recognized it as the appropriate time to put on his game face. His mind hardened. The reality was they had nothing on him. He'd burned the boat and the drugs. The evidence, if any was left, was on the bottom of the sea floor.

Cole didn't want to piss them off, but he wasn't going to roll over either.

"I'm confused. Are you talking about my fishing trip?" Cole looked at both of them back and forth.

"Quit the shit, Cole. We've been watching you."

Cole tilted his head to one side and asked, "Who are you guys, anyways?"

"Three letter agency. You can guess from there."

The first guy pressed both his hands onto the table in front of Cole and leaned in. "Cole, you're left high and dry on this one. You've got nothing, so why not see if we can help you?"

Cole thought for a second. It was plausible that David would have tipped them off. He was in hot water over the Panama thing. Cole pieced bits of it together quickly in his head. On this last run, the stoner was his only crew, the boat didn't have as many bales as it could have held, and he'd been busted only a few hours into his trip. Perhaps David had bowed to pressure from his bosses or the other cartels to get rid of Cole. Still, the feds weren't really going to help him. If anything, they were looking for some charges to stick Cole with and put him away.

The second agent in jeans smashed his fist against the table. "You little piece of shit. You're scum, you know that? We've watched you since you left Florida and knew you were a piece of shit from day one."

Cole asked, "How did you know about me leaving Florida?"

The first agent in jeans intervened, saying, "Mickey told us all about you heading south, Cole. We've kept tabs on you for a while now. But your connection in Panama is the one who really sent you down the river."

Cole sat back in his chair, thinking back to Mickey. *Had Mickey really turned his back on me?* Cole asked, "How do you know Mickey?"

The first agent replied, "Are you surprised? Mickey's one of our guys, but he's not the point right now. You are."

Cole could see that they were pissed. He didn't want to risk another punch to the face.

The agents in suits sat back against the wall, but the second one in jeans seemed genuinely irate.

"Sorry guys, but I don't think I can help you. Come to think of it, I'd like to speak with an attorney."

He'd said the magic word. Mickey complicated things beyond Cole's comfort zone. Now, everything was potentially on the table. With the mention of a lawyer, the first two agents stood up and walked back towards the door, followed by the other two in suits who hadn't said a word. One of the guys in jeans turned to Cole before leaving.

"Cole, you're playing with life and death with these guys. I hope you know what you're doing."

They left him for nearly four hours in that conference room. It was almost midnight when one of the agents in jeans walked back in by himself.

"Cole, you're smart, I get that. But I don't think you understand everything that is going on here. They don't want you around anymore, so they gave you to us."

Cole nodded, "I was fishing. That's my story."

The agent wasn't pissed this time. He handed Cole an ice pack for his eye and said, "I know, man, but let's be honest. You look like shit. If you'll work with us, we can help you. I mean it."

Cole nodded again, put the bag against his still-swollen eye, and asked, "So what now?"

The agent looked at Cole for a second, took a breath, and said, "You can sit in jail and wait for a trial. Or you can turn this thing around."

Cole thought it over in his head. His decisions over the past year had proven time and again to be reckless. He'd gotten carried away with it all, that much he was sure of. Runs to Cuba were crazy enough, but spending half a year running drugs out of Central America had nearly cost him his life. Worse yet, he was nothing short of a traitor to his own country, all in the name of sticking it to Potts and *Delaney*. On top of that, he'd abandoned Isabella for stupid and selfish reasons.

Cole asked, "So how do I turn this around?"

The agent pulled a key from his pocket and unlocked the handcuffs on Cole's wrists. Cole rubbed his hands together as it sunk in that he still might have a chance. He was seconds away from spending the rest of his life in jail and butterflies formed in his gut. Even heavier on his mind was the thought that David had left him for dead. Cartels dealt in death on a daily basis and Cole was convinced, now more than ever, that he was a target.

The agent walked him down the hall and opened the door for him, out onto a patio. They both walked out into the nighttime air and the agent extended his hand.

"I'm Tony, by the way." He passed Cole back his wallet and a few things that had been in his pockets when he'd been caught. There was some change and his key to his room at Bakoua. It made him think of Isabella, although he tried to keep those painful thoughts buried as best he could. She was most certainly worried about him by now, as he'd promised he'd be back by now.

Cole shook Tony's hand, saying, "Thanks."

Tony started laying out a plan. "Cole, you've got some connections that we want to know about. For an American, you've been deeper inside one of the major drug cartels than any guy we've ever gotten our hands on. The honest truth is that it's pretty impressive what you've done. We want to exploit that to hit back at the cartel—and we need you to help us out. We want to get you back on the right team."

"What specifically do you want me to do?"

Tony laughed and replied, "There's a lot you're going to do, but for now I need a show of good faith. I need you to call your guy, tell him you're fine, that you got away, and talk with him for a minute or two while we trace the call."

Calling David was the last thing Cole wanted to do, and he took a few minutes to stare out over Key West. *Why had I ever left this town?* Cole cursed his own decisions, and at the same time wondered if he could still turn it all around.

Tony was still trying to convince him. "Cole, this can be a turning point for you."

Cole asked, "Does it keep me out of jail?"

"Yeah, it will. We need to keep tabs on you, but you'll be more or less free to do your own thing during the downtime."

"What do you mean, downtime?"

Tony nodded again, realizing Cole still didn't grasp the entirety of the plan. "Cole, you're going back in at some point."

Cole shook his head and asked, "Back in? You're going to send me back to Panama?"

"Yeah, Cole, you're going to have all the support you need, but you're going to be at the tip of the spear on this one." Tony took a deep breath. "You don't seem like the kind that minds a little bit of danger."

Cole stared out again into the nighttime sky. He thought of Isabella and how she was expecting him back that evening. He felt his stomach tie in knots when he thought of her in his bed without him.

"When do you want me to actually go?"

Tony thought about it for a second and replied, "It will be a few weeks, maybe a month at the most, for us to put things in place and get a team ready."

Cole nodded and motioned to go back inside. Once back in the conference room, Cole and Tony talked it over some more and then went down another hallway, into a secure comms room, and Tony sat Cole down by a large phone, saying, "Let's do this."

With some hesitation, Cole dialed David.

If David had been behind it all, he hid his surprise when he answered the phone and the two started talking. Two agents stared at computer screens as Cole talked with Tony standing right behind him.

David told Cole to once again lay low. When David sounded like he was going to end the conversation, Tony patted Cole's shoulder and motioned with his fingers for more time on the call.

Cole asked when he could return to Panama, and David again told him to lay low for a bit. Cole suspected it was all a lie on David's part, but played along and finished up promising to stay in touch. To keep David on the line, Cole asked if he'd seen Maria. David laughed and said he hadn't, reminding Cole again that he shouldn't have blown his money on a girl like that. Cole smiled to himself, knowing it was the only thing he could feel good about from the months in Panama. With any luck, Maria was back in Colombia and with that, Cole was lost in better thoughts for a brief moment. One of the agents gave a thumbs up and Cole ended the call, setting the phone down and sitting back in his chair. He wondered still if Maria was back with her family. If so, he at least had gotten something right.

Tony asked, "Now, how does that feel, Cole?"

Cole reclined further back in the chair, looked up at the ceiling for a second, then back at Tony, saying, "Hard to say right now. I've got a lot to process."

The two walked back to the conference room and took seats. Tony laid out some expectations. They had a room for him at the Truman Annex, which housed the Joint Interagency Task Force South headquarters. He could come and go as he pleased, but had to check in each day and couldn't leave Key West without Tony's permission. Cole nodded silently along as Tony went through the details. With his belongings in hand, Tony also gave Cole a phone for keeping in touch. Cole had to have it on him at all times. Silently, all Cole could think about was Isabella and how he was going to get back to see her, but he nodded along at Tony's terms. He thought briefly about telling Tony about her, but dismissed it as a bad idea.

Well after midnight, Tony dropped Cole off at a barracks room at Truman Annex and said he'd be in touch the next day. Cole settled into a spartan room with a small bed, a dresser, and a table in the corner. Cole still had the same clothes on from the boat. His wallet was damp from jumping in the water, and he sat on the foot of the bed, dropping his head into his hands and cupping his swollen eye with his left hand. The magnitude of his situation was overwhelming. Tony wanted to send him back to Panama. It was the last thing Cole wanted to do, but at the same time he owed Tony for giving him a second chance. Moreover, it offered some closure and, if it worked out, a chance to move on with his life. He thought for some time then eventually laid down and even with his mind racing, Cole fell asleep on top of the sheets, still in his salt-crusted shorts and shirt.

The following morning, Cole walked to Blue Heaven for breakfast. Along the way, he picked up a disposable cell phone and charged it up at the bar while he ate, figuring that Tony could trace every call Cole made with the other phone. Walking back to Truman Annex, he pulled Murph's number from his wallet. The paper still wet, Cole carefully peeled it apart, and dialed.

When someone answered on the other end, it was not Murph.

"Who is this?" Cole asked as he stopped walking.

On the other end of the line, a man cleared his throat and replied, saying, "This is Scott's brother."

Cole had never known Murph as anything other than Murph. The first name threw him off and Cole asked, "Where's Murph at?"

Murph's brother paused before saying bluntly, "Murph is dead."

"What?" Cole asked.

Murph's brother explained that the State Department had visited him two weeks ago with what was left of Murph's belongings. Apparently, he'd been shot down flying out of Venezuela on suspicion of carrying drugs. The Venezuelans had turned over what they collected from the crash site to the U.S. Embassy, and Murph's phone was one of the only things left.

Cole's mind raced back to his last conversation when Murph was leaving Martinique. He'd mentioned the trip for David and Venezuela specifically. Cole struggled to swallow with his mouth completely dry and realized that Murph's flyby of the Bakoua was perhaps his last stunt before being killed. With the phone pressed to his ear and his other hand against his forehead, Cole apologized to Murph's brother and hung up.

After that, he tried to call the Hotel Bakoua, worried even more now about Isabella, but between a poor connection and the language barrier, he couldn't get through to anyone speaking English. Cole was lost between anger and fear, feeling himself slip into a panic. He knew it was time again for action.

Back at his room, Cole sat once more at the foot of the bed. It took time for Murph's death to sink in. Cole knew that it was more than unfortunate. With his friend dead and Cole set up to rot in prison, it seemed all-the-more plausible that David was cleaning house. If David knew Cole had been in Martinique, that meant Isabella wasn't safe either.

Cole dialed Tony and when he answered, Cole said, "I'm in, Tony. If I was on the fence before, I'm not anymore. I'm onboard to bring these assholes down."

Tony laughed at Cole's enthusiasm before inviting him down to the JIATF-S building to get acquainted with some of the team. With that, Cole moved quickly down the road and Tony met him by a door leading into a windowless and nondescript building. After clearing a few more checkpoints, Cole found himself in yet another secure comms room littered with computers, video screens, televisions, and about a dozen men and women working at a hurried pace. Tony had Cole sit against a wall and instructed him to watch the show.

On the screens in front of Cole, he watched streaming video from aircraft like the ones that had chased him off of Panama. There were real-time feeds from both the Caribbean and Pacific coming from what must have been six or more planes. Radios crackled with chatter from across the Caribbean basin. On another screen were the positions of aircraft as they conducted their searches, and on yet another screen, was a satellite map of Panama City. Tony motioned for Cole to pay attention to that screen more than the others as a blip moved around overlaid on the city grid.

After 20 minutes, Tony walked over to Cole and pointed again back at all the monitors. "This is because of you, Cole. Your guy David is a big deal, and we're now networked into the inner workings of a major cartel. Our aircraft are on top of every one of his boats right now."

Cole asked, "So you're going to bust them?"

Tony shook his head, saying, "No, not all of them. We don't want to tip David off just yet that we're on to him. We'll make it hurt, but he'd ditch the phone if we blew our cover like that. For now, we're just watching, trying to learn his movements."

"So why not just shut him down now?"

"This is the big leagues, Cole. We play for keeps and we aim for the top. David's not the top."

Cole was quiet for a moment, before asking, "So you willingly let drugs slip through?"

Tony exhaled and replied, "Yeah, for the greater good, sometimes you gotta let one slide." He patted Cole on the shoulder and went back to work.

Over the next week, Cole was in the command center almost daily. Twice he called David to ensure they were still tracking the right guy, and both times they were spot on, tracking David's phone as he made his way in and around Panama City. It was like a game of chess and Tony was lining up his plays. Cole admired the steel resolve Tony showed with the other agents. He led them, but in a subtle way that commanded respect and at the same time created an open dialogue among the agents in the room. Cole admired him for it.

Some of the other agents ignored Cole. One or two of them showed outright disdain for his presence, but most just went about their work with a shared determination to slow the flow of illegal drugs into the United States. Looking at the array of equipment and realizing the magnitude of the operation, Cole was amazed he'd gotten away with so much. Underneath the sunshine, the palm trees, the beaches, and the blue water, the Caribbean was a modern battlefield.

Tony asked Cole questions every now and then, but mostly he followed the monitors' activity and jotted things down on a notepad. On the second day, he sat down and asked Cole about David's phone calls.

"Do you know who David works with?"

Cole shook his head and answered, "No, I never met many guys outside of David."

Tony thought for a moment and explained a bit more of the game to Cole. "He calls a few numbers, most of which we can track to Panama, Bolivia, and Colombia, but there's one number he's dialed three times that is encrypted beyond anything we can track. I think it's encrypted on the other end. Do you have any idea who that might be?"

Cole again shook his head and answered, "No, sorry."

"No problem, but that guy is our target from here on out."

On the third day, Cole was restless for some action and when the opportunity arose, he pointed out the small river where he ran back and forth from in Nicaragua, explaining to Tony and the other agents the frequency of the runs and the types of pangas used. Seemingly on a whim, Tony moved a U.S. Navy ship to monitor the river mouth, and by the next morning when Cole walked in, the ship had busted a load of cocaine during the night. Cole smiled a bit, thinking that perhaps he'd bought some rest for the older couple that had always taken care of him. With a ship off the mouth of the river, David would have to find a new hideout. It felt like a win and Cole was happy.

That night, Tony invited Cole out to dinner to celebrate the bust. In high spirits, Tony offered to buy at El Siboney and Cole wasn't about to refuse the offer. Ordering the same plate of grouper he'd eaten so many other times, Cole bid his time and made idle chatter with Tony.

He finally asked, "So, Mickey is one of your guys?"

Tony laughed, replying, "Yeah, he's been with us for years. He used to run dope like you and something scared the crap out of him. He ran north and ended up caught up in some low-budget dope ring. I got my hands on him and he turned pretty quick. We pay him a bit, just enough to get by, and he keeps up on some connections that help us from time to time."

Cole smiled briefly, then fought back the urge to let Tony in on Mickey's little secret. Cole remembered how Mickey dressed and lived, well below his means as a Cuban migrant smuggler. Even if Mickey had turned to the right side of the law when it came to drugs, he kept up his skills organizing the runs to Cuba and back. If Mickey could run a migrant network under Tony's nose, Cole was that much more impressed with the short little man with greying hair. Cole wasn't mad at him. It was, after all, purely business once Cole had headed south. *Hell, Mickey warned me*, Cole thought before he took another sip of his beer.

Tony asked, "Are you surprised about Mickey?"

Cole grinned, took a longer sip from his beer, swallowed, and replied, 'Nothing surprises me anymore."

After each had put down a few more beers, Cole laid out his cards. "Tony, I need to get back to Martinique."

Tony almost spit out his beer, before putting the bottle back on the table and shaking his head. "Not a chance Cole. You're a flight risk."

Cole pleaded with him and explained the entire situation with Isabella, offering to do whatever it took to get back down to Fort-De-France to check on her. Tony shook his head each time.

Cole finally threw his hail mary, saying, "If I don't have my head on straight for going back to Panama, this isn't going to work, Tony."

Cole thought he made a good argument, as Tony was quiet for a minute. Taking another sip of his beer, Tony stared into Cole's eyes.

After a pause, he changed his previous tone, and said to Cole, "If, and it's a big if, I let you go down there, I'll go with you. But for now we've got work to do."

Cole hid the smile he felt and nodded to affirm that he understood everything Tony said. The two finished dinner with lighter conversation and parted ways outside of Truman Annex.

The following morning, Cole again was in the comms room at JIATF-S. An aircraft was pushing a video feed of the river mouth where the ship had made their bust the day before. There was a bit of commotion amongst the agents and Cole stared at the video, trying to figure out what they were seeing. Tony came over and put his hand on Cole's shoulder, saying, "It looks like they burned the place."

Cole asked, "What place? What are you talking about?"

Tony pointed back at the monitor, saying, "The camp you guys were using, someone went in last night and burned it all to the dirt, probably to send a message or something. Go pack your bag; we are going to go take a look for ourselves."

Cole asked, "What about the people living there?"

Tony just solemnly shook his head, saying, "We don't know, but it doesn't look good."

CHAPTER 16 - PAYBACK

COLE HURRIED BACK to his room and packed the few things he had with him. Meeting Tony back at the command center, they climbed into a waiting SUV and sped over to the Naval Air Station in Key West. This time, a King Air, one not unlike Murph's, was waiting for them. Tony and Cole climbed in and the plane taxied out to the runway, turned around at the end, and the propellers spun up. The plane shook and after a momentary pause, the pilots released the brakes and it surged down the runway, lifted off, and pointed to the south. The familiar thud of the landing gear caused a lump in Cole's throat. It reminded him of Murph and brought with it a somber reality. Cole looked out the window at Key West below. He dreaded a plane ride south and longed for the quiet side streets of a Key West morning. Going south was the last thing he wanted to do, but Tony was calling the shots at this point, and Cole was something between a prisoner and a free man.

The plane droned over the Bahamas for what seemed like an eternity. Tony sat patiently across from Cole and combed through a folder with a red 'Secret' sticker on the front cover. At times, he showed Cole a map, and asked vague questions about routes Cole had taken or people he'd interacted with. But for most of the flight, Cole sat silently and stared down at the hundreds of barren rocks that made up the bulk of the Bahamas island chain. It was nothing like the palm-lined beaches one would see in a travel brochure. Cole shook his head softly, thinking, *This damn Caribbean.*

The majority of the Bahamas, like most of the Caribbean, was a far cry from what Cole had thought years before. Each island they flew over looked much like the one before—large and shallow lagoons surrounding brown rocky outcroppings. Beyond each reef line was the deep and dark blue water and white caps from the sea breeze that stood out even from 20,000 feet above.

On every few islands, there would be a runway or a few stuctures, but few had any signs of life on them. It was as inhospitable as another planet. After nearly two hours, the plane banked back around to the west and a larger land mass jutted up from the sea.

Tony looked up for a moment and out the window, then nodded back to Cole, saying "Gitmo."

Guantanamo Bay, or Gitmo, as the military referred to it, was a familiar place to Cole. *Delaney* had made many port calls there and Cole remembered it from his former life. Gitmo was hot and desolate, sitting on the dry side of Cuba and lacking water for much of the year. It resembled a desert in more ways than one would think. Surrounded by a high barbed-wire fence, with armed guards in watch towers, and a minefield that separated America from communist Cuba, Cole was less than ecstatic to stop there.

"How long are we staying?" Cole asked.

Tony, without looking up, replied, "Not long, just enough to get some gas I suppose."

Cole didn't ask any more questions and instead sat back as the pilots banked around to land into the stiff winds that almost always blew in hard from the east. It forced pilots to come in with a steep turn, directly over the minefield to avoid Cuban airspace. The pilots did a good job of it as they fought to keep the wings level and touched down without much fanfare, taxiing in to an abandoned ramp. Once shut down, Cole and Tony stepped out and waited in the empty terminal while the crew fueled the plane.

It was a spartan waiting area with a few rows of seats, worn tile floors, and a few sailors mulling about. Plaques and framed pictures lined the wall from one end to the other, documenting the history of one of America's last southern bastions from a bygone era. As Cole walked, there were black and white photos of old planes and their crews from the height of the Cold War along with more recent pictures, all telling the story of Guantanamo Bay. Much of it made the base seem outdated, but Gitmo had strategic importance if things ever heated up in the tropics. On the far end, ornate wooden boards listed the bases' past Commanding Officers and Cole paused to peruse the names that dated back to beginning of the 20th century.

He stared at the names of admirals and captains, then reflected on his own service, or lack thereof. In his worn shorts, running shoes, and linen shirt, Cole looked nothing like the spit-polished officer he'd once hoped to be. His hair was a ragged mess and his still-black eye only accentuated the gritty self-induced homeless-esque persona that he'd embraced. At least for now, he was again on the right side of the law, but staring at the names of a century's worth of naval leaders, Cole could not help but feel some shame overtaking his conscience. The Caribbean Cole knew was a far cry from what these names on the wall had known over the past century, yet somehow Cole's kind and that of the names on the board were intertwined in the fabric of the islands and the waters of the Caribbean.

Before Cole's mind could wander much further into the past, Tony called for him and they stepped back out onto the ramp, into the stiff easterly breeze, and up into the King Air. With engines running, the pilots again taxied to the runway and lifted off, flying up and over the small bay and back to the south, away from Cuba.

It was late afternoon when Cole saw land again through his window. The plane descended low, perhaps 1,000 feet over the shore line, and circled a runway tucked against the coast. Without any sort of air traffic control to speak of, the pilots banked and weaved a meandering circuitous course around the field, to check it out before lining up on a short final. Their improvised approach re-minded him of Murph landing his own plane back in Martinique. Touching down firmly, the pilots were quick on the brakes and brought the plane to a stop, shutting down on the bleached and cracked runway. Looking around, Cole could see that jungle more or less extended right up to the edge of the concrete. They were, by any account, in the middle of nowhere.

Tony stood up and advised Cole to let him do the talking. When they stepped out, two trucks pulled up to the plane, each loaded with local men in green uniforms with rifles in various positions across their shoulders or in their arms. They stood silently in the truck bed waiting for Tony or Cole to make a move. Cole looked back to see both pilots leaning against the wing in their best attempt to look calm.

Cole could feel the tension, though. He'd been in enough encounters such as this to know that one wrong move would end poorly for those with the least amount of firepower. Clearly, Cole and Tony were the minority. Tony waved casually and approached the closest truck. A young man jumped out from the back and met Tony half way. The two shook hands and Cole felt the tension break just a bit. Tony passed the man an envelope from his back pocket and Cole could see that Tony had a pistol tucked in the small of his back.

The soldier opened the enveloped and played with its contents for just a moment before waving Cole over. By the time Cole shook his hand, the man was smiling. Cole and Tony climbed in the back of one of the trucks then set off down a dusty and rutted road into the jungle that surrounded the airfield. Cole looked around at his new travel companions who did little to even acknowledge Cole's presence.

"Was that a bribe?" Cole asked as the truck bounced and shook down the dirt road.

Tony smiled and replied, "Just buying us some security, that's all. Nicaraguan Army. We're on good terms with them for the moment."

Almost a half an hour later, Cole recognized the burned-out remains of the old folks' compound as the trucks approached. Both trucks pulled up and circled the smoldering pile of ash before coming to an abrupt stop. The men in green uniforms hopped out and formed a loose perimeter around the complex. None of them talked much, but they all held their rifles—mostly derivatives of AKs—at the ready. *Disputed turf*, Cole thought. Just as David had told him when Cole ran the money back to Panama.

Tony motioned for Cole to follow him around to the back. Once there, Cole saw the burned bodies of what must have been the man and the woman. Smoke still rose from their shack a few feet away and its smell did a merciful job of hiding the stench of the old couples' burnt flesh.

Tony crouched down and examined both of the remains. They were charred black beyond recognition and were contorted from the immense heat that had burned their flesh. Cole did not want to believe what he saw. Tony looked closer at the back of their heads and moved the bodies slightly with a stick.

From his crouched position, Tony spoke. "Both had bullets to the back of their heads."

Cole said nothing, but stood motionless as the guilt burned at him even more than the Central American heat. Cole had been the one to point out the river mouth, and now the couple was dead because of it.

Tony looked back up to Cole and could see the remorse on Cole's face.

"They were shot first, Cole." Tony said it as if that made it any more bearable.

Cole shook his head. "Tony, they suffered more than you know."

Tony then nodded in solemn agreement and looked away, knowing that Cole was not looking for anything to dull the pain.

"Does anyone ever get anything right with this shit?" Cole was mad and ran his fingers through his matted hair.

Tony replied, "It's a nasty business. I won't argue that with you." There was a pause before Tony continued. "Someone has to fight these guys, Cole. If we don't fight them, they win."

Cole thought for a second, looked down at the bodies, and asked, "Is this winning?"

With that, Cole walked back to the remnants of the shack where the woman had done her cooking and the man had sold his assorted goods. He fought back a tear, and kicked through the ash and charred debris. Cole took a few minutes before he crouched down in the black and grey dust and picked up the framed picture he was looking for. Wiping away the smoke stains from the glass, he could see it was indeed the picture of the boy whose parents now laid dead only feet away. The entire family was gone.

Las Drogas, Cole thought.

Cole walked back over to the remains of the mother and father, laying the picture down in between them. From the truck, two soldiers brought shovels and proceeded to dig a grave in a far corner of their plot of land. Tony continued to look around and he put a few bits and pieces of debris in evidence bags. Cole walked over to the soldiers and extended his hand, asking for one of the shovels. One soldier was more than happy to oblige and Cole helped dig a grave for the two most recent victims of a silent war that Cole now wished more than ever to have never known from either side of the law.

As sunset approached, Cole and the soldiers buried the remains. Cole had placed the photo on top before helping to fill in the dirt. None of the soldiers seemed to show much remorse, and it occurred to Cole that it was not for a lack of compassion, but rather a more normal occurrence for this part of the world than Cole knew. Driving back to the airstrip in the twilight, Cole and Tony talked more.

"Was this a message to them, or to us?" Cole asked.

Tony shook his head, saying, "I don't know. It was a message to someone. I think your boy David has gone off the reservation. This isn't standard cartel stuff anymore."

They paused again and as the truck neared the airstrip, Tony explained his rationale to Cole. "I do this kind of stuff to keep it off the streets of America. I know it's not pretty, Cole, but it's happening. If we don't try to stop it, no one will, and these cartels will not stop on their own. It's a nasty business, on their end and on ours. But someone has to do it."

Cole nodded, accepting Tony's explanation.

When they returned to the plane, the pilots were already busy starting the engines. Tony and Cole climbed up and Tony went forward to talk with the pilots, returning a minute later and sitting down next to Cole.

Tony asked, "You feeling adventurous?"

"Why?" Cole asked.

"The pilots topped off the gas tanks with some local fuel, and they told me they're not entirely sure it's good shit. It would kind of suck to crash halfway across the Caribbean at night."

Cole asked, "So where are we going?"

Tony smiled, saying, "I figured we could go check on your girl why we're down here. If David is out for blood, it's probably time to get her somewhere safe."

Cole's eyes grew wide and he didn't know what to say.

"Or we could sleep here tonight in the plane and wait for morning. It might be a bit safer in daylight."

Cole laughed under his breath and stared at Tony. "Are you fucking with me?" If Tony was screwing with him, Cole was ready to start swinging. After the death of the old couple, Cole was not in a mood to joke around.

Tony patted Cole on the shoulder and answered, "No, I'm not fucking with you, Cole. I think you could use a break for a day or two."

"Then what the hell are we waiting for?"

Tony motioned the pilots to get going and before long they accelerated down the pock-marked runway and lifted off, turning east into the night sky.

Tony nodded off during the flight, but Cole found it impossible to sleep. Isabella was only a few hours away from him. It had been almost two weeks since he'd last seen her. Cole knew he was a mess, but he smiled and imagined that she would laugh at his roughed up appearance. Now more than ever, he longed for her companionship. *How good it will feel to lay down next to her,* he thought. He smiled at the thought of her hair tickling his face.

It was after midnight when the plane touched down and taxied off the runway not far from where Murph had put his plane to bed the last time. The airport looked and smelled the same. Had it not been for Isabella, the mood would have been somber at best. Thoughts of Murph flying out of Panama haunted Cole as Tony and him stepped out of the plane and the two pilots went to work putting the King Air to bed. The gravity of losing a good friend sunk in even more and Cole tried his best to shake those thoughts from his mind.

Finding a cab outside the gate, Cole said, "Hotel Bakoua."

The cab driver nodded and they were off. It was the same as when he'd left almost two weeks before. He stared out the window at the palm trees swaying under the easterly winds. So much had changed in two weeks and so much of it had been out of Cole's control. The familiarity of the island soothed his mind, but thoughts of Isabella still gnawed at his stomach. Simply seeing her would be such a relief. Before long the cab pulled up through the gate and Tony paid the driver in U.S. dollars.

Walking up to the front desk, the woman at the counter recognized Cole immediately and went into the back room. She emerged a minute later with Cole's bag and set it down on the floor, yelling at him in French. Cole had no idea what she was saying, but she made quite a commotion, enough that an older man appeared from the offices down the hall and spoke with her before turning to Cole and Tony.

He spoke English, "Mr. Williams, you cannot stay. Here are your things."

Cole didn't understand. "Why, what happened?" Cole was reaching for his wallet to settle whatever trouble there was.

The man shook his head and scowled at Cole.

"Mr. Williams, men came after you left and went through your room. They told us you are a criminal. We cannot allow you to stay here with us. You must go."

Cole was floored. "Is Isabella here?"

The man shook his head. "No. She has gone back to France. She was worried about the baby. The men were not nice to her. Mr. Williams, you must leave or I will call the police."

Cole's eyes grew big as he asked, "Baby? What baby?"

Tony took a step back and looked at Cole for a reaction. Even the always calm Tony realized the magnitude of the man's words.

The old man pointed for Cole to leave, replying, "She is pregnant Mr. Williams. And she left to go back to France. That is all I know. Now I am sorry but you must leave."

Cole took a deep breath and nodded slowly, "I'm sorry to have caused you any trouble."

Still struggling for words, he slung his bag over his shoulder and walked around the hotel, down to the beach, and sat under a tree for some time. Tony silently followed and sat a few feet away, waiting for Cole to process the past few minutes.

If Isabella was pregnant, she hadn't said anything to Cole. It didn't make any sense to him, until he thought about how she'd cried the day he left Martinique. Maybe she had hid it from him to protect him, but the thought troubled him even more. There were a lot of things Cole had screwed up, but he could not let himself ruin her life, or that of a child.

Cole took a deep breath and grit his teeth. The sun would be up in a few hours and Cole had nowhere to go as thoughts of Isabella and now of their child weighed on his mind. With Isabella gone, there was no point to any of it. He was certain she'd been hurt badly and he knew he alone bore the blame. It pained him even more than when he'd left her the first time.

Tony finally spoke up. "Cole, this isn't what you want to hear, but has it occurred to you that she is better off without you?"

Cole was furious for a second and stared back at Tony. He felt his core tremble.

Tony continued. "I'm not trying to be an ass, Cole, but your life is a series of bad decisions right now. If she is as good as you say, you are better off leaving her alone until you can sort this thing out."

Cole inhaled just a bit and held his breath. There was truth in what Tony was saying. Cole exhaled and said softly, "Let's walk some more."

Cole picked up his bag again and the two of them walked the side street over to the marina. Everywhere Cole looked he remembered her. The familiar restaurants were all closed, their waiters and bartenders having long ago finished sweeping up and putting things away for the night. Cole found a spot and sat again up against some trees with his back against his bag. He sat there for a second, then pulled it around to his side and opened it up. Inside were most of his clothes, his boots, and his hat. He tried to smile for a second at the sight of his leather boots, but any fond memories didn't stick.

Rummaging through it some more, he pulled out one of Isabella's shirts. It smelled like her perfume. He held it against his face and took a few deep breaths. It was all he had left of a girl who had all but changed his world. If he knew how to cry, he would have, but his emotions were far too hardened after the last year. He knew he couldn't stay in Martinique, nor could he return to his previous life in Key West without getting David off his back.

David would kill him at the first chance, of that much Cole was certain. He didn't want to think of what David might do to Isabella. He put the shirt back in his bag and looked out across the marina. The boats were mostly dark, with a few still showing a dim light in their cabins. On the far side of the marina, he saw two guys his age loading a sailboat from two pushcarts parked on the pier next to it.

It was almost one in the morning. Cole watched the two of them for some time as they loaded bags of groceries and filled the water tanks from a hose on the pier. Tony had walked off at one point and made a slow lap around the marina to give Cole some time alone. After half an hour, Cole watched both men pull the hatch closed and one of them reached down to fire up the engine. They ran it for a few minutes then cut it. Cole watched intently as one of them set the key in a cup holder next to the helm. They walked the deck once more and, satisfied that the boat was secure, both hopped over to the pier and walked away.

It was most likely a chartered sailboat for a week. In the morning, some family would arrive from the States or Europe and spend the week sailing around the islands. The two guys onboard were the crew who would do the legwork. In the Caribbean, chartered boats like that were good business. For a few thousand dollars, it was an easy and exciting way to cruise the islands. Cole pieced a plan together in his head. Across the marina sat a fully provisioned sailboat. The crew was off to get their last night of sleep before setting sail for a week. Cole looked around at the cafes and restaurants that were all dark for the night. Except for Cole and Tony, the marina was quiet. He instinctively began to connect the dots.

Tony walked back towards Cole, but said nothing for a minute or two. He looked across the marina at the same sailboat Cole was focused on. Finally he grinned and spoke up to break the silence.

"Cole, don't tell me you're thinking of stealing that sailboat."

Tony was spot on. Cole was surprised that he'd been read so well. "How did you know what I was thinking?"

Tony shook his head and looked across the marina at the sailboat. He laughed out loud. "It just fits you. It's exactly what I would expect from the kid who rolled into my office as a soaking shit sandwich. You're a cowboy and I'll say it again—she is better off without you right now. There's hope for you yet, Cole, but you're not there right now."

Cole looked down at the ground and accepted Tony's advice. It was true after all. It was in Cole's nature to be an outlaw. That cavalier attitude had gotten him kicked out of the Coast Guard. It had also made him one hell of a smuggler, but at the same time had nearly cost him his life. As hard as it was to admit, there was blood on his hands as well. It had all led him to Isabella, but at the same time his life had led him to one too many bad decisions.

Tony extended his hand to Cole, helping him up. "Let's go find a hotel for the night. We'll figure this out in the morning."

Cole nodded and slung his bag over his shoulder once more. In a way, it felt as if he was giving up.

Tony asked, "Am I going to have to put you in handcuffs?"

Cole smiled a bit and shook his head. "No Tony. I'm done running."

CHAPTER 17 – PARA BELLUM

TONY AND COLE BOARDED the King Air the next morning and flew back to Key West. Cole spent much of the flight staring out of his window at the Caribbean below. They flew over the same waters where Cole's year of bad decisions had come to a head. Somewhere below the blue water sat the remains of his last Go-Fast and the body of man he didn't know but for whose death he bore responsibility. Unlike the shootout in Panama, Cole felt genuine remorse for the stoner who had died when he burned the boat. And on the other end of the Caribbean were the corpses of a husband and wife buried in shallow grave with not so much as a stone to mark their final resting place. And somewhere further south and east sat the remains of Murph's plane, probably littering the side of some unnamed valley in Venezuela. It was difficult for Cole to let go of Isabella, but in the face of so much death and so many mistakes, it was in fact best for Cole to leave her alone.

In France she would be safer than in Martinique. And it seemed as though David had no trouble keeping tabs on Cole's movements. If Cole left her alone, she was that much further removed from the danger Cole had put her in. He hated the thought of abandoning her, especially if she was pregnant, but as painful as it was, Cole knew for once he was making the smarter choice. So many of Cole's decisions were made in the moment and he rarely thought beyond the matter at hand. While his life was his own to ruin, Cole knew he had inadvertently brought down others with him. Moreover, the drug smuggling was not simply a risk or an adventure he bore alone, but rather a cancer that had spread through all of North, Central, and South America. He'd had enough.

Back in Key West, Tony put Cole in touch with a few more guys from JIATF-S. Over the course of a week, they gave Cole a crash course in the counter-narcotics game. Cole was up and running each morning with the sun and each day ended around sunset, having spent the majority of the day either in the command center or in the various offices at JIATF-S, learning the trade. He understood more about the structure of the cartels than he ever knew while working for them and the plan Tony had in his mind began to take shape.

They monitored David's phone 24 hours a day, and twice that week David had called the same blocked number. Each time he ended a call, there was flurry of activity among David's contacts. The entire staff in the command center speculated as to who was on the other end and how David and his unknown partner were able to encrypt the calls.

After the second call that week, Tony looked at Cole and pointed at the computer monitors, saying, "That's our ticket, right there."

Cole sat back in his chair, asking, "What is?"

Tony grinned. The rest of the team was frustrated by it all, but not Tony. If anything, the added challenge of cracking David's contact energized Tony like nothing else. "The only reason they'd go through the trouble of encrypting a line like this is if the guy on the other end is a big deal. We're going to get that phone and it's going to take us straight to the top. David doesn't know it, but he's giving away more than he thinks."

Cole was impressed with Tony's drive. "So, how do we get the phone?"

Tony took a deep breath, looked at Cole, and replied, "You're going to get it for us."

Cole said nothing. He was reminded of Tony's earlier comments about going back to Panama. Now it was clear. Everything up to this point had been part of Tony's larger goal of cutting off the head of the snake. Taking down lieutenants and guys like David had an impact, but not one the size Tony was looking for. If they were able to go over the top of all of them and bring down the boss, it would throw the cartel into disarray, at least for the time being.

Cole asked, "So what happens if we get this guy?"

Tony stopped what he was doing and explained, "When you take out leadership, the cartel will fall apart for a period of time. They won't move as much and they won't produce as much, because they'll be busy killing each other while someone tries to reestablish leadership. We target the top and prosecute them if we can. It sends a message, but it also has an immediate impact on the flow of drugs."

Cole nodded and thought about the risks and the rewards.

Tony walked over to Cole and sat in a chair next to him. "If we do this, it's a home run, Cole."

"So what do you need from me?"

Tony pointed at the desk with a phone. "It's time to call David again. See if you can set up a meeting."

Cole walked over and sat down, dialing David's number once more. When he answered, David sounded like his usual self. Cole kept his composure and the two talked for a minute before Cole got to the meat of the conversation.

"David, I'm sick of waiting. I'm coming back down to Panama."

David laughed and agreed to meet with him. "My friend, it's been a while since we've had a drink. Why don't you let me know when you're back in town and we can catch up."

Cole agreed and hung up the phone, turning to Tony.

Tony nodded, "Well done."

Cole leaned back in the chair and wiped his face with his hands for a second, then dropped them both back in his lap. "I guess I need a plane ticket."

Tony let out a half-smile and nodded. "Yeah, I think we can make that happen."

He walked over to another phone in the command center and made a few calls. While Tony was busy, Cole took the time to explore his thoughts. David and his cartel were not going to let go of Cole so easily. They had tracked him since the beginning and as much as Cole had thought of himself as a buccaneer of sorts, the truth was he'd been a pawn. Murph's death, the old couple, the drive-by in Panama City, and the guy on the boat were all casualties of a war that included Cole. Some were collateral damage, while others were simply targets from the beginning.

Cole knew his time was running out. He could feel it, even from Key West. The right thing to do, as hard as it was, was to try to end it. If Tony was correct, and David's phone was the key to tackling the cartel, Cole was the right guy for the job. He had the contacts, the access, and the know-how to get close to David without too much suspicion. At the same time, Cole knew he had a target on his head.

He thought back to Isabella. If the cartel was shaken up enough, Cole could slip through the cracks and distance himself enough to resume a normal life, hopefully with Isabella. If not, he would end up dead in a ditch like so many others like him. It was a risk he was now willing to take, not so much for the adventure, but rather for some justice.

Later that afternoon, Tony took Cole out for lunch. They ate at El Siboney again and in a quiet corner of the restaurant, and over a few beers, Tony laid out a plan.

"You'll meet David by yourself—somewhere public. Don't do anything out of the ordinary. Get him talking, have a beer, and just keep him close to you. "

Cole suggested Habanas.

Tony nodded, "Yeah, perfect. That will work." Taking another sip of his beer, he continued, "I've got a team that will be watching you the whole time. They're some rough dudes, and they'll have your back from the second you land until we get you out of there. I'll be down there along with a few others, but you'll be moving on your own. OK?"

"Yeah, got it. Can I meet these guys?"

"No, it's better if you don't spot them. Your movements will be normal that way. Trust me; we'll keep you safe. When the time is right, you'll know it. My guys will move in, grab him, and we'll move with a purpose to get the hell out of town."

Cole was silent for a moment, taking a long sip from his Dos Equis, before asking the fateful question, "So when do we leave?"

Tony laughed and replied, "We leave tonight, but you will leave tomorrow morning. We'll see you again once you're down there."

After parting ways at El Siboney, Cole walked the streets of Key West by himself for the better part of the evening. Cole knew there was a chance it would be his last night on the town. It occurred to him to drink his face off one last time, but over the past two weeks Cole had lost much of the urge to do so. Instead, he meandered down to the boardwalk and then over to Mallory Square one last time. Looking out at Sunset Key and further north to Wisteria Island, Cole smiled as he remembered his first days off of *Delaney* and how he'd stood in the same spot, wondering what the future held in store for him.

Waking early the next morning, Cole went out for the run he'd gone on so many times before. He made it over to the airport and ran hard until his lungs were close to giving out. By mid-morning, he was showered and cleaned up, ready for the flight to Panama City. He wore his boots with a faded pair of jeans, figuring that he would do well to look the part. He had a small bag with him and carried little more than one spare change of clothes. There was no telling what was in store for him beyond a day anyhow.

At the airport, Cole remembered his last flight to Panama, and how he'd almost turned the whole thing off in the same terminal he stood in now. By the time Cole boarded the small commuter jet and the plane had climbed out over the Keys, he'd run the full gamut of emotions, realizing that his life would be far different had he listened to Mickey's advice. At the same time, he never would have met Isabella. His time in Martinique had made so much of the past year's troubles worth something. She gave his life some meaning.

With another connection in Dallas, Cole settled into his seat as the plane climbed up and flew south towards Panama City. He managed to sleep for most of the flight. It was late afternoon when the plane touched down, and as he walked through the familiar terminal to the line of cabs outside, Cole stopped briefly at an ATM and withdrew 500 dollars. Once outside, he dialed Tony.

Picking up quickly, Tony asked, "Everything good?"

Cole replied, "Yeah, I'm on my way to Habanas. I'll call David in a few minutes."

"Sounds good, Cole." Tony sounded calm. "We're all set on this end. If things get out of control, lock both your hands together behind your head like you're stretching. Otherwise, just keep David there and wait for us to move on him."

"Got it. See you in a bit."

Signaling for a cab, Cole sat in the back and called out to the driver, "Habanas."

The driver laughed and grinned, looking at Cole through the rear-view mirrors. "Si, many pretty ladies, *mi amigo*."

Cole couldn't help but smile. He wondered once more about Maria. By now, she was most certainly back in Colombia.

The driver once again grinned at Cole, saying, "*Las chicas*."

Cole took a deep breath and nodded, repeating the driver's words, "*Si, las chicas*."

Cole dialed David as the cab drove west towards downtown. David answered, "Cole, how the hell are you, my friend. Are you in town?"

"Yeah, driving into town now. I'll be at Habanas in an hour or so."

"Great, great. I'm running around at the moment, but I'll meet you there in a bit. Grab a drink and enjoy Panama. You've been away for too long."

Cole laughed into the phone to feign being calm, and replied, "No problem. I'll see you in a bit." With that, he ended the call.

In less than an hour, the cab pulled up to Habanas and Cole stepped out onto the familiar street. He paid the driver and walked over into the lobby of the Marriott. Once inside, he withdrew another 500 dollars from an ATM, and then walked across the street to Habanas with almost 1,000 dollars in his pocket.

Just after sunset, not late enough for the real party to start, Cole took a beer from the bar and made his way to some of the plastic seats at the front of the club. The lights danced around the walls and ceiling and a few girls had already taken up their spots for the night. Music pulsed from the speakers, some older men sat and smoked cigars, but for the most part the bar was still calm. Taking his first sip, he looked around to see if there were any familiar faces. There were none, but he made eye contact with no less than six stunning women. One of them came up to him—just like they always did—and sat in his lap. With one hand on her thigh, Cole made small talk with the girl and nursed his beer.

After a few minutes, he leaned into her ear and whispered, "*Pistola?*" He had to find a handgun somewhere in this godforsaken place.

She looked at him with a funny look for a moment then shook her head, stood up, and walked away. *Damn it*, Cole thought. He was ready to fight for the right side of the law, but there was no one around that Cole knew or trusted, and a pistol would make him much more comfortable. He couldn't see anyone at the bar that resembled the guys Tony had mentioned. After only a few minutes by himself, Cole felt vulnerable.

Just as he was beginning to second-guess the entire plan, a second girl approached and sat in Cole's lap. She was a bit older than the first and not quite as pretty, but she leaned in to Cole's ear and whispered, "*Quieres una pistola?*"

Cole grinned and wrapped his left arm around her hips. Yes, he wanted a pistol. "*Si.*"

The girl looked at him for a second more, then said in broken English, "One thousand dollars."

"Five hundred dollars and I need it now."

The girl looked away for a moment, thought, then looked back at Cole. "Seven hundred and fifty, *mi amor.*"

"Deal," was all Cole said to acknowledge her. He handed her the bills from his pocket and she tucked them away discretely in her purse.

She kissed him on the cheek then disappeared. Cole shook his head at his predicament. Here he was, once again more or less trusting his life to a hooker. In all likelihood, she would hold up her end of the bargain. After all his dealings in Panama, the women of the night had proven themselves more reliable and trustworthy than most of Panama's more upstanding citizens. Cole let out a half-smile and took a long sip from his beer. There was no turning back.

Almost an hour passed before Cole saw David approach Habanas from the street. With him were four other men, none of which Cole recognized. David's partners broke off once they walked up the steps to the bar and David approached Cole by himself.

Cole stood up and shook hands with David, saying, "Wasn't sure I'd see you again."

David dismissed it and shook his head, "Don't say such things, Cole. How have you been?"

The two sat down. "It's been a rough stretch, to be honest. I damn near lost everything on that run from Martinique."

David nodded. "Yes, my friend. That was a tough spot you were in, but by all accounts you did well. Did the Americans get anything out of you?"

"No, I burned the boat. The other guy I was with died, but the boat sank with the drugs and they had nothing on me, so here I am."

David was silent for a moment. "Yes, and here you are."

There was an awkward silence. Cole looked around to see that David's partners were by the bar, but all looking directly back at Cole. Again, there was no one in the immediate vicinity that looked like Tony's guys. Cole felt his heart beating in his chest. He swallowed to bury the lump in his throat. *Control yourself*, Cole repeated in his head several times.

David asked, "You're looking around like you are uncomfortable? You are with friends, Cole. Relax. We are just talking business."

Cole nodded and finished his beer. David motioned with two fingers to one of his guys, who brought two more Dos Equis over from the bar. Cole and David tapped bottles and both took long sips before setting them down on the plastic table.

David continued, "So, you are looking to get back into the business?"

"Yeah, not much else I can do these days."

David nodded. As he did, the prostitute reappeared from the street and walked over to Cole, again sitting in his lap. David laughed and leaned back in his chair.

"You've missed Panama that much, Cole?"

The girl set her purse down beside Cole's right foot and kissed him again on the cheek, then leaned her head against Cole's and smiled at David.

David laughed even louder and took another sip from his beer.

In Spanish, he said something to the girl and motioned for her to go away with his hand. She pulled herself close against Cole and made a kissing motion with her mouth to Cole's cheek, before standing up and walking back into the crowd. Cole took a long whiff of her perfume as she stood up, having missed the smell of a woman over the past few weeks. At Cole's right foot, he felt her purse against his leg. Taking a sip from his beer, he looked down and saw the worn wooden grip of a revolver in the purse. He was now back on solid ground.

David spoke up. "Cole, you've got a lot of guts to come back down here. I think I can find something for you, but maybe we should go somewhere else to discuss it."

Cole asked, "What do you have in mind?"

"Nothing to be concerned about, but we should go somewhere a bit more quiet." With that, he motioned with one finger to his men, who spread out among the bar and formed a loose circle around Cole and David.

"What the fuck is this, David?"

David was still calm and sitting back against his chair. "Cole, let's not do this here, at a place of business. Let's go for a drive and we can talk."

Cole's stomach was in knots. A drive with David and his goons meant one thing and Cole wasn't going to die that way. He grit his teeth and took a deep breath, staring directly at David. "I don't think so, David. I like it right here."

"You don't have a choice, my friend."

Cole reached up and put both his hands behind his head, locking his fingers together, and leaned back in the chair.

Nothing.

After a moment or two, Cole looked around and there was no change in his surroundings. Cole thought, *Where the fuck is Tony?*

David looked at Cole for a moment, then asked, "What are you doing, Cole? You are acting strange."

Cole took a deep breath and replied, "Nothing. Just getting comfortable."

As he let his arms drop back down, Cole leaned forward and reached slowly with his right hand for the purse. By that point, David was on to him and had reached behind his back, pulling out a handgun and slamming it down on the table, its muzzle pointed at Cole. Both beers fell over and spilled out onto the floor as the bottles rolled off one side. David hid most of the gun with the palm of his hand, but he clearly meant to send a threat.

"Don't be dumb, Cole. Not here." David was now all business. Cole had not seen this expression from David before. It was time to act.

Two of David's men approached the table and as they closed in, Cole's instincts took over. He dove to the side of the table, pulling the revolver from the girl's purse as he fell to his side. Now laying on the concrete floor, he could see David's legs moving to stand up, and Cole wasted no time firing a shot through the table and into David's torso. With that, David fell back down against his chair and then onto the ground, landing on his butt. Still holding his gun and sitting upright, David's eyes were big and a look of disbelief spread across his face as he strained to take a breath. Cole steadied the revolver with both his hands and focused once more on David's chest.

In an instant, David pointed his gun at Cole and the two of them opened fire at the same time from less than four feet away. The muzzle blast from both guns blinded Cole for a second. Cole then tried to breathe and felt an immense burning pain from the left side of his rib cage. David, by that point, was slumped over on the ground, and Cole opened his mouth to take a labored breath. As Cole scanned for David's goons and readied himself as best he could for the impending shootout, a volley of fire opened up at the bar.

There were screams and from his prone position, Cole watched drinks spill to the floor and feet running back and forth. More fire erupted from all directions. Holding his pistol in his right hand, Cole covered his face his with left arm and curled up to get as small as he could in the middle of the firefight. It was only seconds, but it seemed much longer before the gunfire stopped. Cole looked back at David and could see that he was dead. Cole's second shot had been a good one as dark blood pooled under David and slowly spread out onto the concrete. Across the bar, three more of David's men were on the floor as well. Cole's ears were ringing, but he could hear American voices as two men ran up the steps and onto the dance floor.

One of David's men moved and two more shots rang out as one of the Americans dispatched him for good.

Cole heard an authoritative voice call, "Clear!"

A second voice called out the same, "Clear!"

The music was still thumping in the background, but most of the lights had either been shot out or otherwise knocked out during the scuffle. Cole groaned and crawled toward David with his revolver still in his hand. One of the Americans approached and kicked the plastic table away, holding an MP-5 to Cole's chest for a second before relaxing and dropping it to his side, where it hung in a single-point sling. He reached down and helped Cole up to his feet.

As he put one of Cole's arms over his shoulders, he said, "It's all right, brother. We're gonna get you out of here."

Cole dropped the revolver, took one step, and then stopped. "No, hang on." Cole leaned down to David's lifeless body and reached into his pocket, pulling out David's phone. "This is what we came for, right here."

The American, dressed in nondescript cargo pants, hiking boots, and a polo shirt, nodded and helped Cole back up and over to the steps. Cole could feel that he was weaker now than when he'd been grazed in the shoulder. Each breath was painful and he could only take in a bit of air. At the base of the steps, a third American stood in the street, an MP-5 in his hands and pointed down the road. He too was dressed in plain clothes, but had a serious look about him, ready to fight if the need arose.

Without taking his eyes off the street, the man asked, "We good?"

The other, propping Cole up, replied, "Yeah, we're good, but where's the fucking van?"

"On its way," said the first.

With that, they tucked back a bit against the wall of Habanas. The third American came down the steps with an M4 at his side and his hands full of phones and wallets. He tucked them inside a bag then moved to cover the opposite side of the road. Cole looked back up at the club. David was lifeless and laying on his side where Cole had shot him. Blood now ran down onto the sidewalk. Across the bar, three other bodies were slumped over on the ground and farther up the sidewalk, the fourth one of David's men laid dead on the street.

Cole's vision was a partial blur by this point, but he could see that the street and the club were empty. Panama had wisely abandoned Habanas, at least for the time being. Across the street at the hotel, there were no guards at the doors, and Cole wondered if that had been part of the plan to begin with, either on the part of David or Tony.

Just then, a van pulled quickly around the corner and came to a stop in front of Cole and the others. They piled in, pushing Cole into a seat by himself and propped him up against a window. Behind him sat Tony with genuine concern on his face. One of the men jumped in the passenger seat, another sat in front of Cole, and the third took a seat by his side.

Tony asked the one next to Cole, "How is he?"

The man replied, "He'll live if we move quickly, but we're gonna need the helo. He needs the ship." The man was already pressing a bandage against Cole's chest and wrapped it around to Cole's back.

Tony nodded and took out a phone. Dialing quickly, he held it up to his ear and yelled, "Plan B, get the sixty to the soccer field. All personnel accounted for, one with a gunshot. Have the medics ready." Tony put the phone away and the van was already speeding through some side streets.

Tony patted Cole on the shoulder and left his hand there for moment, reassuring Cole, "You'll be all right, Cole. Just a little bit longer."

Cole clenched his teeth and nodded, pulling David's phone up to his face and flipping it open. He pushed the send button and the call log popped up. There were a slew of numbers and none seemed any more remarkable than the others. One, reading 'unknown,' caught Cole's attention, and he showed it to Tony.

Tony nodded and smiled, saying, "Go for it."

Cole pushed send a second time and the phone rang. As the van sped around a corner and steadied on a main road, Cole held the phone up to his ear and listened. After a few more rings, a man answered on the other end.

"David, what the fuck is going on down there? Did you shoot him?"

He had a thick Hispanic accent. Cole waited, saying nothing.

After a pause, the man asked again, "David, tell me that you finished it?"

Cole recognized the voice. "Mickey?" Cole asked.

"Who the fuck is this?" It was most definitely Mickey's voice on the other end—and half a world away, for all Cole knew.

"It's Cole, Mickey." Cole paused, thought for a second, then continued with the only thing that came to mind, "This shit ain't personal, it's just business."

With that, he hung up the phone, partly in disbelief. Looking at Tony, Cole could see that Tony was also bewildered. The van turned another sharp corner and the man seated in the passenger seat yelled, "One minute out."

Tony asked, "Are you shitting me? That was Mickey on the other end?"

Cole nodded, saying, "Yeah, even I couldn't make this stuff up."

Tony took out his phone again and held it up to his right ear. With his other hand covering his left ear, he yelled into the phone, "Go find Mickey. Now. Get every guy you've got on it and go find that little bastard."

As the van pulled up to an unlit soccer field, the men all hopped out and helped Cole over towards some bleachers, sitting him down on the lowest seat. Cole pressed his hand against his torso and felt warm blood, his own blood, running down his hand. He tried to hide it, but Cole felt unmistakable panic setting in. As he sat on a bleacher in a soccer field in Panama, his time to die was fast approaching. He turned his thoughts to Isabella and smiled for a second before an immense sadness overtook him. Cole wished that he'd been able to say goodbye to her, or to tell her that he loved her, or to have apologized at least for everything he'd put her through.

Moments later, and from the far side of the field, a helicopter came into view, its rotors whining loudly as it came into a hover over the field, flinging weeds and trash into the air before settling down on the grass. Tony and the men hurried over, now carrying Cole, and they all climbed in. Within seconds, the helicopter was up and airborne. Cole, dizzy and weak, asked to no one in particular, "Where are we going?" Before anyone could answer, Cole slipped out of consciousness.

CHAPTER 18 – THE PACIFIC

HE WOKE IN A BED, but was unsure where he was. He'd been cleaned up. He was in a hospital gown and looked around at his hands then wiggled his feet under the sheet to assure himself that he was still in one piece. He then took a few labored breaths, and it felt far better than it had in the van. After some time, a Navy corpsman walked in, and Cole pieced things together.

He asked, "Where am I?"

The corpsman just looked at him and replied matter-of-factly, "You're on a cruiser, Sir. I'll go get your partner."

The corpsman disappeared, and a few minutes later Tony walked in and pulled up a chair beside Cole. "How are you feeling, Cole?"

Cole tilted his head to one side and sighed. "I've been better, but I'm alive. So where the hell are we?"

Tony smiled. "We had the Navy standing by in case we had to get out quick. I figured you stood a good chance to do something unexpected, so we developed a few contingencies."

Cole laughed and replied, "I've never been so happy to be underway in my life."

"Good thing we did, seeing as how you went a bit nuts back there."

Surprised, Cole said, "Pretty sure I'm alive because of it."

"Yeah, there may be some truth to that." Tony nodded, "So how the hell did you get your hands on a gun anyway? That wasn't in the plan."

Cole laughed even more forcefully and grimaced from the pain in his chest before replying, "It's Panama, Tony. What did you expect?"

"I told you we had you covered."

"Yeah, well, I had myself covered, too." The two of them paused for a moment before Cole asked, "So, what about Mickey?"

Tony leaned back in his chair. "We got him. They caught the little piece of shit passing the sea buoy on a jet ski headed south with a backpack full of cash. The Coast Guard ended up pepper-spraying him after he started waving a knife. My guess is that he was trying for Cuba."

"So he was running things the whole time?"

Tony nodded, "Yeah, it's looking that way. Right under our damn noses, he was running things for years. He had every one of us fooled, but that's how this business is sometimes."

Cole thought for a second and said, "Yeah, he had me fooled, too."

Tony stood up and patted Cole on the shoulder again, then turned and started walking out. "You did good, Cole. Sit tight for a few days and we're gonna get you back to the states, get you stitched up, and then off to recover and get your strength back."

Cole asked, "Where to?"

Tony was already at the doorway. Stopping and turning to face Cole, he smiled and said, "I hear France is nice this time of year. You know anyone over there?"

ABOUT THE AUTHOR

Brian Boland is a 2003 graduate of the United States Coast Guard Academy and holds a Master of Arts in Military History from Norwich University. After an initial assignment at sea, he completed Naval Flight Training and was designated a Coast  Guard aviator in 2008. With more than a decade of operational experience, he has deployed extensively throughout the Caribbean, Central America, and the eastern Pacific, supporting search and rescue, migrant interdiction, and counter-narcotics missions.

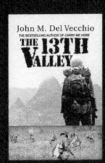

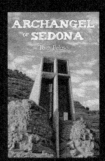

CPSIA information can be obtained
at www.ICGtesting.com
Printed in the USA
LVOW13s0020010217
522742LV00011BA/702/P